Praise for Cooper Not Out

'Five stars. This book will fill your heart.'

Herald Sun

'In the way that *Ted Lasso* isn't really about soccer, *Cooper Not Out* isn't really about cricket.'

Kerryn Mayne

'*Cooper Not Out* is the story Australia needs right now. This beautifully written book highlights life's simple pleasures, like a game of country cricket, but its emotional complexity is what makes the book really sing . . . Frankly, it's a ripping read that will make your heart swell. Roy Cooper is a hero for our times.'

Tracey Spicer, AM

'I am gobsmacked. I love cricket. I love stories. I love books so I have just won the trifecta! Think *The Castle*, think *Phar Lap*, think *Rocky* all rolled into one. I laughed, I cried, I couldn't put it down. This beautifully written tale has every-thing – it's funny, heartwarming, nostalgic and most importantly manages to brilliantly create an atmosphere of anticipation that keeps you coming back for more. I'd give it 6 stars if I could!'

Better Reading

'Bowled over by a cricket story . . . What unfolds is the most wonderful innings, a line-up of characters you'll never forget, an ending as thrilling as a tied Test. It's a book that takes you back to a more gentle time, fills you with nostalgia, from the mentions of music, to recounts of real-life cricket happenings that Smith has woven into his novel . . . *Cooper Not Out* is, however, much more than an ode to cricket. It's a reflection on friendship, on fatherhood, on gender inequality, on stereotypes, on what it means to be a real man . . . an uplifting, inspiring, fun story, to make our hearts sing . . . I didn't want this book to end. I wanted it to drag on for the full five days, to go into overtime, to mix my sporting metaphors. In the words of the late, great Richie Benaud, it's simply marvellous stuff.'

Karen Hardy, *Canberra Times*

'Cricket is not for me, but reading about it is another matter. The game has inspired some of the nation's best sports writing and Justin Smith's *Cooper Not Out* takes the game into literary terrain, in a novel that plays with anything but a straight bat . . . Smith's irreverent, uplifting sports comedy is a nostalgic celebra-tion of cricket that gives a cheerful up yours to the misogyny and homophobia of the era.'

The Age and *Sydney Morning Herald*

'I've read many a cricket book in my lifetime . . . but I haven't read a cricket book as downright fun as *Cooper Not Out*. Here, Justin Smith transports us back to the heady days of summer 84/85 and the Windies tour of Australia . . . This book is exactly what it says it is: a feelgood, charming story about an unlikely hero, full of scones and delightful characters.'

Readings

'This is one of the best books I have read in a while. It's a big call, but it just filled my heart. It made me smile often and it brought out a nostalgia in me that I wasn't prepared for. I absolutely loved cricket as a kid, something that I allowed to forget as I grew up. But this book reminded me how much I loved it, particularly cricket in the 1980s when I was such an avid fan. Having said that, this book will resonate with anyone, cricket fan or not . . . Thank you, Justin Smith, for writing a book that drew me in so completely by the sweetest story, well told and filled with memorable characters.'

Merc's Book Nook

'If you grew up in Australia in the 1980s, this book will fill your heart and tug at your nostalgic soul.'

Mercedes Maguire, *Herald Sun* and *Daily Telegraph*

'I'm calling it . . . this is THE book of summer. Set in the Aussie summer of 1984, cricket is a big player in the story but there's so much more. Small-town police sergeant Roy Cooper is the hero I needed to read about right now. The story is uplifting, poignant and beautifully Aussie! ***** 5-stars from me because it's so beautifully written and a feel-good story that's going to appeal broadly. Sport is a gateway to so many feelings and experiences, and Justin has told a story that made me feel so much while reading it.'

Emily Webb Reviews, Goodreads

'It's summer, and who doesn't love a story about small country towns, cricket and the triumph of an underdog.'

Gourmet Traveller

'This warm bear-hug of a book had me grinning from the first page.'

Maya Linnell

'Justin's magical way with words had me enthralled from the first paragraph.'

Irene Forsyte

'*Cooper Not Out* is a well-written gem.'

The Examiner online

JUSTIN SMITH

GOOD AS GOLD

PENGUIN

MICHAEL
JOSEPH

MICHAEL JOSEPH

UK | USA | Canada | Ireland | Australia
India | New Zealand | South Africa | China

Michael Joseph is part of the Penguin Random House group of companies
whose addresses can be found at global.penguinrandomhouse.com

Penguin
Random House
Australia

First published by Michael Joseph in 2023

Cover illustrations by Shutterstock
Cover design by Christa Moffitt, Christabella Designs
© Penguin Random House Australia Pty Ltd
Typeset in 12.5/18 pt Adobe Garamond Pro by Midland Typesetters, Australia

Printed and bound in Australia by Griffin Press, an accredited
ISO AS/NZS 14001 Environmental Management Systems printer

A catalogue record for this
book is available from the
National Library of Australia

NATIONAL
LIBRARY
OF AUSTRALIA

ISBN 978 0 14377 833 2

penguin.com.au

MIX
Paper | Supporting
responsible forestry
FSC® C018684

We at Penguin Random House Australia acknowledge that Aboriginal and Torres Strait Islander
peoples are the Traditional Custodians and the first storytellers of the lands on which we live
and work. We honour Aboriginal and Torres Strait Islander peoples' continuous connection
to Country, waters, skies and communities. We celebrate Aboriginal and Torres Strait Islander
stories, traditions and living cultures; and we pay our respects to Elders past and present.

For Merryn, Emily and Hannah. Always.

And for Nick Rye and Ray Kitchingman.
There'd be no book without them.

The first Melbourne Cup was run on the 7th of November, 1861. The prestigious new horse race offered 930 gold sovereigns to the winner, but before the prize could be given, it was stolen.

And this is what happened.

*

Five miles from the gold-mining town of Mull Creek, there were three fires burning, and each camp had no knowledge of the others.

At the first was Jesus Whitetree. And Jesus loved gold.

For the time and place he lived, Jesus had an unusual name. But he didn't know that. There were many things he didn't know. He didn't know his age or the date he was born, although he guessed that he was about fifty years old. Maybe a little older. All he knew was fifty was half of one hundred, and one hundred years was a very long time. And he felt like he'd lived at least half of a very long time.

But he was wrong. In truth, today was Jesus' birthday, and he was just eighteen years old.

He had never seen a calendar and he'd never heard much about dates and months and years. He knew the days of the week and he could recite them, but he always made a mistake in the order. He would put Friday before Thursday, and he thought Tuesday was the first day of the week. The errors had been implanted in him when he was very small, and no-one corrected him nor cared that he got it wrong.

And he'd never seen a map or a globe of the world, so he didn't know where he was on this planet. He didn't know the country he lived in and whether it was surrounded by other countries or if he was on an island. And he didn't know the names of any of the towns he'd been through or if he'd crossed any borders.

On the occasion of his eighteenth birthday, it was the year of 1861 and Jesus lived in the British Colony of Victoria on the island continent of Australia.

It was getting colder but it wasn't winter yet. The sun was gone and Jesus had a good fire. The flames glowed orange on his white face and behind him it was black. It was so dark that it seemed like the only things that existed were the objects touched by his fire's light. The logs crackled and moved and he thought it sounded like a song he'd heard a long time ago, but the fire never sang it long enough for him to remember how it went.

He'd be asleep soon, but just before he closed his eyes, he would say his name three times. He'd say it first in a whisper. Then a little louder. And then louder again.

'Jesus Whitetree. Jesus WHITETREE. JESUS WHITE-TREE.'

He did this every night so he wouldn't forget. He'd only had the name for a short time. Maybe a year. Maybe not even

2

that long. No-one else knew it and he was afraid he'd wake one morning with the fire dead and realise he'd forgotten his own name.

Before he named himself Jesus Whitetree, he had no name at all. He'd lived in a brick building that may have had many rooms but he was only allowed in one. It had a ceiling so high he couldn't see it and was filled with other children who didn't have names either. It was so crowded that their bodies were always touching. Jesus couldn't remember a time when he was not touching someone. Their shoulders or their arms or their feet. But it was always cold, no matter the weather outside, and he felt alone. And from his place in the middle of the room, where he slept and ate and waited for nothing, they were watched by men who wore long robes and only ever talked to each other, never to the children.

But one night, he ran away. And he kept running. As fast as he could and as straight as he could. He never made a turn. He was too afraid to. If he turned, and then turned again, he would be going back towards the brick building. He didn't want that. He'd rather bury himself in the dirt until he couldn't breathe. Or jump from a high branch and break his head.

So he always checked the position of the sun and the stars to be sure he was travelling straight. And when he thought he was far enough away – where he knew the men in robes couldn't hear him – he gave himself the name Jesus Whitetree.

He wanted a good name. He deserved a good name. He had been alive for fifty years and he'd always been cold, but now he had his own fire each night. So he should have a strong name. And he should like the way it sounded in his mouth.

He thought of little else for a week, before he settled on Jesus. He'd heard the long-robe men talk about a person of that name. Jesus was not one of the robe men, but they seemed to really like him. He had people who followed him, so he was never alone. And he had died but then he was alive again. The men said his name over and over, so Jesus knew he wouldn't forget Jesus.

Then he needed another name to go with Jesus.

He remembered that he was sick once. It was a long time before he ran away. And he guessed the sickness lasted almost two years. It made him sleep and he'd dreamt of being wrapped in something white. It covered everything. It wasn't like light and it wasn't like cloth. It was something else. It was all of those things but not really. He didn't know. But it was white. Everything was white. And he didn't feel cold when he could see the white. It was the first time he didn't feel alone and cold. And when he was well again, nothing in the brick room was white. It was only in the dream. But Jesus always remembered what it looked like.

So he thought he could be Jesus White. But that was missing something. It needed more. He tried to imagine saying the name to another person and what their face would be like when he did. He wanted them to remember it. Because he himself might forget.

He added 'tree' because they were all around him, and when he was running away from the brick building, the trees helped to keep him hidden. Every time he heard a voice behind him, or the sound of feet or horses, there was always a tree to stand behind until he could start running again.

So he would be Jesus Whitetree.

The name made him feel lucky. No-one else in the world was allowed to pick their own name. He may never have had a mother, but now he had his own name.

'Jesus. Whitetree,' he said again. He did it four times this night to be sure.

He poked the fire and put on another log. The sparks danced up into the darkness as the flames gave a different song. His eyes closed. Jesus may not have known where he was in the world, but he wasn't lost. And he may have had no-one to love, but he loved gold, and before his next birthday, he would have more gold than he could fit into his dreams.

*

Two hundred yards away, at the second fire, was the Jack Pink Gang. Jack Pink was a thief and a liar but he hadn't killed anyone yet. Although he soon would.

He sat close to the fire, as he did every night. Jack hated the dark, and he often cursed and wondered why so much of God's day needed to be covered with black. He was almost twenty-six years old, and the top half of his face was handsome but he had no chin. When he was a boy, other children said he looked more like a rat than a person, but by 1861 he'd grown a long beard to cover the mistake.

With him at the camp were two men and a woman.

One of the men was Ben Carrigan. He was gigantic. His shoulders were wide and they cradled a huge head and no visible neck. He was a foot taller than the tallest person anyone had ever seen. And when strangers first met him, they always felt fear first and then hoped he was just a gentle soul trapped in a towering body. But he wasn't. Carrigan was a man of pitiless violence and unsteady temper, with a fickle sense of loyalty and a savage addiction to opium and Indian rum.

At the fire, Carrigan sat in the dirt with his arms and legs crossed. He looked like a giant schoolboy on the floor of a classroom.

The other man was Samuel LaBat. He was a writer and a poet. LaBat was thin but still looked dangerous, and he was always shabby, no matter how new or clean his clothes were. LaBat had been an effective criminal as a child. He was small and could enter buildings without making a noise, and the occupants would only discover they'd been robbed hours or days later.

When LaBat was a boy, he'd been educated by a generous uncle who'd taught him writing and reading and history. The uncle thought himself to be a forgetful man, because he misplaced or lost most of his possessions while young Samuel lived in the house.

LaBat had been a member of five gangs before he joined the Pinks. But he was never the leader, and he never wanted to be.

He spoke with intelligence and a gentlemanly culture, yet his appetites were uncomplicated. LaBat loved only two things: stealing and writing. And he only loved writing because he was afraid to die. He'd always been afraid to die. Ever since his first memory of life, he was afraid of not living. And so he searched for ways to save himself. The only people he knew who were immortal in this world were the writers. The things they put on the page could be found in a thousand years and the words would not have changed. They would be just as alive as the night they were written. It was why LaBat always kept a small Bible in his saddle – not because he believed in any god, but because it was the oldest book he knew, and anyone who'd written in it was immortal. He wanted the same immortality. So he wrote.

And LaBat always wrote in red ink. To him, it was like he was using his own earthly blood to create something that would be seen in the next life, and the next after that. Tonight, the supply from a small bottle in his coat pocket was low, so he was careful in choosing each word.

The woman at the fire was the mother of Jack Pink. Everyone knew her as Mother Pink. And despite the maternal softness of her name, she had the reputation of being an unbreakable old street whore. She was a round woman with auburn hair that fell to the middle of her back, and a burn scar under her left eye. The wound was two decades old, yet it still glowed with the redness of a fresh infection.

She dressed in laced garments that were impractical for her travelling life, and she sat at the fire on a white wooden stool that had once belonged to a child. That child was long gone and the woman now covered the seat with her round backside. And she looked out past the flames into the night. Unlike her son, she was not afraid of the dark. She was only afraid of being without her son.

All three men at the camp owed something to Mother Pink.

Ben Carrigan had once been in the goldfields working for two Chinamen who gave him a steady supply of opium and enough money for grog. The Orientals spoke no English, and during a pre-dawn miscommunication, Carrigan killed them both. The first one was with a cooking cleaver to the face. The screams woke his partner, who Carrigan grabbed by the neck and squeezed, hoping to extract the location of the drugs. But, again, there was poor communication and the man could only gurgle until his own death.

The police didn't pursue Carrigan for the murders, so he had no need to run. But he did need opium. And Mother Pink gave it to him. Just like the Chinamen, she kept the location secret, but she'd heard the story of their deaths and was careful to avoid the same misunderstanding.

Samuel LaBat had been jailed for stealing a horse that he didn't need. It belonged to a magistrate and was the only light-buckskin horse in a settlement full of brown animals, so he was easy to find. Mother Pink had known of LaBat's ability with pen and paper and decided she had need of his skills. She was also aware of the judge's weakness for golden hair and uncovered knees. So Mother sent a talented colleague to persuade him to release the poet.

LaBat thanked Mother for giving him his freedom, but there was something more he needed from her. He needed her stories. If his writing was to be immortal, the words had to be good. They had to be about love and struggle and violence and deception. And when LaBat met Mother Pink and Jack, he knew they would make great stories.

Jack Pink himself didn't owe a financial debt to his mother, nor was she supplying him with drugs or the promise of stories. But he could not live without her. If he was alone, the world would be too dark and he would die.

That night, the Pink Gang was quiet by the fire. It had been a longer day's ride than usual.

'All right now, you boys,' Mother said to Carrigan and LaBat, 'it's time for Jack to sleep.'

They knew what that meant. Carrigan got up on his massive legs and LaBat put down his pen and paper, and they both walked away from the fire, just as they did each night.

'You can have a treat when you come back, Benny. All right?' she said to Carrigan as he walked into the dark, breaking the bark and sticks with his wide feet.

Mother got up and went to her son and sat with him and touched his face.

'You're so warm, darling,' she said. 'You're very, very hot. You sit yourself so close to the flames. Were you cold today?'

'I was,' Jack said. 'Why is it getting so cold?'

'It's almost winter, darling. Remember? This is when it gets colder. It's hot in the summer and cold in the winter.'

'I don't like it.'

'We'll get some more blankets. We'll do that tomorrow. Would that be good?'

'Yes, please.'

'"Yes, please",' Mother repeated and she smiled. 'You have such wonderful manners, Jack darling. I told you, you can always get the things you want with manners. Now it's time to sleep. Busy tomorrow.'

Mother Pink took a lace napkin, and put it across her shoulder. She pulled Jack closer. Her son was full grown and muscular, but at night she was able to hold him like a child.

She unbuttoned the front of her dress and took out a plump white breast. She put a hand behind Jack's head and lowered him down until his beard-covered lips found her nipple.

Mother Pink started to hum a song as her son fed and she combed his hair with her fingers.

'We're going to have such fun tomorrow,' she said, almost singing her words through the tune. 'Aren't we?' She took the napkin and dabbed the corner of his mouth.

'We'll ride into town. And we'll use our manners. And we'll get just what we want. Do you know your name?' It was a question she asked him every night, and he moved his head to nod without leaving her breast. 'Yes, it's Jack Pink. You know. And everyone else will know soon. Won't they?'

The hummed song hung over the camp as Jack Pink's eyes closed and his belly filled.

From the trees, Samuel LaBat was not permitted to watch. But he watched anyway, as Carrigan walked further into the bush to urinate.

LaBat grinned, knowing that there would be a time when he could describe the breast-feasting scene. But he knew he'd never be able to tell it while he rode with the gang. Although he himself travelled with two revolvers, he didn't like the idea of fighting Carrigan and Jack Pink. Or Mother. They were all too dangerous.

But everything about them made a good story – starting with Jack's conception and birth.

As a young woman, Mother Pink had worked in Melbourne. She was born somewhere along the Murray River, but went south alone while she was still a child. One night when she was nineteen, she took money from a cobbler in exchange for sexual pleasure, but all her attempts failed and then he refused to pay. She came at him with a blade but he pulled a burning log from the fireplace and pushed it in her face. The pain of the burn put her into a coma that was so deep it was thought that she had died. And while she was in her sleep, she was visited by a policeman and his dog. They stayed with her for two nights, and when they left, the seed of Jack Pink was in her belly. Mother slept as her son grew inside her and only woke when the birth began. And she woke screaming. But it wasn't the contractions that made her cry out – she was still screaming from the burning log.

LaBat loved that story, although he was planning to change the assailant from a cobbler to a woodcutter. Cobblers were not known to be dangerous men. Someone who worked with an axe would be better.

But still, LaBat thought, it was a hell of a yarn. Everything about the Pinks was a hell of a yarn.

*

At the third campfire was a police constable named Harry Logan, his dog, and an Aboriginal girl.

The policeman and his animal had nothing to do with the impregnation of Mother Pink. Harry had never patrolled in Melbourne, and he'd never met the woman or her son. Although he'd certainly heard of them. Every policeman, and anyone who'd read a newspaper, knew about the Mother Pink Gang.

That night, Constable Harry Logan was unaware of how close he was to the criminals. He couldn't see their fire or hear Mother's song or feel the indelicate footsteps of Carrigan. But Harry wasn't searching for them and he hadn't been warned they were in the area. The last he'd heard, the gang had gone south, stealing lambs and trading in rough grog. But that had been more than a month before.

Either way, they were not in Harry's thoughts. Instead, he was distracted by a large splinter of red gum deep under the skin of his right palm.

He got a candle from his saddlebag but the light wasn't strong enough. The morning would have been better, but the wound was too painful and he wouldn't be able to sleep until he got it out. So the candle would have to do.

On the other side of the fire, the girl sat in the dirt, hugging her legs with her chin resting on her knees.

She was grinning. Her name was Mary.

'What are you doing over there, Constable boss?'

'Nothing,' said Harry. 'Go to sleep.'

'I bloody well tried.'

'Well, try again. Or stay awake. I don't care. Just stop talking for a while. I need to do this.' His face twisted with concentration.

'What are you doing, Constable boss?'

'Nothing, I said.'

'You just said you need to do something.'

'Just . . .' Harry looked at her over the fire. 'Just . . . give me a minute, will you?'

'Yes, boss.'

'And I told you to stop calling me boss.' Harry winced as he felt for the wood in his hand. 'I'm not your boss.'

'You got me chained to a tree, boss. I reckon that makes you the boss.'

Harry looked up and Mary smiled, her teeth and eyes flashing in the middle of her face.

'Do you ever shut up?'

'Dunno. Maybe,' Mary said. 'But for you, Constable boss, I bloody shut up.'

There was an iron shackle around her ankle, and a chain leading to a tree ten feet away. Mary had old scars on both of her shins, but they were healed and toughened and didn't hurt. They just got itchy sometimes.

Harry put his hand closer to the candle. Almost close enough to burn himself. He saw the injury. It was more of a chunk than a splinter, and there was no end to pinch out with his fingernails. He tried again and gave a small yelp.

'That doesn't sound too good over there, boss.'

'Be quiet.'

'You want some help? I can help. You want me to help? What is it? What's the bloody problem?'

'Look, if I tell you what it is, will you shut up long enough for me to get it done?'

'Yes, Constable boss,' she said and crossed her heart to show she was serious. She didn't know what the gesture meant but she'd seen someone do it once. And she made more of a circle than a cross.

'Right, I've got a splinter and I'm trying to get it out. All right? Is that enough information for you?'

'Yes, boss.'

'Good. Now please shut up.'

Harry's dog was not much more than a pup and had been sitting with Mary as the sun set, but was now moving around the dark looking for food and small animals to chase. Mary scratched her bare foot and rotated the shackle so she could cross her legs. She listened to the fire and the sound of water boiling on the coals and tried to stay quiet for a minute. But she didn't try very hard.

'Constable boss?'

'What?'

'What hand got the wood in it?'

'This one,' Harry said, grunting and frustrated.

'I can't see. Hold it up.'

'It's this one. The right one.'

'Oh, okay.'

'Be quiet now.'

'What you got to get it out?'

'This.'

'What's that, boss? I can't see.'

'This . . . this . . . a needle.'

'That should do the job.'

'Yes, it should but it's a . . .' Harry tried to concentrate.

'A what? What you using?'

'. . . a flamin' bag needle.'

'A bag needle, boss? A bloody bag needle? One of them big bastards?'

'Yes. And it hurts, so would you just be quiet?'

'What hand you shoot with, boss?'

'What?'

'When you hold that gun of yours, what hand you use?'

'Why?'

'What hand, Constable boss?'

'My right hand.'

'Well, that's tough work – you using a big bastard needle and you doing it with ya wrong hand.'

'I'm all right. I just need a minute.'

'Come on, boss, let me help you.'

'No.'

'I got two good hands. See.' Mary held up her palms and waggled her fingers like she had puppets attached. 'They work real good. And I got good eyes too. I can see with that little candle. No problem.'

'No.'

'What you worried about? You think I get over there and hit you on the head with a rock, or something? I don't do things like that. You're the boss.'

'I'm not letting you loose, Mary. I told you that. It's too hard to catch you.'

'You think I'd run away on you?'

'Yes.'

'Nah, I won't. Promise.'

'No, I said.'

'Really promise, boss. Like a really big promise. This dog of yours would chase me anyway.'

The dog walked back to the fire and found a place to lie with Mary. He put his head on her lap and she patted him with easy affection.

'That dog?' Harry said, letting out an exaggerated scoff.

'Yeah. This bloke here.'

'You think that dog is going to chase you through the bush and drag you back here to me?'

'Oh yeah. He's your dog, boss. You're the boss.'

'Not likely – he likes you more than he ever liked me. If I took off them chains, it'd be the last time I'd see the both of you.'

'Oh, don't say that,' Mary said and lifted the animal's head with both hands and looked into its face. 'You love the Constable boss, don't you, mate? You think he's a good fella.'

'Damn it!' Harry said, as he slipped and pushed the red gum further into his flesh.

'Come on, boss. You come over here then. You bring that needle and the bloody candle and I'll get that bugger out for you. Me and dog. Won't we, mate?'

'Yes all right, damn it,' Harry said, defeated. He stood and moved around the fire to sit with Mary.

'You'll have to come closer there. Can't see, boss. You hold the light close and where's that needle?'

Harry gave Mary his hand and became her patient as well as her captor. Her skin was much cooler than his and the feeling soothed the pain. Apart from grabbing her by the shoulder three days before, and putting the iron around her leg, this was the first time he'd touched her.

'Poor old fella,' she said. 'You got half a bloody tree stuck in here. No wonder the bastard hurts.'

'Watch your language, Mary,' Harry said, but his voice was softer.

'Hold up that flame a bit more there, Constable boss.'

'This is your fault.'

'Me?'

'Yes, you.'

'What did I bloody well do?'

'You wanted a bigger fire, so I had to go out in the dark and get more wood and this happened. And before that you didn't like the tucker I made and I had to find something else. You wouldn't just let me sit here in peace, would you?'

'Don't move, boss.' Mary began to use the needle. 'Hold still. Come on, give me that hand back. It'll just hurt for a bit. Just a little bit. And hold up that thing, boss. I got good eyes, but they not that bloody good.'

'Just get on with it, please.'

The dog stood to watch.

'You got a razor, boss?'

'I'm not giving you a razor.'

'Come on. You got a real smooth face all over. No whiskers. I know you've got a real good one.'

'Yeah, I've got a razor, and yeah, it's a good one, but I'm not giving it to you.'

Harry Logan always kept his razor shining and sharp, and shaved every morning. Even when he was sleeping out in the bush. His wife wouldn't kiss him with any beard or stubble, and he had enjoyed kissing the beautiful face of Alice Logan more than doing anything else in this world. So he shaved every day. Even though there were no more kisses. And there was no more Alice Logan.

'I just need it to make a little cut right here in the skin,' Mary said. 'Just a little tiny one with that razor. And then dig this mongrel bastard right out. Yes?'

'No.'

'But it's gonna take longer and hurt more,' she said, starting to work on his hand again. 'What you think, boss? You think I'm gonna use the razor to cut your bloody throat?'

'Yes, I do.'

'Oh no, he don't like me, dog. He thinks I'm gonna kill him. I don't do things like that. Tell him, dog.'

Harry lifted the candle higher to see Mary's face. She was a beautiful-looking child, and she would become a pretty woman. The elegance of her cheeks and nose and mouth didn't match the worn clothes, knotted hair and love of all swear words.

'How old are you?' Harry asked her.

'Don't know.'

'Have a guess.'

'Don't know,' Mary said and she shrugged without looking up from the hand. It was a question she'd given up asking herself. And guessing didn't change anything.

'Fifteen?' Harry said.

'Sure. That'll do.'

'Sixteen?'

'Don't know.'

'Hey, go slow with that thing. It hurts.'

'Don't go moving again, Constable boss. It'll hurt more if you do.' Mary stopped and huffed before she abandoned the needle. 'That's not bloody working.' Then she put her face into Harry's hand and bit into his palm with her young, strong teeth.

'Bugger me! Hey! What are you doing?' The dog barked from the noise and quick movements.

Harry felt the sting of the red gum as it was pulled out of him, and Mary lifted her head and smiled with the splinter between her front teeth.

'Here you go, boss,' she said with her jaws still together. Then she spat the wood into the fire and the coals sizzled with her saliva. 'Give me a look there. Show me. Ah, that got the bastard. He's all out now.'

Harry stared at his hand. He could still feel Mary's face there, and the wetness of her mouth on his palm. He liked the feeling, but there was nothing sexual in the pleasure. He knew there were men like that, but he wasn't one of them. This was about the touch of a child and human warmth.

The feeling stayed with him through the night. The pain was gone and the fire burned as they all slept.

*

The magpies woke Jesus Whitetree, and he remembered his own name.

He liked the mornings. In the big cold brick building, he could never see the light until it reached the high windows. But now he could see all of it. He could watch the sun rise through the trees of one horizon, and watch it all day until it fell into the trees on the other side. He had waited fifty years to see a proper dawn, so he welcomed each one.

And he had slept well. He didn't dream of anything white or beautiful, but the dreams weren't bad either.

He stood and yawned and flapped the dirt from his clothes, and piddled without moving from his camp. There was no need for a fire. There was nothing to cook and Jesus had no tea to boil.

He felt his own body, pushing his fingers into his ribs, and he wished he was stronger and bigger. It was just food. That was all he needed. Hot food. And twice a day. Then he'd be strong.

It will come, Jesus thought. Soon it will come. Keep walking in the straight line. Keep walking straight and there will be gold. And the gold will bring the food and a place that is softer than the ground, and the sun and I can lie together all morning. Strong and lazy.

He lifted his nose and pulled in the air. He did it every morning, hoping to smell gold. He didn't know if it had a smell but most things did. He knew the scent of wood and meat and leather. They were all important things in this world, so something as great as gold surely would have a smell too.

And it must be the greatest of all the smells.

Jesus also knew that gold was kept underground. But he had nothing to dig with. So he kept walking and thought about all the gold that could be under his feet. He'd tried to get to it with sharp sticks and his hands, but it made his fingers bleed and he wasn't strong enough yet. He needed food, and he needed a shovel. And if he had them, he'd stop and dig, get some gold, and then he'd buy an axe and cut down some trees and make a house. He'd cook chickens and have them with potatoes, and make a chair to sit on.

But he didn't have these things yet, so he just walked. A straight line. No turning. And if there was gold under him, he'd just have to come back to get it one day.

Yet even without food or a shovel, Jesus Whitetree was already lucky. If he'd started his walk any earlier that day, he would have run into the Jack Pink Gang. Or they would have run into him. Instead, he only saw the steam and smoke from their dying fire and the flat grass where they'd been sleeping.

*

Like Jesus, Jack Pink liked the mornings, but it was for a more desperate reason.

He was a very different man once the nights were gone. In the dark, he was a frightened boy who couldn't talk, and couldn't think of anything beyond his own fears. And since the night of his birth, he could only sleep feeding at his mother's breast. But with the sunshine, he stood at his full height and feared nothing. And the green eyes that were too afraid to open at night were now sharp and eager to take everything they could from this world.

The gang woke at first light, packed fast and saddled the horses.

'Carrigan,' Jack had said. 'Don't move slow today. I want to get into town.'

Carrigan nodded and rushed to finish his breakfast of opium and bread crusts.

'Find LaBat and tell him to move too. Wherever he bloody is. And have him check his weapons. And then get Mother up on her ride.'

Mother Pink rode a horse that was far bigger than she needed. And as she got older, the more she relied on Carrigan's help to get into the saddle. Riding a tall animal was a habit that had begun when Mother was only a child. She had stolen a Clydesdale to carry her south to Melbourne, and although it was slow, it had made her feel safe and important.

Ben Carrigan rode a stock horse that was more than sixteen hands, but it still looked like a pony when his legs were on either side. And LaBat had a buckskin. It was the same one he'd already stolen and which had put him in jail. But after Mother had him released, LaBat made a calculation that no-one would think him stupid enough to steal the horse a second time. So he stole it and was not suspected.

Jack Pink's horse was raven black, except for a white patch low on its right back leg. Because of its colour, Jack couldn't look at the animal after the sun was set. If it needed tending at night, it was done by Mother or the boys. But in the day, Jack and his animal moved like the same being, and they were so fast through the scrub or the open ground that nothing could catch them.

This morning, the gang moved together with Jack in the lead.

'I need to find a word,' LaBat said, cutting the silence.

'What word?' asked Mother.

'We need something to go with Jack's name – we can't just have Jack Pink. There's got to be something else. I need something like . . .' LaBat held out his arm as if he was about to start a song.

'Like what?'

'Like . . . MAD, or something.'

'Mad?'

'Yeah, MAD Jack Pink.'

'No. I don't like that.'

'Yes, you're right, Mother – not MAD. But something like that. LUCKY Jack Pink. Or BRAVE Jack Pink. Or FAST Jack Pink.'

'Oh, I like BRAVE.'

'Yeah, but it's a bit dull.' LaBat got a pen and some paper from his bag and let the horse take itself. 'I want something with a bit more . . .' And he held out his arm again.

'But BRAVE is good. And it's the truth.'

'Well, it doesn't have to be true, necessarily. We just need people to remember it. What about CUNNING?'

'CUNNING? What does that mean?'

22

'CUNNING? It means smart and tricky. Like a fox?'

'No, I don't like it?'

'What's wrong with it?' LaBat was already wagging his pen to make a note of the word.

'No, it sounds rude.'

'Does it?'

'Yes. It's vulgar.'

'Why?'

'Because it sounds like that word.'

'What word?

'You know the word . . .'

'No, I don't.'

'Well, I'm not going to say it. And I don't want you boys to say it either.'

'All right,' LaBat said, and scratched a single red line to remove 'CUNNING' from the list. 'No matter. I'll think of something.'

'Why do you need another word, anyway? He's got a beautiful name.'

'He does,' LaBat said, smiling at the woman's energetic affection for her boy, and remembering Jack's late-night feeding at her bosom.

'Yes, it's very good, Mother. It just needs a little more music to it. It's only got two syllables. You see,' LaBat turned to Carrigan as though the big man had asked him a question. 'See, you've got a good one – Ben Carrigan. Four syllables. It rolls from the mouth nicely. And it has a strong downward inflection at the end.' Carrigan looked back, his eyes half-closed from the effects of his breakfast.

'And you, Mother Pink,' said LaBat. 'See, three syllables. It's a great name. But Jack Pink is a little . . . I dunno. It just needs . . .'

'Well,' said Mother, 'do whatever you need to do. That's your job. Just make sure that people remember him.'

'Will do,' LaBat said and turned to Jack. 'What do you think, Jack? It's your name, boss. What do you reckon?'

'Shut up, LaBat,' Jack said. 'We're nearly in town. Are you loaded?'

'I am, boss.'

'Well, that's enough cunning for this morning's job.'

*

The dog woke first and turned over in the dirt. Mary put her arm around its ribs and collected its warmth.

'Morning, mate,' she said before her eyes opened.

She could hear Constable Harry Logan snoring. Just as she had through the whole night. And she'd come to know the pattern – it was a minute of throaty vibrations, then silence, then a gasp, then some mumbles, and back to the vibrations.

'He's a loud bugger,' Mary whispered to the dog. 'How did I ever let that bloke catch me? Hey? Have a look at him, mate.'

Harry was using his saddle for a pillow and the blanket had fallen off his belly. His mouth was open and his chin rattled like a piece of machinery that had come loose.

'He's not much of a tracker, mate. He's always gettin' lost. He's slow and he's noisy and he can't even get wood without hurtin' himself.' Mary got up on her elbow and looked at the dog. 'But he still bloody caught me. Or was it you, hey? Did you sniff me out? That's all right, mate. I forgive you.'

Mary kissed the top of the dog's head and it licked around to find her face. She scratched her shins and settled the iron at her ankle.

'Hey,' Mary whispered to the dog. 'Where's he keep them keys, mate? Do you know?'

The dog was no help, but they sat together until Harry woke himself between a gasp and a mumble. His eyes sprang open and he looked surprised until he remembered where he was and who he was travelling with.

'Morning, Constable boss.'

Harry said nothing, but when he was better awake, he made a small fire and cooked bacon. He knew Mary liked it so it would keep her quiet for the few minutes she was eating, and she'd give her rind to the dog once she got all the meat off.

In the mornings, it was rare for Constable Harry Logan to rush. He would shave after breakfast, covering himself with a deep lather before beginning the slow process under his right sideburn. And with each stroke, he would think of Alice.

Then he'd saddle his horse. And what a beauty she was.

She'd been with him for almost five years and although he always thought of her as *his* horse, in truth she belonged to the Crown. She was strong but elegant – a true thoroughbred – and her grey coat reminded him of the white ashes of a dying fire. She had black stockings to the knees and black feet and a single dark mark between her eyes. But it wasn't just her beauty that made Harry love her; it was because the animal was his last earthly connection to Alice Logan.

She had adored the horse.

When Harry had first collected the grey from the police stables, Alice kept telling him how beautiful she was, and although it was regulation to brand all police horses with a Crown, she made her husband promise he'd never let them do it.

So far, he had kept that promise.

Every morning at their home, Alice would give the grey treats and call her 'my sweet one'. Then she'd rub its head and gently blow air into its nostrils.

'What are you doing?' Harry had asked her.

'I'm getting her used to my smell. So she knows it's me.'

'If you keep feeding her, she'll know it's you all right, Alice girl.'

And Harry's wife had such a wonderful smell. It was the first thing he'd noticed about her. She smelt like warm butter and pears. And as they fell in love and married, he realised her scent didn't come from a soap or perfume. The smell was just a part of her, like her long dark hair and brown eyes.

When Alice died two years after they got the grey, Harry thought about all the breath his wife had put into the animal's nostrils and imagined that all the warm butter and pears were still in there – as though she'd been deliberately transporting small pieces of her soul into the horse so it would be there when she was gone.

So every morning, when Harry put the blanket and saddle on, he'd think about Alice and the things she'd say as he was leaving for work.

'You take care of him today, sweet one,' she'd tell the horse. 'Don't let him get you lost. Bring him home to me.'

And he'd lift his nose, hoping to get a smell of Alice leaking from the animal. But it never came.

Harry didn't give a name to his grey horse, but he thought of her as 'Alice girl' or 'the sweet one'. It was something he'd never be able to explain to another person. And he didn't want to.

That morning, after they were packed, Harry mounted up and Mary walked beside him in chains and bare feet and the dog rambled around them and sniffed most passing trees.

'Where we goin', Constable boss?'

'I told you yesterday.'

'You said we were going into a town yesterday.'

'Yes, that's right.'

'But we didn't go to a bloody town yesterday.'

'I know that. It was a bit further away than I thought.'

'So where are we going today?'

'Town.'

'You sure, boss?'

'Yes, I'm sure. Stop talking.'

'Which bloody town?'

'Mull Creek.'

'What's in town? Why we going there?'

'I need to go to the police station and check in, all right? We'll stay there tonight. And then I'll take you back.'

'Where we gonna stay?'

'You're gonna stay in the cell.'

'What about you?'

'That's none of your business.'

'You not going to sleep with me at the lock-up?'

'No.'

'Good.'

'Why is that good?'

'Well, you deserve a nice soft bed, Constable boss. That's all,' Mary smiled at the thought of a long sleep without Harry's night noises.

27

The dog fell behind and Mary called it back.

'Come on, mate. Hey, boss?'

'What?'

'How far until we get back to the farm?'

'A couple of days. Four maybe. Why?'

'Just asking.'

'Don't you think about running off on me, Mary. Not while we're in town. Not while we're any place. And stop smiling.'

'I'm just smiling, boss. It's just a beautiful day. Don't you think?'

'It's not funny, Mary. You can't just steal whatever you want whenever you want.'

'I didn't steal. I told you that.'

'The world doesn't work in that way. There has to be laws. What would it be like if everyone just took what they wanted? It's not my fault you're here.'

'I didn't bloody steal.'

'That's not what I hear.'

'I promise you, Constable boss. Biggest promise ever. I didn't steal nothin'.'

'Just stop talking. I'm not supposed to talk to you.'

'Why's that?'

'The Police Regulations of 1856 state that I'm not to engage nor converse with prisoner unless absolutely necessary.'

'What does that mean?'

'It means shut up.'

'What did I steal? Come on then, what did I steal?'

Harry didn't answer. They walked out of the shadows of the bush and into the sun and Harry stopped to let the horse eat the dry grass. Mary sat with the dog and she glared at Harry with exaggerated anger.

'Don't look at me like that. You know what you did. You took money off the landowner, and you stole his deceased wife's jewellery. And you took his horse.'

'That's not true. That bloody horse followed me. Nothin' to do with me.'

'It's not right, Mary. You just can't do those things. That old farmer was good to you, I hear. He gave you a job and tucker, and you stole from him.'

'What job?'

'Your job. At the farm. They said you were cooking and working in the house.'

'I didn't have no job, boss.'

'They told me you were in the kitchen.'

'Nah.'

'Well, doesn't matter. You can't steal.'

'Where's that jewellery, then? I ain't got it,' Mary said and held out her hands and pulled at her clothing to show nothing would fall out. 'Look, boss. Where?' She shook her wrists and tugged at her naked and undecorated earlobes.

'I don't know.'

'You take me to a judge, boss, and then I'll tell him.'

'We're not going to the judge. Believe me, you don't want to go to the judge.'

They started walking again and Mary lifted the chain to take the weight from her ankle.

'Job?' Mary said after a while. 'I didn't have no job. What bloody job I have? The boss chained me up in his room all day and only let me off at night to get into bed with him. Bloody job? I didn't have a job.'

Harry's face twitched, disgusted at the thought of an old, drunk farmer in bed with the girl. But he wondered if the story was true. She'd told him a dozen other tales since he caught her and it was getting hard to know the difference.

'Well, all I know is it's my job to take you back. That's all. It's better you go back. You don't want to go to jail. You're too young for jail. You wouldn't like it. I'm taking you back and you have to work off what you stole.'

'Work off? Is that what you call that thing, Constable boss?' For the first time, Mary almost sounded angry. 'Work off? I guess I'm too bloody young for jail but not too bloody young to get workin' in the old farmer's bed.'

Mary spat at the ground and they walked in silence again, before Harry stopped and lifted her into the saddle with him.

'Come on, Mary,' Harry said. 'Look, we'll be in town in a few hours. And I'll get you something. A sweet or something. How's that?'

*

Not far from Harry and Mary, Jesus Whitetree found a gun.

He'd stopped at a creek. It was flowing and the water looked clean in his hands, so he drank until his belly forgot how much it wanted food.

He checked the sun again to get his direction right. Activities like drinking, sleeping and digging were distracting, and it would be too easy to walk back from where he'd just been. So he always checked.

Jesus walked for another hour before he noticed the earth under his feet was different. The colour was lighter and it made more dust when he kicked at it. He looked around and the trees and bushes hadn't changed, and the weather was the same, but he knew he was in a new place. He wasn't frightened. He liked new things. It meant he wasn't going back to the old.

He wondered if the new ground would be better for holding gold. He knew some types of dirt were better than others. Some had nothing and others had more gold than could be carried.

A breeze came at his face and Jesus pulled it in. But he smelt no gold. Instead he got a terrible stink that robbed his throat of the cool water and replaced it with a kind of poison. It was the smell of meat. But it wasn't fresh and cooked; it was rotten and he had to cough it out.

He held down his breath and walked over the mound to see where the offence was coming from. On the other side was a man and his horse. Both dead.

Jesus stared at them. He wasn't shocked or frightened but it took several minutes to comprehend what he was looking at.

The animal was on its side. Its life was long gone. The muscles had melted and its skin sat on the bones like a blanket thrown over a row of sticks. And the dead man was still in the saddle with a leg either side.

Jesus took a handkerchief from his pocket. He tied the emerald green cloth around his face like a bandit and walked towards the death.

The man was wearing a long brown coat, a white shirt, and a tall hat that remained in its place. As though he was still alive and concerned for his appearance. But he was surely dead because his bearded face was sunken and his eyes had been taken by insects. His mouth was open in a yawn and Jesus could see the white of his jawbone under the patches of skin.

Jesus knew what death looked like. He'd seen it before. But he'd never seen a dead adult. It's the same, he thought. It's just that the bodies are bigger. And their clothes are better.

As the disturbed flies hummed around him, Jesus wondered who had died first. He could see no wounds on the man or the horse, but he guessed the animal had gone first and its death made him sad. It would have been a pretty horse. The legs were frozen on the ground like it was in the middle of a stride, and its neck was straight and nostrils were high like they were still feeding the lungs with air for a hard run.

Jesus had never ridden a horse, but he knew he would be a great rider when his chance came. And it would come. All he needed was a horse. This one would have been perfect.

'Fifty years is too long to live without a horse,' he said to the animal.

He took off his handkerchief and put it over the face of the horse, covering its eyes. And he left his hand there, almost as though he was giving a prayer. But he wasn't. He just wanted to touch it.

Jesus knew it was wrong to leave them like this, so he put his arms under the dead man's shoulders to drag him out, but as he heaved, the rotten body came away at the stomach and Jesus pulled the man in half.

The stench of the open corpse attacked Jesus' face, but he sucked some air into his cheeks and kept dragging the top half until it was under a white gum tree. Then he went back for the legs.

Jesus had wanted to bury the man but he couldn't. The new ground may have had more dust, but underneath it was just the same hard dirt that he'd been walking on for weeks. So he assembled the two halves of the body and folded the arms over the hollow chest.

The man's brown coat looked like it had many pockets, and Jesus could see that some were full. Perhaps they all were. And he wondered what was in them. A bright silver watch and chain? A proper eating knife? Some food – yes, maybe a little dried beef? Or was there gold? Gold! Yes, why not gold? This seemed like a man who had gold. Jesus couldn't smell anything over the dead stink. But there might well be gold in the pockets.

He wanted to open the coat to look. But he didn't.

Jesus went back to the horse and noticed the saddle for the first time. It was beautiful – just perfect for an animal like this. The leather was carved with long flower patterns and shining from the wear of long rides.

He unbuckled the girth, and although he tried to be gentle, the dead ribs of the horse cracked as he pulled back on the strap. He dragged the saddle out and Jesus fell in the dirt with the last yank. It was heavier than he'd expected and he rested with it on his lap. It was warm, almost like it was the only part of the great horse that was still alive. He put his nose to it and got the sweet waft of leather and animal sweat.

He felt around the saddle, then he touched something that wasn't warm. It was the kind of cold that could only come from metal. And he touched it again without looking. It had a handle that his fingers curled around.

It was a revolver.

He pulled it from the saddle holster and held it in front of his face. He couldn't believe it was in his hand. It was dark grey – almost black – and the handle was white, the same white as the dead man's jawbone.

Jesus knew nothing about guns but he knew what it was.

What he didn't know was this was a Colt Model 1851 Navy revolver, with a handle carved from East African ivory. To Jesus, the concept of an elephant would have been impossible to comprehend, but the feeling of holding a piece of its tusk was like nothing else he'd ever known. It was something magic, yet it was still natural. As though it belonged in his hand.

He sat with the saddle and the gun, thinking for a long time before he got up and walked back to the body. The shadow of Jesus was long in the late afternoon and he paused before he spoke to the two halves of the dead rider.

'Hello, sir. Umm, my name is Jesus Whitetree. First, I would just like to say that I'm sorry that you are dead. I'm very, very sorry. And I am sorry that your horse is also dead. I hope you did not suffer with any pains before you died.'

Jesus coughed and he rolled his fingers over the handle of the gun.

'Second, I'm sorry but I will not be able to bury you today. I simply do not have a shovel. But I will cover you in fresh leaves. One day soon, I hope to purchase a real good one, and if I do, I will return to make you a real grave. I hope this is okay.'

Jesus blinked as he considered his next few words.

'Now, I have made a decision not to remove the things in your pockets. There may be gold and there may be food, and

I'd like both, but that would just not be right. They are yours. However . . .'

He paused and looked at the sunset.

'. . . however . . . I'm gonna take the saddle and the gun. Thank you.'

*

While Jesus held his revolver for the first time, Jack Pink arrived in Mull Creek.

The town was born in a valley, and for decades it was nothing more than a few huts and some skinny cattle surviving around a trickle of water. But in 1851 there was a major strike of gold, and since then Mull Creek had become a busy and wealthy place. There was more of everything. More animals, more people, more Chinese, and more mines.

The Pink Gang rested on the ridge above, before they moved off and followed the track down to the middle of town to find Mull Creek's biggest store. The sign on the front read 'THOMPSON & SON'.

'Good morning to you, Mr Thompson,' Jack said, coming in the door first. Mother Pink, Carrigan and LaBat followed and spread out.

'Good day,' the storekeeper said with a practised courtesy that he gave to all strangers.

Jack walked to the counter and stared at the man before he smiled.

'Good day,' the keeper repeated. He was a shorter man with round red cheeks and sandy hair.

Jack waited and smiled again, but this time, as though he was posing for a portrait.

'What are you in need of today?' said the keeper.

'Ah,' Jack said and held up a finger. 'You don't remember me, Mr Thompson? Come on now, you must.'

The keeper looked at Jack, and he kept his courtesy until he saw the big woman in lace at the back of his shop with a burn mark on her cheek – it was a face he hoped he'd never see again – then he looked back at the man with the green eyes.

'Jack? Is that you, Jack?'

'That's better. Thank you, Mr Thompson. I have to say, I was beginning to feel a little injured that you didn't know me. But I understand, my whiskers have come a long way down since I was last here.'

'Yes, perhaps,' Thompson said, trying to steady himself, but he heard the shaking in his own voice.

'Mr LaBat,' Jack said to the writer while keeping his eyes on the shopkeeper. 'May I introduce you to an old friend of mine? This is Arthur Thompson. He's owned this store for eleven years. Is that right, Mr Thompson? Eleven?'

'Twelve.'

'Twelve? Well, hell, I didn't think it was that long. And you wouldn't think it, LaBat, but it started out as just a shack – right in this same place here.' Jack pointed to the floor. 'And back then, there was nothing but some tobacco and a couple of shovels and pans. But look at it now. There's nothing you can't get at Thompson's. Isn't that what people have been saying? Hey? There's nothing you can't get at Thompson's. That's a good reputation to have, ain't it?'

Mother Pink moved through the store and skimmed her fingers over a roll of dress material. And Carrigan waited by the door.

'LaBat, notice how I call this gentleman "Mr Thompson". That's because I wasn't much more than a lad the last time I was here. And it was "Mr Thompson" back then. Do you mind if I call you "Arthur"?'

Thompson shook his head.

'You don't mind? That's grand. Well, Arthur, I like the new sign you have at the front of the shop – Thompson & Son. That is wonderful. I said to Mother, "I didn't know Arthur had a son." And she heard how Mrs Thompson was walking about with a nice big belly. Now, I don't have a great brain like Mr LaBat over there, but I'd say she had a boy. Would that be right?'

'Yes.'

'Well, that's just mighty. What's his name? It's okay, you can tell me. I'd like to know.'

'Arthur.'

'Arthur,' Jack said and smiled at his mother, who was now smelling a bar of soap. 'Isn't that lovely. Another Arthur Thompson in Mull Creek. But I have to say, Thompson, that's very ... umm ...' Jack clicked his fingers. 'LaBat, what's that word?'

'What's that, boss?'

'You know the word – when bad things are always happening to other people, but someone reckons it won't ever happen to them? What do you call that word?'

'Optimistic.'

'Ah yeah, that's it. I like that word. You're optimistic, Arthur. Very, very optimistic. There are thousands of tiny little babies

37

that don't live to their first birthday – I mean, Mother knows of a family who lost four children – but that doesn't bother you. You're so . . . optimistic that you put a sign out the front saying, "Thompson & Son". That's optimistic. You're optimistic.' Jack pointed at Thompson as though he'd won a prize. 'Blessings to you, Arthur. Because, I mean, the winter is coming and you know how tough the cold is on the little ones. But that didn't stop you. No, sir.'

While Jack let the thought sit with the shopkeeper, the wooden boards of the floor above creaked. Jack looked to the ceiling, like a cat hearing a mouse in the walls.

'Ah, there's the wife now,' he said. 'Checking on young Arthur, no doubt. Just to make sure he's all right. How many times does she do that in a day? If I had to guess, I'd say a lot. Am I right? Hey, Arthur? She's just checking he's still . . . you know . . . still breathing. Maybe she's not as . . . optimistic as you are, Arthur. What did she think of the sign outside? I bet she told you to wait. Am I right? Did she tell you to wait until little Arthur was older?'

Thompson didn't answer. His eyes moved to the other faces in his shop, searching for kindness. He knew enough about Mother Pink to know it wouldn't come from her, and the others wouldn't be riding with her if they had any tenderness to their character.

'No, I bet she wasn't keen at all,' said Jack. 'But, you know what, I think I would've been just like you. I'd be too proud to wait.'

'Jack . . . please don't . . .'

'Don't what? Hey listen, I'd like to help out where I can, so would you like me to get Carrigan here to go up and check on the young bloke?'

Thompson watched Jack's eyes move to the man at the door. The shopkeeper had never seen a bigger person. He felt like he'd walked into the tent of a travelling circus that boasted of having the world's only living giant.

'He loves children, does Ben Carrigan,' said Jack. 'I know he doesn't look like it, but you'd be surprised.' Jack flicked his head to give the order and the big man walked to the stairs. The steps groaned as he went up.

'No, Jack, please. Don't . . .' Thompson said, coming out from behind the counter. He was no longer able to hide his fear.

'It's all right, Thompson. You just stay there. We'd like to help. Ben will take care of it. And you and me can do some trading. How's that sound to ya?'

Jack let the silence sit and he kept his eyes on the shopkeeper. The soft click of a revolver came from under LaBat's coat from the back of the room, just to keep Thompson still. The floorboards above groaned from the presence of Carrigan and there was a woman's startled voice. No-one downstairs could understand what she said, but there were noises of panic, and there was a quick wooden bang, as if someone was moving furniture and had dropped it for the last few inches.

'He loves children.'

'Please, Jack.'

'No problem, it's what old mates do for each other.' Jack walked around the store. 'You know, LaBat. You would think Arthur Thompson and I have been friends forever. But it's not true. We weren't always so close. There were a few troubles along the way. But that's okay, all friendships have to walk on some rough ground now and then. Don't they, Arthur?'

There was a cry from the baby and the woman's voice again. She was pleading.

'Yes,' Jack continued. 'When I was a young bloke, Arthur and I had a dust-up, I guess that's what you'd call it. I was in here one day – you know, when the shop wasn't much more than a humpy – and I was just having a look around. I didn't have any money but I was only a lad and I was dreaming about the things I'd buy when we had a few coins. Right, Ma?'

Mother Pink nodded and gave Thompson an unwarmed smile.

'Yeah, anyway,' Jack said. 'I was walking around, just like I am now. And Arthur there says, "Pink boy" – that's what he called me – he says, "Pink boy, what have you got in your pocket?" I said, "Nothin'." But he says, "Yes, ya bloody do – you've got one of me pen knives in there . . . and tobacco." I said, "No, Mr Thompson. I don't. Really." But I knew he didn't believe me, because he comes at me and he grabs me arm. Do you remember, Arthur?'

Thompson began to tremble as he tried to think of a way to free his family of the situation.

'I reckoned you would,' Jack said. 'Anyway, I was just a boy so I took off and ran home.'

There was another thump from upstairs and Thompson's wife cried out her husband's name.

'Hang on, Mr Thompson . . . Arthur. Let me finish the story first. This is coming to the important part. Anyway, Labat, that night, the constables come to our home, and they turned the place over, making a terrible mess for Mother to clean up, trying to find that knife and tobacco. And they just don't believe us. No matter what we said.

'And from that day, they just didn't leave us alone. Remember, Ma? But, you know, that's not your fault, Arthur. I don't blame you for that. You just wanted your knife back. But I have to tell ya, that caused a few problems for Mother and me around the place. The troopers started saying things to blacken the good Pink name and we had to get out of town. T'was all we could do.'

Jack walked back to the counter and leaned towards Thompson.

'But, do you want to know what's funny, Arthur – I *did* have that blasted knife. Can you believe that? LaBat, can you believe it? It was in my pocket that whole time. I am buggered if I know how it got there. But it was there. And the tobacco too.'

Jack laughed and gave his own head a comical slap as punishment for being so forgetful.

'That little thing has caused a mountain of trouble since then. Just a little old pen knife. Hasn't it, Ma? By God, I could tell you some stories, Arthur. But I've come here today to give it back to you. Because that's what a good friend would do. I wanted to come here and make things right.'

Jack patted the outside of his clothes, pretending to search for the knife.

'But I don't actually have it on me,' he said and pointed to the ceiling. 'I gave it to Carrigan. He's got the knife with him. And I told him to give it to your son. He's up there making sure he . . . *gets* it. I thought it would be a nice gesture. You know, like passing it on to the next generation. Father to son. I imagined you'd like that, Arthur. You being so . . .'

'Optimistic,' said LaBat from the back.

'Optimistic. Exactly. Thank you, Mr LaBat.'

Jack stared at Thompson, while in the room above, his wife began to howl.

'Now, Arthur, we're going to grab a few things. But I have to be honest, I'm kind of in the same situation I was all those years ago. I'm embarrassed to say it, but I just don't have the coins. I hope that's all right. But at least now you know I can be trusted.'

*

At their fire that night, most of the Pink Gang ate well. Mother made damper and they used it to sop up their stew and have with sweet syrup.

With a full belly, Carrigan needed more opium than usual, but the fresh stock of grog helped settle him for the evening, and he sat with his legs crossed and swayed while he watched the logs burn.

LaBat leaned into the flames and wrote for three hours. His ink bottle was full again and he dipped his pen to record the day's events.

Meanwhile, the hero of the tale – Bold, Brave, Fast, Lucky, Cunning Jack Pink – ate nothing and was trembling under his new blanket with only his nose showing.

Mother stuffed her pipe with Thompson & Son's tobacco, before she sent Carrigan and LaBat into the trees. Then she held Jack and could feel the night terrors under his skin.

'It's all right, darling Jack,' she said, moving him onto her breast. 'Everything is all right. What are you thinking about? Are you thinking about the baby?'

Jack nodded his head as he locked onto her.

'Well, I don't want you to think about that anymore. You'll be asleep soon.'

The fire crackled and Mother fixed the blanket to keep her son's head warm.

'Do you like your blanket? Yes, it's a beauty, isn't it? You did so well today, darling. I was very proud of you. So strong. So smart. And you used all your manners. That's what's important.'

Jack's eyelids fell and Mother hummed.

*

Constable Harry Logan and his prisoner got to Mull Creek the next morning. Although it was another day later than expected, because Harry got them lost again. He thought Mary would make fun of him, but she didn't. She just grinned every time he looked up from the fire.

On their last ride before town, Mary shared the saddle with Harry. She rode with her thin arms around his waist, but they stopped just before they got to the valley, and they looked down from the same ridge where Jack and the gang had sat the afternoon before.

'Righto, Mary,' Harry said. 'You'd better get down and walk. The locals don't like their police going easy on criminals.'

'Yes, boss.'

Mary looked over the town. It was bigger than she'd imagined. Harry had told her about the buildings, the goldmines and the streets full of people, but sitting at the peace of their campfires, she couldn't make a true picture in her head. She'd seen other towns before, but they weren't big like this. They were just like the rest of the bush, with only a few buildings in the middle. But this was different. It was as though the town was a big lizard, and the tops of the houses and shops were like the scales, and the mineshafts were horns on the head.

'Tell me when you're ready,' Harry said.

Mary lifted the chain to take the weight off her ankle. 'Hey, Constable boss, you know what they call us?'

'Who?'

'The people down there. You know what they call my people?'

'What's that?'

'They call us the "Yes People".'

'Yes, I've heard that.'

'They call us that 'cause we say yes to everything. We're so friendly.'

'Come on. Time to go.'

'I'm ready, boss.'

They walked down into Mull Creek, passing the miners and the farmers with their wagons until they got to the streets.

'Don't worry, boss. I'm not smiling. And I do it like this. Watch.' Mary dragged her feet on the well-used road, bent her shoulders, put her chin on her chest and talked as though she had only learnt to speak two weeks before. 'I'm the Yes People. The boss done caught me. Poor, poor me. I didn't say "Yes" the proper way.'

'Stop that, Mary. Walk properly.'

'With the bloody chains on?'

'You know what I mean. Just be . . . sensible.'

'Yes, Constable boss.'

'And don't call me . . .' he stopped before he finished. He'd forgotten that he'd given up that fight.

44

Harry Logan was nervous. Towns had always made him uneasy, and that feeling grew with the population. It had been two years since he'd been to Mull Creek and it was now twice the size. And although he was glad to complete this part of his mission, he would have liked to have avoided the town.

Two women stopped in the street and watched Harry and Mary pass. They were the kind of women who didn't live in Mull Creek before the gold strikes: back when there was no money, no religion, no culture, and no children to teach. They nodded at the Constable and gave him tight smiles of approval at the way he was handling the natives. Harry returned the gesture without pride.

Mary saw them and started to drag her feet again. She stuck out her bottom lip and looked at the pair as though she'd just been whipped with a green sapling. But then she flashed them her best smile and winked, making a clicking sound as she did.

'Morning, ladies,' Mary said.

The women huffed and found something else to look at.

The Mull Creek Police Station was in the same place as Harry remembered, but it was now made of brick, there were more places to tie the horses, and the entrance seemed less like a bush hut and more like a real home for the constabulary. But the first face Harry saw was the one he'd expected. Sergeant Tom Addington.

'Well, bugger me,' Addington said. 'Have a look at this, would you? Harry bloody Logan.'

Tom Addington had been in the town long before the first strike and Harry had known him even before that. Harry would never have thought of Tom as a fat man. He'd always been a little lumpy and unconditioned, but now his belly was filled with gold and his face was red and round like a plate.

Anyone who knew Mull Creek knew Tom Addington.

'They told me you were getting in a week ago,' Tom bellowed. His voice was always louder than it needed to be. 'Where're you been? You get lost again?'

'Good day, Tom.' Harry shook his hand and didn't explain himself. '"Sergeant Tom" now, is it? Do I need to bow or anything?'

'No, but I think you bloody well should. I thought I was gonna be a constable forever.'

'How did you manage it?'

'I just waited for everyone else to die. And I've got a bit more help these days. By God, I need it. The town's gone mad. People everywhere. Come on, let's go get a drink.'

Tom Addington walked past Mary to get his cap from the wall. He didn't look at her, he just took a key off the same hook and tossed it to Harry.

'The cell's at the back there. My bloke's having a snooze. He'll keep an eye on things.'

Harry took Mary to the lock-up. They walked past a constable who was snoring on his back, and Mary shook her head at the thought of trying to sleep near another noisy trooper.

The cell door was heavy and it took Harry two hands to close it. He looked through the hole and Mary could only see his eyes.

'I won't be long. You all right in there?'

'Yes, boss,' she said, standing in the middle of the dark cell.

There was no fire and no dog, and Mary could feel the chill coming off the brick and onto her bare shoulders. And for the first time in a month, she couldn't find anything to smile about.

'See ya, Harry,' she said to herself when he was gone.

*

Harry Logan had forgotten how much Tom Addington liked drinking, but he was soon reminded at the bar of the hotel. The sergeant's face didn't react to the first slug from his glass, so Harry knew it wasn't his only grog for the day. The bar was busy, like the rest of the town, and Addington made no effort to hide his uniform or pay for his drink.

'Well, you picked a good time to get here, Harry,' Addington said. 'You missed all the excitement.'

'What's that?'

'We had a famous visitor here yesterday.'

'Famous?'

'Yep.'

'The governor?'

'Oh, better than that, my old mate. Mother Pink was in town.'

'Bugger me.' Harry looked over his shoulder as though the woman might be behind him. 'Mother Pink was here?'

'Yes, Harry.'

'Was she alone?'

'Oh no, we got the pleasure of the whole gang. Don't worry, she's gone. At least, I hope she bloody is.'

'Did you see them?'

'Nah.'

There was no hint of shame on the sergeant's face. Another law officer might have been embarrassed if the Pink Gang came and went without his knowledge. But his new rank, and the constant presence of alcohol in his blood, had made Tom Addington immune to shame.

'Arthur Thompson saw them, though,' Addington said, looking at the barman and pointing at his empty glass. 'They bailed up his shop. And they scared the ghost out of him. He needed eight mouthfuls of rum before I could get a word out of the bastard.'

'Mother Pink back in Mull Creek? I didn't think that would ever happen. I thought she was south these days. What happened at Thompson's shop?'

'They threatened to kill his baby boy. It's only a couple of months old. They put a knife to its throat. And then they ran off with half his store.'

'A baby? A knife? Bugger me.'

'That's what he told me. I don't think he would have made it up. I don't like Thompson – he's always talking crap about getting robbed – but his wife had the same story. She needed ten mouthfuls. The boy is alive, thank Christ.'

'Hell.' Harry tipped the liquor into his mouth. He felt a lift in his unease at being in a town again. Goldmines and brick buildings made people evil, and if he wasn't convinced of that before, he certainly was now.

Addington waved at the bar to hurry them for another round.

'Who's she running with now, Tom? Who's the gang?'

'Well, Thompson said her son was there. Jack. And he did all the talking. Which I find very flamin' hard to believe. He was a stupid little shit when they were here years ago. Do you know him?'

'No, I can't say I do.'

'And they had a big bloke with them. He was the one with the knife. Name of Carrigan.'

'Ben Carrigan?'

'I don't know. Just Carrigan is all I've got.'

'Really big, is he?'

'Yeah, that's what Thompson said. A bloody mountain. Do you know him?'

'I might. And if it's the same Carrigan, then I'm not bloody surprised Thompson was shaking. He's lucky the child didn't get eaten. He's a rotten bastard. And he's been shot at least three times and he's still walking around. What are you gonna do?'

'What do you mean?'

'Are you going after them?'

'Shit no.'

'You're not?'

'Nah, I can't. There's only the two of us here. And the Company wouldn't like it – there's too much money in town these days. We can't just leave the station. The second we do, there'll be a brawl in the street and every bastard will join in and the mines will get shut for the day and the Company will scream blue murder. Nah, can't have that. Do you want the job?'

'What job?'

'Track down Mother Pink.'

'No, thank you.'

'Come on, you were a pretty good shot, if I remember right.'

'I'm not that good.'

'And you can ride hard.'

'No thanks.'

'And I see you've still got that magnificent grey out there with you. What a lovely horse that is, you lucky bugger. How did the depot let you have an animal like that? Beautiful. Too good for you. On her back you'd chase them down.'

'I'm not doing it. I like the odds a little more in my favour.'

And more than being outnumbered, Harry knew his own sense of direction would never get him close to the gang. Unless it was an accident. He was a capable policeman when he was in front of a criminal, but someone else needed to find them first.

Addington drank and shrugged. 'Fair enough. I don't blame you. But listen, would you do me a favour, though?' Addington leaned forward. 'Can you stay for a week? Or maybe two?'

'What for?' Harry felt the nerves jump again.

'The Company's worried about the gang coming back. That Thompson bail-up might have just been a practice – you know, to see if we'd put up a fight. So the bosses are jumpy. The Company would feel better if there was another trooper around. And I told them you were coming in.'

'I dunno, Tom.'

'Come on, mate. Give us a hand.'

'I've got to get the girl back.'

'What girl?'

'My prisoner.'

'The native?'

'I've got to get her back to the farm.'

'Oh, bugger that. Just leave her in the cell. Ya worried about some old grazier having a cold bed for a couple more weeks? Come on.'

Harry took a drink. 'All right.' He wasn't persuaded, but he knew Tom Addington could order him to stay if needed. So, more arguing was pointless.

'Good. Thanks, Harry. Hey listen, there's something else I need to ask you about. You didn't come across a fella by the name of Noble in the last couple of weeks, did ya? Andre Noble. Wears a long brown coat and a tall hat.'

'No, I didn't see anyone like that.'

'Well, you'd know it if you did. He stands out. He carries a Colt with an ivory handle. And he's got a saddle with flowers carved in it. Real fancy bugger'

'Is he a crook?'

'Oh nah, he works for the mining company. He's like a private detective for them. He's a mean bastard. But he's high in the organisation. He's one of the boss's sons. And he was coming up from Melbourne. He should have been here months ago.'

'Long brown coat, you say?'

'Yeah, all the company blokes wear them. You'll see when you meet them.'

'What's his name? Andre Noble?' Harry started to make a note in the small book from his pocket. It was a habit.

'Yep, that's right.'

'Nah, haven't seen him.'

'Right then, Harry.' Addington had the last of his drink and turned the glass over to show he was finished. 'I'll get you a room upstairs here. The beds are good and soft. And I'll get you a girl.'

'No, thank you.'

'You don't want one? Why's that? Did you get yourself another woman?'

Another woman, Harry thought. Another woman? Tom Addington knew Harry once had a wife. He'd even met her twice before. And he knew that she'd died. Another woman?

The memory of Alice, the rum in his belly, and the thought of spending two weeks in Mull Creek drowned him in sadness. He hated being alive without Alice Logan.

Another woman?

The question made Harry remember something else about
Tom Addington: he talked about horses like they were women,
and women like they were horses.

*

Jesus loved his revolver. It was not just the greatest, and only,
possession he'd ever had, but it was also the greatest object he'd
ever seen.

Since finding the gun with the white handle, it hadn't left his
hand. He slept with it, he cleaned it with the frayed ends of his
dirty shirt, and he studied the purpose of each mechanism until
he could find them without needing to look.

And he practised shooting for the first two hours of every
morning. He would find a tree that was the width of a man's
chest, then he would take ten steps away, turn as fast as he could,
lift his arm while cocking the hammer and pull the trigger. But
he had no ammunition. No lead balls. No powder. And no caps.
When he'd found the revolver, every cylinder was empty.

Almost as much as gold, Jesus wished he had a bag full of
ammunition so he could feel what it was like to fire the gun, so
he could do some proper practice. But even without shooting it
for real, Jesus knew he was fast. His arm would whip up and he'd
aim down the black barrel with a single open eye, and it would
always be in the middle of the tree. But he longed to know the
kick of it and see the bark split open from the blast.

Jesus liked the saddle too. Not as much as the gun, but it
was still pretty. Each evening, when the sun was about to go, he

would sling it over a horse-sized log and ride it until the last light with the revolver in his hand.

But the saddle was heavy, and when he started walking again, he tried to carry it every way he could. He held it in front with both arms, he put it on his shoulder, and he sat it on his head. Nothing was comfortable. Nothing was easy. And he wouldn't drag something so magnificent behind him through the dirt.

Jesus wished he could find an animal to carry him and the saddle. It didn't have to be a horse. It just needed legs and a good back. But the only creatures he'd seen were all small and they'd scurry at his presence, or they were flying above, too high to catch.

But as difficult as it was to carry the saddle and the gun together, Jesus somehow knew he was moving towards a moment when he would need both. He'd never heard the word 'destiny' but the concept was with him. There was something that was going to happen, and it was always meant to happen. It was like a story that had already been told around a fire some place, and now it was here. And the gun and the saddle were part of the story.

Just like he was.

*

After noon the next day, Jesus arrived in Mull Creek. And he was about to be arrested.

Just like Mary, he'd seen towns before but only from a distance, and he'd never seen one like this. He knew there was only one thing that could make a town this grand. It must be gold.

Jesus had stopped on the same ridge, just like the others had before him, but he didn't stay long. He just changed the position of the saddle on his shoulders and walked down.

This is it, he thought. This is the place. This is why he was walking in a straight line. This is why he escaped. This is why he found the saddle and the gun and the dead man and his horse. This is the reason. To be here. For the gold. To sleep in the white blankets and eat and buy a shovel and get a horse and fill his gun with ammunition. Gold. For the gold.

The town made different sounds to the bush. There were no more birds or wind blowing through the high leaves. Now he heard music, metal clinking, rolling wheels, and hundreds of voices.

But Jesus had been in town no longer than fifteen minutes when he was grabbed and taken to the police station.

He'd been standing in the street and looking at the faces. It had been a long time since he'd seen a living face. And there were now so many, but none of them were looking at him – even when he smiled. He wondered if all the walking had made him disappear. Perhaps he had become a ghost. He didn't remember dying, but maybe he had. Or maybe he was never alive.

But before he could ask himself another question about his existence, one man looked at him. He was tall and wearing a long brown coat – just like the dead man on the horse.

'You! You! Stop!' he said, charging at Jesus. 'Why do you have that saddle?'

*

54

Jesus sat in the police station with Harry Logan and Tom Adding-ton. There was a big table in the middle of the room, with the police on one side and Jesus on the other. And at the back of the room, Mary watched through her cell door.

'Now listen up, lad,' Addington said. 'I've never seen you before. I don't know anything about you. So, before you say one word to me, I need to tell you something, and it's the most important thing you have ever heard. It's this: I know when someone is lying. Right?'

'Yes,' Jesus said.

'Call me Sergeant Addington.'

'Yes, Sergeant Addington.'

'So, if I ask you a question, and you tell me a lie, I'm gonna know straight away. And I mean straight away. I'll know the very second. It's a talent I have. Isn't that right, Constable Logan?'

'Yes, Sergeant,' Harry said. He knew Addington had no such talent, but it was his job to act like it was true.

'Are you with me, boy?'

'Yes, Sergeant Addington.'

'Right. And do you know what horseshit is?'

Jesus was puzzled and turned to look into the street, as though he was going to be asked to run and get some.

'No, not that kind,' said Addington. 'It's the kind you speak. Horseshit? We had this American bloke here a couple of years ago. He was from Boston.' Addington twisted his mouth when he said 'Boston' and put on an accent that would have been unrecognisable to anyone from Massachusetts. 'He was out here for the digs but he didn't find anything. Anyway, he said every-thing was "horseshit".' Addington did the voice again. 'It was horseshit this and horseshit that. That's what people in Boston call a lie. Horseshit. Understand?'

'Yes, Sergeant Addington.'

'Good. Because if you tell me any horseshit, I'm gonna know. And it's gonna be bad. Not for me. But for you.'

Addington walked to his desk and took out a strip of leather as long and wide as his arm.

'Now,' Addington said, pulling on the strap to get the feel, and to make sure his suspect got a good look. 'Over at the schoolhouse, old Mrs Sullivan has a strap just like this and she keeps it for the naughty children. But I've got to tell you something.' Addington put his face close to Jesus and whispered as though the teacher might hear him. 'She is bloody useless with it. Let me show you. Hold out your hand. It's okay . . . just hold out your hand.'

Jesus put out his hand and Addington turned it over so the palm was facing up.

'She does this,' said Addington, and let the leather fall limp on Jesus' skin. 'I bet you didn't even feel that, did ya?'

Jesus shook his head.

'That's how she does it. But that's not the way I do it.' Addington lifted his coat and showed Jesus his naked waist. The sergeant's skin was soft, white and puffy, with splotches of a red rash.

'See that bit there,' said Addington, poking his finger into the fleshy part of his own side just above the hip. 'That's where you've got to slap it. Right on that spot. And it stings like the devil has bit ya.' Addington sucked in air and showed his teeth as though it had happened to him and he was remembering the feeling.

Jesus looked around the room. There were eyes behind the cell door watching him. They were bright. Almost glowing, as though there was a candle behind each eyeball. Jesus looked at the other policeman. He wasn't smiling but he was cleanly shaved and had a kinder face than the sergeant.

'Look at me,' Addington said, testing the feel of the leather again. 'You're just a little skinny bloke, and you don't have the same fat bits as me. But let me tell ya, it won't make any difference. It will hurt just the same. Do you believe me? Look at me, boy. Do you believe me?'

'Yes . . . sir . . . Sergeant Addington.'

'Right, well let's not piss about with it then. I'll ask the questions, and if I smell horseshit, I'm gonna slap you with this. Right? I can't put it any plainer than that.'

'Yes.'

'Good. So, what's your name?'

He looked around the room again, before he said, 'My name is Jesus.'

And that's when Jesus got his first belting.

Tom Addington was not a religious man. He only went to church to suppress the boredom of his Sundays and to wink at the widows. But the boy was not only lying, he was using blasphemy to do it. So Addington jumped at him, with his heavy boots stomping the wooden floor, and grabbed the lad. He bent him over the table, lifted up his filthy shirt, and gave him seven whips with the belt. Right in the spot he'd promised. Harry Logan looked away but the sound was enough to make him wince.

The sergeant had been right. The pain was awful. Jesus felt like he'd fallen on a fire and couldn't get off. He couldn't remember when he'd last cried. But he cried now. As Addington pushed him back into the chair, and his irons clanked, his eyes filled with water and he blinked them into tears on his cheek.

Jesus realised the gold town had no gold for him. No horse, no ammunition, no shovel, no food. Just pain. And this was the first time Jesus had ever told anyone his name, and he'd been whipped for it.

'Look at me, boy,' said Addington. 'See what I mean? I wasn't lying, was I? It hurts, don't it? Now, I reckon I know what you're thinking right now – you're thinking, how do I stop him from doing that again? Well, I already told you – just tell me the truth. That's it. So, what's your name?'

The pause was too long, so Addington grabbed him once more. Harry got to his feet and put his hand on Addington's chest. He wasn't too physical; it was more to guide the sergeant away before the next strike. He would never get rough with another uniformed man and he didn't want to undermine a superior officer's authority in front of a suspect. But Tom Addington had drunk too much, and this was just a child – a skinny child who hadn't washed or eaten for months, by the look of him.

'Sergeant Addington,' said Harry, 'let me have a word with him.'

Addington didn't disagree. He was satisfied with the punishment he'd already given. And he could always do it again later, or whenever he bloody wanted. He was the officer in charge – he could beat the child through the day and into the night if he had a mind to.

Harry pulled his chair closer to Jesus, and he let the silence hang in the room. When he saw most of the pain leave his suspect's face, he said, 'Do you need water?'

Jesus nodded and Harry poured some in a tin cup.

'All right now. You're in trouble, son. Right now, it is only a little bit of trouble. But if we can't sort this out, it's gonna be a whole mob of trouble. Now, is that what you want?'

Jesus shook his head while he tipped the water down his throat, spilling it at the corners.

'Good. Me neither. So let's just start again.' Harry dipped a pen into the ink and let it hover over the paper. 'What's your name?'

Jesus looked at the sergeant.

'It's okay,' said Harry. 'Just look at me. Tell me your name. Just the truth.'

'It's Jesus.'

Harry grimaced, as though he could hear the crack of the leather again, but Tom Addington only groaned.

'Jesus?' Harry repeated in a whisper.

Harry Logan had more religion than Tom. His mother had been strict and she was able to recall quotes from the Bible to fit any sin or situation. Harry knew it wasn't blasphemy to use the name the suspect was giving. He was on duty so he would be forgiven. And he would pray about it later. He would pray for himself and the skinny boy.

'Jesus?' said Harry again. 'That's your name?'

'Yes, sir.'

'All right then, what's your other name?'

'Whitetree.'

'What?'

'My name is Jesus Whitetree.' He was in pain but Jesus still liked the way his name sounded.

Addington snorted a laugh that had no humour, and the leather strap squeaked as he wrapped it around his hand to get a better grip.

'What?' said Harry.

'Jesus Whitetree.' There was something more bold in the way he repeated it.

'Jesus . . . Whitetree?'

'Yes, sir.'

'All right.' Harry sighed and pushed the paper and the pen to his suspect. 'Write it for me, if you please.' Harry looked at the boy's face. And he knew that look. He'd seen it many times before. 'You can't write?'

Jesus shook his head.

'It's all right,' Harry said in a softer voice. He took back the paper and wrote the boy's name. 'Do you know the date of your birth? When were you born? Christmas, I suppose?'

Harry allowed himself a small joke that was wasted and ignored by everyone else, except for a small giggle coming from behind the heavy cell door.

'How old are you?' Harry tried again, but before Jesus could answer, the front door opened with a bang and a man in a long brown coat and a tall black hat came in. He was the third man Jesus had seen dressed this way. One was dead and the other had him arrested. Maybe most of the world was full of men who looked like this. And this Brown Coat was unhappy. His face was free of every emotion except impatience.

'How old are you?' Harry said, ignoring the guest and keeping his mind on his work. 'Look at me, son . . . Jesus. Look at my face. How old are you? I would guess sixteen.'

'No.'

'No? How old then?'

'I'm fifty.'

'Fifteen?'

'No, I'm fifty years old.'

Harry scratched his scalp and heard Addington swear. Either this child is stupid or he likes to get beaten, Harry thought. But he'd seen Jesus' face after the strap, and he knew he didn't like being whipped. And the boy didn't seem stupid. A bit slow but not stupid. He couldn't read or write, his clothes were almost rags, and he looked at every object in the room like he'd never seen one before. But Harry knew what stupid looked like and this wasn't it. It was something he couldn't yet describe. He only knew he didn't want to see the boy beaten again.

'So,' Harry said, slow and clear. 'Your name is Jesus? Jesus Whitetree? And you're fifty years old?'

'What the hell is this nonsense?' the Brown Coat said, before he turned to the sergeant. 'Addington, outside.'

Tom Addington followed the Brown Coat into the street.

Harry scratched again and looked at Jesus. Apart from the eyes of Mary, they were now alone.

'All right, mate. I don't know what your game is, but I'll tell you what's gonna happen. I'm gonna put you in a cell back there. The bed's not bad. It's better than the dirt. And I'm gonna bring you something to eat. Do you like chicken?'

Jesus almost fainted at the thought. Food. A chicken. Browned skin with white greasy meat underneath.

'So, you'll have something to eat. You'll sleep. And then we're gonna talk again. Right?'

'Yes, sir.'

'Jesus, help me,' Harry muttered to himself.

*

Out in the street, Tom Addington was getting a belting of his own. It wasn't physical. It was verbal. But it was no less brutal.

'What have you found out, Addington? Not much by the look of it.' The Brown Coat had no respect for the sergeant's rank, experience, or leather strap.

'Don't worry,' Addington said, feeling the eyes in the street starting to look at him.

'Christ, I told you never to say that to me.' The Brown Coat didn't care who was watching or listening. 'Didn't I? Never say, "Don't worry." It's my job to worry. And it's my job to worry about you not doing your job. So, what have you found out about this boy?'

Addington only stared back. He didn't want to give answers. Nor did he want to chase bushrangers, question suspects, and talk in the street. He just wanted to drink and have an easy life.

'What has he said about Andre Noble? Why does he have the saddle?'

'Nothing yet. But he'll talk.'

'Addington, I don't think you've developed a proper appreciation for this crime.' The Brown Coat pointed a finger back to the police station. 'That boy could have killed a Company man. An important Company man . . .'

'I don't know if he did.'

'Did what?'

'I don't know if he did kill him. I mean, have a look at him –
he's tiny. He's just a skinny boy.'

'I don't care how big he is, and I don't care how ragged he
is either. Starving and desperate people can outfight the biggest
men and the best shots. I've seen it.'

The Brown Coat turned his head and looked down the street.

'This is not the bush anymore, Addington. Do you understand that through all the fat in your head? We have doctors,
teachers, lawyers, priests. This is a modern town. And we
built it.' The Brown Coat tugged his lapel as he said the
word 'we'.

Addington knew that 'we' did not include him. He was just
another servant to the mining company. As low as the lowest
worker down a mine.

'And do you know why they're here, Addington? Gold. There's
gold. That's it. That's all that stops us from sleeping on the bark
every night. Gold and quartz. But the gold is in the ground,
understand?' The Brown Coat pointed at the dusty street. 'We
need men to get it out of the ground. And we need women to feed
those men. So, do you think a family will come here if they're
worried about getting stabbed or shot?'

'No.' There was only one right answer for Addington to offer.

'Gold and families. That's Mull Creek. That's what makes
a town, Addington. But yesterday a gang rode in here, bailed up a
store, holding a knife to a baby's throat – a baby, Addington . . .
a baby. Then they ride out as calm as you please. And then today,
this boy walks through the middle of town with Andre Noble's
saddle and his Colt. It doesn't sound like anyone is too fearful of
the local constabulary, does it?'

The Brown Coat straightened himself as though he was almost finished with the sergeant and was ready for the next job on his list.

'We're trying to get the trains here, Addington. Do you think they're going to lay the track to a place that stabs babies?'

'I'll solve this,' said Addington.

'Do it. Find Andre Noble. And if he's dead, we're gonna hang that little bastard in there.' It was the first time the Brown Coat had given something that looked like a smile. 'We need people to know that it's what we do to thieves and killers.'

The Company man touched his hip to feel his own revolver underneath. It was something he always did before he walked away.

'But until we do hang him, Addington, make sure you keep all this business out of the newspapers.'

*

After the robbery at Thompson & Son's, the Pink Gang committed seventeen more crimes in just one week.

Some were minor offences, done so much from habit that the gang were unaware they were even breaking the law. But others were bold and violent, and committed in the light of the full sun. This included four highway robberies. Two of those were on farmers bringing goods into Creswick, a gold and sheep town ten miles south-east of Mull Creek. One had a wagon full of wool and the other had potatoes and two sacks of sugar.

And the other hold-ups were on a spice merchant and lone woman on a horse.

The merchant had been travelling with three large bottles of perfume. The scent was so strong, it could be smelt through the glass, and as it mixed with his peppers and cinnamon, the gang detected his path long before they saw him. LaBat climbed into the wagon next to the merchant and put a revolver barrel to his cheek, while Jack Pink used polite words to describe how the robbery would progress.

'A very good afternoon to you, sir,' he said, with a hand on his hip and the other resting on the handle of his holstered revolver. 'I'm Jack Pink and these are my companions. Before we begin with any business negotiations, do you happen to have some kind of weapon with you? A knife or firearm? Ah, you do? Well, don't touch it – that could be a little dangerous. Just point and my friend here will take care of it.'

After the wagon was secured and in the possession of the gang, Jack walked the merchant into the trees. He made him kneel and Jack stood behind him, cocking his revolver beside the man's ear, before poking the barrel into the back of his neck. For the next fifteen minutes, Jack whispered to the merchant about the sad nature of death. He spoke of the blackness and the silence and the inevitability of the crypt. He did this until the man wet himself. Then Jack uncocked his gun and left the merchant crying in his own horror.

The lone woman on horseback was dressed more like a man, and it was only after she got close that the gang saw the waves of blonde hair under her hat. On the instruction of Mother Pink, Jack had memorised three lines of Shakespeare from LaBat for just such an occasion. He recited to the woman about love and moonlight, then robbed her of her jewellery and a small calibre travelling pistol.

A day later, they stole an iron safe from the burnt remains of a hotel. The pub had caught fire two nights before, and when the gang arrived the owner and his wife were sifting through the ash remains, looking for things they could use in their new life. Jack approached him and listened with a caring expression as the publican explained how a patron's dog had knocked over a table holding a full lamp. The burning fuel spread across the floor so fast that they had no hope putting it out. And the dog had been the first one through the door.

Jack nodded with sympathy and put a comforting hand on the publican's shoulder, while the man explained that the safe was the only thing to survive the inferno. Then Jack pulled the revolver from his coat and ordered Carrigan to lift the safe into their new spice wagon.

The gang also stole three horses, two sheep for meat, one goat for milking, and a crate of stout from the rear of a Ballarat public house.

And with each crime, Mother Pink stood at the back and watched, LaBat made notes, Jack did the talking, and Carrigan frightened the hell out of the victims.

It had been a fruitful and exhausting spree, and Mother had LaBat write a description of all their deeds so she could give it to the newsagents. Over her long years of life, she had been in the newspapers on many occasions, and she considered herself an expert in the news business. She knew what it took to make an exciting story. They liked the tales of fear and violence, but they also wanted a bit of detail. If they could print that the criminal was wearing a red scarf, it made the tale more believable, and they could then exaggerate the rest. And now she had her own writer to give them plenty of colour and description.

Mother Pink waited a few weeks, to give the papers enough time to go to print, then she sent LaBat on a three-day ride to collect all the editions he could find.

Mother was excited at the thought of seeing her son's name glowing in the newspapers – knowing that thousands of eyes across the colony would read it too. It would be seen by the lying solicitors, the snobby women in the tearooms who had nothing to be snobbish about, the graziers, the landlords, the troopers, the miners, and the fools who spent their lives working for other people. They would all know about the dangerous and handsome bushranger called Jack Pink. All the men would wonder if they could outfight him and the women would get a thrill in their hearts at the thought of the rogue visiting them at night.

Mother knew how people thought. She knew what made them frightened, what they would pay money for, and what made them want to kill. Her years of bedding men, and knowing what brought them delight and satisfaction, had given her a rare wisdom.

On the night she waited for LaBat to return with the newspapers, it was windy and they made camp on the top of a hill. Jack didn't like the wind, so Mother had Carrigan build a big fire before it got dark, and now the flames were twisting in a bright orange dance, and sparks were flying off into the scrub. If the weather had been hotter, they would have started a bushfire, but the night's chill euthanised the embers before they could cause mischief.

The fire made a hiss and Mother welcomed the noise as her only company.

Carrigan was happily drowning in drugs and sitting on a log looking into the dark – seeing things no sober person ever could. And along with his opium and rum, the big man had started scoffing handfuls of the stolen sugar from the sack. Mother hoped he was not birthing a new addiction that she would have to satisfy.

Her son was by the fire and covered with three blankets. No part of his body was visible – she could only see the trembling lump in the middle. Mother knew it wasn't just the squally weather and the darkness that was making him afraid – she'd noticed a change in these last few weeks as the gang pulled their guns and took their pleasures. With every new crime, Jack became more bold during the day, yet more fragile at night.

Mother feared what Jack would be like if she wasn't here. It had been two years since he'd had a night without her. And it almost killed him. She'd been playing cards in the McManus' horse shed, where they had bare-knuckle fights in the late afternoons and then gambling into the night.

Mother filled herself with gin and the irresponsible atmosphere, before she met a gentleman with a quick wit and stiffly waxed moustache. He gave her another drink and asked her to return to her old career for just one more night. She negotiated the price, placing the figure well above reasonable, but he agreed.

Although it had been many years since she'd practised professional lovemaking, she still performed well, like an old stonemason who only needed a chisel in his hand to remember how it worked. Her banter and manoeuvres were skilled, and the encounter was not only profitable but physically satisfying, for both Mother and her client. So much so that when it was done, she fell into a deep and naked sleep in the man's clean bed. She woke just before dawn, realising her son was alone in their shack. She stole the remainder of the gentlemen's purse and rode hard to be with her boy.

When she found him, Jack was soaking in sweat and blood. He'd stabbed himself twice in the gut. Mother used the moustached man's money to pay a capable doctor to save Jack's life. He almost died many times in the month that followed, and she held him for every minute. She realised that her son had almost been taken from the world without people knowing his name. It would have been such a waste. They would never have known about the intelligent and gallant man she'd raised. So when he was well again, Mother made three promises. She vowed to never leave him alone in the dark again, to never use her body to comfort another man except her son, and to make sure the world would remember the name of Jack Pink.

As she waited for LaBat's return, she watched the shaking mound under the blankets until her breasts began to leak, the milk creating two wet patches on her lace bodice.

'Come, Jack. Come, my beautiful boy. It's time to sleep.'

She picked him up and his eyes were scrunched closed to keep out the night. She locked him onto her bosom and his face started to ease, and for the next two hours he was half-feeding and half-asleep.

Mother heard a horse coming. The rider was noisy and made no attempt to hide his presence. So she knew it would be LaBat. The scruffy writer had run with enough gangs to know that it was impolite, and frequently dangerous, to sneak into a camp of armed bandits. And when he got to the fire, Mother made no attempt to cover her feeding son. The Jack Pink Gang had been together long enough now to have no secrets.

'Welcome home, Samuel,' she said and her eyes flashed at the stack of newspapers under his arms. 'You got them then, I see.'

'I did.'

LaBat sat at the fire. His face was cold and reddened from the wind. He poured some boiling water into a cup and filled the rest with rum. He sipped on the first bit until the temperature was right, then he poured it down his throat.

Mother waited until her poet was warm and settled before she nodded at the papers.

'So?' she said.

'Mother, I have to tell you something, and you won't be pleased.' He pulled a knife from his belt and cut the bailing twine holding the bundle together.

'What? Have they said something slanderous about our Jack?'

'No.'

'What then?'

'They didn't say anything at all.'

'What?' Mother snapped. Her reaction disturbed Jack and his mouth made a popping noise as it came off the breast. She eased him back on and spoke to LaBat in a forced whisper that was almost as loud. 'What the bloody hell are you talking about, LaBat?'

'Jack's name is not in here, Mother.' He put his hand on the papers as though he was swearing on a Bible.

'I don't understand what you're saying. Did they call him something else? Did they call him Gentlemen Jack?'

'No.'

'Bold?'

'No.'

'Cunning?'

'No.'

'What then?'

'Nothing,' LaBat said, reaching to prepare more hot rum. 'They don't call him anything. He's not in the papers. They didn't write about him.'

'Have you checked every word?'

'I have.'

'There must be something in there. Then why did you come back with all that?' Mother pointed at the pile.

'Because I knew you wouldn't believe me.'

LaBat was right. If he hadn't returned with every edition, Mother would have given him half a bowl of stew, let him sleep for an hour, and then sent him back out to fetch them.

'This is just . . . I don't know . . .' Mother looked for a handful of words that could best describe her mood. 'I'm upset. Very upset.'

'I understand. However, *you* have made the headlines,' LaBat said.

'What?'

'You're in here. They wrote about you.' He swore on the Bible again.

'Damn it. I knew it. What does it say?'

LaBat took the edition on the top of the pile and stood to take it to her.

'Don't give it to me,' Mother said. 'You know I can't read at night. Just tell me what it says. They call us the bloody Mother Pink Gang, I suppose? Don't they?'

'No, they don't mention the gang either. Just you?' LaBat wet his thumb, found the page with a small article that he'd circled in red ink, and read to her. '"It is as a warning that we inform the towns surrounding Ballarat about sightings of the famous Mother Pink. The notorious lady of the night . . ."'

'Shit!' Mother Pink cried, and spat into the fire with anger.

'"The notorious lady of the night, who was given the name of Gertrude Louise Pink at the time of her birth, has been recognised and suspected in the momentary disappearance of a goat from a property on Millers Road at Mount Rowan on the night of the 22nd day of this month of May. The goat, which is of the British Alpine breed, was seen being taken away by Madam Pink and being led into nearby bushland. However, the beast was found grazing the following morning on the roadside in front of a neighbouring property. We are told it appears to be unharmed."'

'Is that it?'

'No, there's a little more. "Mother Pink has been known to engage in much felonious activity in her long life. She has been past convicted of prostitution, the serving of sly grog, theft, theft and robbery, assaults on women, assaults on the police, arson . . ."'

'Bitches!' Mother spat again and LaBat knew to skip forward in the catalogue of her criminal life.

'And then it says, "Pink is to be recognised by her portly body, erotic attire, and a highly noticeable scar on her cheek."'

'Portly?' Mother asked. 'Portly? Flaming portly? What does portly mean?'

'Ummm,' LaBat paused before he lied. 'Pretty. It means pretty.'

'Oh,' Mother eased for a moment, then became angry again. 'This is bad, LaBat. Bloody terrible. Why are they not writing about Jack? And why is it about the bloody goat? This is your fault, LaBat. I blame you.'

'My fault?'

'This was your job.' She pointed a finger at him and he could almost feel it pushing a hole in his chest from the other side of the fire. 'I hired you to make Jack famous. I told you I wanted every idiot in this colony to know the name of Jack Pink. And you have failed.'

'Mother, I did everything you wanted. I wrote all the letters and gave them to the newspaper people. And I might say, my words are far better than this rubbish.' He waved the pages at her and considered throwing them on the fire to make his point.

'I don't care how good they were. Your words didn't work. Your precious, precious words. What am I going to tell Jack in the morning?'

Carrigan came and sat by the fire. He didn't acknowledge his gang mate's return.

'All right then. We failed. I failed,' LaBat said, holding up his hands in surrender. 'So, what are we going to do?'

'Well, you promised me a poem, LaBat. You were going to write a poem for Jack. You said poems were the way to get people to remember him. So, where's the bloody poem?'

'I'm working on it.'

'Work harder.'

Mother went quiet and shook her head as she pondered the changing world. 'I honestly do not know what has happened to this colony. You hold a knife to a baby's throat and you can't even get it in the bloody papers. Back in my day, they would have talked about something like that for a year. Times are different, LaBat. Very different. Everything is about the gold now. Just gold. They don't care about people anymore. And it just makes me so sad.'

'We need something bigger.' LaBat made another hot cocktail and stared into the fire as he pondered a solution. 'We need an audience. We have to do something in front of so many people that they can't ignore it. Thousands. Do you know what I mean? Bugger the papers – what we need is witnesses.'

'Thousands? Yes, I like the sound of that.'

'A big crowd. And we need to frighten the devil out of them. People always remember something when they're afraid. Fear is hard to forget.'

'Yes,' Mother said, nodding and allowing him a smile. 'That's very good, LaBat – a big crowd. Yes, that's what we need.'

Mother looked down at her beautiful boy. He was asleep. His mouth had fallen open, lips shining from her milk. She felt a thrill in her blood. How wonderful it would be to see him standing in front of thousands of people – handsome, and well armed. They'd scream and tremble at the sight of him. They would never forget it. And they would tell the story for the rest of their lives. To hell with the newspapers. It wouldn't matter what they wrote. The world would still know Jack Pink.

'Gold and fear,' LaBat said, still looking into the flames. 'We just need a crowd. That's the problem. Where do we find a crowd? A crowd with gold?'

And as the flames danced in the wind, LaBat was unaware that the answer was hidden within the pile of papers at his side.

While he'd been searching for news on the Jack Pink Gang, he had missed the racing announcements. But he would read them in the morning, and then he would find a solution, courtesy of the Victoria Turf Club.

*

Back in Mull Creek, the newspapers were just as scant on detail as LaBat's collection. There was nothing about the gang. They even failed to mention the goat.

There'd been some town gossip about what happened at Thompson & Son's. The story varied from an attempted kidnapping to whispers about a nameless bushranger who carved his initials into the child's belly with a sharpened fingernail.

The mining company and Sergeant Tom Addington were successful in keeping it away from the newsagents and the Police Gazette. And when Thompson's customers asked him about the episode, he confirmed nothing. The storekeeper knew better than to go against the wishes of the Brown Coats. If he wanted their protection, he had to shut up. Thompson's business was successful, but the Company only needed to open their own store and he would be ruined.

So as much as Thompson was haunted by the voice and the cold eyes of Jack Pink, he kept quiet. The only way he changed his life was at night. He no longer slept with his wife; instead, he set up a thin mattress beside his son's cot and lay there till dawn with a loaded shotgun.

Until Pink was dead, or he found a way to forget him, Thompson would be suffering in his own hell.

But down the dusty street, at the Mull Creek Police Station, Jesus Whitetree was experiencing some paradise. His bed was soft, and twice a day hot food was brought to him. He didn't need to find it, catch it, or worry if there would be more. This is how I will live when I have gold, he thought.

Yet there were things he missed.

He missed his own fire and saying his name three times before sleep. He missed walking in a straight line, knowing he was getting closer to gold with each step. And more than anything, he missed his gun. It hadn't been his for very long, but it was still his. When he was sitting alone in the cell, he could still feel the white handle in his palm, and the tip of his index finger tingled at the memory of it resting on the trigger. He had thought about the saddle too, but as beautiful as it was he still had no horse.

It was the revolver he really ached for.

But before his longings could be allowed to grow to desperation, he would be distracted by food again.

Each meal was served in his cell by the kind Constable Logan, who always followed the food with a dozen questions about where he got the saddle and his gun, and about the dead man in the brown coat.

After a week of regular food and questions, Jesus was unlocked from the cell, a chain was put around his ankle, and he was taken back to the big table in the police station's front room. And when he sat down he could smell the food even before the bowl was in front of him. Chicken and potatoes. Wonderful, wonderful chicken and potatoes.

Constable Harry Logan sat Jesus down and put three spoons on the table. Then he unlocked the heavy door of the other cell.

Jesus knew there had been someone in there. There was talking, but it wasn't loud enough to hear the words because the walls were made from brick. He thought it was either a child or a woman. And as the Constable led her out, Jesus could see it was both.

Harry sat her at the table and put an iron around her ankle. She was smiling, almost like she was about to start laughing, and she looked up at Jesus as though they'd met many times before and she'd been waiting to see him again.

'This is a bit bloody special,' she said, grabbing her spoon.

'Watch that language, Mary, please,' said Harry, moving to the pot on the small stove.

'Yes, Constable boss.' She smiled at Jesus and poked out her lip to acknowledge that she knew she was in trouble but also that she didn't care.

Jesus had seen Aboriginal people before, but never one this close. He didn't know why they were black. Some birds were different colours but that didn't make sense for people. They could have been born white and then something happened to make them change. Or maybe they were waiting to become white one day. But as he looked at the girl, he couldn't imagine her being any other colour than the one she was. The black wasn't just sitting on the surface of her skin – like Jesus thought it would – instead, it was as though her whole body was made from the same thing that gave her the colour. Everything was black – except a full set of teeth that flashed between her lips, and the white in her eyes.

Mary was still smiling at him as the food was put down. The chicken was made into a stew with pieces of potato and something green. She gave it a good sniff and her face reacted to the magnificent odour. The expression that Jesus saw was the same thing he was feeling inside, but he didn't show it like her. He liked her face. It was pretty and bright and half of it was taken up with a smile.

'This smells so good, boss,' Mary said. 'You know it's my favourite. Have I been a good girl or something, hey? What's this all about? This is bloody special. We got the best tucker and we sitting here like kings and queens? What's bloody going on?'

'Just eat, will you?' Harry sat down and polished his spoon with the bottom of his coat. It was a habit that had playfully annoyed his wife, and now he did it every meal so he could think about her again.

'Oh, don't you worry about that, I'll be eating all right.' Mary ate with her utensil in the left hand, lifting the liquid like soup, while she grabbed at the solid chunks of meat and vegetable with her other fingers.

Harry chewed slowly and Jesus waited.

'Eat up,' Harry said to him. 'It's all right.' And the order was obeyed.

Mary slurped and chomped and made groaning sounds to appreciate the taste. 'Did you really kill someone?' Mary said to Jesus with a full mouth.

'Me? No.'

'Are you sure? It sounds like the Constable boss thinks you did. Did you kill someone by mistake?'

'No.'

'Did you hit someone on the head with a bloody axe?'

'No.'

'Did you scare a bloody horse and he throwed someone off and their bloody neck got broke?'

'No.'

'Oh, let me think,' Mary said and put more food in. 'Did you poison someone?'

'No.'

'Did you make them some tucker and then they go to sleep and then wake up in the middle of the night and they bloody drop dead.' Mary grabbed her own throat with both hands, stuck out her tongue, and acted a quick pantomime.

'No.'

'Is your name really Jesus?'

'Yes.'

'Where's the dog, boss?' Before Harry could answer, Mary lifted her head and called out, 'Mate! MATE!'

The dog opened the front door with its nose, ran to Mary, put his paws on her leg and took a nugget of meat from her hand.

'This is bloody special,' Mary said again. 'What a family we are. Hey Jesus, Jesus, did you break someone's heart? Is that what happened? Did you say something bad and they dropped bloody dead because they were so sad?'

Jesus thought about it before he replied. 'No, I don't think I did.'

'So there you go. I don't reckon he killed anyone, boss. He don't look like a bloody killer.'

'Language, Mary.'

'That's my name,' she said to Jesus. 'It's Mary. I didn't kill anyone either.' She held up her leg to show the shackle. 'But you'd think I bloody did.' She looked under the table to see if Jesus had one and just nodded when she saw he did.

Harry wasn't angry at Mary's questions to Jesus. It was what he was hoping for. Over the last week, Harry had tried every policing technique he knew to get something from the boy. He left him alone to think. He questioned him for hours. He talked to him when he was tired. He talked to him when he was fully awake. He was friendly, then he was impatient. But nothing worked.

The skinny boy just stuck with the same story about finding the body of Andre Noble and his horse dead, and how he buried him under leaves, and took the gun and the saddle. Harry knew the story wouldn't be accepted by Sergeant Tom Addington and the Brown Coats.

Addington had wanted to keep whipping the prisoner and then drag him to the location of Noble's body. But Harry knew the lad wouldn't survive the beatings or the journey. There was no muscle or fat on his bones.

Since Jesus had been arrested, Harry had thought more than once that the boy and Mary had similar bodies. They were the same height and both skinny. And if they were in the same clothes, and far enough away that he couldn't see the colour of their skin, he wouldn't be able to tell them apart. Mary had the build that all the native girls had at her age, and couldn't be fattened no matter how much bacon and stew he put in her. But Jesus was just starving. It was a miracle the boy had been able to walk more than ten feet on his own, much less carry the ornate saddle of Andre Noble.

But Harry had to do something. He'd promised to get answers for Addington within a week. And his time was almost done.

So he decided to release Mary into the situation. He guessed that she'd be half-crazy with boredom in the cell and wouldn't miss a chance to ask endless questions.

Harry was right. And while Mary talked, he watched the face of Jesus.

'Where do you come from? Do you have a dog too? Can you ride a horse? What's your mother's name? How high can you climb up a tree?'

And despite all her words, Mary could still eat faster than anyone. Including the dog.

Although Harry didn't discover anything new, he remained convinced that Jesus wasn't a killer. His eyes were too clear, and he continued to look at everything with the same naive wonder. Where Mary seemed much older than her years, Jesus was far younger. He was a child.

Two days before, Harry had given Jesus a shave and a haircut in the cell. There was not much to scrape off the face, just the fluffy gatherings of a teenager. He'd asked Jesus to hold the mirror and the boy stared at his reflection like he'd never seen himself. He rolled his head around, keeping his eyes still, and studying each part of his face.

Murderers didn't look at themselves like that. People who had killed were often so ashamed they couldn't look at all.

So even if the boy had killed Andre Noble by accident, there would be some remorse. But there was nothing. This boy was free of guilt.

Lucky little bugger, Harry thought.

But luck would not be enough to save him. And neither would Harry Logan's instincts or opinions. Unless he could get some evidence to clear the boy, or find the real killer, or if Andre Noble wandered back into town with the dreamy look of a man who'd been distracted by women and grog, there was no hope for the scrawny lad.

And Harry knew how the process would unfold. If he didn't save the boy, there would be a trial. It would be tainted by the Company, there would be no-one to speak for Jesus, and the evidence would be scant but still damning. Then he'd be hanged. Either at Melbourne's Pentridge Gaol or by gallows made by the Brown Coats out in the street.

And if they couldn't find him guilty of murder, they certainly had enough evidence for theft. Then the Company would make sure he was beaten to death in the first month of his sentence. They would not permit Jesus to live. They'd want everyone to see what happens when a person kills or steals from a Brown Coat. And from what Harry had pieced together, Andre Noble was a particularly powerful Brown Coat. He was strong, quick and dangerous. He had no permanent home, and he was willing to do anything to protect the interests of the mines. He would have made a good criminal, but he didn't need crime to get what he wanted. He had something better. Gold.

If Andre Noble really was dead, it would be no loss, Harry thought. If there were more people like Jesus, and fewer like the Brown Coat, the colony would be the better for it. Harry Logan remembered the way things were in Victoria before the first strikes of gold. There was an innocence. Much like Jesus. But that was lost now. Where there was once just farming, building and creating families, now there was digging and greed. But Constable Harry Logan knew it wasn't his job to be sentimental, nor to make men better than they were. That was for the priests and the politicians to do. Although they never did it well enough.

Mary picked up her bowl with both hands and tipped the last bit of soupy stew into her waiting mouth. It went down with a final slurp and a triumphant groan.

'Boss, I got to tell ya, your cookin' is getting real bloody good.'

'Thank you, Mary,' Harry said, trying to sound dismissive and weary, but in truth he enjoyed preparing food, and seeing Mary attack it like a snake wrapping itself around a rat brought him a pleasure that he would keep to himself.

'You got a lolly in your pocket, boss?'

'No, I don't.'

'Oh, come on, something sweet?'

'No.'

'Please, Constable boss, you gotta have something. This is a real special day. Look, the whole family is here.' Mary pointed at Jesus, the dog, then herself.

Jesus – who'd picked up the pace of his own eating – looked up at the policeman. 'Should I be calling you boss? Like her?'

'No,' Harry said. 'Please don't.'

The well-fed frame of Sergeant Tom Addington came through the door, followed by his constable. It was one of the rare times Harry had seen Tom's subordinate awake. Usually he was working through the night, and spending his days asleep on the bunk outside the cells.

'What the bloody hell is all this?' Addington said, looking at the table gathering. 'Is it Christmas?' It sounded like a joke, but Addington wasn't smiling and no-one answered.

Jesus stopped eating, Harry started clearing up the bowls, and Mary retracted the proud look on her face. She knew better than to be seen enjoying herself around people like the sergeant.

Addington didn't look at Mary, but acknowledged the iron on her black leg and gave Harry an approving nod.

'Harry, let's go and have a drink,' the sergeant said. 'I need to tell you something.'

Addington walked out into the street and towards the hotel. Harry followed but turned at the station door and went back to take two sweets from his pocket and put them on the table between Jesus and Mary. One was orange and the other bright green.

'Oh yes, boss. You're a bloody good bloke.'

*

At the pub, Constable Harry Logan was given his orders.

'Right, Harry. We need to get cracking on this thing. It doesn't look like Mother Pink is coming back here. They've moved on. So I need you to find this Andre Noble's body. Get that boy to show you where it is. He looks right enough to travel.'

'I'm not sure yet, Tom.'

'He's right,' Addington said as a statement of fact. 'You've fed him enough. We're not trying to get a pig ready for the sales, we're trying to solve a murder. So get him moving. Leave tomorrow. What else have you got out of him?'

'Not much.'

'No names?'

'Nah.'

'Is he still calling himself Jesus?'

'Yep.'

'He'd have to be the biggest idiot in the Empire. And there's plenty to choose from, I've met a few. But stupid people still kill, so unless you've got a banquet prepared for them, you can go first thing. All right?'

'But, Tom, this is a felony, isn't it?'

'Yeah, so?'

'Won't the superintendent want the detectives working on the case?'

'No. I don't want to get anyone else involved. The Company is after me enough as it is. Look, I'd be happy to try and keep belting it out of the boy, but he's just not giving it up. We need to find that body. Do this for me, Harry.'

Harry could only nod. He began to think about the days ahead, and the impending death of Jesus Whitetree. He knew he would find nothing that could save the boy. If there was a body, they'd hang him. If there was no body, they'd hang him.

They drank in silence until Addington broke it with a final order.

'And take that girl with you. She's pretty enough but she's running down the pantry. And I'm sick of the smell of her.'

*

The sun lifted into another day and Jack Pink woke before the others to saddle his horse.

The black animal had no name. Jack gave it no affection and none was sought. It didn't need reassurance and it was afraid of nothing. It just remained still while Jack tightened the girth and put the bridle over the pointing ears.

In the saddle, Jack didn't need to kick his boots into the horse's belly or slap its raven coat with his reins. There was just a pause before both horse and rider expelled a foggy breath and then charged into the dawn like they were leaving a gun barrel.

They shot across the open ground and into the trees, and as they got closer to the dense bush, the sound of the hooves echoed back into Jack's ears. They rushed between the rough trunks of the box gums, jumping over the fallen branches and ducking under those still hanging low.

Jack pulled his revolver from the holster – drawing the gun across himself – and aimed without firing. Then he put it back and did it again. Then again. And when he and the horse were at full speed, he pulled it again and fired.

He always went for a small target, like the knot on a tree or a twig, and if he ever missed, it wasn't by much. He would kill an animal if he saw it, but most were already frightened off by the galloping vibrations.

Jack fired his six shots. He was moving too fast for the smoke or the smell of the powder to hit his face. They just hung behind him until they drifted up into the leaves. Four shots did as intended and two went an inch to the left.

Horse and rider came from out of the bush and into the open ground on the other side. Jack dropped the reins but the horse kept the speed, and without needing to look down, he released the loading lever of his revolver and replaced the empty cylinder. Then another pause and another foggy breath before they turned and went back into the trees to fire another six.

No man had taught Jack how to ride. He'd had no identi-
fiable father in his life, and there'd been no old stockman from
a neighbouring property willing to pass down his skills. Jack
had had no likeable qualities as a boy, and the men who met
him had been filled with a sense that any lesson they'd give the
chinless lad would be either wasted or misused.

There was only Jack and his mother. She showed him how
to saddle an animal and the rest he learned just from watching
others or from falling off.

In his early years, he wasn't much of a rider, and then he
was given the black horse. Mother Pink presented it to him one
morning when Jack had just turned twenty. From their first
moments, they became like two metals melted together.

They were strong. Scorching. Uncatchable.

In the trees, Jack had one last practice shot. There was a slim
dead branch protruding low on an otherwise healthy trunk.
Jack cocked the hammer, aimed with both eyes open, and fired.
The lead ball made the branch disappear, as though it had been
cracked off by the tail of a stock whip.

Then Jack came out of the bush, into the open again, and
rode back to the camp even faster than when he left.

Two people saw Jack and his horse on that morning ride. One
was a farm worker who was late getting to his job, and the other
a travelling miner who'd spent the last six months panning, but
was now returning to his fiancée without a fleck of gold for their
wedding.

Neither witness really knew what they saw. They heard the
shots and the sound of the running horse, yet there was nothing
to see but a black flash.

*

Jack walked into camp with the terrors of the night now flushed from his body, and he found the mood of his gang to be joyful. Mother was almost dancing, LaBat was grinning, and Carrigan held a dozen eggs in his massive hands following a dawn raid on a farm.

'Ah, good morning, my sweet boy,' Mother Pink said, as Jack warmed his fingers at the fire.

'Morning, Mum.'

'How was your ride, love? Were you fast?'

'Yes, Mum.' He took a cigarette that she'd already rolled for his return.

'Wonderful. I'll make you some eggs for your breakfast. But first, Samuel and I have some very good news.'

'It's a great day, boss,' said LaBat, jumping in. 'It's one of those days that makes you want to find something to steal or shoot. Do you know what I mean?'

LaBat often felt the need to become a salesman before giving information. But it was wasted on Jack Pink.

'What is it, Labat?'

'I think we might have found a big event that's worthy of your talents and attention.'

'Something wonderful, Jack,' Mother Pink said. 'Something that will make you . . . unforgettable. Just like we talked about.'

'Listen to this, boss.' LaBat squinted at the small text and began to read. '"News from the Victoria Turf Club" – that's the headline. "At a committee meeting of the Victoria Turf Club, notice was given of a motion that the club should hold a race of similar bearing to the famed Chester Cup."'

'The Chester Cup?' Jack repeated, lighting his smoke from a stick in the fire.

'Yep. From back in England. A big race.'

'What's all that to us? You want me to race?'

'No, Jack. But there's few that could beat you and that black girl of yours. But just have a look at this,' LaBat snatched another newspaper from the top of the pile. 'This is a better one: "The Victoria Turf Club voted to present a handicap event in November. The prize will be paid in sovereigns."'

'Sovereigns? Gold? How much?'

'We don't know yet, Jack,' Mother said. It was the first thing she'd wanted to know too.

'But it's got to be big, boss. I mean, it has to be. They'll want owners and trainers from all over the place. And if they want to get some runners from Sydney or even from across the water, they'll have to make the purse pretty bloody good.'

Mother moved a hot pan full of bacon to some cooler coals so she could open the eggs. 'It's going to be a lot,' she said. 'We're the golden colony now – if we only give a pissing little prize, we'd be lucky to get a stable from Ballarat to enter. Everyone knows there's money around. They can't hide it from us anymore. And they tried. Oh they tried. Them wellborn hogs that wanted to keep it all. But we could see it coming out of the ground. We're not stupid. Are we, Jack?'

'No, Mum.'

'It would have to be five hundred, at least,' said LaBat.

'Five hundred?'

'Oh yeah, Jackie lad,' LaBat said and gave Jack Pink a wink. It was the wink of a salesman. And LaBat regretted taking liberties the moment he did it. Jack gave the writer his cruellest expression and the fear burnt a hole in LaBat's gut. He knew Mother Pink could say anything she wanted to her son, but LaBat could not. And he didn't want the kind of trouble Jack Pink could provide. LaBat had watched the tall bushranger closely in the last few weeks as they committed their binge of crimes. And despite the moonlight frailties and the need for a full belly of breast milk, Jack was more dangerous than any person he'd ever known.

Some people were dangerous because they could shoot fast or throw hard punches. Some were dangerous because they had power and money, and they could hire dangerous men when circumstances required it. And some were just dangerous because they attracted trouble like crows on a carcass.

LaBat was bad because he was too lazy to work, and because crime was entertainment. Carrigan was bad because he had a corrupted appetite that could only be fed through seedy means. And Mother Pink adopted badness as a way to survive. She'd be dead without it.

But Jack was different. He was bad because his soul was bad. Either the gods had created him to counter all the pure things on earth, or he was a terrible mistake. But he was bad either way.

'So what's your plan then, LaBat?' Jack said, standing at his full height. 'Spit it out of ya mouth.'

'Well,' LaBat said. His mouth was suddenly dry. 'I think . . . we're going to rob it.'

'What do you mean?' asked Jack. 'You want to rig it? You want to pick a winner and nobble the rest?'

'No, I mean we steal it. We rob it. We grab everything. We

get the prize money, then we bail up the bookies, the toffs, their wives, the owners, the trainers, jockeys, the lot. If someone's got a coin on them – we'll take it.'

'Don't you just love it, Jack?' said Mother, giving a plate of food to the boys and a bag of sugar to Carrigan.

'It will be the pillage of a lifetime, boss,' added LaBat.

'And everyone will see you. Let the newspapers try and ignore you then, hey? My beautiful Jack.'

Beautiful Jack looked at his plate. He had three eggs but one had a broken yolk and the other had a fleck of ash.

'So let me get this right,' Jack said, looking up at his gang. 'This is your plan: we ride into the biggest gathering the city has ever seen, hold our guns on thousands of people, rob the bookies, clean the pockets of every man and woman there, take the prize money, and then just ride out.'

'That's it,' LaBat said, licking the bacon juice from his fingers. 'What do ya think?'

The bushranger gave his quick reply before he ate his only unspoiled egg.

'Yep. Good.'

*

While the Jack Pink Gang made their plans to rob the first Melbourne Cup, the motley family of Harry Logan, Jesus White-tree, the dog, the grey horse and Mary set out from Mull Creek to find the body of Andre Noble.

Harry hired a sulky from the town's blacksmith. Tom Addington usually took it for free, but Harry gave the smith a fair price and paid a week in advance. He harnessed the cart to his horse and waited for Mary to get ready.

For a person with no possessions and wearing her only clothes, it always took a long time for Mary to get herself right to leave.

When she was set, Harry flicked the long reins and they all moved out. The Constable and Jesus sat on the uncushioned seat, and Mary walked beside in chains with the dog, until they were outside of town then Mary climbed up into the cart and Harry chained his two prisoners' legs together.

The sulky was only built for two people but the slim back-sides of Jesus and Mary were able to fit next to Harry with a few inches to spare.

Harry was still concerned about the size of the boy. Despite the policeman's efforts, he still looked like a starved sheepdog. But Harry had no such concerns about himself – with all the cooking he'd been doing in the Mull Creek police station, he'd noticed a swell in his own belly and some minor difficulty in buttoning his pants. Even with the daily interrogations of the lad, it had been a lazy couple of weeks in Mull Creek for Harry Logan. The bed of his hotel room was thick and soft, and the evening drinking sessions with Tom Addington ensured that he never had to wait long to fall asleep.

And one night he was a visited by a woman. Either Addington had ignored Harry's rejection of female company, or perhaps a woman simply liked the look of the clean-shaven constable and followed him up to his room. It was possible. Harry was still a good-looking man, and his police uniform gave him a soldierly quality that was attractive to a woman surrounded by the unwashed sunburnt miners of Mull Creek.

The woman had light brown hair and she was pretty enough, and she had curves and bumps under her clothing that promised warmth and tenderness on the cold night. But just like every other person in the world, she was not Alice Logan. So nothing happened.

Harry knew that if he got close enough to breathe her in, she wouldn't smell of warm butter and pears. It would only make him feel more alone. And he couldn't risk feeling more alone.

The sulky rolled away from town, travelling the same route Jesus had taken two weeks before and moving almost at the same speed. Mary was enjoying the novelty of the ride, and she spent the first hour swinging her head to look around.

'Do you know them fellas, Constable boss?' she asked when they were well clear of Mull Creek.

'What fellas?'

'Them fellas back there.' Mary poked a thumb over her shoulder and Harry looked back. 'Do you know them?'

Four hundred yards behind, two men and their horses were following the same track.

'No, I don't.'

Harry lied. He knew who they were. They were Brown Coats. He'd seen them twenty minutes before Mary and they were maintaining the same speed as the sulky, always staying four hundred yards away. Thieves would have hidden themselves in the trees, but the Brown Coats didn't care if they were seen. It's what they wanted. They weren't there as protectors or escorts. They were overseers.

Harry knew the Company didn't trust him. They'd think he was too soft to dispense the kind of justice they paid Tom Addington for. Harry understood their suspicions and he didn't blame them. He was aware of his own leniency. And he'd already been thinking of how he might let the boy go if he couldn't find enough evidence to clear him of the killing or the robbery. But any plan would be difficult with two Brown Coats as his shadow.

Mary started to sing. It was a quiet song that was more of a whistle through her teeth than something with words. And it was a tune that had no sadness. Harry flicked the reins again and wondered how she could sing such a beautiful thing while she was chained.

And Jesus just listened, happy to be moving again.

In the back of the sulky was Andre Noble's saddle, rocking like it was another passenger. Harry brought it in case he needed to show a witness, or anyone who might have seen the Brown Coat in their travels. Constable Harry Logan was a competent policeman who knew that most people weren't keen observers – they had their own lives to think about. But sometimes an object or a word could help them remember. And small details were often enough to lead to bigger answers. It would be better to show the saddle than describe it.

Also in the back was a short-handled shovel. Jesus had asked Harry if they could bring it along. It was the only request the boy had made since he was arrested, so Harry just agreed.

Harry knew it was unlikely they'd find Noble alive and healthy. Not just because the boy said he saw the dead body, but because people like Noble didn't run away. Their lives were too good. Only people with bad lives ran away. And Harry had known plenty like that. Including his two passengers.

That night, they made camp. Harry unhitched his horse, and the animal put its heavy head to Harry's chest, as though she'd been missing the feeling of him on her back. Harry rubbed a hand between her ears and under her jaw – where she liked it – and he whispered something to her. Like Mary's song, it was just noises more than proper words.

He kept Mary and Jesus chained together.

'I'm sorry about this, boy,' Harry said and shrugged. 'But I'm going to keep this on ya leg.'

'Oh and don't you worry about saying sorry to me, boss,' Mary said, her sarcasm always coming with a grin. 'I'm all okay.'

Harry didn't reply, but in truth he'd wanted to apologise to her every night since they met.

He went to gather firewood and hurt his ankle trying to kick a stick in half.

'You right there, Constable boss?' Mary said, hearing Harry's stumble. 'Don't get no splinters or nothing. It's getting too dark for me to see good to get the bastard out.'

When Jesus closed his eyes, he could still feel the rocking of the buggy, as though they hadn't stopped moving. He'd never travelled like that before. He didn't need to do anything – just sit there as a tree got closer and closer, then watch it move past, and then another would come. And every hour or so, the Constable would stop and ask him for directions to the dead man's body and the horse.

With his eyes still closed, Jesus wanted to say his name three times. But he just thought it instead.

He felt Mary move next to him. For a moment, it reminded him of the high brick walls and being surrounded by the other children and being touched every moment of the day. But it was different. It was better. Mary was warmer and being near her made him feel peaceful, even though she was never silent. She was always talking or singing or making clicking sounds with her fingers. But she still made him feel calm. And he liked the things she said.

They ate and the fire glowed on their faces, and four hundred yards away was the camp of the Brown Coats. They'd made a huge fire and they were still not hiding. Far from it, Harry thought. They wanted him to know they would be watching him tonight, and all day tomorrow.

Then the world slept for a while.

But just before midnight, there was a howling sound from the Brown Coats' camp. It wasn't an animal, it was a man trying to sound like one. And that made it even more frightening. It was a long wail that bounced off the dark walls of the night, followed by laughing and hooting.

The noise didn't wake Harry, it only interrupted his snoring for a moment. But it woke Jesus and Mary. It yanked them out of their sleep and they sat up at the same time and the irons jangled on their legs. They listened for a minute, then Mary put her mouth to his ear.

'Jesus,' she whispered, so close that her breath was like thunder. 'Do you hear them men? Them men are coming for you. Do you know that? You figured that out yet?'

'Me?'

'Shh. Yep. Don't you know that? They not coming for me or the boss. And they not coming for the dog. They coming for you. They want to hang you.'

There was another howl. A shorter one. Then more laughter. Jesus looked to the raging fire and the silhouettes of dancing creatures moving past the flames. The sight and the noise and Mary's words made him rattle with fear. The feeling was so strong that he wondered if he'd ever feel peace again.

'But don't you worry now,' she said, comforting him like a mother that he'd never known. 'You and me are gonna run. Run away? Understand? We're gonna bugger off. We're gonna be like two rabbits. Them bastards can really run.'

Jesus nodded and looked into the dark, as though he was searching for a clear path to start running. 'All right. I understand.'

'Not now,' Mary said, grabbing his arm. 'Silly bugger, they'll be watching for that. And we got these mongrel chains on. Nah, we're gonna wait. Okay, just wait. We'll do it when it's good.'

Jesus nodded again and there was another howl. There was a lot to be frightened of. It was dark, he was chained and there were men who wanted to grab him and choke his neck with a rope.

'Don't worry,' Mary said. She was so black, he could only see the outline of her face. But then she smiled and her teeth shone like the burning wick of a lamp. 'I'm gonna save you, Jesus. And you're gonna save me.'

Mary lay down in her bed of dirt as Jesus stayed sitting up, thinking about death by hanging.

'Anyway,' Mary said with a cheerful yawn. 'Goodnight.'

*

The next morning, they had a cold breakfast at dawn, Harry checked the directions with Jesus, and they moved out.

Harry hoped the early start would put some distance between them and the Brown Coats. He knew they would have been drinking all night. It was the kind of men they were. But it still wasn't early enough to escape their followers. With the first shadows of dawn, Harry could see the Brown Coats riding behind him, just like they had the day before. Hour after hour. And Harry cursed the thought of another morning and afternoon of being chaperoned.

'Jesus?' Harry said, breaking the silence.

'Yes, sir.'

'Are you sure we're going the right way? We seem to be doing circles.'

'No, sir. I remember this place. I know that tree.' He pointed. 'And those bushes. And that log with the big knothole in the middle.'

'Are you sure?' Harry put his hand to his forehead so he could look around. The policeman had no idea where he was, and Mary giggled at his confusion. If this bloke didn't have a smart horse and a dog, she thought, he would have been dead years ago. Or some of her people would have found him wandering around with a long beard, no boots and a torn uniform.

'Jesus, it's important that we find this body,' Harry said, giving the boy his sternest constable face. 'You know where he is, I don't. If you say go that way, I go that way. If you say go over the hill, I do it. If you say you recognise a tree, I believe you. I have to believe you. I don't have a choice. But you do. Understand?'

'Yes, sir.'

'So, we're going the right way, are we?'

'He said yes, boss.'

'Shut up, Mary. Jesus, are we going the right way?'

Jesus paused and looked at the horizon. 'Yes, sir. This is the way.'

'Right then.'

He knew it was impossible, but Harry felt like the Brown Coats could hear his words, and the men would stay with him for every turn of the small wagon's wheels, and when the trip was over, Jesus would hang.

'So, we'll get there today?' Harry asked.

'Yes, sir,' Jesus said.

'Are you sure about that?' Mary asked, staring at Jesus with her wide brown eyes. 'Today? Really?' And she jabbed an elbow into his fatless ribs. 'Today, ya reckon? I don't bloody know about that.'

'Shut up, Mary. How would you know? You don't even know where we're going.'

Jesus looked at Mary and then back at the policeman. He only had the truth to tell, but it seemed to make Mary unhappy. 'Yes, sir. Today.'

'Right.' Harry flicked at the reins and they moved.

Just before noon, the track they were on came to an end, and in front were just trees and grass and bush. Jesus remembered the place well enough. He'd stopped there for a dig, but he found no gold four inches under the surface, and he broke the stick he was using, so he'd walked on.

'Right now, which way?' Harry asked. He stopped the sulky and yawned and rubbed the glare out of his eyes.

Jesus was about to point east and give a clear answer, but then he felt the spiky elbow of Mary again. Her eyes were wide and she twisted her mouth like she had words but couldn't get them out. She waggled her finger to the west for only Jesus to see. Jesus must have looked confused because she twisted her face harder and shook the digit again.

So Jesus did something that he'd never done before. He told a lie. He remembered the howls from the night before and the talk of hanging. And he remembered the words of Mary. 'I'm gonna save you, Jesus. And you're gonna save me.'

'It's this way, sir,' Jesus said, pointing in the same direction as Mary's finger. She didn't jab him in the ribs, so he must have got it right this time.

'Are you sure?'

Jesus paused before he lied for the second time in his life.

By his count, he'd only done two things wrong since his birth fifty years ago: he'd stolen a saddle and revolver from a dead man and he'd lied to a constable.

'It's this way,' Jesus said, pointing again.

Mary wanted to go west. So they went west.

*

That same day, Jack Pink wasn't travelling at all. He was spending his afternoon punching someone in the face. It wasn't supposed to be a fight to the death, but the crowd watching on were cheering as though death was a possibility.

The face Jack was punching belonged to Donal Magee. They called him the Fist of Fiery Creek and he'd once been the best bare-knuckle fighter anyone had known since the colony began. He was famous for winning a contest that lasted seven hours and twenty minutes. No-one who was there could believe what they'd seen, and after Magee raised an arm in triumph, he slept for five weeks in a rope hammock without waking. It was a mighty victory. But that was a decade ago and there'd been many fights since.

Magee was now deaf from two split eardrums and his eyes were ruined by all the blood that had leaked between his lids.

Jack took advantage of all his opponent's disabilities as he imposed damage on every part of Magee's body. He cracked him high on the cheek, then forced his chin further to the side than nature intended, then belted the meaty part of his jaw just under the ear, and then straight on the nose to make it gush with blood and snot.

The fight had started in the normal fashion – shirtless and bare-knuckled – as the two came together in a ropeless ring marked out only by spectators.

Unusually for an Irishman, Magee had been trained under London Prize Ring rules, and he walked to the centre with his fists dancing in front of his face like two swarming flies.

Jack's technique, however, was far more primal. He kept his hands low and invited Magee to take an early lunge at his bearded face. And the invitation was accepted within seconds of the first round, as Magee opened with his trusted combination of a quick left followed by a harder right.

Neither connected. Jack swayed back before countering with his own left jab. He landed it in the centre of Magee's face and stunned his opponent into a pattern of torment that continued until the Fist of Fiery Creek was in the dirt.

It was no-one's job to stop the fight and the crowd was far too drunk and happy to want it to end. They loved the sound of bare flesh being smacked together and the groans of air exiting Magee's body as the untamed bushman Jack Pink pushed his raw knuckles into the gut.

It wasn't the most sporting event, but it was certainly the best fight they'd seen in a year. By a long way. And no-one was happier than Mother Pink. This was her kind of crowd. They were mostly men, and the only women there were those unfit for school halls, churches and markets of respectable trading. They were often called the 'wrong women'. And Mother Pink was as wrong as any of them.

But she didn't cheer and holler with the crowd, she just smiled, sipped her gin, and watched her boy in the middle, slapping and punching Magee and grabbing him by the hair.

Mother had organised the fight after discovering Donal Magee was living in Ballarat. Life as a brawler had not been prosperous, so he wandered east with a gold pan and a pick with a broken handle. She knew his skills had diminished, but the old scrapper could still bring in a crowd.

It would be a profitable afternoon, and the extra funds would help get the gang closer to Melbourne. Mother was taking a handsome cut of the house bets, and she put every penny she had on her son to win.

She had no doubt of victory, but to help the outcome, she'd prevented Jack from taking his usual morning ride. She didn't want him expelling all his night demons riding his black horse. She wanted him to use the face of Magee instead.

Because the newspapers hadn't much reported on the Pink Gang's recent crimes, Mother was unconcerned about being recognised in public. There were even some uniformed troopers drinking and watching the fight. One of them was a former client of hers. He looked much older but she still knew him and remembered his fondness for making love while standing up. Now he had a limp and looked like he'd struggle to either stand up or make love.

As instructed, Carrigan remained at the back and collected

the gambling money. The big man would be a solid deterrent against any disputes, although there would be none because there was no denying who was winning the fight.

Samuel LaBat scribbled out some notes and thought the fight had the makings of a mighty poem. He'd been promising Mother a verse for months, but he'd been unable to get one started. And there were plenty of words that would rhyme with Magee, Pink, fist and blood.

The writer also spent much of the bout moving through the crowd, gathering information on the new horse race in spring. He bought a round of dark ale for a retired jockey called 'Pixie' Richards, who was pointed out as an authority on the sport, and his size suggested he knew the game.

Although Richards was tiny, he had a deep Scot's voice, as though he was a puppet being operated by a much larger man.

'So it's all true then?' LaBat asked. 'This big race? What do you know about it?'

'Oh aye, it's true enough, boy,' said Pixie, tipping down the first half of his free drink. 'Will be mighty. And them stuck-up bastards at the Jockey Club will hate it.'

'Why? I'd think they'd be keen on a big race.'

'Oh, they're keen all right – keen to have it for 'emselves. But the Turf Club got there first.'

'They don't get along then?'

'Oh no, boy. The clubs fight like angry cocks.'

'I see,' LaBat said and made a note. He recorded all rivalries. He never knew when he might need the information.

'So then, got a horse, have ya?' Pixie drained his mug and waited for another.

'A horse?'

'Yeah, a horse? Have you got a horse for the race?'

'I'm thinking about it,' LaBat said, lying and waving to get fresh drinks. 'Maybe.'

'Well, you'll need one. They don't let you run it alone.' Pixie reacted to his own little joke. His laugh was even deeper than his voice. It sounded like someone banging on the first two keys of a piano.

'Yeah, right, a horse. Got it,' LaBat said without smiling. He didn't like to be laughed at.

'It's a handicap race, see, boy? Do you know what that is? It ain't about the fastest animal. They weigh down the fast ones. But it's a bloody long race, so you're gonna have to have a nag to last the distance. And you'll need a mighty rider. It's gonna get tight on that track . . . there'll be a lot of flesh out there . . . a bloke could get lost very bloody easy. Have ya your rider?'

'Rider?'

'Jockey.'

'Jockey?'

'Oh aye, they sit on the horse.' Pixie laughed again.

'No, I don't.'

'Got a trainer?'

'No.'

The low piano keys kept banging and LaBat thought how joyous it would be to stick the little shit with a knife and listen to some higher notes instead.

'Anyway, ta for the grog, but I don't think I been much use to ya,' Pixie said. 'If you want to run the Melbourne Cup, you're missing some of the essentials.'

'The Melbourne Cup? Is that what they're calling it?'

'Aye, what else would they call it?'

'I dunno . . . but . . . look, to be honest, I'm more interested in the betting side of things. Not the actual racing.'

'Oh, right then. I understand. But I don't know much about the starters yet. It's like I told ya – it's a handicap, so anyone could take it. If you want to get some coin, I wouldn't use a penny on that race. You might just as well stand in a sheep shed and take bets which one'll get clipped first.'

'But it's going to be a big betting race, isn't it? That's what the newspapers said. A lot of people will be betting.'

From behind them, Donal Magee gurgled with pain as Jack gnawed at the flesh of his eyebrows.

'Oh aye, there'll be a lot of bets, don't worry about that.'

'So why are people betting if it's so hard to pick the winner?'

'Because they know nothing 'bout racing. They're just like you. It's a show, understand? Just a show. They just want to sit in the sun, look at the girls, wave to the gov'ner and bet on something they know bugger all about.'

'Then it wouldn't matter where the horses come from then?'

'Oh no, boy, they'll still want good'ens. The best. That's part of the show, see? You don't want a mob of scabby old bloody bush runners. They'll be thoroughbreds.'

'Have another ale. What about the prize money? What do you hear?'

'A thousand.'

'A thousand? That much? In gold?'

'That's what I hear. Aye. A thousand special sovs, made just for the Cup.'

'A thousand? All gold? That sounds lovely, doesn't it?' LaBat said to himself, rather than his drinking companion.

'But if you want to make some money, don't worry about that race. I'll tell ya of some others.'

Pixie kept talking but LaBat was no longer listening. He was thinking about his share of the thousand pieces of gold. He imagined it piled in a wooden chest with a heavy lid and a single fat lock to keep the bounty safe. He knew it wouldn't be as romantic as that. They'd probably be kept in flour bags with a bit of twine around the top. But he didn't care how it came. A thousand gold sovereigns was a thousand gold sovereigns. They could keep it in a bucket of kookaburra shit, for all he cared, as long as he got his cut.

And it wasn't just the sovereigns – there was all the money from the bookies and the purses and wallets in the crowd.

LaBat was ready to be a rich man. As much as he liked stealing, he was looking forward to a life beyond robbery and sleeping on the ground. He planned to take his share and ride to New South Wales, where no-one knew his face. He'd find a beautiful woman – or maybe two of them – and they'd feed and love him until he was fat and exhausted. Then he'd write the story of his life. And it would be more than just a poem or a smattering of words in a newspaper, it would be a book. A magnificent book. It would be read in every colony and over the seas. He would be wealthy and sleeping with naked women, and his words would make him immortal.

He would live well, and then he would never die.

LaBat took a slug of rum and silently toasted the race to himself. Thank God for the Melbourne Cup.

He looked over at the fight. Jack was still pummelling the

head and torso of Donal Magee. Jack was like a sea storm, well beyond the control of men. And the faces of the spectators told LaBat everything he needed to know about the boss: Jack Pink frightened people. As much as the crowd was enjoying the fight, they were all afraid that the tall bushman might turn on them and make their face into mash as well.

They felt the same fear that LaBat had felt.

That was just the kind of fear the gang needed to rob the Melbourne Cup.

It was late afternoon when Mother Pink went into the ring and stopped the brawl, as Carrigan collected the winnings in an empty sugar bag and the crowd gave a final cheer. They were all drunk and it had been a bloody day.

It would be dark soon and Mother's left bosom started to leak as they rode hard to get back to camp before they lost the sun. There was not a single drop of blood on her boy's face, there was only sweat, but she knew he would still need some extra attention tonight.

Donal Magee was carried off in a wagon of hay, with his feet dangling off the back. He would never see another morning. He stayed in the fist-induced coma for two weeks until he finally died. Jack Pink would never know it, but the Fist of Fiery Creek was the first man he'd ever killed.

Yet he wouldn't be the last.

*

While Jack Pink was killing Donal Magee, Harry Logan was still driving the sulky west.

He was going where Jesus told him, with no idea he was being guided by the secretly pointing finger of Mary. And as they travelled, the land changed. It became quieter. They'd not seen a town since they made the turn. Not even a single dwelling or a shed. And they hadn't seen another person walking or riding the unmarked tracks.

It was just them, with the Brown Coats following behind.

In this new part of the world, the birds didn't sing as loud, as if they were unsure of their own voices. And the sky was cloaked in darker grey clouds that moved like they were bringing rain, but none fell. It was like a promise. Or a threat.

Mary and Jesus swayed with the wagon, still chained together, and just before noon, when she knew Harry was distracted, Mary grinned at Jesus and rolled her eyes in her head, then stopped and stared at him, then rolled again. He knew she was trying to tell him something. It wasn't just directions – now she was trying to tell him something different. She lifted her eyebrows, then dropped the left one and then the right. She suddenly looked impatient, then she smiled again. All the time keeping Jesus in her eye.

Finally, he realised what she was telling him: tonight was the night. They were going to run. This was it. And Jesus was glad of it. Since last night, he'd thought of little else but his own hanging. He kept touching and pinching the skin on his neck, and making gulping sounds as though he'd forgotten how to breathe. Air had become precious, and the thought of a tightened rope snatching it from him became an immovable terror.

Jesus lifted his own eyebrows to show Mary he understood. And that he'd be ready. Mary winked and the plan was set.

*

If they'd travelled east like they were supposed to, the small caravan of a widowed policeman, his dog, his grey mare, two armed mining executives, a murder suspect and a native girl would have already found the body of Andre Noble and the meatless carcass of his horse.

Harry thought finding the body would be the best hope for the fate of Jesus. He was hoping to secure some evidence that Noble hadn't died by the boy's hand. If there was no body to inspect, Jesus would look guilty from lying. But Harry also thought the only thing that could save the boy was discovering the corpse with the real killer standing over it, holding a signed statement, and a priest to verify the confession.

An hour before dark, Harry realised they weren't going to find anything that day. He stopped the sulky, rubbed his face with frustration and looked at Jesus.

'You said we were going to get there today,' Harry said. 'Well, just so you know, we're not going to.'

'It's just a bit further, boss.'

'Shut up, Mary.'

'It must be just a little bit further,' Jesus said.

'We had this conversation yesterday – exactly the same – and now we're having it again. And I'm about to lose the sun.' Harry rubbed his face again. He suddenly felt exhausted. 'Just tell me, are we going the right way?'

'Oh yes, Constable boss. Absolutely.'

'Shut up, Mary. Jesus, are we going the right way?'

Jesus touched his neck, thought of the rope, and kept lying.

'Yes, sir.'

'This way?' Harry pointed.

'Yes, that way.' Jesus pointed with him.

'So why aren't we there?'

'I'm sure we'll get there tomorrow. No bloody problem, boss.'

'Mary, if you open your gob again, you're gonna go hungry tonight.'

'Yes, boss. Oh, can I have a green sweet?'

'Yes, but shut up. Jesus, why aren't we —' Harry stopped his question when he heard stomping hooves behind him. It was the Brown Coats.

For the first time in the journey, they closed the gap and rode up to the sulky. And just like the howling from the night before, they were unsubtle about their approach as they pulled up either side of Harry.

For the last two days, their faces had been hidden by distance and the shade of their tall hats, but now they were clear. One had red hair and orange splotches covering his cheeks, and the other had a beard that was the same colour as the dark clouds. Despite their differing features, they seemed like brothers. More than brothers, it was as if they were sharing the same rotten soul.

'What is this, policeman?' asked the red-haired one. He said 'policeman' as two separate words, so it came out as 'police-man' and was clearly done for mockery.

'Where are we, police-man?'

'We're . . . we're here?' Harry said. He knew it was a stupid thing to say, but it was the only response he could think of to a question that he had been asking himself. 'Where else would we be? I don't know what you're asking.'

'You know what I am asking. Where is the body, police-man? Listen to me, you have made three turns that you didn't need to make. We should be there by now. Your sergeant said it was a day's ride, and no more. But it's been two days and this day is about to end.' He looked at the clouded sun dropping into the horizon. 'So I ask again, where are we?'

Harry had no better answer so he picked up the reins and flicked them, but the Red One bolted forward to grab the bridle of Harry's horse.

'You,' said the other man with the face of a cloud. He was pointing at Jesus. 'Speak. Answer. Where are you leading us, boy?'

Lying to the kind constable hadn't been easy, but he knew there would be understanding and forgiveness if he ever got caught. It was different with these men, and Jesus felt his throat choke.

'Where is the body? Where is Andre Noble? Where are we going?' Cloud Face asked again. His horse turned under him but he kept his eyes on Jesus, whipping his head around to maintain the stare. His coat fell open, showing a holstered black-handled revolver at his side. Then Jesus saw a flash of white coming from the man's belt. It was the gun of Andre Noble. It was *his* gun – the gun of Jesus. The sight of it brought an unexpected dose of comfort. Just knowing that he and the gun were in the same place let the air flow back through his neck.

'Where? Answer me!'

'I ask that you direct any questions and queries to me,' Harry said.

'Where are we going!?' the Brown Coat yelled. There was nothing for the roar to echo off, so the words just shuddered across the open land. 'You are being pushed around by these children, police-man. They are in charge. And they have fooled you. So tell me where you are going? I'll not keep asking.'

Harry then adopted a tone he'd used many times before, with drunks, vagrants, reluctant witnesses and startled thieves.

'Now look here,' said Harry. 'If you men want to follow behind, that is up to you. But I am here conducting a police investigation surrounding the disappearance of one Mr Andre Marcel Noble within the colony of Victoria. I am doing this at the behest and orders of my superiors, and therefore the governor of said colony according to the laws of Great Britain and Her Majesty the Queen. This young male is part of that investigation, and I'm instructing you to cease any and all interference in the questioning of witnesses or the gathering of evidence as part of the aforementioned case.'

Harry Logan knew he was just talking bullshit, but it was always the best way to remind others who the Crown law officer was in a conversation.

But the Brown Coats were not intimidated. They were unafraid of police, governors, laws, or even monarchs of England. They had gold. They needed nothing else.

'When, police-man? When will we get there, boy?'

'Well, as I have stated, you are welcome to follow,' Harry said, moving the sulky. 'But now I am going to those trees and make camp for the evening. Tomorrow – I expect – I will receive further information to aid with my investigation. And it is *my* investigation. Please remember that. Not yours.'

'Tomorrow. It had better be tomorrow,' said Cloud Face, more to Jesus than Harry as the sulky rolled away. The rage of these men was clear, and they were now tired of following.

Mary hadn't looked up while the men talked, but she felt inspired by the boss. She was proud of his bravery and lifted her head to catch the eye of the Red One. She gave him a short but knowing smile and half a wink.

The Red One was stunned and then angry, but these emotions lasted less than a second before he smiled back at her. And it was an awful smile. It wasn't to show happiness or even contempt; it was like he was passing her a curse. And it frightened Mary more than anything ever had before.

Mary had seen a lot of faces, but she'd never been truly afraid of any of them. She was clever and she knew how to embrace a friend and avoid an enemy. But she'd never seen a face like this before. She was angry at herself for being so bold with the wrong person. She was not used to feeling terror or regret, but now both swirled inside her. She only hoped that when she ran away with Jesus that night, she would outrun the curse too.

Cloud Face called out as the sulky moved off.

'Tomorrow! Police-man! Tomorrow!'

*

It was tomorrow. But only just.

On Harry Logan's pocket watch – a gift from Alice on their third, and last, anniversary – it showed twenty-three minutes past midnight. But Harry didn't know it. He was asleep.

Jesus was asleep too, and he'd already had a dream about an itchy rope stretching his neck as his feet flicked and searched for the ground underneath him.

Only Mary was awake.

Two hours before, she'd whispered her plans to Jesus: they would limp away through the dark and hide in a hollowed log for the day, and then they'd travel through the night again until they could find some farm tools to take off the chains. Then they would run hard. Just like rabbits.

Mary kept a big piece of meat from her meal and she'd give it to the dog to distract him while they left camp. There was a strong moon that night, which would help Mary and Jesus get away but would also make them easier to find if Harry came looking.

Mary had wanted to sleep, but she also wanted to be awake two hours before dawn. That's when she'd wake Jesus and they'd go. Two other things were preventing her from resting. One was the terrible memory of the Red One's smile, and the other problem was more immediate – Harry had chained her and Jesus to a log, and she wondered how they'd get free.

Most nights, Harry would just run the chain around the trunk of a tree a couple of times, and it would be held there by its own weight more than anything. But tonight, it looked far more secure. He'd given it some extra attention. It was going to be difficult.

She looked at the log and the chain again, hoping she would be able to solve the problem when the time came. Then she put her head down and the dog rolled over and spooned against her, and she whispered a prayer that the chain would be gone when she woke. She put her arm around him and the smell and warmth dropped her into a deep and unexpected sleep.

Then Mary woke up. She was snatched out by a noise but didn't know what – it was still sitting in her dreams. She sat up and looked at Jesus. He was asleep and still tethered to her ankle, and Harry was asleep on the other side of the dying fire, rattling out his familiar snores. But that wasn't the noise that woke her.

114

She looked at the long chain and followed it with her eyes to the log, expecting to see it still locked around the dead fallen branch. But it wasn't. Mary rubbed at her eyes and wondered if she was still asleep or being tricked by the moonlight. But it was neither – the chain was off the log and lying in the dirt attached to nothing. She pulled at it and it came to her like a snake until she held the final link in her fingers.

What had happened? Who did it? Was it Harry or Jesus? Was it the dog?

Mary was properly awake now and remembered the prayer she whispered before sleep. Had it worked?

She hadn't prayed to anything in particular – just to whoever or whatever was listening. And she didn't really believe in prayers. When she was very little, before she was stolen, she had an aunty who believed that all the good things that happened came from the spirit of the long-necked turtle. Her aunty's word for the spirit was *murrup*, and it was one of the only old words Mary could still remember.

So she'd prayed – and if the long-necked turtle was listening it couldn't hurt. And now she was awake and the chain was free.

Mary had never seen a miracle before, and it should have frightened her, but it didn't. It was what she'd asked for and it happened. That was not something to be afraid of. And if it was done by the spirit of her ancestors, or a reptile that once made the sky, or by the god of people like Harry Logan, it didn't matter. Maybe they were all the same thing, anyway. Whatever it was, Mary knew they were helping her tonight.

And now it was time for the plan. She would wake Jesus. She would feed the dog. She would wait until Harry's snoring reached the right pitch. They'd lift their irons and stay close so they wouldn't clatter. They'd walk until they couldn't hear Harry anymore. Then they'd walk further, and when the sun came up, they'd hide. And if Jesus wanted to know how she got the chain off, she would tell him. She'd tell him about the long-necked turtle and everything. It would sound silly. She knew that. But she'd tell him, anyway.

Mary turned to wake her friend, but a noise stopped her. It was the same noise that woke her up.

Before she could think what it was, or touch the shoulder of Jesus, a hand came from behind and covered her face. The flesh of the palm almost choked her and the fingers spread out like the legs of a massive spider.

It was the Brown Coats. The Red One had her, and Cloud Face grabbed Jesus, and they were dragged into the trees together.

Mary screamed but it was only inside her head. She didn't have enough air in her throat to even make a muffled cry. She opened her eyes and could see between a gap in the two spider legs, and the chain that she'd prayed over was now dragging behind after her.

The miracle was gone. It was never there. There was only the curse.

*

The story of Mary and Jesus would have been a more pleasant one if they weren't grabbed by the Brown Coats. But that's not how the story goes.

116

They were taken from the moonlight and pulled into the dark cover of the trees, and the hands that grasped Mary felt like they were made of steel rather than bone.

Mary had always thought of herself as a strong person – even with her skinny limbs and underfed ribs. She'd sensed a fighting energy in her body that could battle against hard men and wild animals when needed. But as the fingers of the Red One gripped her and lifted her off the ground, she quickly understood how weak she was against him.

Yet she still fought. And she twisted herself around until she could see the outline of the Brown Coat's face. That was a mistake. Without effort, the Red One changed his hold, clutched Mary's throat with just one hand, and cocked the other one back for a punch. Then he threw it without pause.

Mary couldn't see the fist coming from the shadows, but she felt it. It landed half on the cheek and half on her nose, and it exploded in her skull. It was like she'd been hit by a falling tree, and it took away all sight and sound for a moment.

And with that giant punch, she realised something terrible was going to happen.

Just like the illusion of her own strength, Mary had always felt nothing truly awful would occur in her life. There had been bad things – some could be considered unbearable by other people – but she had survived them and always believed she was ready for the next one. But with that punch, she knew she was about to endure something that she may not survive. And perhaps it was something she wouldn't want to survive.

Mary felt her body hit the ground and her eyes came open. She turned her head and she could see Jesus. Their ankles were still chained together and Cloud Eyes had him pinned to the ground.

Jesus was still trying to understand what was happening. Less than a minute before, he was asleep. And it was a deep one. The worries of the day had left him exhausted. Then he had the flash of a dream about being kicked by a horse and bitten by a snake at the same time. That's when he woke up. And he had woken in this hell.

Cloud Face was just as strong as his evil colleague, and he twisted Jesus' arm high into his back. It felt like the end of a burning stick was being poked into his shoulder. The more he fought, the deeper the stick went.

Mary loved that Jesus was fighting so hard, but his strength didn't match his courage, and she knew they would die like this together. She had imagined them being friends for a long time. Maybe even forever. She wanted them to run together and stay close even when the chains were gone. And they would light their own fire and laugh all night. And if there were troubles to come, they'd fix them together. They'd be mates.

But now it wasn't going to happen, she thought.

And where was Harry? Where are you, Constable boss? Come on, ya bloody snorin' bugger. And where's the dog? Hey, mate, where are ya?

She realised the dog would be dead. These bastards would have tricked him with some food – the way Mary herself planned – and they'd have killed him.

Mary had an awful sadness that mixed with her rage and physical pain, and she knew nothing would save her from what was about to happen. No policeman, no friend, no dog, no turtles – long-necked or otherwise – and no gods. She had gone to sleep praying, she thought she'd woken up to a miracle, and now there was only this.

She tried to get up but felt the Red One's grip again. And then there was another punch. She knew it was coming, even without looking. It hit her on the left eye. It was just as hard as the first and her head filled with dots of light.

She almost prayed for another punch – so hard that it would take her away from everything.

Then she heard another crack, but this one wasn't at her face. Then another. It was the sound of wood and bone.

'Bastard!' she heard a voice. It was Harry Logan. 'You bastard! You mongrel bastard!'

There was another collision and Mary saw the Red One falling towards her. His eyes were stunned open and he landed on Mary with no strength in his body. She pushed him off and looked up to see Harry standing over them with his shotgun.

He was holding the barrel and using the butt to smash the Red One's head. She'd never seen the boss frantic and angry before. He lifted the gun again and cracked it into the freckled face. The Brown Coat expelled a grunt before he fell in the dirt, knocked out.

Harry spun the weapon to now use it as a gun. He pointed it at Cloud Face who was jumping up to get off Jesus, but still keeping a knee in his back. The Brown Coat went for the revolver in his holster. He was quick, and he had it cocked and pointed before Harry could get the hammer back on his shotgun.

Constable Harry Logan was a good shot, and he knew how to use his hands in a scuffle, but he'd never had a fight to the death.

Very few in the colony had. There were many revolvers and rifles and shotguns, and there were a lot of rough faces that looked like they'd used them to kill, but almost none had. The most Harry himself had done was a warning shot above the head of a horse thief who surrendered the very moment he heard a ball of lead fizzle over his hat.

And it was the same for Cloud Face. Despite his speed, he'd never killed anyone. He'd never been in a real gunfight. But he was in one now. And currently, he was winning it, because his weapon was ready to fire and Harry's wasn't.

Jesus kept struggling – thrashing his arms around – and Cloud Face pushed him down harder with his knee and his spare arm, but still kept his aim on Harry and was about to fire. He was going to get his first kill. And he was starting his list with a police-man.

Jesus reached up with a last frantic grab for Cloud Face's shirt, but he found something else instead. It was something so familiar that it was almost part of his own body. And as dark as it was under the trees, and as desperate as his situation was, he knew exactly what he was holding. It was the gun that once belonged to Andre Noble. Now the gun of Jesus Whitetree.

Jesus recalled every piece of it. The only thing that was different was the weight – it was heavier. No-one else who'd ever touched the gun would have noticed the difference, not even Andre Noble. But Jesus could. It meant the gun was loaded.

All the hours of practice from when he first found the Colt Navy were still inside every muscle of his hand. His thumb pulled back the hammer – all the way to where it needed to be – and his finger was already at the trigger.

Cloud Face didn't feel it when the revolver of his dead comrade was being taken from his belt. He only heard it being cocked. He looked down at the boy and saw a flash of the ivory handle and the black hole at the end of the barrel. He had been unafraid of the boy. He was skinny and dim and half-dead from a lack of food, and holding him down was as easy as wrestling an injured baby possum. So Cloud Face showed no respect.

And that's what got him killed.

He leaned back and swiped at the revolver, as though he was taking a toy from a misbehaving baby. But the swipe missed, and this child was too determined.

Jesus kept the gun on Cloud Face and lifted his leg, kicking the Brown Coat in the middle of the gut. Cloud Face fell back and swung his own gun on Jesus, but the finger of Jesus only needed to squeeze and the hammer sprang forward and the powder blasted.

Jesus knew nothing about the anatomy of the human body, and if he'd ever been asked to find the location of a man's heart, he'd only have guessed and most likely been wrong. Yet that's where he shot Cloud Face. The lead ball cut through the skin and bone and into the fist-sized muscle underneath.

Cloud Face didn't fly back into the dirt. Instead, his back bolted straight – like he was a soldier greeting an officer – and he stared forward as though he was watching something coming for him. And something was coming. It was his own death. Then he whispered the name of the man who had just killed him.

'Jesus. Oh my dear Jesus,' he said.

But he was talking about someone else.

*

The Red One was still alive. His body twitched and a line of blood rivered from under his hair and dripped into the dirt. Harry bent down and took the revolver from the man's belt. The Brown Coat was unlikely to wake from the coma soon, but the last few minutes had been so terrible that it felt like everything bad was possible.

No such precautions were needed for Cloud Face. He was well dead. And as Harry looked at the body, he was amazed at the quick skills of Jesus. He would never have trusted the boy to save his life in a fight. But that's what had happened.

Jesus got to his feet. He was holding his gun and being careful not to pull on the chain attached to Mary. He could still feel the vibration in his palm from the recoil, the smell of burnt powder in his nose, and his ears were ringing. He knew there'd be a bit of noise when a gun fired, but it was much more than he'd expected. And he thought there would've been more blood when a man got shot, but there was just a small black mark in the middle of Cloud Face's chest.

Jesus was yet to understand what he'd just done. He'd taken a life but his brain and soul couldn't process it. He was just glad he wasn't dead and the terrible things that were happening to his friend had stopped.

Harry went to Mary to help her stand but she signalled that she didn't want to be touched. After a minute, she fixed her clothes as best she could and got to her feet, and the three of them just stood and looked at each other. They were all like different people now. What they meant to each other the night before had changed, and the sadness of that change was over-whelming to Harry. He wanted to ask Mary if she was hungry.

He wanted to cook for her and listen to her slurp her food and then swear and say something silly and then tell her to shut up.

But that wasn't going to happen again.

It must have been closer to dawn than they all thought – or they'd just been standing for a long time – because the first hints of the sun came and they could see the mess that was around them.

Harry approached Mary as though he was walking up on a frightened animal. Her eyes were wet, and it could have been from tears or pain, or just her body's reaction to being punched in the face. Harry knelt at her feet and unlocked the iron from her ankle. He was careful not to pinch her as he twisted off the cold metal. He did the same for Jesus, then he took two quick steps and threw the irons as far as he could into the longer grass. They landed with a heavy rattle as the links settled into the place they would rust.

Harry came back and stood in front of Mary, and without using words – just their eyes, shrugs, pained smiles and nods – they spoke.

I'm sorry about what happened. Are you all right?

I don't know yet. Yeah, I'm all right.

I'm sorry. I took your chains off, see.

I know.

But I'm also the bloke that put them on, so it doesn't mean much, does it?

Don't worry about it.

I'm sorry that I chained you up and dragged you around the colony and let those bastards follow us. Now look at all of this. I should have known. I know what people are like – I've seen too many of them. And I let it happen. I'm supposed to look after children and women. Please take the horse.

Your horse?

Yeah. Take her and go.

Where do you want me to go?

I don't know, but don't come back here.

It was another minute before Mary moved. She wiped her face and went to the sulky and got Andre Noble's saddle and carried it to Harry's horse. It took her three swings before she got it on the back, and then she fixed the bridle. The animal greeted her by giving her a gentle nudge. Mary touched the soft patch between the flicking ears and breathed in its beautiful smell.

Harry made himself busy by acting like a policeman and picking up all the firearms and putting them in a pile. And Jesus stuffed his gun into his pants. It was still warm from the shot.

Mary got up in the saddle and the horse was unbothered by having a new owner. The scent of Mary was familiar to her big nostrils. Then Mary spoke the first words of the morning.

'Come on,' she said to Jesus. 'It's time to go.'

He climbed up, but started with the wrong foot in the right stirrup and had to try again. Mary moved forward to make room for her friend, and just like the sulky seat, both their backsides were able to fit in a place that was designed for just one man.

She took a last look at the constable and wished the dog was still alive and sitting next to him, sniffing the air and waiting for his tucker.

'See ya, Harry,' Mary said in a voice that was not much more than a croaky whisper.

Then she kicked the horse with the heels of her bare feet and they leapt forward and bolted. The hard gallop of his horse was the only sound in the morning and Harry could do nothing but stand and see them go, riding until they were swallowed by dust and breaking sunlight.

There was a noise behind him. It was the sound of a stick snapping, and he turned and reached for his revolver and drew it at what was coming.

'Bloody hell!' Harry cried out. He was startled and all the fear and anger of the last half an hour came out of him.

It was the dog. He was limping but, at the sight of Harry, his tail swayed. It was a slower wag and not as enthusiastic, but it was still a wag.

'Bugger me, mate. You scared the hell out of me. You all right? Hey? You all right?' Harry rubbed the head and the tail picked up speed. He got on his knees and felt around the dog. He was tender at the back leg and yelped a little, but nothing was broken.

'Good boy,' Harry said, then he answered a question he knew the sniffing dog was asking. 'She's gone, mate. She's gone. They're both gone.'

Harry went over to the Brown Coats and felt sick at the sight of them. The Red One groaned, his chin vibrated and his head rolled in the dirt. He was starting to wake. With no urgency, Harry lifted his revolver, cocked it and fired, putting a ball through the freckled forehead.

What a bloody terrible morning. The only bit of good luck was that he'd brought a shovel.

*

Jesus had never been on a horse before. Just like he'd never fired a gun, won a fight, or killed someone.

He couldn't believe he was the same person he was two weeks ago, walking alone and saying his own name in the quiet before sleep. His new life was dangerous and fast.

And the feeling of the horse under him was like nothing he could have imagined. It was as though he was riding the fastest cloud of a moving storm. The trees that had always gone by so slow were now just a blur of bark and leaves. He'd seen people ride before and it had always looked frightening to him, but he wasn't afraid now. The horse's back straightened into a gallop, its head darted forward, and the hooves stroked the ground like it was touching air rather than earth.

Jesus held onto Mary, but only gently. She hadn't spoken since they'd left the camp and she'd barely moved. She kept her head straight and held the reins with a grip that didn't change for hour after hour.

Jesus touched his gun. He thought the metal would have gone cold in the fresh morning, but it hadn't. And it stayed warm as they rode through the day. But he didn't need the temperature of the gun to remind him how he'd just killed a man before dawn. He knew he'd never be able to forget it.

He had been told that killers went to hell when they died. They were thrown down with the thieves and liars. But he knew nothing could be worse than watching what was happening to Mary. That was already hell, and Jesus had to kill to get them out of it.

He had five shots left in his gun and he wondered if he'd ever need to use them. Would they be for more practice? Perhaps

I should, he thought. It was only practice that had saved him and Mary. He was grateful for every minute he'd spent aiming and cocking and spinning the cylinder along his palm. He only wished he'd had the gun before Mary got hurt. He wouldn't make that mistake again. He vowed to keep it with him always. And if he needed to use every one of the five shots to protect them, he would.

They rode on.

At first, Jesus felt like they were being chased, but as the day got older, it was more like they were being pulled towards something. And it was something good. Or at least it was better than what they were leaving behind. Jesus wondered if Mary was thinking about the same things as him.

She wasn't.

Mary was trying to think of nothing at all. She just wanted to ride and she wanted to do it as fast and for as long as she could. And Harry's beautiful grey horse seemed to want the same thing.

Jesus thought they'd stop riding when it got dark, but the moonlight only seemed to make the animal faster. Tonight there was no fire, no meal, no warm dog, no chattering Mary, and no Harry to tell her to shut up.

But there were no chains either.

*

When the horse finally stopped, Jesus woke and it was the morning.

They'd arrived in another different world. They were at the bottom of a hill next to a creek flowing lazy, and a one-room bush hut. But it was clean inside and a fresh white blanket was tucked into a small bed. It looked like someone's home, but it also seemed to have been prepared just for them.

Mary still hadn't spoken. To Jesus, her face was older now. Not fifty years old – she wasn't like him – but she was older than she was. And the smile was gone. She didn't look at the hut, she just waded out into the water until she got to the middle. It was no deeper than her knees but she lay down with her head above the surface. The water moved around her body and burbled like it was getting used to the new object. Its routine had been disturbed. But then it settled back into its flow, as though the girl was a rock that had been there for ten thousand years.

Jesus looked after the mare. He took off the saddle and helped it find water and grass. Mary stayed in the creek until the sun was high, then she lay on the bank to dry and went into the hut, pulled back the clean covers and got into bed, where she slept for four days.

Jesus lit a fire in the hut's small hearth and kept it going through the nights. He wanted Mary to be warm and he didn't want her to wake up in the dark.

He ate what he could find on the bushes and in the creek, and sat with her for the first two days. Then he started to look at the hill. He began to feel like there was something on the other side. Something waiting for both of them. And it wasn't something he needed to be afraid of or something he'd have to shoot.

He could hear a humming sound. At first, it was barely there and he wasn't sure he was really hearing it. But once his ear found it, it was impossible to ignore.

So on the third morning of Mary's sleep, when he was sure she wouldn't wake, he walked up the hill. It was far steeper than it looked and it felt more like a mountain than a hill. The noise grew and he got to the top and looked down the other side. It was a town. But it was bigger. Just like the hill was too big to be just a hill, this town was too big to be a town.

It was a city.

Mull Creek had been the biggest place he'd ever seen and he remembered how the gold town looked like a large animal, and the houses were scales on its back. But it was nothing like this mighty animal. Its scales couldn't be counted and they sprawled back to the horizon. And the humming noise lifted. It was the sound of people all living together. Thousands of them. Jesus had known the world was full of people, but he didn't know they all lived in the one place. And this was the place.

On the fourth day, Mary woke just before dark. Jesus made a meal from a good fish he'd trapped in one of the creek's shallow pools, and Mary ate it without enthusiasm. Then he stirred the fire to make it last and they sat together but they didn't talk – there were just the clicks and spits of the burning wood. There were no Brown Coats or police, and it should have been a wonderful night. But Mary just looked into the coals, with one eye almost swollen shut from the attack, until Jesus put his own head down to rest. He was almost asleep when he heard a voice.

'What?' he asked with his eyes springing open.

'I said, "What do you reckon?"' Mary's voice was low, and if the night wasn't so quiet he would never have heard her.

'What about?' He smiled to hear her speak.

'I dunno, about anything.' She didn't smile back. 'Please talk, Jesus. Say something. I don't care what you talk about. Just say something. Tell me about things that you like. What do you want?'

'What do I want?'

'Yeah, if you could have anything, you know, what would you want? Anything.'

'I dunno.'

'Yes, ya do. Everybody knows what they want.' She scratched at her unchained ankle. 'Don't ya wanna tell me?'

Jesus looked at the fire.

'Please talk to me, Jesus. Tell me anything.'

'I like . . .'

'What? What do you like?'

'I like gold.'

'Gold? All right. What do you like about it?' Her voice was still quiet.

'I dunno, it's just . . .'

'Have you got some gold in some place?'

'Nah.'

'Did ya have some?'

'Nah.'

'But ya want some?'

'Yeah.'

'Fair enough. Do ya wanna be one of them mad blokes diggin' in dirt?'

'Yeah, I suppose. But I never had a shovel.'

'What would you wanna be like them for?'

'I just . . .'

'. . . ya just like gold? I understand. Do you like the colour?'

'I dunno. What colour is it?'

'What do ya mean? Don't ya know the colour?'

'What colour is it?'

'It's . . . I dunno . . . it's just . . . gold colour.' Mary rested her chin on her knee. 'I don't know how to say it. It's just gold. How would you say the colour of the sky is?'

'Gold is blue?'

'Nah, it's not. But how would ya say blue? Gold is gold. Just gold.'

'Have you seen some?'

'Yep,' Mary said. She had seen a few flecks, resting in a fat white palm. But it was years ago, and she wasn't impressed by it. Although the owner of the palm certainly was. 'But you haven't?'

'No.'

'But ya still want it? Ya never seen it and don't know what colour it is, but ya want it?'

'Yeah.'

'Why?'

'I dunno.'

'Yes, ya do.' Mary's tone wasn't bossy. She just wanted to keep hearing her friend talk. 'Tell me. Please.'

'It's just . . . you don't need much. Just a little is enough. And then you can sleep anywhere you want. You can eat all the time. You can get what you need. Everything is better with gold. And you don't have to keep looking.'

'Looking for what?'

'Looking for gold. When you've got it, you've got everything.'

Mary looked at the revolver tucked into Jesus' pants. 'The fella who had that gun and that fancy saddle – that Andre Noble bloke – did you shoot him over gold?'

'No.'

'It makes people do bad things.'

'I didn't. I promise. I just found him.'

'All right,' Mary said, and believed him. She lay down.

'Mary, what's that place on the other side of the hill?'

'It's the city.' Her eyes were closed and she answered with the curled lips of a person about to sleep.

'What city?'

'Melbourne.'

'Are you sure?'

'Did you see lots of houses?'

'Yep.'

'And big chimneys with smoke goin' up and making their own clouds?'

'Yes, yes, that's right, it's just like that.'

'Then it's Melbourne. What else would it be?'

Jesus thought for a moment. 'Did you know it was there?' he asked.

Mary didn't answer him. The sticks in the fire shifted as though they were ready for sleep too.

'What do *you* want, Mary?'

'Dunno.'

'Yes, ya do.'

She wanted to tell him. She wanted to say there was no good in wanting anything. She had nothing before, yet the Brown Coats still found something to steal. So she wanted nothing. She wanted less than nothing. She wanted so much nothing that she became like the gap between the trees or the place where the wind stopped. But how could she tell that to Jesus?

'What do you want?' He tried again. His face was so bright. He looked like all she had to do was say it and whatever she wanted would be waiting outside the hut.

'I think I want to help you get some gold,' Mary said. 'How does that sound?'

They slept, and in the morning they both lifted Andre Noble's saddle onto Harry Logan's grey horse.

'Bugger me, this bastard is bloody heavy.'

Jesus smiled. His friend was swearing again.

They rode over the hill and down towards the biggest town they would ever know.

*

Harry Logan had been swearing too, but there was no-one to hear it.

He dug two graves for the Brown Coats. He knew he could have made do with just one and shoved them in together like diseased sheep in a pit, but that didn't seem right.

The dog watched from the edge as Harry lay them down, folded their arms, put their handkerchiefs over their eyes, surrounded them with their possessions, and covered them over.

Harry kept nothing of theirs. He knew better than to make the same mistake as Jesus. Stealing – even from a dead man – always caught up with the thief.

He smoothed over the graves with the back of the shovel and hoped the weather would soon make them look just like every other piece of ground. He left them with no headstone, but he did give them a prayer. It was a muddled benediction made from the few things Harry could remember. It began with 'Our Father who art in heaven' and ended with the last two lines of 'Silent Night'. It wasn't very good, but he knew it was more than they would have given him. And Harry wasn't really praying for them. They couldn't be helped. Souls like theirs would be stewed in hell before the bodies went stiff. He was really praying for himself, just to hear some gentler words.

He'd done so many things wrong in the last day that he feared for the eternal stains that would be on him. Worse than anything, he had failed to protect Mary. And then he killed a man. But there was something else that was chewing at him – he had let his prisoners go. Even though he knew it was right, it wasn't his job to let people go. He was supposed to catch them and take them to justice.

The colony needed laws and police. Without them, there would only be men like the Brown Coats and women like Mother Pink running across the land, taking whatever and whoever they pleased.

Harry worried that he was a different man now. He didn't know what he was. He wasn't a good policeman anymore. He was something else. And he prayed he'd figure out what that was. But before he could, he'd need to tell a lot of lies. And he would have to keep telling them until he was in the ground himself.

Harry boiled some water and shaved, so he could feel clean and to think about something else, then he mounted the Red One's horse. The animal had an unwelcome disposition, just like the man who'd owned it, as though he'd branded it with his own wickedness.

The dog had stopped limping but still wasn't at his strongest, so Harry went slow. They kept going west. He could have gone back the same way they'd come but he knew he'd probably get lost, and even if he didn't, it would take him back to Mull Creek. And he didn't ever want to go back to Mull Creek. When it came time to tell his lies, he'd prefer not to do it with Tom Adding-ton over glassfuls of grog. Instead, he wanted cold and formal surroundings so he could lie in a cold and formal fashion.

He rode with the trees so he wouldn't be seen. His luck had been bad enough recently, and he didn't want to be spotted by another travelling Brown Coat. The bastards seemed to be everywhere.

Just before the day ended, Harry found a town. It was so small it had yet to be named, and a mile before the first house, he stopped and shooed the horse away. The animal knew it wasn't wanted and it turned and bolted with the saddle and all, as though it was carrying the ghost of the Red One. Harry knew it would have been safer to shoot it, but he didn't kill horses. Until that morning, he hadn't killed anything.

The town had one street and no visible citizens. He walked until he found the blacksmith.

'Good evening, sir,' Harry said.

'Christ, you frightened the blazes out of me,' said the smith. He wasn't working – he was sitting on a hay bale drinking rum and lighting a pipe. Harry couldn't tell if this was the end of a hard day, or if the man had been sitting like that since morning.

'My apologies then. I need your assistance. I require a horse.'

The smith stood and looked out onto the road. 'You don't have a horse?'

'No.'

'I've never seen a trooper without a horse. What happened?'

'It's dead,' Harry said. It was a rehearsal for the many lies he would have to tell more important people than the blacksmith. 'I was in pursuit of a fleeing suspect when it was wrong footed and fell, breaking its leg.'

'The suspect broke its leg?'

'No, the horse.' If everyone he had to lie to was this stupid, it would be easier than Harry thought.

'Oh, right then. What did he do?'

'Who?'

'The suspect. What did he do?'

'Just kept running. Got away from me.'

'No, what did he do? What's he a suspect for?'

'Murder.' Harry regretted it the moment he used the word. Murder made people curious. If there was a killing anywhere, the whole colony wanted to know the details.

'Bugger me, is that right? Murder? Who did he murder? Or is it a woman? Did a woman do the killin'?'

'I'm not permitted to say.'

'Oh, go on.'

'No, I'm sorry, it's official constabulary business and I'm not able to —'

'Shit,' the smith said, kicking and spitting. It had been three years since anything interesting had happened. The town was unaffected by gold, and there was nothing to steal and few women worth killing for.

'What do want from me, trooper?' The smith had lost patience.

'I need a horse.'

'I have nothing for ya. I have no stock for the selling.'

'Right, well I can't pay for it, anyway.'

The blacksmith spat again.

'I require a horse to return me to my station,' Harry said. Another lie.

'But you won't pay for it?'

'No, not right now, you'll have to tally up with the Crown later.'

After more spitting and negotiation, Harry had a new horse. It wasn't the oldest horse he'd ever seen, but it was the oldest he'd seen with a saddle on its back. He felt sorry for the creature – it looked like an old woman forced into a wedding dress for a marriage that she no longer had the energy for.

'Is this girl gonna make it?' Harry asked.

'Probably. Depends. Where ya goin'?'

'Ballarat.'

The blacksmith bit into his lip while he considered the distance. 'That's a bugger of a long way. But yeah, she should just about it make it.'

'I'm grateful,' Harry said, not meaning it.

'And if she doesn't, you can always find some other poor bastard and give him one of these.' The smith held up the piece of paper Harry had given him. It was a note stating that he'd be compensated for a horse and saddle by the police force of the Colony of Victoria. The smith waved the useless document like it was a weed he'd just pulled from his vegetable garden.

Harry mounted, and the old girl under him mewled as she accepted the fate of her wedding night.

'So long,' Harry said, and the smith turned without a word. Harry called him back. 'One more thing, if you please.'

'What do you want now, trooper?'

'Which way to Ballarat?'

*

It was getting cold and the rain had been stubborn for a week. The Jack Pink Gang had left Ballarat and were moving south-east towards Melbourne.

Mother Pink was their human map. Her internal compass was far better calibrated than Harry Logan's. And she'd travelled these roads many times. Sometimes she was running away and sometimes she was chasing, but she always knew where she was.

On the wettest of days, the gang took shelter inside a church at Bacchus Marsh. It was a thriving town despite its lack of gold, because it was surrounded by full crops and healthy farms, and its location made it a perfect stopover between Melbourne and the mines.

The church was made from corrugated iron and the rain drummed at the roof while the gang hung their clothes to dry along the pews, and sat together half-naked in the back rows. Their only other company was the Reverend. He was dry, fully dressed and putting a fresh coat of white paint on the window frames while balancing on a wooden box. It was a poor day for painting, but the young Anglican vicar had an infinite energy for the maintenance of his church.

And there was nothing else to do.

He didn't ask of the gang's faith or their circumstances, because it didn't matter – he never turned people away. His wife warned him how this trusting nature was one of his many faults. Bacchus Marsh was a town with an impassable divide between Catholics and Protestants, so she thought her husband should be more discerning about who he allowed into the building. The Reverend had long suspected that his new bride had no real belief in God, nor the resurrection of His only Son, but was instead merely a passionate warrior in the politics between the faiths. If she were a man, he thought, she would be his superior.

Jack Pink sat with his feet resting on the pew in front, his bare chest still shining from the rain. He was staring at a large crucifix on the wall of the altar. Samuel LaBat was reading the vicar's copy of a Melbourne newspaper and Ben Carrigan was cradling a bag of sugar.

The sweet granules were now never far from his clutch and Mother Pink had become concerned by the giant's new addiction. Not because it might damage his health, but it had made him less reliant on her opium. And sugar was too easy to get. It was something he could do on his own. So watching Carrigan consume handfuls of sugar was a reminder of how much power she'd lost over him. But he was still with the gang and he was still showing loyalty to Jack. And he was still a frightening sight.

Mother fixed her hair as best she could in the reflection of the church windows. The rain had flattened it and the make-up at her eyes had come loose and made two black streams on her cheek. She'd stripped down to an unchristian degree – showing much more flesh than lace – and the Reverend watched her move through the rows, grateful it wasn't a Sunday and his wife was away teaching the Bible at the town's only school.

Mother had a piece of paper in her hand, filled with words in red ink. LaBat had been promising her a poem about her beautiful boy. And this was it.

She held it away from herself with an outstretched arm so her old eyes could focus, and she read it aloud to her gang and the painting priest, with the words pinging off the iron walls:

THE GOLDEN HAND

Let me tell you how it went,
And the words will flow like flood;
It's a tale of big men throwing fists,
With tears and heart and blood.

They called him the Fist of Fiery Creek,
He was known from bush to sea;
And before one day in Ballarat
No-one got the best of Donal James Magee.

He was strong and hard;
His punch was like a curse;
But he never thought he'd ever find
A man who had one worse.

Then from the north near Stoney Creek,
Where the miners dream of drink,
There came a bushman to best them all,
And they called him Fast Jack Pink.

Mother Pink stopped reading. 'We're not from Stoney Creek. Why did you say that?' she asked LaBat, who'd been enjoying Mother's lusty delivery of his words.

'It doesn't matter,' LaBat said.

'It *does* matter. I had a cousin at Stoney Creek. A haughty bitch. I don't want to say we're from Stoney Creek.'

'Yeah, but it sounds better. That's all that matters,' LaBat said. 'Stoney sounds like he's tough. Made of rock. Solid. Hard.'

'We're from Middle Swamp.'

'Yeah, see, that doesn't sound quite so good, does it? Would you be afraid of someone from Middle Swamp?'

'But it's the truth.'

'Truth?' LaBat winced at the concept. 'Bugger truth. The people who read this won't know that. They just want a proper yarn. And that one there is gonna be a beauty.' LaBat pointed to the page in her hand.

'And why are you going on about how good Magee is? This should all be about Jack, shouldn't it?'

'Because the bigger and better the foe, the greater the victory. See? We need the hero to slay the dragon.'

'And why are we calling him "Fast" Jack Pink?'

'Fast is good. It means a lot of things. It's frightening, without saying it's frightening. It's subtle.'

'Oh, okay.'

Even as he was writing the poem, LaBat knew he'd have to explain it all to Mother. She was no fool. She had a greater understanding of the true nature of human beings than anyone he'd ever known, but she was bloody useless at storytelling.

'Just keep reading, Mother. Please. You'll see.'

And she did. The rest of the poem was a brawny retelling of the brawl between Jack and Magee. It was a fabrication of half-truths and romantic brutality that made the bushranger sound far more noble than violent. And it included nine more words that rhymed with Pink.

Mother started to enjoy herself. She strutted out a performance like it was an opera for a full house, and the volume of her voice lifted as she twirled towards the pulpit to deliver the final verse.

So when you're asked who is the best,
Twice you won't need to think;
'Cause them that saw him won't forget
The sight of Fast . . . Jack . . . Pink!

Mother threw up her arms at the final mention of her lovely boy's name. Only LaBat applauded, but his two hands were enough to fill the church. When his clapping ended, the front door of the iron building flew open. And standing there was the Reverend's wife. She was drenched from the rain and stunned by the sight inside her church. There was a huge man licking his lingers, two others without shirts, some trollop with bulging breasts giving a sermon, and her husband teetering on a box with a paintbrush. She left as quickly as she came in, and the vicar knew the incident would take a month to explain, and another month before she'd speak to him again. It was lucky there was still plenty of painting to do. He would tell her that at least they weren't Catholics.

'Very good, Samuel,' Mother said to LaBat, as though the interruption didn't happen. 'It's wonderful.'

'Thank you, Mother.'

'I think I like "Fast Jack Pink". Yes, very good. That's just lovely.'

'Yeah, I'm thinking about changing the title to "the Golden Knuckles".'

'Oh well, whatever it is, I think it's grand.'

Yes it is, thought LaBat, with his eyes to the corrugated ceiling. It is grand. He imagined people holding his printed words and reading them to each other around the fires and pubs and tables, and then folding the pages to keep and show their children one day. Then their grandchildren. LaBat felt the genesis of his immortality.

Jack hadn't moved during the recitation. He was still looking at the crucified Saviour on the wall and realised his arms were spread out on the pew in the same fashion. It was a thought that would haunt him in the dark later that night.

When the entertainment settled, it was time for business. Mother and LaBat sat in front of Jack and leaned back to speak.

'Listen boss,' LaBat started. 'Everything is looking good for the Melbourne Cup, but I think we've got a problem.'

'What's the problem?' Mother responded for her son.

'We just need more men. I've been gathering information from everywhere I can, and I don't think we're going to be able to do the job without them.'

'Oh nonsense,' said Mother. 'Once the crowd get a look at Jack . . . Fast Jack . . . and they see Carrigan, they'll scream like drowning children.'

'Yeah, but it's going to be a ruddy big crowd, Mother. They'll be thousands of them.'

'We already knew that. So what's the problem?'

'It's a hell of a lot more than we first thought. Have a look at this.' LaBat held up the newspaper. 'All anyone is talking about is the Cup. There's nothing else. I thought we could handle it on our own, but it's just too much risk.'

'Well, I'm not afraid, and Jack ain't neither,' Mother said and fixed her hair again.

'It's not about being afraid, Mother. It's about getting the money and the gold. Look,' LaBat said, pointing a finger all over the paper. 'The horses. The trainers. The jockeys. The dressmakers. The betting. The Governor. The Governor's wife. The track. The traders. The contractors. There's nothing else in here. It's just . . . it's just . . .'

'The Cup?' Jack said in a whisper through his beard.

'Exactly, boss. The Cup.'

'Reverend!' called out Jack. The word cracked like a whip and startled the priest. He'd been content to remain unnoticed by the gang as they put on a show for themselves.

'Can you help us out here, Reverend?'

'Yes, if I can.'

'Well, Reverend . . . it is "reverend" isn't it, not "father"?'

'No, reverend is fine.'

'That's good. I've never had much use for fathers. Tell me, what do you know about the Melbourne Cup? How many of your mob are going?'

Jack waved his hands over the pews.

'About half, I should say.'

'What's half? And watch your brush there, Reverend, you're dripping paint on ya floor.'

'That would be forty.'

'I see. And how will they be when they get back here – after they've had all that gamblin' and grog and sin? Do ya think you'll be right to save 'em? Ah, you'll fix 'em up again, I bet. You'll make 'em all clean. They'll all be like children and virgins once more. It's a lucky thing they've got you. Imagine the world without a pure little spot like this to come back to. You've done well, Reverend.'

The priest didn't answer. He suddenly felt ill. But not from the vapour of paint or the meat of his last meal. He was ill because he realised he'd let the devil in the door.

'Forty,' LaBat repeated to Jack. 'Forty just from this little church, boss. Add that all up. There'll be thousands at the Cup. Thousands.'

Jack leaned back and crucified himself again and kept a smile on the painting vicar.

'All right, LaBat. Get more men.'

*

Mother lost the argument. But there were no problems with her pride, because she lost to her son.

And so the Pink Gang expanded.

Mother was helpful in picking the recruits. She'd told LaBat that they were in the perfect town for finding desperate people. There were two kinds of traveller coming through Bacchus Marsh – those going from Melbourne to the goldfields, and the ones coming back.

The first kind used Bacchus Marsh as a place to rest, stock supplies and try for a last bit of entertainment before the merciless business of chasing gold began. The gang didn't need these people. They were too optimistic. But those on the return journey were different. Most came back without riches. They had wrecked bodies and stained spirits, and they limped back to Melbourne to beg for work and the forgiveness of their families. Only a few returned wealthy, and they were so surprised to have found gold that they flashed their money around Melbourne with rampant enthusiasm. And it was the sight of that enthusiasm that kept the coaches rolling in both directions.

But it was only the broken ones the gang needed.

The search took almost a month, and the weather was cold and the rain remained wilful. The Pink Gang moved between the shelter of the church and the Border Inn, where they took two rooms upstairs. At night, Mother would nurse Jack to sleep in the soft, trimmed lace bed with a low lamp burning until dawn. Carrigan did as he was told by staying out of trouble. And LaBat almost fell in love twice.

Three times a week, the coach to Melbourne would come in and the gang would be waiting. Some of the travellers were just too broken. They looked like they'd struggle to feed themselves, much less hold a gun or carry a bag of gold. Others were too virtuous, and just as Mother was skilled at picking the lust and greed in people, she could also see the goodness. And it was of no use to her.

The rest of the passengers were bureaucrats and Chinamen. They were even of less use.

But after three fruitless weeks, finally the Thursday-afternoon coach wheels rolled through the deep puddles and delivered the Fox family.

The moment Mother saw them, she knew they were right for the job. The sister and two brothers stepped out and searched around as though they'd been to the town before, yet were still lost. That was the look Mother was waiting for. That was the look of broken people. The look of those who'd once had a good plan but now had nothing. Worse than nothing. They had no bags, just a sack between them, and they crossed the muddy road. Not because there was anything for them on the other side, but because there was nothing else to do.

And Mother was there waiting for the three of them.

Winston and Wellington Fox were short and chubby twins in their late twenties, with meaty hands, bald heads, and cupid faces that made them look like giant babies. And because there were two of them, their strange features were even more striking and comical.

Their sister was Camilla Fox. In contrast, she was slender and taller than most other women, and she had plenty of hair. It was black and fell almost to her backside. It reminded Mother of the coat of Jack's horse.

Despite their uppity names, there was nothing in the Fox family to suggest good breeding or education. In the bar, Mother Pink ordered food and loosened the siblings with strong drink, and discovered what she'd expected: they'd travelled from Melbourne to find gold and found only dirt, and had lost the few possessions they had dragged from the city.

Their early life was brutal. The Fox parents had been servants in a wealthy Hawthorn home, but were both killed in a firebox explosion, when the siblings were little more than babies. So they only had each other.

The boys said little, and although they had basic manners at the table, the world had left them uncultivated and distrustful. Camilla had more to say and there was a brightness in her speech that showed LaBat a wink of intelligence. Just like hair, it was something she had that her brothers didn't.

And Mother also liked the shape of the girl. She was bony, yet strong. Mother had seen that type in fights and they were always dangerous. They were biters and scratchers and gougers, and they were hard to hold back from a brawl. Camilla had the qualities of an excellent street whore.

'Here's to the family Fox,' Mother said, lifting her rum.

LaBat drank while looking them over, and nodded his congratulations to Mother.

The Fox family had everything the gang needed. They were almost broken and without options. They were like empty lamps – all wick and no oil. Mother would be their oil.

They were perfect.

*

While the Pink Gang were celebrating their new incarnation, Mary and Jesus rode into Melbourne on Harry's grey horse.

To Jesus, the place was even bigger now that he was inside it, and every piece of ground was taken up with something. It was either a shop, a house, a church, a factory or a stable, and in between there were roads full of people moving in and out of doors like birds that couldn't settle in just one tree. Some buildings were grand and others were broken and filthy, and there were ones almost as tall as the brick walls he'd been born between. But as different as they were, they were still all part of the one town. Jesus had never known there could be such a place, and he wondered how long people had been living this way.

He and Mary got down from the saddle and walked the streets. Mary held the reins and Jesus held his gun, but still kept it hidden. He'd taken the white blanket from the bush hut and wrapped it around the pistol and kept it to his chest. Mary told him it looked like he was carrying a baby in his arms. But he made sure the end of the ivory handle was always free, in case he needed to grab it.

And just like the gun, Mary and Jesus were hidden too. They were unnoticed. Even with a beautiful horse and a fancy saddle, they barely got a second look from the thousands of faces. There were just too many other horses, wagons, carts and riders. Mary and Jesus could have been locals or strangers, it made no difference to the busy people of Melbourne.

Jesus felt as if he'd been holding in his breath since they entered the city, and when he finally let it out, he choked on the stink that greeted him. It attacked the back of his throat like a biting cattle dog at the hoof of a cow. He'd smelt all kinds of awful things in his fifty years of living – human shit, rotten food and wet hay – but he'd never known anything like this. Not even the body of Andre Noble was this bad. He looked at Mary and he knew she was being attacked by the same cattle dog.

A well-dressed woman moved past them, and her soapy perfume brought a few seconds of relief before the harsh pong returned. Jesus wondered if the smell was permanent or whether they had just arrived on a bad day for the wind. But of the hundreds of faces he could see, no-one else was suffering like Mary and Jesus. So he knew it was nothing special. It was just Melbourne. As it was yesterday. And as it would be tomorrow.

'There's a river down here,' Mary said, pointing ahead through the street. 'We'll go there. What do you reckon?'

Jesus couldn't see it and he wondered how Mary knew, but he followed her and, sure enough, there was a river. The shadows of the buildings ended and there was grass again, leading down to the water. They sat on the bank and let the sun hit them.

'This poor bloody river's got the same stink,' she said, as two empty bottles floated by, bobbing in the current and

JUSTIN SMITH

moving like they were in a slow race. 'This one used to be a real good one.'

'Have you been here before, Mary?' he asked. 'Do you know this river?'

'Nah,' she said.

Her voice was still low and she hadn't smiled yet from her swollen face. People are like rivers, Jesus thought as he let his head fall back. It doesn't take much to change them.

The grey horse started to chomp into the green feed on the bank.

'That sounds good, Harry Horse,' Mary said.

'Who's Harry Horse?'

'This one. The boss never called her a name, so it's Harry Horse. Got to call her something.'

Mary put her head down too and listened to their animal chewing on the city grass. The sound woke her appetite, and a stretching noise came from her empty belly. She wished she could roll over and find a meal coming from the ground.

She thought about food and she thought about chains and, like Jesus, she thought about the people who made the rivers stink. Then she thought about Harry, alone without a dog or a horse. And she hoped he wasn't lost.

*

Harry wasn't lost, but once he was in Ballarat and standing in the office of the Superintendent, he wished he was.

Harry remembered William Pepper from the miners' riots of '54. The man was an inspector then, and was known for being a grim and unforgiving character, with a strange lisp that made him look like a child trying to form its first words.

The Superintendent's office was decorated more than anything Harry had ever seen. Every inch of the room was adorned with a brass trinket, a medal, or framed citation. Pepper sat behind his desk and took a sip of tea, as though he was practising etiquette for a coming engagement with the Queen, while he sneered at the disappointing constable standing at attention before him.

'This is a most unappealing situation, Logan,' Pepper said, looking at the report on his desk.

'Yes, sir.'

'I don't need you to agree with me, Constable.'

'No, sir.'

'It simply won't do. I was not told of any murder case. I know nothing of a body, nor of a subsequent investigation, nor of a search party. I was not informed and the Gazette was not informed. This is not how things operate in my district.'

Before he arrived in Ballarat, Harry had many hours of riding to rehearse his story. His dog and the blacksmith's old horse had heard it at least three dozen times. Harry knew he couldn't lie about everything, so there had to be just enough truth in there for when Sergeant Tom Addington was eventually questioned. But not enough truth to get him and Jesus charged with murder, or get Mary caught again.

Fortunately, before being sent into Pepper's office, Harry had been made to write a report on the events that saw him lose his prisoners and his horse. It helped him get it all straight before it reached the Superintendent.

Pepper looked at Harry's report again and had another sip for Her Majesty.

'So, let us be clear, Constable. You had two prisoners, a boy called Jesus White . . . Whitetree, who was being questioned over the disappearance of a Mull Creek mining executive, and you had a female native already in custody for theft and destruction of property?'

'Yes, sir.'

'Mary?'

'That is correct. No other name. Just Mary.'

'And you were searching for the body of this executive? Andre Noble?'

'Yes.'

'With the assistance of two other executives acting as a search party, yes? But on the afternoon of the fourth, the children escaped while you were briefing the executives on the investigation?'

'Yes, sir.'

'And the executives gave chase after your prisoners?'

'That's correct, Superintendent.'

'But you didn't?'

'No, sir. There was —'

'Don't speak further. I'm attempting to understand this blasted mess. Just answer my questions. You haven't seen any of these people since?'

'No, sir.'

'Not your prisoners and not the other members of the search party?'

'No, sir.'

'And where is your mount? The horse, where is she?'

'As stipulated in my report, sir, my horse —'

'It's not your horse, Constable.' The Superintendent held an erect finger in front of his own face. 'Be clear on that. The animal is the property of the Colony of Victoria. It's the Governor's horse. Her Majesty's horse. And, in their personal absence, it is my horse.'

'Yes, sir.'

'So where is it?'

'Sir, during the disruption of the escape, and the chase that further ensued, my . . . your . . . horse was panicked by the noise and ran off. I can only assume it followed the others.'

'You can only assume?'

'Yes, sir.'

During his many rehearsals, Harry had first planned to say that Mary and Jesus had taken the horse. The story would make more sense if they did, but he also had to allow for the possibility they might get caught one day, and he didn't want horse theft to be added to their list of crimes. Especially not a police animal. To a man like Pepper, stealing a Queen's horse would be worse than murder.

Harry remained convinced that Jesus had nothing to do with the death of Andre Noble, but now that the boy was an escapee, he looked even more guilty. Harry only hoped Jesus and Mary had pointed his grey horse north and ridden hard to the river and out of the colony.

In his report, Harry wrote, 'The aboriginal female had made it known to myself that she had relatives in South Australia, and she had often expressed a desire to visit there one day.' This was bullshit, and Harry hoped he hadn't overcooked the tale. But looking at the face of Superintendent Pepper, he could only see anger and intolerance, rather than suspicion.

'Logan, I am looking at your file here, and I am surprised. I can see no past indication that you were such an ineffectual policeman. Perhaps it is only good luck that has prevented your superior officers from discovering your true incompetence.'

'Yes, sir.'

'But clearly you're not at all satisfactory.' Pepper turned the pages of Harry's file. 'It's a jolly good thing all other constables are not like you, otherwise the Governor's house would currently be occupied by drunken, unlicensed miners and prostitutes. So what am I to do with you?'

Harry knew it wasn't a question for him to answer.

'You are a mounted policeman without a mount. That does me no good. I also see that you were granted permission to marry. Where is your family located?'

'I have no family, sir.'

'No wife?'

'No, sir.'

'She ran off on you too, did she? No luck with horses or women?' Pepper's lip curled into a bitter smile over his own joke.

'No, Superintendent. My wife is . . . deceased.' Harry felt the same bite of pain he always felt when someone mentioned Alice Logan. She was only supposed to be in his heart and dreams – she was not for people like Pepper to speak of. But the Constable had no power to change the conversation.

'Dead?' said Pepper, looking at the file, only saddened that the record had not been updated properly. 'Well, that makes matters easier, I suppose.' He closed the file and folded his hands together on the desk to deliver his orders. 'Constable, I require you to report to the Richmond Police Depot for duty – no later than ten days from this date today.'

'Richmond? Sir?'

'Yes, that is correct.'

'Melbourne?'

'Yes. I have no need for you here. I require mounted men in my district. In the city, they are in great need of men for foot patrol.'

'Foot?'

'Well, you don't have a horse, do you? What other kind of policing were you thinking of doing? Did you think I would give you another horse to lose?'

'No, sir.'

'When you arrive at your new station, I want you to make a further report to my counterpart about the escaped prisoners – including a full description. You are dismissed, Constable.'

'Yes, sir.'

'And don't take a mount. You will travel on the public coach.'

*

The next day, Harry was on the way to Melbourne.

The crude suspension was no match for the mud holes along the well-used track, but after the first six hours his body moved without knowing it, like a sailor who'd found the rhythm of the waves.

The coach was carrying more gold and mail than people, and the driver was a busy and intolerant man who had two rifled companions with him to cover the front and rear.

Three years before, a coach heavy with gold had been bailed up by its own passengers in the middle of a journey. Whether the four men purchased their seats with a clear plan for robbery, or perhaps just got bored between Leigh Creek and Ballan, no-one ever knew, but the gold was gone and so were the men. Since then, the coach company had been careful about who it selected as passengers for journeys heavy with gold. So it was just Constable Harry Logan, a young woman and an ageing Chinaman as the only human cargo.

Harry was not in a rush to get to his destination. With every landmark he passed, and every sign nailed to a tree, he could feel Melbourne coming at him like a spreading virus he was destined to catch. He not only hated the place for what it was, but for what it was going to be. It would be his new home. And probably his last home.

Home? Harry thought about the word. Only once did it ever have meaning. A prisoner didn't call his cell a home and a soldier didn't call a mound of dirt he was using for cover his home. They were just places they had to be. So the city would be a place Harry had to be. It was no home.

And worse, he would be living out his days in Melbourne on foot. He'd known other police who were taken from their mount and made to walk the beats, and the indignity of it was unbearable. They never returned to the saddle, they were never promoted, and their lives ended with busted feet and knees that ached even in their sleep.

And Harry missed his grey horse. The sweet one.

He missed their quiet mornings together, the long rides alone, and the thought that the breath of Alice Logan was travelling with him always. He didn't regret giving her to Mary and Jesus.

He only wished that night had not happened. And he knew that when he began his first patrol in Melbourne, the feeling he had now would only be deeper.

Harry sat in the coach with the dog beside him and its head on his warm lap. It was enjoying the ride. Its journey was a blissful procession of naps and pats and attention. The back legs and belly were still tender from the Brown Coat's kicking, so the boss just rubbed its head and ears. Harry thought about Mary and the injuries she would have, and it made him so sick and guilty that he wanted to cry out, like he had something wedged in his throat and he had to scream to get it loose.

Harry looked at the other two passengers. The woman wasn't a child like Mary, but her eyes were still fresh and bright with immaturity and hope. On her lap, she had a collection of letters, and as they travelled, she'd pick one out and unfold it like it was a delicate, ancient parchment, then she would read it, touching her fingers on her lips and smiling. Then, after her eyes reached the bottom, she'd look out from the carriage with the same blissful expression. And when the effect of the words faded, she would select another.

Harry had no doubt the girl was travelling towards the author of the letters. And the pages were of love. Clean, gleaming, undamaged love.

But she didn't ignore Harry. After each adoring trance, she would return to the company of the coach, remembering where she was, and allow the policeman a smile. It was as though Harry was getting the last scraps of each letter. But it was enough. He would take whatever morsels of love he could get. Even if they belonged to someone else.

The Chinaman didn't ignore Harry either. Whenever their eyes found each other, the man would give his head a quick bow and his permanent grin would widen. It was clear he had no English to use but would have liked a conversation. He had no letters to entertain his spirits, but instead a basket of food that he shared with Harry and the young woman. It tasted good and had a sting of spice that made the dog's tongue flick.

The hands of the oriental were soft. He hadn't been mining. Perhaps he was a cook. In Harry's experience, all the Chinese could cook, and the men were often better than the women.

The Chinese had few friends outside of their own people, and Harry couldn't see that changing soon. They were disliked for bringing opium, crime and cheap labour into the colony. But he also knew Victoria was full of people who came from somewhere else and they all brought bad things with the good.

The dog sighed and put its chin back on the boss's thighs, and Harry's own head fell back for sleep. He snoozed in happiness with the smell of spice in his nose and the feeling of love oozing from the young woman's skin, and he began to dream. He dreamed they were no longer going to Melbourne, but were instead travelling to another place in the world where there were no Brown Coats or Superintendents with decorated offices. But the dream was all too quick. There was a sharp sound – like a whip or a gun – and the coach pulled to a stop with some swearing from the driver. Harry grabbed the dog as they flew forward in the seat.

There was the sharp sound again.

'Stay in here,' Harry said to the others, as he transformed from passenger to policeman.

He got out to see that he'd woken in Bacchus Marsh. The town was frantic and the sound of gun shots was coming down the street.

An old man ran past with a bucket.

'What's happened?' Harry asked.

'Mother Pink, Constable. You've just missed the Mother Pink Gang.'

Harry looked down through the chaos.

'She's put the church on fire.'

*

With his revolver and shotgun, Harry ran into the middle of town. Everything was moving at an unnatural speed, like ants disturbed by heavy boots. Harry knew the town of Bacchus Marsh because he'd been here half-a-dozen times, even once with Alice, and although the place was busy, it functioned without panic. But not today. The old man was right. The iron church was on fire.

There was a frantic woman at a water pump, working the handle like she was pumping water from the hull of a sinking boat, as townspeople arrived with buckets. Harry followed the parade of full receptacles, and watched the empty ones come back the other way for more.

At the church, the flames inside were roaring out from the white framed windows and the front door. Harry knew that even though the church was covered with corrugated metal, everything else would be wood – the floor, the beams, the pews, everything. And it would be good and dry and unable to put up a fight against any decent fire.

'Is anyone in there?' Harry called to a family going by – they all had buckets to suit their age and size. 'Is anyone hurt?'

'Don't know, Constable,' the mother called back.

Harry could see no other uniforms and he thought about giving orders to co-ordinate the battle, but he didn't need to. As frantic as the citizens were, it wasn't the town's first fire.

Yet they weren't going to win this one.

Harry got close enough to feel it touch his cheeks, and he could hear the hungry blaze inside. To him, burning buildings sounded like distant trees falling or someone in a neighbouring house moving their furniture. He'd seen homes, sheds and stores go up before, but he'd never seen a church on fire.

The same old man who'd told him about the fire rushed by with a full bucket.

'I'm a Catholic, Constable, but I'm still here to help,' he said to Harry, as though he'd momentarily considered letting the Protestant building burn.

'What the bloody hell happened here?'

'The Gang, Constable. Mother Pink. They've been here for weeks. They lit up the church, bailed up the store, stole three horses and shot out of town.'

'Is anyone hurt? Any wounds?'

'No, sir. None that I could tell you about. The Sergeant went after them with his men. The Father . . . I mean the Reverend . . . seems a bit spooked.'

Harry looked where the old bloke was pointing. The Reverend and his sobbing wife were holding a large cross. They were clutching it like two koalas in a tree. The Saviour wouldn't have looked so big hanging on a wall of the church, but next to the Reverend it was enormous and three feet taller than both of them.

Harry was already shaken by the sight of a burning church, but seeing the priest and his wife with blackened faces clinging to the cross felt like it was the end of all days, and that the whole world was dry enough to burn.

'I'm a Catholic m'self,' the old man repeated, turning back for more water. 'But I'll still help.'

*

Mother Pink released a howl that sounded like sexual pleasure, and she leaned forward, slapped the reins on her horse's neck and grinned into the wind.

The gang charged through the bush with the police chasing. Jack was leading with Mother, LaBat, Carrigan and the Fox family forming behind in various states of excitement.

But Mother felt no fear. They would not be caught. The police weren't cowards, but they were men who were given orders, followed them, and then wanted to go home and loosen their boots. They didn't want to have fights and they didn't want to fall from their saddles.

Mother had many clients in uniform and she knew the way of things. Being too brave meant injuries, and if a trooper was hurt, he was ordered to report to the police hospital, where he'd lose half his pay for the privilege of their care. And most came out sicker than when they went in. So they rode with care, always watched where they walked in the dark, and tried to stay clear of people who might shoot them.

For Mother, the trick in getting away was to ride hard through dense bush, and hope the blokes chasing her knew as much about the police hospital system as she did.

She howled again. Mother had many reasons for embracing the joy of life. They'd had a delightful afternoon terrorising and robbing the Reverend and his wife, and she'd tested her new army in battle. They were perfect. Especially the new recruits. They were fast, cruel and didn't ask unnecessary questions.

Inside the church, Mother had ordered him to stand in front of his pulpit, as she gave Camilla a revolver.

'Now, dear girl, point it at him. At his chest. Good girl. That's right. Now pull the hammer back. One click, that's it. Now it needs to go back a little further. Until it clicks again. Oh yes, that's it. How does it feel? You're smiling, so it must feel good. Does that feel nice? Do you know what you have there in your fingers? That's his spirit you're holding there. And you can either keep hold of it in your beautiful hands, or you can pull that little trigger right there and release it . . . release it into the heavens. You can do whatever you want. That's the power of the spirit.'

Mother watched Camilla's face. She wasn't stunned or frightened. She was having fun. That's what Mother was hoping to see – some fun. What's the point of anything if it wasn't fun?

Mother put her palm under the butt of the revolver and lifted it until it was aiming just a few inches above the Reverend's head.

'Now, sweetheart.'

The gun blasted into the back wall and the dark powder's smoke went over the Reverend's face like it was a running ghost.

Oh yes, Mother thought. How bloody wonderful. If the girl would point a gun at a priest, she would do anything.

Jack was perfect too. He spoke to the godly couple in a whisper – reciting Bible verses and sermons from the Reverend's own notebook – until the two almost collapsed with fear.

Then Carrigan and LaBat cleaned the place out of money, a small barrel of port, and anything that looked shiny, before Winston and Wellington started a powder fire under the middle pews.

And while the fire took hold, Jack was still reciting – determined to finish his lesson before he let the Reverend and his wife leave. And Mother watched the couple struggle to get the crucifix down from the wall. The vision made her laugh.

'Save the Saviour!' she called out as she ran past the flames.

Mother slapped her horse again as they left the town and the chasing troopers well behind. The newspapers could not ignore them now. There were too many witnesses.

She needed to make the colony afraid of her boy, and this would do it. Once they heard about the burning church, and read LaBat's poem of the bare-knuckle fight, they would be good and scared.

We're ready, Mother thought. We're ready for the Cup.

*

In Melbourne, Mary and Jesus were surrounded by food. It was hanging in markets, carried on wagons, and being sold in every shop. It was everywhere except their hands and bellies. They were starving.

The bad smell of the city should have helped keep their appetite down but it didn't. Their hunger was more determined than the stink.

They didn't beg from the people walking by and they didn't ask for scraps at the back of stores. There were too many others doing that and they were having no luck. And Mary and Jesus were careful not to meet new people.

Mary thought about stealing what they needed, starting with warm bread and a roasted leg of pork she could see in a Bourke Street shop. Why not, she thought, we're already criminals. She could have asked Jesus to pull out his gun and point it at a store-keeper's face while she loaded up her arms. But she knew he wouldn't do it. He'd never use it on an old man working behind a counter. It's why she liked him.

And Mary herself was not a natural thief, although she'd stolen in the past and knew that she might need to again, but stealing from people who had stolen from her was not the same as walking into a shop with a gun. Sometimes it was hard to know the difference, but even with her belly squealing from emptiness, she did.

No wonder Jesus wanted gold, Mary thought. There was no need to steal, and there was no confusion about what was right and what was wrong, you'd just buy what you needed. And when you needed more, you'd buy it again until your stomach was silent and all problems were done and gone.

But with or without gold, they had to remember they were running from something bad. There were three dead Brown Coats, and Jesus and Mary had something to do with each one. So somewhere, someone would be chasing them. And the next chains that went on their legs would never come off.

When she was hungry and there was nothing to do, she thought about Harry Logan. The Constable boss. She remembered the warmth and the food and the dog, and the way Harry's eyes crinkled when she'd tried to confuse him, and how he'd yelped when she pulled out the splinter with her teeth. And she remembered the way he looked at her on that bloody shithouse morning when she was taken by the Brown Coats. No-one had ever said sorry to her. Not for anything. But Harry did. Or at least he'd tried to.

She thought about all the things Harry had that she didn't. He had a uniform, a horse, two guns, a good razor, plenty of food in his sacks, and places to be. But it always felt like he was wearing chains too. Not like hers, and not like Jesus', but different ones.

And Mary wondered what she would have done if she turned around on that cold Melbourne day and found Harry holding the irons, offering to take her back to travel the dirt tracks with him again. She really didn't know. Freedom had to be better. Although starving and dying wasn't.

But thinking about Harry was not going to fix their problem. They had to eat. They had to put something in their bodies or they would die in the smelly town surrounded by food and strangers.

Weeks after they arrived in Melbourne, on one icy morning, Mary, Jesus and Harry Horse looked in the window of their favourite tearoom along Bourke Street. It was their favourite, not because they'd been inside but because the windows were big and they could see everything. Today, like the other days, the room was full. Everything was full. The seats were full of well-fed bottoms and the tables were full of food.

There were giant slices of cake, bulging sandwiches, and smaller treats in the colour of strawberry and lemon and orange that were so shiny with sweetness, it looked as though all the sugar in the world had been squeezed down to fit on the table.

The waiters were in white, and they piled the food onto tiered plates that climbed above the fat diners' heads and poured steaming tea into fine cups.

On some previous mornings, Mary had made Jesus laugh by telling stories about what was going on inside, and she'd performed mocking voices as the lips at the tables ate and talked.

'Oh hello, yes, it is soooo nice to see you. Would you like some tea? Oh, yes please, that would be just soooo bloody lovely. Oh my, it is so very cold today? Oh yes, rather cold, I do so agree. It is soooo cold that I think my bosoms have frozen. My goodness, that is so frightful. Oh yes, I think I shall have two cups of bloody tea today. I shall have one to warm this bosom and then I shall one to warm that bosom.'

It had always been a good show.

But today there were no funny voices and there were no laughs. They were just too hungry. All they could do was watch.

Jesus knew that everything happening at the tables was because of gold. They were dressed from gold. They were smiling from gold. And they were eating gold. He didn't need to wish for everything in the world – he just needed gold, and the rest would come. But although he was surrounded by it, the metal had never seemed further away.

And while Jesus and Mary watched through the window, they were being watched themselves.

Mary first saw the pair of blue eyes in the reflection of the glass. When she turned, they were the eyes of a child, and were so bright that once Mary saw them they couldn't be ignored.

Mary and Jesus had become used to the colours of Melbourne's streets, like the red bricks and the green paint, but very few things that were blue. And certainly not as blue as these eyes.

The eyes belonged to a little girl. She had a round face and short blonde hair like Mary had never seen before. She was alone but not lost, and she wasn't starving like Jesus and Mary, and she had clothes that were simple but warm and well made.

Mary first wondered if the blue eyes were looking at them or staring into the tearoom window, just like they were. But they weren't. They were looking right at Mary and Jesus. And when Mary met the eyes, the child didn't look away. She wasn't shy or afraid. The round cheeks lifted into a smile and then the child waved. Mary waved back but didn't smile. Jesus smiled but didn't wave. Each only had the energy for one gesture.

The child stayed for a few more moments before she gave a last wave and walked away. Mary and Jesus remained at the window until the food was cleared away, then took Harry Horse down to the river, so at least one of them could eat.

The next morning it wasn't as cold but they were still starving and looking through the window at the same people at their regular tables. Mary saw the blue flash again and turned to wave. But now the child wasn't alone. She was with five other children. They were about the same age – seven, eight or nine years old – and some were boys and some were girls. There was a chubby redhead, a tall one with long brown hair, and another with a scarf and a nose reddened by the cold. They all looked at Jesus and Mary and waved.

The next morning they were there again. And there were even more children. Eleven waved and smiled, with the blue-eyed one in front. But this time, they didn't stay on their side of the street. They crossed the cobbled road and walked to Jesus and Mary.

'Hello,' said Blue Eyes. 'May we touch your horse, please?'

Jesus and Mary looked at each other to check it was reality. It didn't feel real. Perhaps they had died of cold and starvation under a bridge the night before, and their bodies were floating in the Yarra but their souls were making a last visit to the tearoom before they went to heaven, and now they were being surrounded by angels to take them away.

But it wasn't a dream and they hadn't died, and they could see that Blue Eyes was very real.

'May we touch your horse, please?' she asked again. 'Would she like this?' Blue Eyes reached into a bag and pulled out a large green apple. 'And would you like an apple too? I have plenty. Here.'

Perhaps they were angels after all.

Jesus and Mary took an apple each and thanked the child. They bit into the fruit like their souls were trapped inside and they could only get them out with their teeth. And it was glorious. The apples crunched in their jaws before sliding through their unused throats and into their desolate bellies. They could feel the sweet juice mixing with their dying blood and it made them live again. It was life. Big, plump, green, juicy life.

Mary knew she should have been more suspicious of the gift. If she wasn't dying, she would have been.

'Would you like another? They are good, aren't they?'

Blue Eyes held an apple on her flat palm under Harry Horse's nose. The big tongue and teeth found it and took half with the first chomp. The child rubbed her small hand between the horse's eyes as the others surrounded the animal. They were gentle and each was stroking a different part. But they didn't touch it like children who'd caught a kitten, they were more like visitors to an art gallery who had come to admire just one piece.

Harry Horse had another apple but it took this one whole and juice squirted out from sides of its mouth, like it had been smashed with a mallet. And Jesus and Mary ate their second with the same speed as the first.

'Please take the rest of my apples,' Blue Eyes said before leaving.

'Thank you,' Mary said simply, as she kept chewing.

'If you're here tomorrow, I'll bring some more. Plenty more. Goodbye.' And the children went and soon dissolved into the crowded street.

Jesus, Mary and the horse went down to the water and ate the apples as if they were royalty at the head table of a feast. The nectar made them feel drunk, so they danced on the bank of the Yarra River.

They were alive and the city belonged to them.

*

The next morning, Mary was mocking the tea drinkers again and Jesus was laughing. They'd finished the last apple an hour after midnight, and they were still half-sloshed on the juice. And still celebrating being alive, or at least not being dead.

But they knew their bellies would become empty again if the blue-eyed girl didn't appear. They'd talked about selling Harry's horse – or just the fancy saddle on her back. Both would bring a good price. But Jesus and Mary were still being chased by the police, and they'd have a better chance getting away by riding, rather than running. And the horse was beautiful.

Jesus and Mary knew she was the most beautiful thing they'd ever own, even if they found gold one day. And although Mary still wanted nothing in her life that could be taken from her, in a smelly city that blocked the sun for most hours of the day it was difficult to part with beauty. Particularly when it could save their lives.

As a tubby woman pushed a giant wedge of cake into her face, Jesus and Mary saw Blue Eyes' reflection again.

'Good morning,' the child said. She greeted them like friends, but she was looking at the horse more than Mary and Jesus. And she was surrounded by even more children than yesterday. There were almost twenty now.

'I'm very sorry, but I forgot to bring the apples today. Silly me. Silly, silly.' She held out her hands to show they were empty.

Jesus and Mary were disappointed. And they were also ashamed. Their lives had become so desperate that they were waiting on a small child to feed them. They were lost again.

'Would you like to come home with us? The apples are there. We have a very big barrel full of them. And we have beef and bread. And we're having soup tonight.' The other children nodded, confirming the menu. Blue Eyes walked to Harry Horse. 'And we have oats,' she said in a playful whisper. 'Bags and bags and bags and bags of oats.'

She looked at Jesus and Mary again. 'Please come home with us.'

*

So Mary and Jesus followed the parade of children. They crossed the bridge and walked south. And while they did, Constable Harry Logan's coach was coming into town.

They only just missed him.

If Mary and Jesus had waited at the corner of Swanston and Flinders streets for just ten minutes longer, Harry would have seen his former prisoners, his horse, Andre Noble's saddle, and a crowd of children surrounding them like they were on a school outing.

And they would have seen him too, with the dog's head sticking out of the carriage watching the street activity.

Harry had had very little luck in the last few weeks, but he was lucky that day. If he'd seen them, he may have been overwhelmed by duty and brought them in. Then they could all stand before a judge and let the Crown decide what they had done right or wrong. Or he may have just asked for his horse back – although he'd already told his superiors it was gone, so trying to come up with a plausible story about its return might bugger up all his other lies. Such was the confusion that was now his life.

But Harry didn't see Mary and Jesus, so he was spared the decision.

He got down from the coach and offered his arm to the young woman coming off the step. Harry hoped the rest of her life would be as joyous as the promising content of the letters, but there was no-one at the stop to greet her. Harry wondered if she'd written them all herself.

Harry hadn't been to the city for eight years and he'd forgotten about the smell. It leapt into his nose like an adulterer jumping through a woman's bedroom window.

He and the dog walked along the narrow streets and were soon lost. Harry thought he knew the way to the Richmond Police Depot, but he discovered that he didn't even know where Richmond was. He asked for help from a street florist. A crude map, and a handful of even cruder flowers, cost him a shilling. Harry knew he'd need to study the city's layout or he'd be broke in a week.

*

At the Depot, Harry presented a letter to the Inspector, as ordered.

Inspector Frederick Rourke was a slim man with an untidy desk, who greeted his new constable with a warm handshake. Harry stood before him with a straight back and his hat under his arm.

'Don't worry about any of that shit, Harry,' the Inspector said, as though he'd known him for years. 'Have a seat. How was your ride down? Bumpy, I expect?'

'It was a little, sir.'

'It'll be a bit smoother travelling once the trains start rolling. But that won't be all champagne and pudding, let me tell ya that. It'll just bring more crooks and long-bearded bastards down here for us to deal with. There'll be carriages of them. It's dangerous bringing the city closer to the bush. I don't need to tell you that. I suppose you missed all that in Bacchus Marsh?'

'No, sir, I was there.'

'You were at the church, Logan?'

'Yes, sir.'

'Burning down a bloody church,' the Inspector shook his head at the thought. 'You wouldn't read about something like that, would you? Mother bloody Pink, hey? You know, she was the first person I ever locked up. I was a young constable and she put up a hell of a fight.' Rourke chuckled at the memory of it. 'I think I've still got the woman's teeth marks on my shins. It wasn't *her* first time, I'll tell you that. And she's still around. And that lad of hers sounds half bloody mad. The colony is going to buggery. Anyway, let's have a look at this letter of yours.'

Rourke opened the orders and leaned back in his chair. As he read down, he glanced up at Harry after every few lines.

'Superintendent Pepper doesn't like you very much, does he? I wouldn't let it trouble you too much – he hates everyone. You should see what he wrote about me once. But he does have lovely penmanship. So at least the words look real pretty while he tells you how shithouse you are.'

The Inspector finished reading and rubbed his face.

'You have had some adventures, Harry. Are you sure it's not going to be too boring down here?'

'No, sir.'

'Are you gonna be all right just cuffing drunks and dodging prostitutes? I know it can be hard for you mounted blokes to come down from the saddle. And the letter says you're going to be living here at the Depot.'

'That's right.'

'But the file says you were given permission to marry.'

'She died,' Harry said, wanting to end the conversation as fast as he could.

'Oh right then. I'm sorry to hear that. The same thing happened to me. Bloody lonely, isn't it?' The Inspector wasn't after an answer or pity. It was just a statement of fact: being a man with a dead wife was bloody lonely.

'You might need to get yourself a new uniform, Harry,' Rourke said, looking him over. 'You look a bit . . . bushy. And the Super here notices everything. He's not as big an arse as Pepper, but he doesn't miss much. I don't want him crawling up my backside, okay? So get some new gear.'

'Yes, sir.'

'And you won't need them guns. Just handcuffs and a baton for the city. And what's his story?' The Inspector pointed at the dog and smiled. 'Hey, where are your bloody papers, mate?'

The dog went to the Inspector for a pat and more attention.

'Sir he's —'

'You know you're not allowed to have an animal at the Depot?'

'Yes, sir, I did know that.'

'Have you got any family at all around here?'

'No?'

'Well, just try and get rid of him when you can. I mean, don't shoot him or anything silly, but just find him a good place. Until then, if someone asks, tell them we're training him to sniff illegal rum or dead bodies or something like that.'

'Yes, sir.'

'There's a good mattress out there for you with the rest of the boys, and give me a yell if you need anything.'

Harry unpacked and found that little had changed at the Depot since his days of training. But there were a lot more police.

That night, when they lowered the lamp flames, Harry lay on his bed with the dog at the end. He was surround by dozens of people, yet the Inspector's words remained true: it was bloody lonely.

*

174

Jesus and Mary followed the children south. The tall buildings were behind them and the rancid waft of Melbourne faded. They walked by a mass of water that didn't move like a river.

'Is that the sea?' Jesus asked. He was still holding his gun to his chest, wrapped like a baby.

'No, that's the lake,' Blue Eyes said, and pointed further south. 'The sea is down there a bit more.'

Half a mile after the lake, they stopped in front of a property that was surrounded by a tall hedge with a solid wooden gate in the middle. Four children ran ahead to open it, so they could all go through.

On the other side, it was a world of horses and children. There were more than a dozen animals and twenty small boys and girls. No-one walking along the road could have imagined the activity going on behind the hedge. There was a large running track with a white painted rail around the outside. There was a long row of stables. And a big house with three chimneys, all with fires burning below.

Mary and Jesus could still see the city that had almost starved them. It wasn't as far away as they would have thought. But the place they were in now was so different it felt as if they'd taken two ships, four coaches, and walked another two hundred miles, but instead, it would be just a short flight for a quick bird.

To Jesus, there was something familiar about all these children. He was like an animal that had no sense of its own appearance yet still knew the members of its species. He didn't know how, but he knew that they didn't have parents either. Just like him. But the children weren't hungry or lost, and even though they were surrounded by a wall, it wasn't made from cold brick, it was green and soft; and it wasn't there to keep them in, it was there to protect them from what was outside.

Just like Blue Eyes, and her gang that had brought them there, all the children were aged from about five to ten. They were dressed in well-stitched clothes, and they all seemed happy and busy.

'May I take your horse?' said a little one, who blinked fast as she talked.

'It's all right,' Blue Eyes said to Mary. 'Let her go. They'll feed her and brush her coat.'

The child took Harry Horse to a stable where she was surrounded by a dozen pairs of small hands. One went under to unhitch the saddle, another stepped onto a box to remove the bridle, a boy went from leg to leg to check the shoes, and another guided the long face into a bag of feed. They moved as though they'd been expecting her.

'Please come inside,' Blue Eyes said and took Mary's hand.

In the house, there were more children, almost as many as there were outside. They were all busy working in the kitchen or cleaning, and others were writing around a small desk surrounded by inkwells and papers.

The house was even bigger than it looked from the outside, and the rooms were filled with sleeping bunks that went all the way to the ceiling. And each bed was made with a blanket of a different colour, so every room was like a giant patchwork.

It was warm inside, but not like the heat of a campfire where the night chill would find the exposed skin only a few feet from the flames. Instead, the warmth was coming out of the walls and even from the children themselves. A little one came from the kitchen with two mugs for Jesus and Mary. The drink was made from chocolate and creamy milk, and it filled them up as though they were drinking the very same warmth from the house.

They'd never been in a building like this. Every other door Jesus and Mary had entered was into a police station or an institution or a homestead where Mary was treated more like a utensil than a person. They were inside, yet they still felt free.

More busy children moved around, and Mary and Jesus began to think they all lived alone without adults. But then a voice came from the other end of the hallway. They couldn't hear what was being said, they just knew it was a man. Jesus pictured a police sergeant with a strap of leather and Mary imagined a Brown Coat. Her heart banged but the faces of Blue Eyes and the other children were unchanged and a little one invited them to sit and rest. Then it was almost dark, and the children from outside came in and filled the house. Although it wasn't crowded. It was almost as if the house grew to accommodate everyone as they all cleaned their hands and got ready to eat.

Bowls of soup were served out from a giant ladle that was almost too big for the small cook to handle, and crusty bread was torn into chunks and handed around. But no-one touched their meal yet, even when the last bowl was on the last lap.

'I'll get him,' the tiniest child of the house said and ran off down the hall – sliding the last few feet on her socks. 'Soup is ready, Captain,' she said into a doorway.

A minute later, the floorboards creaked and the silhouette of a large man appeared. He walked slower than the speeding child but soon he stepped into the light of the room full of children.

'Good evening, Cockies,' he said. It was the same voice Mary and Jesus had heard, and the man nodded to them and smiled.

He wore no uniform and no brown coat, and he had white hair that went down to his shoulders, and a beard of the same colour that grew to the top of his enormous chest. At first, he looked strong, as though he could scoop up all the children at once and lift them above his head, but then Mary saw his hands. They were small for his body, and the fingers seemed stuck together and they curled back into his palms. Yet they weren't like fists, instead they looked broken.

'Good evening, Captain,' the children said. Three helped him into a cushioned chair and three others moved in to help him eat. One held the bowl, another spooned in the soup, and the other dabbed at the beard and moustache with a cloth.

They all called him Captain, and it was the only name the children knew. But he was born as Laurence Flynn. His blood came from Ireland, and although he'd never been there, his voice still transported the lilt of County Cork.

He had received the name Captain from his time at sea, although it came from playful irony rather than respect. He was never the commander of a ship. He was not even an officer; instead, he spent almost two decades as the ship carpenter's mate. And he was a terrible sailor. Those who served with him thought he was more likely to drown than anyone they'd ever met, including people who would never see the ocean. And although they liked his company, his sailing comrades gave him the name Captain as a joke and eventually convinced him to find a new life on the land.

As he got older, his beard and salty wind-burnt face started to suit the joke, so everyone called him Captain. And they all began to believe he was once the master of one of the Empire's mightiest sea vessels. He did nothing to discourage their tales and even began dressing like an old seafarer.

But age hadn't always been kind to him. Perhaps it was all the ocean air of his youth, or the constant sawing of wood, but as his hair went white his hands became useless. Until they were nothing more than passengers hanging from his arms.

The Captain slurped his soup, and as he was fed every spoonful, he showed some form of appreciation to the tykes feeding him.

'Thank you, Cocky. Lovely. Nice. Good. Who did the cooking tonight?' Seven hands went up around room. 'Well done, Cockies,' he said with the last spoonful.

When his bowl was empty, a little girl carrying a yellow flower behind her ear put a chunk of tobacco in a pipe and lit it. She took the first few puffs to get it going, before she rested it in the Captain's mouth. The sweet smoke wandered over his head and all the children moved to face him. They weren't like soldiers waiting for orders, they were more like daughters and sons waiting for a story.

'How did we go this afternoon, Cocky?'

'Good, Captain,' said Blue Eyes, giving her report. 'They're all away and they finished their feed.'

'How's Butternut tonight?'

'He's doin' real good. He might be right for a run tomorrow.'

'That's welcome news, then,' the Captain said, holding the pipe with his teeth. He looked around the room until he found the child he wanted. 'What do you reckon, Cocky?'

A boy with long hair, who was younger than Blue Eyes, said, 'He looks good, Captain, but I wouldn't run him too hard. I'd give him an easy one and then see how he pulls up first.'

'Right then. Good plan.' The Captain's voice was relaxed, almost sleepy. 'So how about we take out Whirlwind, Chasing Prince, Magician and Butternut tomorrow? Everyone all right with that?'

Around the room, on the floor, and high in the bunks, dozens of little heads and bodies nodded and agreed.

'And what about the numbers? How's business?' the Captain asked one of the children who'd been working at the desk. The child stood with an open notebook and gave a report on grain storage, hay, saddlery expenses, food for the pantry, and the bills due at the end of the month.

The Captain listened and smoked until the yellow-flower child removed the pipe.

'Right then, I'll see you before the sun.'

The Captain walked to his room and Blue Eyes followed him down with another child. There was a creak of the floorboards and then the squeak of a bed and the children came out.

Blue Eyes said to Jesus and Mary, 'The Captain was asking if you'd go down and say goodnight to him.'

'Down there? In the room?' Mary asked. She felt the fear again. She'd been in rooms with old men before. But Jesus was holding the gun, still like a baby, and the face of Blue Eyes was as warm as the house.

'I'll come with you. He just wants to say goodnight.'

'Who's Cocky?' Jesus asked. It was something he'd been thinking about for the last hour.

'We all are. We're all Cocky. The Captain's not real good at remembering names. He's good with horse names, but not ours. So we're all Cocky.' Blue Eyes shrugged and smiled. 'Come on, don't be frightened.'

When they got to the Captain's room, he was in bed with a low flame lamp showing just his face.

'Thanks for coming,' he said in a voice that was ready for sleep. 'I'm glad you're here.' He tried to pull the blanket to his beard with a thumb and finger, but the pinch wouldn't take so Blue Eyes did it for him. 'Cocky tells me you have a beautiful horse. Can I have a look at her in the morning?' They nodded. 'Thank you. Goodnight then. Just one thing before you go – you won't be needing that gun, Cocky,' he said to Jesus. 'But if it helps you with your sleep, you keep it.'

And then it was time for their own beds.

Jesus climbed a ladder to the high bunk, where his was made and waiting for him. Though it wasn't the gun of Andre Noble that got him to sleep. It was the well-stuffed mattress cradling him like nothing else ever had, it was the bread and soup inside him, and it was the sound of the children talking freely and softly to each other through their yawns about the end of the day.

Jesus still wanted gold, and he didn't know if he was closer or further away. His last thought of the day was that he was sleeping like a man who already had some.

*

One bunk below, Mary didn't feel the same as Jesus. She had neither gold nor peace, and even though her skin enjoyed the comfort of the mattress and the clean sheets, inside she felt the same as she had every night since the Brown Coats. It was as if they had left something awful in her bones, and there was no way to dig it out. It wasn't like a splinter. And it was always there, but was worse when she tried to sleep and she was without the light or the sound of Jesus talking.

Finally, she slept – she didn't know how long. Then she felt a hand come out of the black to pull at her.

'Shit, who is that?' She waved her arms. 'Don't bloody touch me!'

A small flame filled her bunk with light. It was soft but still bright enough to show Mary where she was, and it lit the face of a small boy standing on the ladder at her bed.

'Good morning,' the boy said. 'It's tomorrow. Come on with me now.'

Mary followed him down and Jesus was already at the bottom with his own escort and dressed in new clothes. There were three children around him, tugging at his shirt, coat and pants to check the size was right. When they were done, they moved to Mary and dressed her.

And they both got new shoes.

Mary and Jesus looked at each other as though an introduction was needed, and not just to one another but to themselves. They'd only known their filthy clothes, and now they were dressed with buttons and soft fabric. And with the same bony frames, they looked like twins. Except for the colour of their skin.

Down the hall, an easy but roaring laugh came from the Captain's room before he appeared.

'Good morning, Cockies,' he said to all the gathered children.

They responded, and were as happy to see him as he was to be alive and awake.

'Thank the good Lord and all his mates for the mornings, hey?' the Captain said, walking outside where it was still dark and there was just the promise of a morning ahead. To Mary and

Jesus he seemed even bigger and stronger than the night before, but his hands were still frozen and useless.

The children started their work. Some held lamps while the others prepared the waiting horses, and the Captain walked into the stables and checked each feed bin. Blue Eyes held a notebook and followed him with a ready pencil.

'The Prince has left a little tucker in there,' the Captain said and the child recorded the information.

He went around to the front of the tall bay horse and stood and looked at the big eyes.

'What's up with ya, Prince boy? Hey? You always lick that bin clean. And I put a little extra corn in that batch. You always like that. Hey?' The Captain looked at the child fastening the saddle. 'He looked all right coming out yesterday, didn't he?'

'Yes, Captain.'

'Have a little stroll for me, Cocky.'

The child took the bridle and walked the horse along the row of single stalls and back.

'Yeah, righto. Thanks, Cocky. He's all right, but give him a little more feed for breakfast and we'll see how he goes. And pull him up if you feel something wrong. You know what you're doing, Cocky. You don't need me to tell ya.'

Chasing Prince and Whirlwind were saddled, and a child went from leg to leg and lifted them to stretch the horses into their gear. Whirlwind was leaner than the Prince and was almost solid black. With their two heads close, they were like opposing knights from a chessboard.

Two children were lifted into the saddles with the help of six others. It was a long way up for the little ones. They were both boys and no more than eight years old. One wore a baggy orange hat that he turned around so the peak was in the back of his neck, and the other was missing more teeth than he had, but it didn't stop him smiling as they walked to the track.

On the way, the horses were made to step over five poles that were lying on the ground, each a couple of feet apart. The Captain watched how they moved through the obstacle, and gave Blue Eyes a nod when they made it through without hesitation or a sideways step.

'Keep 'em going easy,' the Captain said as they went out onto the track and moved into a canter. They were more like partners than opponents.

A little one climbed up the rail until her head was level with the Captain.

'What do ya reckon, Cocky? How does Chasing Prince look to you?'

The child kept her eyes on the track and just nodded her answer.

After another lap the Captain called out, 'Right, Cockies, let them give you a fright.'

The riders lifted their baby backsides higher off the saddles and pushed the horses into a gallop. Hooves thumped the track while their backs flattened into the run. Blue Eyes took a watch from her pocket; it was huge in her small hand and it looked older than the colony. It might have been shining silver once, but now it was almost black from age.

More children came to the rails to watch, including Jesus and Mary.

'Yes, that's lovely,' the Captain said at the sight. 'Would you have a look at that?' He turned to Blue Eyes. 'Cocky needs to trust Whirlwind a bit more. He's too busy trying to teach her how to run. She knows more about runnin' than he does about ridin'.'

She nodded and made a note in her book.

Chasing Prince and Whirlwind finished the track work and the soapy sweat was washed off them. The water turned to steam on their bare backs as they were walked to cool down. The Captain watched them move away with the same care as he did before the run. The Prince looked good but he'd still check her feed bin after breakfast.

Then the Magician and Butternut walked over the poles and onto the track as dawn cracked.

'Cocky,' the Captain said to the one in the orange hat, 'remember to go easy. Real easy? Okay?'

The boy understood and the two went around, warming into a canter. But after a lap, it was clear the horse wasn't ready. The Captain looked at Blue Eyes and could see she knew it too.

'Righto. Bugger. Bring him back in,' the Captain said, wincing as though he felt the pain himself.

Blue Eyes whistled through two fingers and the sharp sound cut the early morning as she waved them to return.

Magician had the track to herself. She was a strong horse of dark chestnut with a white splash down her nose. She went into a gallop and the rider grinned into the wind, showing his lonely few teeth.

'She looks good,' Blue Eyes said to the Captain.

'Yep, if she was a bit smarter she'd win everything. Have a look at her – she's got the muscle, she's got the twitch, she's got a twenty-foot stride, but she's as dumb as a broken axe handle.'

'She might just need some luck,' another little one said.

'Cocky,' the Captain said, smiling, 'the only luck we're gonna have is if she's in a field with ten that are dumber than her. But we'll see.'

The Captain wasn't angry, or even disappointed with Magician. It was just the way it was with people and horses: some had brains and some didn't. If an animal wasn't intelligent enough to know why it was running, there was little he could do to change it. He could feed it, tend to the injuries, run it at dawn, and keep its back warm from the cold, but he couldn't make a horse smarter. And he couldn't make it want to win a race. The animal had to be born with that. And Magician wasn't.

He knew if he could put Whirlwind's head on Magician's body, he would have a beast that could beat anything. But a trainer could drive himself silly trying to think like that.

Jesus and Mary watched with their morning escorts.

'Are these all your horses?' asked Jesus.

'Oh no,' said the child. 'None of them are ours.'

'Who then?'

'Lots of different people. That bay one is Mr Tucker's – he owns a vegetable store. That one there is Mr Shepherd's horse. He's a solicitor. And see that one – Magician – the Governor's cousin owns her.'

'Why are they here? Why are they running around like that?' asked Jesus.

'Racing,' Mary answered for the child. 'They're gonna bloody race them.'

Mary spoke with more confidence than she was really feeling. In truth, she knew little more about horse racing than

GOOD AS GOLD

Jesus, but at least she knew what it was. She'd only seen one race in the past and it was two years ago. She was alone on a hill and could see a crowd gathered near a single big tree in the open ground. They lined up a dozen horses with their riders, before someone lifted a flag then dropped it, and the pack took off. At first it looked like they were trying to run away from the crowd, but then they turned, and kept turning until they came back around to where they started. And the objective was obvious to Mary. To be first.

She remembered being thrilled at the sight of it, and she now felt it again as she watched the children work the horses. It made the curse in her bones ease. It was sport. It wasn't for survival or escape or travel, it was just for the fun of it. And the feeling Mary had was on every other face at the Captain's stables.

'That's right.' The child smiled. 'The Captain is teaching them how to run. Do you like the races?'

'I don't know yet,' Jesus said. He was still unsure of the concept.

When the training was done and all the horses were washed, walked and fed, the Captain approached Jesus and Mary.

'What do ya reckon, Cockies? May I have look at ya girl now?'

Mary just nodded. It had been such a strange morning for her. She'd been woken early, dressed by others, there were shoes around her hardened feet, and she was surrounded by excited and happy people. And the day had only just begun.

Blue Eyes guided them to the last stall where they'd put Harry Horse the night before.

'Oh my,' the Captain said on his first glance of the grey thoroughbred with black stockings. 'Oh my. Can we bring her out?'

The children had already put the bridle on, knowing it's what the Captain would have wanted.

Out in the early sun, the Captain stood silent for a few minutes and looked at the horse from all sides.

'Well, bugger me, Cocky,' he said to Blue Eyes in a soft voice that carried a little shock. 'You weren't lying about this, were ya? She is . . .' The Captain didn't have a word for the horse yet. He touched the coat with the skin of his forearms, running it along her back and over the muscles of her legs.

'Magnificent,' he said, finding the word he needed. He stood on the other side and stared again.

'Where's our Cocky with his magic fingers?' the Captain asked Blue Eyes, and the child knew who she had to fetch. She returned with a smiling boy who went straight to the trainer.

'Morning, Captain.'

'G'day, Cocky. Get down there and give us all the good news.'

The boy had big hands for such a small child, and the digits were long and fine like they were the fingers of an artist. He got on his knees and wrapped his hands around the black leg just above the fetlock.

'How's that, Cocky? How's the cannon bone?'

'My fingers don't touch, Captain. It's a good one, all right.'

'Lovely. And let's have a look at that foot.'

The boy with the magic fingers tapped the leg and the grey lifted her hoof. Just like Mary and Jesus, their horse had been given new shoes too.

'Oh yes,' said the Captain to himself. 'What a foot – lovely and dark.' He put his ear to the horse's ribs and smiled as though someone had begun to play him some music.

'I better introduce myself now,' he said to Mary and Jesus, moving to the head and looking into Harry Horse's face. He locked onto her eyes and moved closer, until the bottom of his white beard was touching her nostrils.

'There's a lot going on up there,' he said to her in a whisper. 'What are you thinking about? Hey? What do you want to tell me? You don't miss much, do ya?' Without looking up, the Captain said to Blue Eyes, 'Look at those ears, Cocky.'

'I see them.'

'She's a smart one. You weren't lying, Cocky.'

The Captain came out of his trance and walked to Mary and Jesus. 'What do you call her, Cockies? What's her name?'

'Harry Horse,' Mary answered, before she realised that she shouldn't say the name of any serving policeman, especially the boss, but it was too late.

'What did you say?'

'Harry Horse,' she said in a mumble.

'Flamin' hell,' he laughed. 'Harry Horse. I think that might be the worst name I've ever heard for a gorgeous creature like this. The poor thing.'

The Captain walked into the stall, looked at the feed bin and nodded at the emptiness. 'You gave her a little extra, did you, Cocky?'

'I did,' said Blue Eyes.

The Captain turned to come back out but stopped at the decorated saddle of Andre Noble hanging on the rail. He was silent as he touched the decorated leather with his elbow, like he was poking a dead animal to see if it was alive.

His face became serious and he looked at Jesus.

'Where did you get this saddle?'

'We just . . . I found it.' It was the second time he'd been asked the question. The first time had led to a beating and almost got him and Mary killed.

'You found it? Where did you find it?'

'It's ours, boss,' Mary said.

'Captain,' Blue Eyes corrected her. 'You can call him Captain.'

'Captain. It's ours, Captain.'

'No it's not,' he said.

The man's welcoming face was gone. But he wasn't angry. He almost looked frightened, as though his new guests had brought a contagious fever with them and soon they would all be infected and buried.

'I know it's not yours,' the Captain said. 'Because I know the man that rode in that saddle. He would never sell it. And Andre Noble was not a man to give things away. I know that, because I know him. And I know that saddle, because I made that for him.'

The Captain lifted his arms to show his limp and useless hands.

'It was a long time ago, but I made that saddle for him.'

Jesus opened his mouth to tell the story, and it was all going to be the truth. But the Captain stopped him.

'Look, just tell me one thing and I'll trust ya for the rest. Is he dead?'

'Yes,' said Jesus. And Mary waited for a new chapter of the curse to begin. But it didn't.

'Good. Thank God,' the Captain said and he smiled again. 'I always thought I'd see that saddle again, I'm just glad Noble's arse isn't sitting in it. Right! breakfast!'

*

Their morning meal was like a wedding feast. They ate at a long table set up beside the house, with the Captain in the middle, Jesus and Mary across from him, and the children sprawled around. There were full plates of meat, eggs, cooked apple and mushrooms, and strong tea poured from metal pots.

Mary watched for a moment before she ate. It was obvious that the meal was a routine, yet it was still special. And it may not have had the linen finery of the city tearooms, but it was far better. Because they weren't just eating to live, or to show that they had the money to spend on fine food, they were eating to celebrate being together.

They talked about the horses they'd worked at dawn, and the discussion was jumbled with stories, half-sung songs, laughter, and the passing of plates. The Captain was a part of all of it. He sucked his tea through a thick piece of straw and the children helped with his food, but they had to wait until his smiling mouth stopped talking before they could put more in.

As the second round of tea came out, the Captain knocked the table with the back of his hand and looked across.

'Right then, why don't we talk some business?' he said. It was an invitation, not an order. 'What's the story with this horse of yours?' he asked Mary. 'Where did you get her?'

'We just . . . got her,' said Mary with a shrug.

'Same place you got that saddle?'

'Nah.'

'Did ya buy her at a sale?'

'No.'

'No, I wouldn't think so. And I wouldn't think you found her out in the bush – no-one lets a beast like that out of their sight. So, come on, where did ya get her?'

'We won her in a bet,' Mary blurted, and she shoved a chunk of pork in her mouth to help disguise the fib.

'A bet?' he laughed hard, just as a child tried to put half a boiled egg to his lips. 'What was the bet, Cocky?'

Mary was feeling good from the morning. Better than she had felt in years. She was warm and fed and she was free. The man they called the Captain wanted a story, so she would give him one.

'Well, there was this old farmer we were working for. We were cuttin' thistles and he bloody says, I reckon you two can't cut all them thistles in one day. And I said we could. And he says, I betcha bloody can't. And I said, how much you wanna bet then? And he says, if you can dig them all out by dark, you can have me horse. And we did and he gave her to us.'

'Thistles?' the Captain said, chewing.

'Oh yeah, but there were millions of the bastards. Little purple heads stickin' up all over the place. We worked our bums off, didn't we?' she said to Jesus, who liked the story so much he almost believed it.

'What did you put up?' asked the Captain.

'What do ya mean?'

'When someone has a bet, they put something up. So, what did you put up for your side of the bet?'

'Nothin',' Mary said, now covering her mouth with a mug of tea.

'Nothin'?'

'Yeah, but I gotta tell ya, that farmer really hated them bloody thistles. I mean real bad.'

'So he gave you that horse for cutting thistles?'

'Oh yeah, it's a crazy bloody thing, I know. And his old missus was real pissed off with him. When we were riding off, she was slapping him on the head with his own hat. It was a sorry sight, boss . . . Captain.'

'It was lucky you already had the saddle then,' the Captain said, smiling. And it was a gentle smile. He didn't believe one word of the story, but he liked the way the girl talked, and her dark face glowed as she did. And he didn't regard her words as lying. He knew what it was like to travel and cover your tracks. Sometimes you needed to have a story to tell people. And the old man had learnt that, just because someone told him a lie, it didn't mean they couldn't be trusted.

The Captain liked the boy too. He was much quieter and a bit slow, and just as Harry Logan had observed, everything was a mystery to Jesus.

'All right then,' the Captain said, showing that the need for explanations was about to end. 'Just answer me this then. Is some frost-hearted, horse-whipping, drunken mongrel, like the bloke that owned that saddle, ever going to come here looking for you and that horse?'

'Nah,' Mary said.

'Good, because now I've got a little deal for ya, if ya wanna hear it. All these horses here belong to someone else and they pay us to train them. Some pay with money and some with food and supplies. I don't expect you to pay, but if you do some jobs around the place – just like the other Cockies – we'll work on your girl and see if she runs half as good as she looks. If she wins any money on the track, we'll go half-and-half. Right up the middle. How about that for a plan?'

Mary had only known life inside the hedge for less than a day, but she already knew it was better than any life she'd had since she was stolen. And for the first time she could remember, she had a choice. A real choice. She could say yes and stay, or say no and leave that morning. It was up to her. And it was up to Jesus. She checked her friend's face, and it was saying yes.

So they both agreed.

'Marvellous. Glorious,' the Captain said, biting into the second half of the heavily salted egg from a Cocky's hand. Then he looked at Jesus. 'Are you a jockey?'

'I don't think so.'

'Do you ride?'

'Mary does.'

'Yeah, well, that's no good. You can get away with being an Aboriginal jockey if ya good enough, but not a female. And you're both.' The Captain shrugged. He didn't make the rules, but he knew how they worked. 'Sorry, Cocky love.'

Mary shrugged back. She knew how they worked too.

'Stand up for me,' the Captain said to Jesus. 'You're a good size. There's not much of ya. We'll get you riding, no problem in the world. If that's what you want.'

The Captain drained his tea through a fresh straw.

'Just one thing – that poor animal has the worst name I've ever heard. We've gotta change it.'

*

The winter of 1861 came just like other winters before it. And though Melbourne didn't let the frost settle on the ground like it did in the bush, it still felt colder to Harry Logan.

He dressed in his new city uniform, checked his reflection, and accepted his new life as a foot constable in the city.

Harry usually worked alone, just him and the dog. His new comrades were unsure of him. There had always been a divide between the Mounted and Foot branches of Victoria Police. They seldom worked together and there was a competitive snobbery that didn't need to be explained to anyone in the job.

It was rare for a policeman to change branches in their career, and no-one at the Depot had ever heard of a bush trooper coming off his horse to walk the Melbourne streets. There were half-stories and full rumours about what had happened to Constable Harry Logan – some were true and some were not – but no-one asked him for confirmation.

Harry was given a patrol between Lonsdale and Victoria streets. He came to know his beat well, and would only get lost once or twice a week. And before long he was regarded as a reliable and fair representative of the constabulary in his part of town. He was a gentleman who was always clean shaven and willing to listen to the troubles of storekeepers and residents. He showed compassion and discretion, yet he was still able to wrestle a thrashing drunk into handcuffs. And he was no-one's fool.

One evening, when there was more fog than clear air, a widow had locked herself out of her own house. She was half-drunk and fully naked, and had the misfortune of living on a road between two popular pubs. She was a big woman and her chalky-white backside was impossible to hide against the dark walls of her building. Even in the bad weather.

Harry covered the crying woman with his new coat and treated her with a dignity that was noted by all who heard the story. It was a great comfort to them, because as funny as the tale was, and as fast as it spread, each person felt they were only a few sherries away from being in the same situation. And if it ever did happen to them, they'd want Constable Harry Logan and his dog to be the ones to find them.

The presence of Harry's pup was still against regulation, but Inspector Frederick Rourke had stopped asking Harry about getting rid of the dog. Instead, he would stroke it like it was his own pet and save pieces of meat from his evening meal. The Inspector was asked about the dog by one of his superiors, and Rourke told him the dog was at the Bacchus Marsh church when the Pink Gang burnt it down and the mutt had got a good sniff of all the gang members. So he explained how its wet nose might be needed in case Mother Pink ever came to the city.

The story was complete bullshit, but it worked. And it worked because in that winter of 1861, the people of Melbourne had become fascinated with Mother Pink and her son Jack, and the mob of villains that followed them.

Harry Logan still had bad dreams about the burning church. But while the image haunted the policeman, it bewitched the readers of the city's newspapers. It was not uncommon for a building to burn, but rarely was it a church, and never was it a church that was deliberately set ablaze. The boldness and the blasphemy of the act made it a deliciously terrifying story.

The more they read about the gang, the more they wanted. The newspapers scrounged for anything they could print about the Pinks. Fresh stories, old yarns, rumours, lies, speculation, locations, acquaintances. Anything. If it was about the gang, it was in the paper.

Samuel LaBat's bare-knuckle poem of the fight between Jack Pink and Donal Magee was published in the paper with a large illustration. The drawing looked nothing like either man, but there were beards and fists and flying teeth and the readers loved it.

One afternoon on his patrol, Harry Logan came across two boys playing. They were having a mock dust-up in front of the markets, and one lad swung at his mate and cried out, 'I'm Fast Jack Pink! The Golden Hand! Come here, ya godless bastard, and I'll snap ya neck with me grip! I'm Jack Pink!'

The boy was not much taller than the street horse trough he was standing beside, but the tales of the bushranger had filled him with a brutal spirit.

And the news of the robbery at Thompson & Son's in Mull Creek had finally escaped the crude censorship of Sergeant Tom Addington and the Brown Coats. It was printed in the city papers, and the women in the tearooms were fanning their faces as they discussed the terrible crime. But they read it to the very last line. Then they would read it again.

And through that winter of 1861, as they relished every new word on the Pink Gang, there was only one other story the readers cared about. The Melbourne Cup.

The colony had known a few race meetings in the past, but nothing had the same fever and anticipation as the Cup. They felt the November event was their reward for all the tough years. Even though the gold had brought wealth, new buildings, better roads, and plans for the rail tracks, the decades had been hard ones for the colony. They had endured long days of digging, sickness and empty larders.

Every person knew someone who had died trying to create the Victoria they had. Some were hit by a tree that was cut the wrong way, some fell from a horse, some died in childbirth, and others worked their bodies into early coffins. But together they had made Melbourne the biggest city on the continent, and the second biggest in the Empire. So why shouldn't they celebrate? Why shouldn't they dress well and drink hard and have a bet, while holding a pretty girl in the sun?

Why not? They had earned it. So the people of Melbourne spent that winter talking of bushrangers and thoroughbreds.

*

It wasn't only city people who were enjoying the newspapers. Mother Pink was relishing every word. It was as though the news was being printed just for her. Everything was about her two favourite subjects: her wonderful and famous son, and the event that would fill their saddlebags with gold.

The papers were still calling them the 'Mother Pink Gang'. It was bloody frustrating but at least her son's name was now appearing more and more with each edition. They were describing his quick hands, his cool disposition, and his well-mannered tongue. And after the Melbourne Cup, Mother thought, everyone would know who the real leader was. The Jack Pink Gang would be born, and if her old body couldn't make it through the next winter, she would have done her job on this earth.

But she didn't want to die. Not yet. She was having far too much fun for it to end. Just like the other citizens of the colony,

Mother felt she was now deserving of her rewards. And the old prostitute couldn't wait for spring to come.

After the church fire and the excitement in Bacchus Marsh, they had let the troopers chase them north for a day, but then they doubled back until they finally reached the sea.

It was LaBat's idea to head for the coast. It had been a hard few days' ride, but no-one would ever think to look for bush-rangers down with the sand and white birds and blue water. And the writer also thought the irony of a beach setting would help him with his next poem about Jack.

At first, the crashing waves sounded like thunder in their bush ears. Mother was the only one who'd ever seen the coast before. It was colder than she remembered, and the constant wind untidied her hair. But she was too content to be fussed with her appearance. The gang she'd made for her son was perfect. LaBat's pen was working well. Carrigan remained controllable, yet frightening, although she had to increase his opium dosage so he would crave less for sugar. And the twins, Winston and Wellington, were following orders with an unquestioning brutality.

But their sister, Camilla, was Mother's greatest discovery. The young woman was greedy for adventure. She had a solid stomach for dangerous situations, and she was blessed with an intelligence that God had failed to give her siblings.

One night at their camp in the dunes, Mother was putting Jack to sleep and she asked the girl to come closer. Camilla hadn't shied away from the sight of a full grown and bearded man nursing at the breast of his mother, nor had she stared like they were freaks in a show.

'Come and sit with us, Camilla darling,' Mother said in her low, campfire voice. 'You are another gift to me. Did you know that? Just like Jack was a gift.'

'Thank you, Mother.'

'There are so many wonderful things coming for us,' Mother said, looking at the sky, as though a prophecy was written in the millions of tiny lights. 'Can you feel it? Can you feel all the wonderful things coming? Can you feel the blessing?'

'Yes, I can feel it.'

'Does it frighten you?'

'No, I'm not frightened.'

'No, I can see. We don't get frightened, do we? People like me and you?' Mother looked down at her son's face. 'Jack's hair has fallen in his eyes. Would you fix it for him?'

Camilla put her thin finger under a wave of the bushranger's hair and guided it back.

'That's a good girl,' Mother said. 'Does he feel hot to you? Is he a little too warm?'

'No, Mother. I don't think so.'

'Check again, please.'

Camilla put her hand on Jack's forehead, then moved the back of her hand along his cheek. 'He feels just right.'

'You have a wonderful touch, darling girl. You've done it just like a mother would have done it. You will be a mother one day.'

'I hope so.'

'Oh, you will be.'

'I hope it will be a boy.'

'It will be.'

'I wonder if it will be like Jack. Do you think so, Mother?'

'Yes, good girl, I know it. He will be exactly like Jack.'

Mother moved Camilla's hand so they could both touch Jack.

'The time will come when I need you to be the mother. Just like this. Just like I am tonight. It's the only way the story can go on.'

'My story?'

'No.'

'Jack's story?'

'Yes, darling, Jack's story. You do want the story to go on, don't you?'

'Yes, Mother.'

The girl now understood. And as they were lullabied by the sound of waves kissing the sand behind them, Mother was almost content. The gang was complete and their plans were perfect.

There was just one thing that had bothered her. In the newspapers, among all the words about the gang and the Cup, there was another name that appeared. It was the name of another wanted criminal. His crimes were not detailed in print, only that there was a reward for 'information that will lead to capture and conviction'. And the reward was higher than her son's.

Who was this person, Mother asked herself with swelling frustration. Who was more valuable than Jack Pink?

Who was this Jesus Whitetree?

*

Jesus had no idea his name was in the newspaper, and he certainly didn't know there was a reward of £100 on his head.

The Crown had never offered a bounty so high, but in truth, it was the Brown Coats of the Mull Creek Mining Company who'd put up the money. And they would put up more if needed. The Company had one executive dead and another two missing, and this boy was responsible for all of it.

But Jesus was safe with the Captain and the children, because the old trainer only read the newspapers for the racing items. He'd lived a long life and felt like he'd heard all the bad news he ever needed. He was done with reading about murders, fires, robberies, accidents, and women having their clothes torn by lusting men. There was nothing he could do about it, so he didn't need to know. He had the horses and the children, and that was enough for the last years of his life.

Also, the Cockies wouldn't be seeing Jesus in the papers. Though they'd all been taught to read and write at the Captain's stables, they simply had no time for the news. And even if they did, the description of the fugitive Jesus was simply 'a man of thin build'. Jesus didn't look like a wanted man and his name was never used at the stables. Mary only ever called him 'mate', and to the Captain, Jesus and Mary became Cocky and Cocky, like all the others.

It had been a good winter at the stables, and within a fortnight of arriving, Mary and Jesus had become just another part of the business. They woke in the dark and the dawns came in with the sound of thumping hooves. Mary liked working hard and the thrill of helping to make their horses run faster stayed with her. She couldn't wait to watch a race and see one of their own animals in the middle of it.

Mary never felt as if she was working for someone else, because everything they did was for each other. The colder and longer the day, the more she liked knowing there was a warm house, food and company waiting for her. And the long days helped to hold back the awful Brown Coat feelings that would come to her at night in her bunk.

The Captain began the training of Harry Horse. They started by getting her used to the smaller saddle and the feeling of a different rider on her back, and then the old trainer let her move around the track with the orange-hatted Cocky at the reins. They went easy for the first lap to make sure there were no hidden wounds, then faster, and faster again, until she was guided into a gallop.

The Captain observed her with the same expression he had when she'd first arrived. She was so beautiful. There was just no other way he could describe her. And the beauty of her, standing still, was multiplied when she began moving around the track.

But Harry Horse wasn't very fast. On the clock, there were much quicker in the Captain's stable, but she ran with little effort and when she finished her track work, her big eyes told the Captain she had much more in her. She just wasn't ready to show him yet.

The grey horse reminded him of a pretty girl who'd give a man only one slow kiss and then say good night, leaving him a promise of a love that was so great it would destroy him if it was taken away. The Captain had known girls like that, when his hair was darker and his hands worked properly. And he'd seen horses like Harry Horse before. They had more to give but they were keeping it a secret.

The Captain didn't know what she had for him. He only knew she was beautiful, and she would need a name more fitting. He didn't have it yet, so through that winter, he started calling her Harry Grey.

And while he worked the horse, the Captain tried to make Jesus into a jockey. This was not so beautiful. It was both a frightening and amusing sight. Watching Jesus in a saddle was like watching a rag doll strapped to a running cat.

But the Captain was determined to make the boy a jockey. He was the perfect size. He was skinny and short, and although he ate like a six-foot woodcutter, the food never turned into fat under his skin. And the stable needed a jockey. The other Cockies were good riders – better than most professionals – but they were too young. Although there were no rules to stop him, the Captain shuddered at the thought of his small children in a field of adults. So he had always paid outside jockeys to ride at all the meetings.

But now he had Jesus. And the boy was old enough. So with a mix of optimism and arrogance, the Captain spent an hour each day teaching his new Cocky how to ride. And he hoped that come the spring, he would be ready.

*

Then it was spring. But Jesus wasn't ready.

The Captain had always believed there was a rhythm inside all animals, even the humans, and he saw it as his job to match the rhythm of the rider with the horse, so they could work together as one. Yet as he watched Jesus bob around the track during the winter, the Captain wondered if he'd found the only animal on the planet with no rhythm at all.

But Jesus was enjoying himself. He liked being high on the horses' backs and he loved the feeling of the wind. He wasn't moving in a straight line, like he usually preferred, but he was still moving. And he was moving fast. The Cockies would lift him up and he'd hold the leather straps – just like the Captain told him – then he'd close his eyes and imagine Mary was up there with him.

And it was those closed eyes that worried the Captain more than anything. He'd tried to explain to Jesus that good jockeys would read the field so they could find the openings, and this was only possible with the full use of their sight.

Mary was more direct.

'Open your eyes up, you silly bastard,' she said. 'What are ya doin'? What's wrong with ya? You might be heading for a bloody tree or something.'

'There aren't any trees,' Jesus said. 'The track just goes round and round.' He wasn't trying to be clever, and she was now used to his innocence.

'Yeah, I know that, but if you're ever in a bloody race, you'll need to be watchin' out.'

'Why?'

'Just try it, will ya? Start with one bloody eye and see what happens.'

And Jesus did try it. But it didn't work. The next ride, both eyes were still shut.

The Captain persisted with the lessons, and not just because the stable needed its own jockey, but because this Cocky never fell off. The Captain had never seen a new rider who could hang on so well. Though the boy had no rhythm, no technique, and ran the track in darkness, he could stay in the saddle as well as anyone the Captain had ever seen.

The old trainer had started him on the slowest horse they had. Then a quicker one. Then quicker again, until he had Jesus at a full hard gallop. He always stayed on. And if he could stay on, then he could be taught.

The first meeting of that spring was at the Caulfield race-course. It was only a few miles from the stables, and the Captain, all the Cockies, Jesus and Mary, and two horses set out in the early morning to be there before the first race.

They decided to run Whirlwind in the second event and Harry Grey in the last.

They knew Whirlwind would be the favourite in her field, but that Harry Grey would have no chance. She'd never raced before and would be too nervous at the jump to make a proper start, then she'd either stay well back or she'd get into the pack like they were wild brumbies across the scrub, but she wouldn't get to the lead. That didn't bother the Captain, he just wanted to watch the beauty run. And he wanted to show her off – although he knew her beauty would be lost on the crowd.

The Captain didn't like the people who went to the races. He hated the drinkers and the punters because they had no interest in the animals or the sport. They could guzzle stout and play two-up anywhere, but they came to the track pretending to know something about horses.

He didn't like the women who dressed up. He didn't like the trainers who mistreated their animals. And he hated the jockeys. Most weren't good riders, they were just lucky enough to be born the right size.

But he needed a jockey, so for the Caulfield meeting he hired Rupert Smite. Smite had been magnificent once, and rode for some of the colony's biggest stables. Now he was more a drinker than a rider. And he was a sleazy little bugger who'd become addicted to sex with very tall women, and these women were expensive to keep entertained.

Jockeys weren't like horses. The Captain couldn't check the clearness of their eyes or the direction of their ears to know if they were ready to race. He just had to trust them. Luckily, he'd known riders who were barely able to stand from the previous night's grog, yet could still find the gaps and take the win.

The Captain only hoped Smite still had a couple of good rides left in him. So Blue Eyes paid the jockey, made him sign a receipt, and the deal was set for him to run the two races.

The Caulfield track was more bush than racecourse. It was a mix of scrubland and sand hills, and lacked the manicured prettiness of a toffs' track. But it would do. And it was a popular race.

The first event was about to start, and the Captain, Jesus, Mary and Blue Eyes went to the course's edge to watch. Far away, around the other side, a steward on a black horse dropped his red flag and they were off.

For Jesus, it was an incredible sight. He'd never seen so many horses running together, and all the colours of the jockeys were like a dancing rainbow as they got closer and charged past.

'What's this?' Jesus asked, lifting his voice over the thunder.

'What's what?' said Blue Eyes, taking out her black watch.

'Is this the race?'

'Yeah,' said Mary, snorting a small laugh. 'What did you bloody think it was?'

'I dunno. I didn't think they all did it at the same time.'

Although he'd heard the children and the Captain talk about racing and jockeys and meetings and courses, Jesus still hadn't been able to put it all together in his head. He'd imagined that one horse would run, then another would have a go, and then another, and they'd just keep going like that until it got dark.

But he was wrong. And he was glad he was wrong. This was far more exciting. The ground vibrated through his boots and the horses went like mad, and at the end the crowd cheered and some punched the air with triumph and others kicked the dirt with disappointment.

So this is racing, Jesus thought. It's no wonder they want me to keep my eyes open.

'Right,' said the Captain. 'That's that done. Now it's our turn. Yes!' He was excited and did a jig as he turned around. 'What do ya reckon, Cocky?' he said to Blue Eyes. 'The track's a bit faster than it looks.'

'Yep, I'd say so. Do you want to strap her legs?'

'Good idea.' And he jigged again and smiled at Mary and she felt it too. 'What a day! I love it!'

The children saddled Whirlwind, stretched her and kept her warm. Then the Captain stood at the head, letting his white beard touch her nose. He said nothing for a minute before he whispered 'So here we are, girl. Will you show them now? Come on. Do a good one.'

Rupert Smite was waiting outside the stall, dressed in his dark purple silk.

'Right, now listen up,' the Captain started at the jockey. If he could have, he would have been pointing a finger.

'I don't need a lesson, old fella,' Smite interrupted. His mouth was always bigger after he had the pay in his pocket. 'Just get me up and let's get goin'.'

But the lesson was coming, anyway. 'She'll want to start hard,' the Captain said. 'But keep her in the bridle. Don't let her get away. If you keep her back, she'll have plenty of lungs for you at the end. Understand?'

'Aye, Captain,' the jockey said, touching his cap with no respect. He got up into the saddle and grabbed the reins with the whip in the right hand. 'Am I doing it right so far? Do I hold onto these things here?'

'You just ride like I told you, smart arse.'

But he didn't.

Whirlwind and eight other horses walked to the start and the steward gave them a moment to get settled. The starts were never perfect, but if a rider couldn't get himself to the line when the flag dropped, that was his problem.

'How are they looking?' the Captain asked, squinting at the distance. His eyes were only strong enough to see half the race these days. The rest was blurred like a wet painting.

'They're good,' said Blue Eyes, watching the trembling mass of man and animal at the starting posts. 'She's found a good spot in the middle.'

All the children came out and lined up along the track to see their horse.

'They're off, Captain,' said one.

They stretched their necks to catch the jump, and the sound of it reached them a second later from across the track.

'How did she get away?'

'Good, Captain. Strong.'

'That's it. That's right. Just do what ya bloody told, Smite,' the Captain said to himself. 'She'll get ya home. Just do it like I said, you arrogant little . . .'

'He's in front,' said Blue Eyes.

'Damn it!'

'Yep, he's way out.'

'Already? Bugger my arse!'

The field came around and the blur became colours and then horses. The Captain saw Whirlwind in the lead by three lengths. He yelled to his jockey, but it didn't come out as full sentences. It was just a blast of swear words.

'Keep her back!' Blue Eyes called out as they went by. And the other children chimed in with similar thoughts.

'He's got the whip on her already, Captain!' said the tiny Cocky with the yellow flower behind her ear.

'Bloody hell, Smite! You useless imp!' the Captain yelled as the field went back around.

Mary was loving it. The sound and the sight of the animals coming by was magnificent, and she could feel the same passion flooding out of her new friends. It was infecting her in the way she'd hoped. It was soaking into her bones.

'What's going on?' the Captain asked, turning to Mary.

'Ummm, she's going backwards,' Mary answered, unsure of how to describe it. 'She's not in front anymore.'

'Of course she's bloody not!' he hollered out to the track.

The race ended with Whirlwind coming in second last. And even though Smite had ruined all hope of winning, he still whipped her right past the finish.

When horse and rider got back to the stall, the Captain was waiting. The children offered no help to get Smite down. They just let him jump and took their poor animal away.

'You bloody useless little bag of possum shit.' The Captain started easy. 'I told you what to do and I knew you didn't listen.'

'Back away from me, old bloke.'

'What did I tell ya?'

'It's not my flamin' fault, is it? If you can't train 'em to run more than ten feet, then that's your problem not mine.'

'Oh they can run all right, Smite. That is, until some pissed midget with a whip gets on their back and flogs them.'

The Captain had never been one for violence. There were times as a younger man when he had to fight, but he never started the brawls. His size scared off most opponents. But now that he only had his mouth as a weapon, he wanted nothing more than to seize the jockey by the throat, pull his pants off and lash him with his own whip until his arse was glowing red.

'Just piss off away from me, Smite.'

'Yeah, piss off,' said Blue Eyes, backing up her friend.

'And your skills will not be required for the next race.'

'Don't think ya getting the money back.'

'Well enjoy it, 'cause it's the last you'll ever get from us.'

Mary just watched. She was already having a great day, but seeing the Captain rip hell into the little bloke with the big gob made it even better.

And Jesus watched and realised there was a lot more to this racing business than he'd thought.

*

It was getting late in the day at Caulfield and all the other races were run. There was only one left.

The Captain gathered the Cockies together and said, 'What do you reckon? What will we do with Harry Grey for the last race? We can just scratch her.' And a few heads nodded. 'Or we can put her in.' More heads nodded.

'Let's give her a run,' said the Cocky with the magic fingers.

'Yep,' said Blue Eyes.

The Captain turned to Mary and Jesus. 'What about the two of you? She's your horse. What do you want to do? If you don't want to run her, she won't.'

The old trainer didn't push. He just waited for the answer.

Mary and Jesus were unaccustomed to being asked questions and given choices. It was a strange feeling. If they wanted, they could all just go home, or they could saddle Harry's horse and watch her run. The decision was theirs.

Jesus was silent. He was unsure of this new life, where his opinion mattered. Mary was less timid.

'Yeah, bugger it,' she said. 'Let's get her out there for a bloody run.'

'Yes!' said the Captain, turning to Jesus. 'You ready for a ride, Cocky?'

'What? Me?'

'There's no-one else, is there? Listen, don't worry. You're not gonna win. So don't think about it. We just want to see how she goes in a field.'

'Me?'

'You'll be right. Just stay on her back. You know how to do that.'

Jesus looked at Mary. Since the moment her eyes had peered out from behind the cell door in Mull Creek, and he was chained to her, he'd come to depend on Mary's wisdom. He wondered how he'd lived for the last fifty years without it. He would let her decide. And she did, with one of her winks. He loved the way she did that.

'Come on, mate. Get up there,' she said to him. 'Try it with ya eyes open, but.'

'Bloody marvellous,' said the Captain and nodded to a Cocky, who pulled out an emerald green silk for Jesus to wear. 'Stick this on.'

The other children ran back to the stables to get Harry Grey ready.

'Just one more thing,' the Captain said. 'I haven't given the officials a name yet. They know we've got a runner for the last race, but that's all they know. So, let's come up with something better than Harry or Harry Horse or Harry Grey. What do you reckon? I've got one for ya. How's this: we call her Thistle Queen.' The old trainer was met with blank faces from Mary and Jesus. 'It's in honour of you winning her in that bet with the farmer. Remember? Sound okay?'

The Captain still thought the story was a load of crap – that's why he liked it so much.

Mary and Jesus agreed to the name. The race was about to start and they trusted the Captain.

'Right then, Cocky,' he said to Blue Eyes. 'You go tell the stewards.'

They all got to their jobs and Jesus was lifted onto Harry Grey, and soon he was at the starting line wearing his silks with a cap and a whip.

'You right there, boy?' a steward asked him, and Jesus gave him a nervous nod.

'Good then,' the steward said, pointing down the track. 'You better turn your girl around. We're running the other way.'

And so, on the 7th of September 1861, the last race at Caulfield began. The red flag dropped, the horses jumped, Thistle Queen took off, and Jesus closed his eyes.

And when he finally opened them again, they'd won.

*

Few people were there the day Thistle Queen had her first win. But it was a hell of race and they wouldn't forget it.

It was almost sundown, and even the hardest gamblers had lost enthusiasm for the day. Most spectators were drunk and had left for the closest public house to pour more rum on their Saturday, and others were asleep on the grass.

The odds on Thistle Queen were long. Although the Captain had a strong reputation in the racing world, it had been a few years since he'd had a big winner. And the punters knew that if he'd had any faith in the smoke-coloured grey, he'd have put her in a better race. So there were only three people who picked the winner that day. One was a young woman who'd told her husband to put two shillings on the nose, because emerald green was her favourite colour. He'd scoffed and teased her – although he himself failed to pick a single place-getter all day. Another was a butcher, who'd come with a plan to bet on the horse with the highest odds in each event, hoping the few pay-offs would cancel out the losses, but until the last race he'd won nothing.

The third winner was the Captain himself. Though he had no real passion for betting, as a man of Irish blood he was inherently superstitious, so he always put a little money on his horses, no matter what the rest of the field looked like.

For Jesus, the race was a thrill. From the darkness of his own eyelids, he heard the pounding of the ground in front of him and he knew he was going faster than he ever had before. He tried to think of all the Captain's lessons, but none would come. Nothing was clear. Only the excitement of it all.

If he thought of anything, he thought about Mary, imagining he was holding onto her as they charged ahead together. Then the thumping got closer and soon it was bursting in his ears, and he could hear the snorting of the other animals and could smell their hair and sweat. He could also hear the jockeys swearing and making frustrated grunts, including Rupert Smite, who had snagged a ride when another jockey broke his leg falling in the fourth event. And Jesus could hear their whips swiping at the flesh of the animals.

Then the noises were behind him and he felt Harry Horse push forward and then slow and stop.

'You can open them now, ya mad bastard.' It was Mary. And when he did, he and Harry Horse were surrounded by the children. They were cheering and hugging each other.

The Captain was louder than any of them. He had loved every stride of the race. The grey horse was even more beautiful when she was surrounded by lesser creatures. She was magnificent. And she wanted to win. That was the secret she'd been keeping from him all winter. When she was in a pack, she wanted to be first. On a bare track alone, there was nothing to run for. She needed a reason. She needed a race.

That night, they all went to a pub. They had a back room to themselves and they ate huge pies made with beef and barley, and a cake that was as good as anything seen through the window of the Bourke Street tearoom. And the Captain permitted himself a whiskey while they all sang and told each other the story of the race over and over.

Jesus' and Mary's heads were dizzy, like they'd drained the Captain's glass and then had eight more. Jesus was still unsure about what had happened, but Mary explained each moment that her friend had missed while his eyes were closed.

'I've got something for you two,' the old man said and he motioned to Blue Eyes who put a small bag on the table. It was the size of a child's fist, and it made the sound only a purse full of money could make.

'That's your half of the prize money,' said Blue Eyes. 'And your share of the Captain's winnings.'

Jesus and Mary stared but they didn't dare touch. They looked at it as though someone had just put a snake on the table. They didn't know what to do. They'd never had money before. They'd never had anything until they had each other.

'Is that . . .' Jesus could barely say the word that was never far from his mind. 'Is that . . . gold?'

'Gold?' said the Captain, laughing and feeling the full warmth of his drink. 'Gold? What do ya think I bloody am? Nah, that's just notes and coins. But lots of them. Money. What do you reckon, hey? Not bad for ya first race.'

Now Jesus and Mary could do whatever they wanted. They could ride Harry Horse back into town and rent any room they pleased, up high so it was above the stink. And they could spend a whole day at a fancy table behind the glass. Just like they'd dreamed of.

But they didn't want to go anywhere. They were just where they wanted to be.

*

After Harry Horse became Thistle Queen, she soon became one of the most popular horses of the Melbourne spring of 1861.

She ran the tracks of the city and the bush, and the same beauty that had entranced the Captain began to capture others. She was fast and exciting and often easy to find among the darker horses.

After Caulfield, she won at Emerald Hill. The course was a little flasher but not much, and it was a bigger event with a stronger field. But the result was the same. Thistle Queen jumped with a perfect start, sat at the back, then charged through the middle, and won by five lengths.

And there were more people there to see it happen.

Those who put money on the high odds were well rewarded, and they went back to town with their winnings and bragged about the new lightning grey with the black stockings, as though they had ridden her themselves.

Then she ran at Heidelberg. But the word was getting out about Thistle Queen and the odds dropped. The bookies wouldn't make the same mistake again. They knew unless the grey was in a field of proven champions, or she was handicapped with an anchor, she was likely to win.

And she did. But only by two lengths this time.

Then she won at Box Hill and Williamstown before she was put into her first handicap at Dandenong. Although Thistle Queen carried more weight than the rest, she was still the favourite. She gave a hard ride but came second to a chestnut colt that had little more than a skinny jockey and a saddle on her back.

But no-one remembered the name of the winner. They only remembered Thistle Queen. And by the middle of October, she was a celebrity of the courses. Even the drunks, hard gamblers and overdressed women that the Captain despised would stop to watch her go by.

The only one who wasn't watching was Thistle Queen's own jockey.

Jesus still couldn't open his eyes. But he still loved the rides. He loved the sounds and the speed and the power of Harry Horse under him. And after every race they would feast at a pub and the Captain would give over another purse of coins.

Life had become full of celebration, food, cool mornings, warm evenings, money and friends.

And one morning after training, they walked the horses down to the beach. Jesus had tried to imagine what the sea would be like, but the reality resembled nothing he could have conjured. He'd thought it would be a fast-flowing blue river, and he'd be able to see the rest of the world sitting on the other side. But instead it was more grey than blue and the current was coming towards him and then going away. Mary said they were called 'waves'. And there was no land beyond, just more sea. Either the rest of the world didn't really exist or it was just too far away.

The Captain walked the horses into the water until their

bellies touched. He said the cold was good for toughening the muscles after a hard run.

And Mary played with the children on the beach. They loved her and the day was sunny. No-one was more excited by a win at the track than Mary, and her pleasure infected the whole stable. And some of the children had taken up swearing, just to be more like her.

Jesus watched his friend dig in the sand, with a dozen little hands helping. He wondered what life would have been like if all the dirt that he'd ever walked on was as soft as sand. How much gold would he have now? But he knew that if the world was sand, he wouldn't be here with the Captain, the children and Mary. And he would never have ridden fast on a winning horse.

For Mary, her life continued to get better with each day, and she filled every hour with work, food or laughing with the children. She hated the quiet moments because that's when the Brown Coats came. Even in death, they knew how to find her, and she wondered if she could ever outrun them. In her bunk at night, while she waited for morning, she felt them grabbing her and punching her face from out of the dark. And if she wasn't dreaming of the Brown Coats, it was the police. But it wasn't Harry Logan chasing her, it was the face of Sergeant Tom Addington from Mull Creek. The fat cruel man would be riding towards her and Jesus with a rope in one hand and his leather strap in the other.

Every night, she felt like they were all coming for her, like a giant falling tree that couldn't be stopped. It wasn't until a young Cocky struck a match before dawn and filled the room with candlelight that the feeling dissolved.

Mary knew her friend in the bunk above had the same feelings, because each night, while she waited for sleep to come, she'd hear Jesus clicking and checking his revolver.

And there were five shots left in the gun of Andre Noble.

*

By the time Thistle Queen ran at Dandenong, the field for the Melbourne Cup had been accepted and their handicaps were announced.

Through the winter, a starting list of fifty-seven horses was cut down to twenty-one, with thoroughbreds like Archer from Sydney and a local horse called Mormon as the early favourites.

When the race was only two weeks away, Mr Edward Donovan from the committee of the Victoria Turf Club put on his top hat and waved his cane at a passing coach on Collins Street. Half an hour later he pulled up at the long hedge in front of the Captain's stables.

The Captain disliked the kind of people who sat on racing committees. They were a fussy and pretentious collection of toffs, who were more concerned with their position than what happened on the course. And in recent years, the Victoria Turf Club had been at war with the Victoria Jockey Club over the control of the sport.

The Captain had no patience for these kinds of conflicts. He'd been around the world twice and had seen people kill each other over things like religion – even when they believed in the same god – and sport was no different. Despite the two clubs existing for the racing of horses, they still found plenty to fight about.

But Eddie Donovan was not the worst of them. His father was a sheep farmer who'd died early from consumption, so the young Donovan sold the herd and went looking for gold. He found enough to change his accent and put him on three committees. Including the Victoria Turf Club.

'Good afternoon, Captain,' he said, dodging the horse dung and a busy youngster.

Donovan was not surprised by the sight that greeted him. Like everyone in the racing game, he knew about the old trainer and his children. The Captain's Orphans, they were often called. No-one really knew how they came to be at the stables, but there were cruel and untrue rumours that the old man was stealing them from the street to work as cheap labour or slaves. But anyone who had seen the children knew they were cleaner and better fed than any child in the care of an institution.

'What a mighty day it is, Captain.'

'Mr Donovan, what is it you need?'

'A cup of tea, a short brandy if you have it, and ten minutes of your time, if you please.'

They sat at the long breakfast table and a child brought a single china cup for Donovan. The Captain never ate or drank in the company of outsiders. Especially to talk business.

'We've been hearing all about your splendid grey. Thistle Queen.'

'Have we? And what do *we* say about her?'

'She's a pretty thing, I hear. An angel that runs like the devil. Who's the owner?'

It was a question the Captain had been expecting since Harry Grey won her first race. Few people cared who trained an animal or who was riding, but they always wanted to know who was getting the prize money.

'No-one special. A couple of blokes are in it together – a squatter and a fella that works with the banks.'

'Wealthy men?'

'Not really. I'm training for my lowest price. Just to help them out, like.'

'No names, then? You won't tell me who they are?'

'They wouldn't want me to say.'

'Men of mystery?'

'Something like that.'

'Can I have a look at her?'

'I don't think they'd be looking at selling her, Donovan.'

'Just a look then, Captain? Please.'

They went to the stables, and Donovan touched the grey coat, then stood back to get the full view. 'She's a real doll, this one. Well done, Captain.'

'They won't sell,' the Captain repeated.

'No no, I understand. I'm not here for that. We have something else in mind.'

'What would that be then?'

'We have our Melbourne Cup coming up. Were you thinking of attending yourself?'

'I was not. I have no care for fancy outings.'

'Well, fancy is just what we're hoping for. We want to put on a real show.'

'I don't do shows. I do the races, Mr Donovan,' said the Captain.

'Let me come straight out with it then,' Donovan said. 'We want a big crowd. This will be the grandest race in any colony. So we need the best field we can get.'

'I see,' said the Captain, not caring, and looking around for a job to do so he could excuse himself. But a man without the use of his hands found it hard to look instantly busy.

'We're worried the numbers might be low. We don't know why. There's certainly been plenty of talk and hoo-ha about the Cup – it was even in the London papers. But it's not only that. We just want the best field we can get.'

'So what do you want from me?'

'Your girl Thistle Queen here has been a bit of a favourite for the crowds. She'll be good for some early bets. We'd like you to put her in the Cup.'

'Isn't the field set? That's what I heard.'

'Always room for another. Especially one like yours.'

'You think one grey will make that much difference?'

'It's worth a try. We just want a good race – lots of colour – so we'll get a few more next year. If we don't, the blasted Jockey Club will move in and take the day. We don't want that, do we?'

Just like religion, men like Donovan always assumed other people were on their side.

'I'll ask the owners,' said the Captain, trying to walk his guest to the gates.

'It's a mighty prize.'

'I said I'll ask.'

'Well, while you're asking, ask them what they think about a thousand gold sovereigns. Nine hundred and thirty, if I'm to be exact.' Donovan's eyes flashed and he went into his pocket. 'Have a look at this.' He opened his hand to show a gold coin. 'Isn't that something? We had them made special.'

The Captain bent forward to see the object as Donovan turned it over in his palm.

'What's that?' he asked.

'The sovereign. A gold sovereign.'

'No, what's that on it?'

'It's a horse's head.'

'Funny looking horse. What's that stickin' out?'

'Nothing. It's the ears.'

'No, it's not.'

'Yes, it's the bloomin' ears.' Donovan sounded annoyed for the first time. 'Two ears. See, one and two.'

'Well, one might be, but the other looks like a spike stickin' out of the front of his head. Is it supposed to be a unicorn or some such?'

'No, it's just a horse.'

'With a spike on its head?'

'Look now, these were made special for us in Sydney. At the Royal Mint.'

'Do they not see many horses in Sydney? Don't they know where the ears go?'

'It's made of gold, Captain Flynn. And there are almost a thousand of them. What more do you want?'

The Captain looked at the coin with the spike-headed creature and the words 'THE MELBOURNE CUP 1861' above its head. He showed no emotion but his heart thumped the inside of his chest. The committee man had a point. What more could he want? It was a thousand sovereigns of gold. He never thought he'd have a horse running for such a prize.

'I'll ask,' he said.

*

That night as they ate roasted lamb, the Captain, Jesus, Mary and the children discussed the Melbourne Cup.

'It's a long run,' said Blue Eyes.

'Two miles,' said the Cocky with the magic fingers. 'She hasn't done one that distance before.'

'But you think she can do it?' the Captain asked through the smoke of his pipe.

'She'll make it, but I don't know how well she'll finish,' said the one with the yellow flower. 'And we can't check her on the clock here, because she only runs proper in a real race.'

'What's the rest of the bloody field like?' Mary asked.

Over the spring, Mary had become more involved in the decisions. She had a good instinct for the sport of racing. She had an eye for studying the competition, was quick to spot an injury, and was as good with animals as anyone the Captain had known. Mary loved the idea of watching Harry Horse running in a long race with a big crowd, and if she won something called the 'Melbourne Cup', it'd be almost like winning the whole city. The city that had almost starved them.

'I don't know – I'll find out,' said Blue Eyes, making a note. She would ride into town tomorrow to gather information on all the starters.

'So, what do we reckon?' the Captain said, looking over the full room.

All the little heads nodded.

The Captain was glad, because his thoughts had changed about the race. After Donovan left, the Captain went for his afternoon sleep, and before he fell under, he thought about the future. The Flynns were an ancestral collection of old women and young men. The females were tough and rangy and adaptable to all seasons, but the men were inclined towards illness and fatal accidents. The Captain had lived ten years longer than the oldest Flynn man he'd known. And in that decade, he'd become far more afraid of death than he wanted to be.

But even worse than the fear of death was his concern for the children after he was gone. The stable would be theirs, but without an adult the place would soon get taken over. And just as it was for racing, the colony of Victoria had a committee for everything – including the Orphan Asylum Committee, which the Captain well knew as an organisation that destroyed far more children than it saved.

Even though the two new Cockies were older than the others, they were still drifters. The Captain trusted them but he didn't expect them to stay.

If he could get a half-share of a thousand gold sovereigns, it would keep the creditors away until the children were old enough to take over the stables for themselves. And they could hire any help they needed.

So that night, they all agreed to run Thistle Queen in the Melbourne Cup. The Captain wanted it for the children's futures. Mary wanted to win. And Jesus wanted it because he heard one word.

Gold.

*

It was good to feel warm again, but the spring always gave Harry Logan an extra slap of loneliness.

It had been Alice's favourite season. And on the first sunny day, his wife would always change from her heavy winter clothes into her only light dress. Harry could see the beautiful skin of her arms and neck in the daylight, and when the breeze caught the thin fabric, it would cling to show her heaven-born figure.

But like the other spectres that haunted him, Harry pushed them down and kept working.

It was a busy time for the police. There'd been new strikes in the fields and more gold had come into the city, carried by people who were unaccustomed to wealth. And with the new gold came the drinking, thieving, whoring, and a general imbalance to life in the streets.

Harry was astounded at how easy it was for city people to get into a fight. In the bush they still fought, but it took longer to build up, like a long damp fuse towards a box of powder. But in Melbourne, a peaceful room with grog, music, and laughter soon became violent. It would only take a few wrong words, or a picked pocket, or a short pour of watered-down gin.

He attended three stabbings, including a woman who was slashed across the forearms by her own sister, although none of them were fatal. But there were no gunshots. He was glad. Harry had only seen two bullet wounds in his life – one was made by the boy Jesus, and the other by himself when he fired into the head of the Brown Coat. And that was plenty. He never wanted to see one again.

But despite the coarse memories, thoughts of Alice, and the lifting crime rate, Harry Logan was doing well. He walked for miles every day, he ate better, and he was as physically strong as he had been in years. And he took happy moments wherever he and the dog could find them.

On the first day of November 1861, Inspector Frederick Rourke waved Harry into his office.

'Do you like racing, Harry?'

'Racing, sir?'

'Horses, Constable? Do you like the horse races?'

'No, sir. I can't say that I do.' And he didn't. Harry had never liked animals being used to amuse people. He hated dogs doing tricks or roosters fighting or one horse being flogged to outrun another horse that was also being flogged.

'Good, I'm glad to hear it. Then you're just the man for the job.'

'What's the job, Inspector?'

'The Melbourne Cup. It's on next week and I need to send a few blokes to Flemington to help out. So I'm glad you don't like it, because if you did you'd be too busy watching the track and trying to slip a punt than doing your job. What do you reckon? Are you right to do that job for me?'

'Yes, sir. Of course.' Harry had no problem taking his orders from Frederick Rourke. Although the Inspector had a casual approach to police regulations, he was the kind of boss Harry trusted and wanted to please.

'And I'm comin' too. Because me, on the other hand, I *do* like the races. And I don't wanna miss it.' Rourke rubbed his hands together with excitement, then gave the dog a chunk of bread covered in fat dripping. 'But we can't bugger it up, Harry,' the Inspector said, dropping his smile. 'There might be a few there full of grog and bad manners, so we can't let it get too rowdy.'

'Yes, sir.'

'Because if we get this wrong, the Chief Commissioner will

cover my arse with gravy and have it for Christmas dinner. The Melbourne Cup is like his baby.'

And it was. Chief Commissioner Fredrick Standish wasn't only the head of the colony's police force, he was also the chairman of the Victoria Turf Club. The Cup was his idea and his passion. And it was on his orders that Eddie Donovan went to see the Captain about getting Thistle Queen into the race. Standish had watched her run at Box Hill and couldn't remember seeing a more handsome horse. Although the Commissioner lost his own coins that day.

'There's gonna be a lot of money at the track,' said the Inspector. 'And the committee want to pay the winner on the day with gold sovs. A bloody stupid idea, if you ask me, but that's how they want to do it. And it's their show. So you'll be there with a carbine and a revolver. Sound okay?'

'Yes, sir. How many in the crowd?'

'We won't know until the day. Not as many as they were hoping for, I hear. That's what happens when you put something on a Thursday. But that's not for lowly fellas like us to worry about, Constable.' The Inspector gave him an ironic salute. 'Just polish your shoes, spit on your buttons, and look good for the big boss.'

'Yes, sir.'

The Inspector spooned out more dripping and held it out for the dog to lick.

'And bring ya mate here with us. But we'll have to make him a special police animal. They don't like dogs at the track.'

*

The Flemington racecourse was a few miles from the city, along the easy-flowing Saltwater River. And on the day of the Melbourne Cup, people got there any way they could. Some arrived by boat, some walked or rode, others used coaches, and the rest came by rail. The tracks to the racecourse had only been put down a year before, and for many this was the first time they'd ever travelled by train. They found it a smoother ride than a horse coach, but it was crowded, and the passengers in the middle were unable to enjoy the scenery as they collided with fellow travellers.

But however they arrived, thousands came to the Flemington racecourse on the 7th of November, 1861.

Some started drinking far too early, and although they'd pleaded with their employers to let them go, their day would soon finish with them asleep on the grass before the race was run. But for most, the Melbourne Cup wasn't a drunken affair. It was sunny and perfect, and they spoke in excited tones as they wandered to look at the turf, the bookies and the sideshows, before finding a place on the grass to spread out the food they'd been preparing for days.

Eddie Donovan stood back and counted all the heads. His wife had been trying to speak with him, but he was too distracted with numbers. His future as a committee member of the Victoria Turf Club depended on getting a big crowd today and impressing Chairman Standish. There was little he could do about it now, but he still counted.

Despite his worries, it was a beautiful sight. There were families on the lush hill, there were well-bred people engaging in polite conversations, and there were happy mobs around the food stalls and the betting area. This is how a race should be,

Donovan thought, allowing himself some congratulations. They had done it well.

He looked to the grandstand. By God, he loved that building. Like the train line, it was new, and if they wanted to have grand races, they needed a grand place for the grand bums to sit. Set on bluestone foundations, the grandstand had private dining rooms, a special area for the Governor and a new jockeys' room below. This was a bloody beauty, he thought. As good as anything in the world.

But the Flemington grandstand wasn't just for people, it was also where they were guarding the prize money. On the ground floor, right under the place where the Governor would watch the race, was a small room with two solid locks. Inside there was a metal box that needed three men to carry it, full of the special gold sovereigns.

When the committee had begun organising the Melbourne Cup, they thought it would be too dangerous to have the money there on the day. The original plan was to deliver the prize to the winner a few days later with armed guards. But then the Turf Club decided to make more of a show of it, and they informed the newspapers that the prize would be presented immediately after the race. And all in gold.

People loved gold. They liked to talk about it, brag about it, and stare at it when they could. It was gold that had made the colony the richest in the Empire. It was gold that laid the tracks and built the grandstand. And it was gold that would help bring the crowd.

Donovan had become annoyed at the emblem of the horse on the sovereign, with the spike sticking out of its head. He hadn't seen it until the Captain pointed it out, and now it was all he could see. He just hoped no-one else would notice. But what did it matter? It was gold. People loved gold.

And there was one more reason the committee wanted the prize money there that day. The Victoria Turf Club didn't have an actual cup to present to the winner. The Melbourne Cup had no cup. It was the one thing they'd forgotten, so they needed something to hand over at the end. What could be better than a box of gold? And to settle any fears about robbery, Chief Commissioner Standish promised to have armed constables guard the prize at all times.

Donovan counted the crowd once more and reflected on the things they'd got wrong and right for the first Cup.

Of the many jobs he had, he was also in charge of getting Thistle Queen to the race. In that, he had succeeded, because on the other side of the grandstand, the grey horse was arriving.

*

Jesus and Mary, the Captain, Harry Horse, and Blue Eyes and the other children paraded into the Flemington course.

The night before, they'd all camped by the river and made a big fire. They sang and told stories and slept with the stars. It was a glorious night.

They were led to their stall by two well-dressed stewards. The stables were new but not as fancy as the grandstand. Even with the odour of hay and dung, there was the smell of sawed wood and fresh paint.

Some of the children stayed with Harry Grey to get her ready, while others ran through the crowds to see everything they could before the race.

The Captain put his elbow on Mary's shoulder and said, 'Listen, Cocky, don't you go too far, hey?'

'Something ya needed, Captain?'

'Nah, but these lot are a bit funny,' he said, nodding his head in the direction of the crowd outside. 'They won't want to see you wandering around. Better just stay here with me, hey?'

The Captain knew it was probably an unfair opinion of many in the crowd. Not all would hate seeing Mary's skin, but the ones who didn't wouldn't protect her from the ones who did. And the Captain had come to like the girl very much. She was funny and smart, and even though she was still a child herself, she'd brought a maternal wisdom to their home.

'They don't like me?' Mary said, grinning and already knowing the answer. 'What's not to like?'

'They just don't like Aboriginals. Especially not at the races.'

'Maybe they just haven't met the right one, Captain. They should keep lookin'.'

The old man laughed, and the noise startled the neighbouring thoroughbreds.

Over the winter and spring, the Captain would smile just a little more when Mary was beside him at the track. The girl had an instinct for racing, and she understood how the small things could change a horse and an event. The feed, the animal's stride, the condition of the track. And she never pretended to know more than she did. If there was something she didn't understand, she'd seek out the answer.

But more than instinct, there was something she shared with her grey horse. They both wanted to win. And the winning happened out on the track. Nowhere else. After every race, when Blue Eyes cut the winnings in half, the Captain noticed that

Mary barely looked at it. And she certainly didn't count it. To her, she'd already received the prize when their horse crossed the line first. She needed nothing else.

Each of the Cockies had come to the Captain in their own way, and none of their stories were happy ones before they lived behind the high green hedge. He knew Mary was no different. He'd seen the scars on her ankles and the hesitation before each cheeky grin, and he'd been told she still wasn't sleeping like she should. Something had happened to her. But with her colour, the Captain would've been surprised if it hadn't. He didn't know what. He only knew he liked her.

And Mary liked him too. He was strong and gruff, and had no shame at needing the children. But there was something else. Something she hadn't fully realised herself. Mary liked the Captain because of his two useless hands. No matter how close she was to him, he couldn't grab her. If one day he changed, and became drunk or angry or worse, he would never be able to hold her. So she could keep liking him. Without fear.

And he was right about the Melbourne Cup crowd, although Mary didn't need to be told. She knew what would happen if she walked out there like the other children. She'd be watched and followed and questioned, and if her answers weren't good enough, she'd be chucked out. And that wouldn't do, because the thought of missing the race was unbearable.

Harry Grey's stall was waiting for her with the name 'THISTLE QUEEN' on the gate. And when she was settled, Blue Eyes took a walk down the stable to see the rest of the field.

She knew each starter, because she'd collected every piece of information she could find. Blue Eyes had spent four days in

Melbourne, hiding under tables so she could listen to conversations between punters at the well-known racing pubs, reading every newspaper, and asking innocent questions of some of the old trainers. And when she got home, she formed a small committee with Mary and Magic Fingers to analyse each horse.

After a couple of scratchings, there were eighteen left on Cup Day, with Harry Grey included. There was Toryboy, Inheritor, Black Bess, Lucy Ashton, Archer, Medora, Antonelli, Mormon, Grey Dawn, Prince, Twilight, Dispatch, Sorcerer, Fireaway, The Moor, Flatcatcher and Nutwith. The youngest horses were three-year-olds and the oldest was unknown, and each was handicapped from six stone to twelve, depending on their recent form.

With all the thoroughbreds looking out from their stalls, it was a magnificent sight. It was enough to make the crankiest old horseman stare in silence, and wish there was an artist in the stable to paint the moment.

It was going to be a mighty run. Very few in the crowd would have witnessed so many perfect animals at once. Most races had no more than five or six starters, and some bush events only had two dashing to the finish.

Without shame or hesitation, the Captain thought their horse was the most beautiful, and if they were betting on looks alone, she would be the easy favourite. But as much as he'd dreamed of the gold prize for his Cockies' futures, he knew they had little chance of winning.

With the handicaps, the distance and the strong field, it would all come down to the skill of the rider. And his self-blinded rider had none. They could have hired another jockey, but Rupert Smite would have been flinging the Captain's name around like cow shit after Caulfield, so they wouldn't get anyone from the top classes. And any other jockey would have been a gamble. If he was going to take a chance, he'd rather do it on his own Cocky. And Jesus had been winning, so why stop now?

'Captain?' said the Cocky in the orange hat. 'The stewards want to know the names of the owner and the jockey.'

'Tell them to bugger off,' said Mary, answering for him, as she brushed Harry Horse for the third time. 'It's bloody anonymous.'

'I tried that, but they said they need to know or we can't run.'

'Just tell them anything,' the Captain said. 'Tell them Harry Grey.'

'Who for? The owner or the rider?'

'Both.'

'So you want me to tell them the owner is on his own horse? Will they believe that?'

'I don't care.'

The Cocky went to inform the officials. They didn't believe it, but they had no way to disprove the name. And it was getting too late to check. It was almost time for the race.

*

A steward escorted Jesus to the new jockeys' room under the stand, where he sat and watched the other riders talking, smoking and sharing the top quarter of a bottle of whiskey.

They all gave him an unsmiling look. He was certainly the right size for a jockey, but none of them had seen him before. And those who knew of the fast grey Thistle Queen had heard nothing about the abilities of the rider. Neither good nor bad.

But they were always suspicious, competitive and nervous people, and today they were in no mood to make new friends.

In his previous races, Jesus had never been with the jockeys like this. He was put on Harry Horse in the stables, walked out, and, after a quick look down the track, he would close his eyes and then they were off.

So Jesus just sat with his bag on his lap. He opened the flap to check his riding gear. The ivory handle of his gun stuck out from its white blanket on a bed of his emerald green silks.

He touched it with just the tip of his finger and wondered where they were keeping the gold.

*

The prize was far closer than Jesus could have imagined. If it wasn't for the solid wall at his back, he would be only four steps away from the metal box of 930 gold sovereigns. And only one step further was Constable Harry Logan and his dog.

Harry had been in the small room since four that morning. He was bored and tired and his only activities were yawning, patting the dog and checking his firearms, which he did far more than needed. And as much as Jesus loved the gold, Harry would have loved a blanket and to sleep for a few hours in the corner of the room.

But the Constable knew of the inherent dangers that came with an armed guard sleeping next to a fortune of gold. And even worse than the danger was the thought of some of the visitors he may get. The Chief Commissioner and the Governor were sitting above, and the Inspector had said there was a fair chance they might come down for a look at the prize. Harry knew if they found an already disgraced and dismounted constable snoring with his cheek resting on the barrel of his carbine, it would be the end of his career.

So he stayed awake, wishing he could shave to freshen his face, and thinking of stories to amuse his mind and keep his eyes open.

But of all the stories he could tell himself, nothing could be more fanciful than what was real: Jesus Whitetree was just a few feet away, Mary was in the stables, and Harry's old horse was about to run in the Melbourne Cup.

*

The Captain's children loved the sideshows. There were games and prizes and dancers, and everything was colourful.

As they ran between the attractions, they stopped to watch two funny-looking men juggling balls by the grandstand. None of the Cockies had ever seen identical twins before, and they wondered if they were all like these two – with their chubby bodies, bald heads, and faces that made them look like giant babies.

The children were fascinated, even though the men were terrible performers. They dressed in drab clothes, they didn't smile and they couldn't juggle. Their entire act consisted of standing beside each other and, with no synchronisation or co-ordination, tossing the balls in the air and attempting to grab them before they hit the ground. The children clapped and laughed as they watched the enormous baby-men chase the balls down the hill.

The twins' only other spectator was Eddie Donovan. He had been counting the crowd again when he stopped and gave the men a long look. One of his other jobs for the Melbourne Cup was to approve all entertainment. Like all his other tasks, he'd taken this one seriously, and he didn't remember hiring this act. But the children seemed to like them and they were doing no harm.

Before the day was over, the giant baby-men would do a great deal of harm.

*

The Melbourne Cup was soon to begin and Mary brushed the coat of her grey horse. There was a hard feeling in the middle of her gut that made her both excited and desperate. Excited at what was about to happen, and desperate for the result. If they could just win, if they could just be faster and luckier than any other bugger, there would be something so bloody wonderful waiting on the other side.

Down the hill, the committee was still looking for ways to make it more of a show, so a steward came to the stalls to explain a new plan. They wanted all the horses to come out in a line, they would be announced to the crowd one by one, then joined by their jockey in full view of the grandstand. It was just for the theatre. The anticipation. The colour.

The Cockies saddled Harry Grey and Blue Eyes tightened the springs of her watch and walked around for a final check. It was time. The Captain stood at the horse's head with his beard touching her nose.

'Show them, beautiful girl,' he said in a whisper.

His head was dropped like he was beginning a prayer. And it was a prayer. As the race got closer, the more the Captain wanted to win it, and he'd started to believe it was possible. To himself, he said, 'Oh Lord, we may not be the most worthy in this stable, but we'd really like that bloody gold. Please let our Harry Grey run faster than this lot, and please help our jockey to keep his eyes open.'

The field lined up and down they went to the grandstand. Each horse was with its trainer, and only Thistle Queen had two people leading her – the Captain and Blue Eyes. And at the sight of the first horse, a slim black animal named Prince, the crowd gave a mighty a cheer. Until then, they'd all been occupied by their own food, grog, conversation and entertainment, but now they were ready for some horses and the big race.

Donovan stood in the front row of the grandstand, and with a voice that he'd been practising in his bath for weeks, he roared out the name of each horse as it appeared. The original plan was for him to announce the names as they went onto the turf, but lining them up like this was much better and he looked over to the Governor to see that he was enjoying the drama.

With each announcement, a jockey would come from the other side of the building to join his horse. The little men were all in their colours of red, yellow, blue and purple. Some strutted and waved at the spectators, while others moved like shy calves at a market. Some horses got a bigger cheer than others, because their names had been printed many times in the newspaper by reporters who used elegant words to describe the thoroughbreds. But now the people didn't need words. They were seeing them, finally. And the crowd waved their bets in the air and pointed as though every gesture could affect the race's outcome.

Thistle Queen was third last in the order, and when Donovan called her name, the crowd responded. It wasn't the loudest reception, but it wasn't the quietest either. Her odds had remained high, but some at the Cup had watched her run in a bush race or two and couldn't remember ever seeing such a graceful animal at full stride. So although they'd put their money on a more sensible bet, they still saved a few pennies for Thistle Queen.

Mary stayed back in the empty stall. She made a seat of clean straw and started tucking into a pie and a bottle of ginger beer that the Cocky with the yellow flower had bought for her. Her plan was to stay there until the race started and then, when everyone was distracted, she'd run down the hill to the fence and watch with the others.

She listened to the names being called and she grinned as the sweet drink and salty meat filled her belly. When Harry Horse's turn came, her teeth flashed with excitement. But something was different, Mary thought. All the other names were said once. Only Harry's was repeated.

'Thistle Queen!' roared Donovan. Then, after ten seconds, he said 'Thistle Queen' again. This time it sounded more like a question than an announcement. Then he said it again.

Back at the grandstand, Donovan was forced to repeat the name because no jockey had appeared to join his horse. When he said it for the fifth time, he looked down at the Captain for some help.

'Better go and have a look, Cocky,' the Captain said to Blue Eyes from the side of his mouth.

Blue Eyes ran off in the direction from which the riders were appearing, and while she did, Donovan pushed on with the last two names. Blue Eyes scrambled through the crowd in a sprint until she got to the jockeys' room. There was nothing. It was as quiet as an empty tomb.

Jesus was gone.

*

Fifteen minutes before Donovan started calling out the horses' names, Constable Harry Logan was almost asleep. He'd had no visitors in the secure room and the faint sound of people enjoying themselves outside only made him more tired. The dog had been snoozing at his feet for two hours, and with only the box of gold as company, Harry's eyelids fell.

But then the heavy door swung open hard and he saw a face. It was the last one on earth he'd expected. It was Sergeant Tom Addington of Mull Creek.

'Harry bloody Logan!' said Addington. 'They told me you were in here.' The Sergeant was smiling and his voice banged off the walls, pulling Harry from a blissful moment between reality and sleep.

'Shit, Tom! Bloody hell, you scared the Christ out of me.'

The Sergeant chuckled at the reaction and sat down without invitation. Harry smelt the familiar scent of Tom Addington. Stale grog and a dusty uniform. If the room was pitch dark, he'd still know it was Tom Addington.

'How are ya, mate?' asked the Sergeant.

'What are you doing here, Tom?'

'They needed a few extra hands for this shindig today, and I was coming down anyway, so I stuck up me hand. There's a few lovely looking tarts out there. I'm glad I didn't miss it. How long have you been in here?'

'Hours,' Harry said through a yawn. 'Since dawn.'

'Don't worry, I've got another young constable on the way to give you a spell.'

'Nah, it's all right. I'll stay here.'

'Nah, come on. You wanna see the race, don't ya?'

Harry shrugged as though he didn't care but, in truth, he was glad he hadn't been forgotten.

'So, I gave you a bit of a fright, did I?' said Addington, putting his hand on Harry's leg. 'Well, good, because I owe you a couple, ya bastard. Do you know how much shit I got in because of you? I've been kicked up the arse so many times that you wouldn't bloody believe me if I told ya. The Company had a kick. The Superintendent had a kick. Every mongrel has had a kick.'

'Sorry to hear that, Tom.' It was the conversation Harry hoped he'd never need to have. He'd told lies in his report, and then told them again to Superintendent Pepper in Ballarat, but now he would have to answer to Tom Addington over the missing Brown Coats and the escaped prisoners.

'What a mess all that was,' said Addington. 'And it's still a mess.'

'The mining blokes never showed up then?' Harry asked. He thought it would be better if he started with a few questions, rather than wait for Addington to do all the talking. Guilty people didn't usually ask questions about the crime they were guilty of. He only hoped Addington couldn't see through it.

'Nah, haven't heard a thing. We thought we might get some news after winter, but nothing.'

'What about the prisoners? Have you seen them?'

'That little bloke Jesus and your bloody native?'

'Yep,' said Harry.

'Bugger all. Not a thing. Gone. Who knows? But we're charging them with murder.'

'Murder? Both of them?'

'Yep. Why not? It's been long enough. The executives are now presumed dead. So dead's dead. And the last we saw of them, according to your report to Pepper, was with your prisoners. So dead means murder.'

It was something Harry had suspected for months, but to hear it made it real. He'd seen the name of Jesus in the paper, and figured it was just something put out by the company. But the thought of Mary and Jesus getting charged, caught and hung for murder was a horror to him. He thanked God that he'd given them a fast horse. They'd be long gone.

'So no idea where they're at?' Harry asked again.

'Nah. And we're a bit short on trackers. Most of them have been looking for Mother Pink's mob.'

Good old Mother Pink, Harry thought. At least she was useful for something.

The door opened again and a young constable who looked just a little more awake than Harry came in to relieve the post.

'Come on,' Tom said to Harry. 'We might slip in a drink before the race.'

*

In the next room, while Harry and Tom talked, Jesus had changed into his emerald-green silks and his white cap. He didn't look like a person wanted for murder. He looked just like a jockey.

The space wasn't really big enough for eighteen people – even little blokes like them – and Jesus started to feel choked by the lack of fresh air. The others were smoking, talking loud and spitting, and it was like the walls were getting higher and closer.

A steward entered and stood in the middle of the room, in his top hat. Surrounded by the jockeys, he looked enormous. He explained the plan. He wanted them all to line up outside, and their horses would be brought to the front of the grandstand, and when they heard the name of their horse, they were to walk around and smile for the crowd and stand with their animal so everyone could get a look at them.

Some of them grumbled at the request. They weren't a bloody circus act, for God's sake, they were professional riders. But they did as they were told. So did Jesus.

He was happy to be outside and the sun warmed his face. The steward explained the plan once more, and the eighteen waited.

Jesus used the time to think about the gold again, and how wonderful it would be to get it. He wasn't good with numbers, but looking at the long line of other riders, he knew enough to know the odds weren't good. But he still had a chance. That's all he needed. And he and Mary would get half. He didn't know how much half of 930 was, but he would ask Mary later.

The crowd was getting excited for the race. Many were on the grass beside the jockeys' room and they applauded at the sight of all the colourful little men lined up. Jesus felt as though he was famous, or even royal, and he hoped they would still be there cheering for him when he won the gold.

But then he saw something that made every vein in his body turn to frost. Two policemen were moving through the excited crowd. He'd seen other police at the races, and it hadn't worried him. But these two were different. Because he knew them.

It was Harry Logan, the kind constable who had shared that terrible morning with him and Mary, and beside him was the round figure of the cruel Sergeant Tom Addington. Jesus remembered the man's leather strap, and the welts he'd made on Jesus' back had been there most of the winter. The sting of the beating still came to him in dreams.

He believed Harry was a good man, but he was with Addington and he had a rifle. Jesus knew they were there to catch him. Nothing else. And since he'd been beaten by the Sergeant in Mull Creek, he had killed a man. He was innocent then and he still got whipped. He could only imagine the lashing he would get now.

Jesus wished Mary was with him to help with a plan. But she wasn't. He would need to come up with his own. He did and it was a simple one. He jumped out of the line and ran as fast as he could.

Harry Logan and Tom Addington didn't notice one of the jockeys bolting. There were too many other things to look at, and Harry was still trying to wake up in the bright sun. The other jockeys didn't care either. They were only worried about their own race. If another rider had forgotten something, or needed a nervous pee before the start, that was their problem. Only a few people in the crowd were wondering why a jockey was sprinting through them and jumping over their picnics.

Two drunken punters on the hill watched Jesus come up towards them. And seeing the determination on his face, they got out of his way.

'Bugger me,' said one. 'Easy, mate. Slow down.'

'Are ya tryin' to win the Cup without a horse?' asked the other.

'Hey, the track is in the other bloody direction.'

They laughed and watched Jesus run to the top of the hill and into the trees.

*

After Donovan had read all the names, there were eighteen horses in front of the grandstand but only seventeen riders. And as beautiful as Thistle Queen was, she looked odd against the rest of the field.

Blue Eyes ran back from the empty jockey room and stopped in front of the Captain. Donovan was making a speech and the crowd was quiet, so the Captain and his Cocky couldn't talk to each other. But without words and only using gestures and their eyes, they had this conversation:

'He's not there.'

'What?'

'He's run off.'

'What the hell are we gonna do?'

'Don't know.'

'Damn it.'

'Wait. I've got an idea.'

And with that, Blue Eyes ran to the stables.

When Donovan was done with his speech, he hurried towards the Captain at the front of the grandstand, looking over his shoulder to see if the Chief Commissioner or the Governor had noticed the missing jockey. They had.

'Where's your rider, Captain?' Donovan said through his teeth. His desperation was clear.

'Give us some time.'

'We're about to start the race. I don't have any time.'

At the stall, Mary was still resting on the straw in the corner. She'd heard Thistle Queen's name called out a few times and then the rest of the field, so she thought everything was as it should be. Until Blue Eyes ran in.

'Is he here?'

'No.' Without saying a name, Mary knew she meant Jesus.

'It's about to start. Have you seen him?'

'No.'

'Quick. Come with me.'

While Blue Eyes was sprinting to the stables, she was thinking of what to do if Jesus wasn't there. And by the time she knew he wasn't, she had another plan. She took Mary by the hand and they ran along the back of the grandstand and into the jockeys' room. As soon as they were in, Blue Eyes began grabbing the jockeys' bags and spilling the contents on the floor.

If she'd grabbed Jesus' bag, she would have tipped out the white handle revolver onto the floor. But she didn't, and she was only on her third when she found what she wanted – a spare set of riding gear. Black cap and green silks. Perfect.

'What the hell are ya doing, ya mad bugger?' Mary asked.

'He's gone. Put this on. Quick.'

Mary did it. She was worried about what had happened to Jesus, but she trusted Blue Eyes.

'And keep your head down.'

Less than a minute later, Blue Eyes and Mary ran to the front of the grandstand where the horses were moving off to the track. Very few in the crowd noticed the last jockey running late, and if they did, they just saw a thin person in green silks getting to their mount. It was all noisy and exciting, and everyone was far too busy checking their bets and pointing at their chosen horse.

Before the Captain could understand what was happening, Blue Eyes helped Mary into the saddle.

'Keep your face covered,' said Blue Eyes, and Mary pulled the cap down as best she could, before pulling on a rein and turning Harry Horse to join the others.

The Captain was stunned into silence, but there was nothing he could do about it. It was too late. It was time for the Melbourne Cup.

*

Mary hadn't been on Harry Horse's back since their long ride from the bush to the city. And she now realised the full beauty and strength of the creature. She could feel the heart, lungs and muscles under her, and it was like she was a foot higher than any other rider.

But her saddle was tiny. She'd never sat on one so small, and thought it barely covered her bum. Andre Noble's was more than three times the size and held both her and Jesus. Thinking about the saddle made her remember her friend. What the bloody hell had happened to him? Jesus wasn't the smartest person she'd known, but he was smart enough to sit in a room and wait for the race. Something had happened, but Mary knew the best thing she could do was get in the race and try to win the gold for him.

They moved to the starting post. She could see the crowd in the distance – soon she'd be riding past them. But she felt less like a jockey and more like a bandit rushing through an unwelcome town.

The other jockeys were making their final checks and steadying the animals. None of them bothered looking at Mary, but she kept the cap pulled over her face and her eyes down in case they became more interested.

Just as the stewards were organising the field, a jockey jumped from his mount to adjust the saddle, but before he could, his horse bolted from his hands. It was Twilight, a brown mare and one of the race's oldest starters. She shot off down the turf as though the race had begun, and kept going past the cheering spectators, many of whom thought the riderless display was just part of the day's entertainment. It wasn't, and the impatient stewards had to wait until Twilight had run the full course and come around to the starting post again.

When things settled, Mary did as she was told and came forward. A steward gave her a quick look but missed seeing her face and he was then busy with the next animal.

They would never be able to get such a huge field in a perfect straight line, but they did the best they could. And when they were ready, the chief steward – dressed in a striped jacket and top hat, and mounted on a horse that looked almost fast enough to run in the Cup – stood at the starting post, holding his red flag.

Mary was placed in the centre of the field, and she felt smothered by the heat and the size of the animals. It was as if she'd been thrown into the middle of a cattle pen full of snorting bulls.

The flag was lifted, but before it could drop there was a false start. It made the crowd erupt and jeer again. It annoyed the already cranky officials, yet only added to the excitement for everyone else.

When they were ready once more, the flag dropped. And they were off in the Melbourne Cup.

*

Many stayed in the grandstand to watch the race. The view was high and clear, and they could see every straight and every turn of the course. And, even better than the view, anyone in the stand could tell people they watched the race with Sir Henry Barkley, the Governor of Victoria.

Two such people were a pair of women sitting a few rows behind Sir Henry. One was old and plump, with a heavy chest and heavier make-up that almost covered a burn scar on her cheek, and the other was young and slim with long black hair. Their ages were too far apart for them to be sisters, and they didn't look like mother and daughter, but they wore identical outfits of black satin and white lace. Just like Mary, their hats covered their faces. They drank the best wines on offer, laughed with the same mix of joy and irony, and watched the people more than the horses.

Eddie Donovan was also sitting near the Governor. And with all the frantic moments before the start, Donovan needed to slow his blood with two quick whiskies. His wife had them waiting for him, and when the last drop went down, he looked over at Sir Henry, who was sitting next to the Chief Commissioner of Police, Fredrick Standish. The two were smiling and pointing at the track. All was well for Eddie Donovan. The race was finally away. And when it was over, it was his job to announce the winner to the crowd. He decided he wouldn't have another whiskey until he did.

Not everyone was in the grandstand. Most of the spectators were on the grass, pushing to get as close to the track as they could. And the Captain and his children were among them. They found a good spot on the left of the grandstand, a couple of hundred yards from the finish post.

'How'd she go, Cocky?' the Captain asked Blue Eyes when he felt the race start through the crowd. 'How'd she get off?'

'Good, I reckon, but I can't see much yet. They're too close. I tell ya, this will be a slow one. Some of that grass must be a yard high.'

Blue Eyes was right. The weather on Cup day was warm and bright, but there'd been good rains in the fortnight before. Some sections of the track had grass that made it look more like a crop than a racecourse.

Further along, closer to the grandstand, Harry Logan and Tom Addington were in the crowd together. Neither was watching the race. Addington was looking at the women and he thanked God for the spring weather. With the horses distracting the crowd, he could let his eyes run all over the girls' bodies and excited faces. He was a little drunker now and he wondered if he could grab one with the reddest lips and squeeze a kiss out of her without being noticed.

As usual, and unlike his Sergeant, Harry Logan was mindful of the job. He was still on duty, he was still armed, and there was still a box of gold at the course. But he felt calm. The people were happy and easy, and he thought the biggest threat of the day would come later when the staggering drunks fell over trying to get home.

Harry had never been in a crowd so big, either as a citizen or policeman, and every eye was on the race. All except two men on the grass behind him.

He noticed they were juggling for a group of children, who were too young to care for the sport of horse racing. The men were odd looking – bald twins with round, chubby baby faces – and they were bloody awful jugglers.

Harry had seen a few jugglers in the city, and they'd reminded him of Alice. Just before they were married, she had told him she was going to teach herself to juggle. A year later, when he came home to her buttery smell, she said, 'Watch this, Harold John.' She picked up a pear, a lemon and a small glass jar, and tossed them in the air. She fumbled a bit and had to catch the jar in her apron before it hit the dirt floor. She wasn't very good, but she was a lot better than these twins at the Melbourne Cup.

At the top of the hill, from behind a tree, Jesus watched the start of the race alone. He was too far away to see if Harry Horse was in the field or if it was just another grey. It didn't matter.

All he knew was that he had to find Mary and warn her about the police.

*

'Where are they up to?' the Captain asked, needing to shout over the crowd.

'They're coming around the first turn,' said Blue Eyes.

On the track, the suffocation that Mary felt before the race had now disappeared. From the moment the flag dropped, all she could feel was the power of the animal underneath her. And she loved it.

It was an even start and the field was together as they came to the first turn. No-one was pushing to get to the front, because it was a long race and any rider who didn't know it wasn't going to last the first mile.

Thistle Queen was in the middle, and only the spectators in the grandstand or the few on the hill could see the flash of bright grey bobbing in the enormous pack of darker thoroughbreds.

As they came into the first straight that ran along the grandstand, Mary lifted her head for the first time and looked down the track. It was a wide and lush green road with no visible end, and thousands of faces were lined along the sides like trees at a riverbank. And just in front of her were a dozen galloping horses and the bums of their riders sitting a foot above the saddles.

Mary hoped she had herself in a good position. She knew what a good position was. But even though her instincts for the sport were strong, and she'd learnt a lot from Blue Eyes and the Captain, it was different in the middle of a race. Mary only prayed Harry Horse would make things right if she got them wrong.

Just hold on, Mary thought. Just hold on. That's what Jesus did. And he won with his bloody eyes shut. How hard could it be?

The thought of her friend made her smile as she rode. Bloody mad bastard, he was. How could he run a whole race in the dark?

And as they went along the straight, Mary closed her own, just to know what it was like. It was frightening. It made the thump of the animals twice as loud. She could hear the breathing of the horses and the grumbling of the jockeys, and it felt like she was going four times faster. Why did Jesus do it? Crazy bugger.

Mary rode through the dark for only a few seconds, and just before she opened her eyes, there was a terrible sound. The rhythm of the running pack was broken, and a horse made a pained and frightened noise. Her eyelids sprang open in time to see three horses fall right in front of her.

The crowd reacted to the sight. Some gasped and turned away – it was too awful to watch – while others stretched their necks to check if it was any horse they'd put money on.

'What's happened?' asked the Captain.

'A fall!' said Blue Eyes. 'It's a fall! A bad one!'

'Who? Us? Are we in it?'

'I don't know yet. There's a few down.'

Shit, thought Donovan in the grandstand. The race had only been running for thirty bloody seconds and they already had a fall. He had a better view than Blue Eyes and could see the jockeys' colours well enough to know it was Dispatch, Twilight and Medora that went down. What a bloody mess.

Mary pulled back hard on the reins, just as Harry Horse made a sharp turn to avoid the wreckage. It was successful, but as hard as Mary's knees and fingers tried to grip, she was thrown from the saddle and tossed into the air.

She was flying for less than a quarter of second, but it felt like she'd become a spirit bird gliding towards the horizon clouds. Until she landed. There was nothing spiritual about that. Mary hit the turf with her face and shoulder first, and the grass that had looked so soft and lush felt like a wall of rock.

The impact exploded in her head as her teeth banged together and her body collapsed on itself. But she got up as fast as she could, fearing the horses behind were charging at her. They were, and for a moment she thought she would be trampled into the grass, before they split.

Mary's legs wobbled from the shock, but Harry Horse was beside her to lean on.

She'd been racing for less than a minute yet it felt strange to be standing still. She looked down the green track and the field was running ahead as if she'd never been part of it, and the sound of the galloping began to fade.

The Melbourne Cup was going on without her.

*

Spectators and officials rushed out to move the injured jockeys and horses. Dispatch and Medora couldn't get up. And they never would again.

Twilight wobbled her first few steps before she bolted towards the crowd, and for the second time that day they saw a horse running free without a rider. Perhaps, some thought, she was just one of those animals that wasn't meant to have something on its back.

'What's happening?'

'Harry Grey has stopped,' said Blue Eyes. 'She's standing there, that's all, Captain.'

'Is Cocky still on her?'

'Nah.'

'Are they hurt?'

'No, I don't think so. They're both just . . . standing.'

'Well, that's that then,' the Captain said. 'We're all done. Bugger it.' He wasn't angry. The old trainer knew what a fall like that meant, and he was glad he still had his horse and rider to take home. But he was disappointed. He'd wanted Harry Grey to run by the grandstand just one time, so everyone could see what a beauty she was.

Eddie Donovan cursed the fall again and resisted having another shot of liquor. Shit, that's four horses out. Yesterday, he'd had a field of twenty-one. They'd had a few scratchings and they started the race with eighteen. Now there were only fourteen. At this rate, he thought, I'll be lucky to get the three place-getters limping to the post. He felt like the commander of an embattled naval fleet, standing on the shore, watching his ships get cannonballed one after another.

Donovan checked the faces of the Governor and the Chief Commissioner. Thankfully, they'd remained distracted by the field that was still running.

Constable Harry Logan was too far away to see the fall. He heard the gasp of the crowd and it made the dog bark, but he decided it wasn't the kind of gasp that needed police attention, so he stayed where he was.

On the track, Mary looked at the injured creatures in front of her. Her stomach was already twirling from gulping down her pie and ginger beer too fast, then getting jostled around and changed into the riding gear, and then being thrown onto a horse. Then she raced and was thrown off. But now the sight of the poor buggered animals trying to lift their heads made her sick.

It had been less than half a minute since the fall, and the field was now long gone down the straight. Some spectators ran onto the turf to help with the fallen horses and riders, and one went to Thistle Queen to secure the reins. It was a woman with a pink bonnet and a mole on her top lip. She checked the animal first, before she turned to the jockey. She was shocked. Although the jockey's face was crusted with dirt and grass, the features and the colour of the skin were clear.

'Goodness me,' she said to Mary. 'What is this? What are you doing here, girl?'

The woman was stern, angry and confused all at once. Mary knew that look. She'd seen it many times before. It was as if the woman had found a snake in her kitchen.

'Answer me.' The mole quivered and the pink bonnet darted around, looking for someone of authority to make things right. 'Tell me what you're doing here, girl.'

But Mary wasn't afraid. Instead, the stunned face and haughty voice of the woman were like a tonic in Mary's blood.

'Haven't ya heard, love?' she said, grinning, as some blades of grass fell from her face. 'The Melbourne bloody Cup is on today.'

Mary swiped the reins from the woman's fingers, leapt into the saddle, cut through the crowd and took off after the pack.

*

'We're back in it, Captain!' said Blue Eyes.

'What?!'

'She's running again! She's after them!'

The field was starting to come out from the Captain's blur. They were still together but beginning to spread out, with

Flatcatcher at the front. They went past the Captain, before fading back out of focus. Then he heard the solo gallop of Harry Grey thirty seconds later. There she was. He watched her go by, and he watched the crowd watching her. He knew she had no hope of winning from this position, but at least they'd get to see her at full stride with her black legs reaching for the next bit of turf. That should be enough to fill some hearts.

Further down the course, Sergeant Tom Addington turned from the buffet of females and glanced at the track.

'Hey, Harry, that one looks a bit like your old grey.'

'Does it?'

'Yeah. A bit.'

But Harry Logan still wasn't looking. After the commotion of the fall, he went back to watching the twins. He didn't like the look of them. Not just because they were awful jugglers, but there were half-a-dozen children around them, including a little boy. He was no more than five years old and dressed in bright yellow with a blue cap. He'd tried to move away from the performers, but each time he did one of the fat twins would shepherd him back.

Far better than most, Harry Logan knew there were some men who shouldn't be alone with children. And no-one was watching these giant babies, so for that moment it was his job.

If he'd been more interested in racing, and less distracted by his duty, he would have seen his former prisoner and his own grey horse running in the grandest race of the year.

Mary had the width of the track to herself, and way ahead she could see the rest of the field. But they didn't look like a mob of individual horses; instead, they were one massive animal with dozens of legs and bobbing heads. And now that she was alone,

Mary felt like she was going even faster than before. She went by the grandstand – the place that would be the finish line after they ran a full lap – and Mary could see the people waving and jumping, and she felt Harry Horse rush through the cheers of the crowd.

Mary lifted herself forward and got as close to the dark grey ears as she could.

'Ya just a bloody show-off, you are.'

They went after the pack and Mary didn't dare close her eyes again.

*

In the grandstand, Eddie Donovan watched the lone grey rush by. She was a beauty all right. And she was fast. If it hadn't been for the fall, she would have been a chance.

The field went into the turn that ran along the Saltwater River, and Donovan could see Archer and Inheritor in front now. They were both Sydney horses and he knew there'd be plenty in the crowd unhappy with a northern outsider winning the Cup. But no-one on the Victoria Turf Club Committee would be disappointed with the result. They didn't want the Melbourne Cup to be just some local bush affair, they wanted entries from all over the continent and the world. If a Melbourne horse won the first year, it would do nothing to spread the prestige of the event.

But they weren't halfway yet, Donovan thought. There was a long way to go and any horse could win it. Except the fallen ones being dragged off the turf. And Thistle Queen.

Jesus ran to the stable and there was no-one there. He knew the Captain and the Cockies would be down by the track just before the grandstand, and Mary would be with them. Where else would she be? He wanted to run down there and warn her about the police, but he couldn't risk being seen and leading them straight to her. If he was going to get caught, he'd rather be caught alone.

Jesus decided to wait in the stall until the race was done. But there was something he needed to get from the jockeys' room first. Something he needed to protect them both. It would be a risk and he only hoped all eyes would be on the race.

Still dressed in his green riding gear, Jesus sprinted back to the top of the hill. He was still too far away to see the race properly, but he could watch the field – and behind them, about nine lengths from the last animal in the pack, a grey speck was moving up. Even with the distance, Jesus knew it was their horse. But he had no idea who could be riding her.

Down by the track, Blue Eyes had climbed up on the top of the fence and held onto a flagpole.

'What's happening?' the Captain asked her.

Blue Eyes shouted down a full report of the field to him and the children.

'Where is she?'

'She's well back, Captain, but it looks like she's still got a bit in her.'

She might well have, the Captain thought, it still wouldn't be enough. There would be some good riders in that mob. They'd have kept their horses in the bridle until now and put themselves in position for the final sprint. Harry Grey was a bloody ripper horse, for sure, but anything she had inside her to win this race would've been used trying to catch the pack.

However, Blue Eyes could see what he couldn't and she gave him a smile. 'She's still going after them. She's moving up, Captain. She's almost at the back.'

Mary had watched the field get closer and closer, but it wasn't until she caught them that she knew she could.

The jockey of the last horse turned to see the grey coming up behind him. For the last two minutes he'd thought he was running last, and he almost smiled to discover that he wasn't. But then he frowned when the grey galloped past him and he was last again.

Thistle Queen moved through the back third of the field, with each rider giving her a similar frown as she went by. Mary heard the jockeys use their whips, and she realised for the first time that she was the only rider without one. But her right hand didn't feel the need of it. Harry Horse had plenty in her and belting her wasn't going to bring it out any faster.

They came into the straight, heading for the grandstand. Eddie Donovan was loving the sight of it. The injured horses had been dragged off the track and forgotten, and the field spread as they prepared for the final dash. He saw Mormon, Prince and Antonelli fighting for a place, but it was Archer that was well ahead with three quarters of a mile to go.

That would be an excellent result, Donovan thought with a smile. If Sydney's Archer had the win, and local favourite Mormon came in second, that would be perfect. And even better, Donovan had put a little of his own money on Archer's nose, so he had plenty to celebrate. He was already counting the winnings in his head, so he didn't notice the flash of grey coming through the middle.

Blue Eyes was still holding the flagpole and she put a hand to her forehead to cut the glare, as though she was searching for land from the mast of a mighty ship. And as Thistle Queen came out of the pack, it was like an island in the ocean.

'Captain!' Blue Eyes yelled to be heard over the lifting crowd. 'She's coming! She's coming through!'

'Come on, Harry Grey!' he said, and the children jumped around him. 'Come on, ya bloody gorgeous thing!'

Mary and Thistle Queen were in the open, with the pack behind and only Antonelli, Mormon, Prince and Archer in front. The riders were cursing and whipping and she could feel the desperate heat coming off the horses. She just held on. She had no other plan. She knew she was nothing more than a passenger, and if she wasn't there, Harry Horse would be doing exactly what she was doing right now, sprinting for the finishing post.

They were almost there, with only Archer in front of Thistle Queen. And Eddie Donovan was loving it. He still wanted the Sydney stallion to win, but how bloody wonderful it was to have a close finish, with a local grey coming from the back to take second place. And it wasn't just any grey nag. It was the grey caught up in the fall, the grey that came from well back to give the crowd a final rush of excitement, and, even more importantly, it was the beautiful grey he was asked to bring to the Cup. So Donovan's future on the Victoria Turf Club Committee was now assured.

Archer raced to the grandstand and Thistle Queen was just a length behind with a hundred yards to go. Mary was so close that had she a whip, she could have touched the sweaty bay arse of Archer. But she just looked to the winning post as the roars of the crowd came from all around her.

263

Archer's jockey felt the new competition and started to whip his ride as if he was trying to thrash a fox out of a bush.

'I'm here,' Mary said to her horse and herself. 'I'm still on. Come on, Harry girl.'

Then she felt herself moving forward. It was like Harry Horse had grabbed Archer and was pulling him back. And as they rushed past the grandstand and the winning post, they were at each other's sides.

'They're done!' yelled Blue Eyes. 'They're through.'

'Who got it?'

'I don't know!'

'What happened? Who won?'

'I don't know!' No-one knew yet.

Even Donovan, who had one of the best seats in the grandstand, didn't know. He only knew it had been a hell of a race.

Down in front, at the winning post, was a top-hatted steward. It was his responsibility to decide the winner. Fifteen seconds before the end, he thought he had the easiest job of the day. But that changed. Now it was the hardest, with every trainer, punter, official, publican, politician and woman waiting for the result.

And in the grandstand, through the excitement of the finish, the Governor of Victoria, Sir Henry Barkley, turned to Chief Commissioner Standish and asked a question.

It was a question asked with wonder and confusion. And it was a question that would never get officially answered.

'Standish, was that a black girl on that horse?'

*

Constable Harry Logan couldn't have heard the Governor's question, but he was about to discover the answer. And when he did, he thought he'd gone insane.

Yes, it was a black girl, all right. It was Mary, the girl who didn't shut up, and liked his cooking, and slept on the dirt with his dog, and made fun of him getting lost, and was grabbed and hurt by the Brown Coats. The same girl he had chained and then let go and thought about every day and hoped had gone north, never to be seen again.

And, yes, it was a grey horse. The one that had been his companion and his deputy. The one that carried the spirit of Alice Logan. The same one he gave to Mary and Jesus so they could run.

So, yes, it was a girl on a grey horse. No doubt about it. But how, how, how, Harry thought with ascending perplexity, how could it be *that* girl and *that* horse? In the Melbourne Cup?

Seconds before he made the discovery, Harry had been standing with Tom Addington, still watching the fat juggling twins. He was just being a good policeman, trying to stop something bad before it could happen. If the odd-looking brothers were going to grab a child, they'd do it when the crowd was most distracted. Right at the end of the race.

When the crowd cheered the winners across the line, the twins didn't even look up at the track, adding to Harry's suspicion. But as he watched, he didn't notice that his dog had picked up the scent of something familiar and had run off through the forest of legs.

In those seconds of unrestrained joy from the crowd, Inspector Frederick Rourke appeared and was as excited as any spectator.

'What a flamin' run. Did you ever see anything like it? How can you not like racing, Harry? After that? What's wrong with ya?'

Rourke had already been a friendlier boss than Harry had ever known, but now he was like a leaping puppy.

'What a horse that grey is. Did you see it, Harry?'

Rourke pointed to the track where the horses were slowing down and coming back to the front of the grandstand. Harry followed the Inspector's finger. And that's where his insanity began, when he saw Mary and his horse.

'I hope he got across the line,' Rourke said. 'I put quite a few bob on that grey. I knew it. I knew there was something special about him.'

'Her,' Harry corrected, but he was too stunned to know he'd even said it.

'Right, *her* then. Well, if she gets up, I'll have made a ruddy fortune. What a horse!'

Harry's shock became panic and he looked at Tom Addington to see if he'd recognised Mary. But he hadn't. He was still distracted by the grog in his head and the women in his view.

'Oh hey, listen, you two,' Inspector Rourke said, as though he'd suddenly remembered he was in charge. 'We need to get the prize money to the front of the grandstand. They want to give it to the winner, so everyone can see it. You know, while the crowd is still carrying on. Sergeant, you and Logan go and take care of it, will you?'

'Yes, sir.'

'And we'll need to post guard. Get all around it. Stand up straight for the Governor, all that kind of crap.'

'Yep, right then,' Addington said, remembering he would need to do a little work today. 'Come on, Harry. Let's get this job done.'

But Harry was too stunned, both in movement and words. He was still trying to understand how Mary got there. He couldn't even invent a scenario in his head where it was possible. And he only began moving when Tom grabbed him by the arm to take him to the room under the grandstand.

And the shock made him forget all about the baby-faced twins.

*

Eddie Donovan was loving it. There was confusion. But it was wonderful confusion. Things couldn't have been better for the man. The race had been thrilling and the crowd was so exhilarated they didn't know what to do first.

He wanted to keep the excitement going, so he sent word for Archer and Thistle Queen to be brought to the front of the grandstand with their jockeys before the weigh-in.

His plan was to place them on either side of the metal box full of gold and then call for silence, just for the drama, before announcing the winner. The people would erupt at the news and he'd have the Governor come down to officially present the gold to the winner. It hadn't happened yet, but Donovan was already congratulating himself for the idea.

The Captain was even happier than Eddie Donovan. He'd never seen a ride like it, and, even better, there'd been thousands there to watch it with him. He'd wanted to show them a beautiful miracle. And he did.

But in his joy, the Captain had a problem. The weigh-in. Thistle Queen was either first or second, and the jockey and the gear would need to be checked and weighed. The field was now walking back from where they'd pulled up, so he only had a minute, or maybe two, to come up with an answer.

'Cocky, go find the Cocky. It's the only hope we got.'

Blue Eyes knew exactly what he meant, and she took off to find Jesus.

While the Captain tried to think of a way out, he was given a piece of welcome luck. An official ran over to tell him Eddie Donovan's new plan of having a presentation before the weigh-in.

'All right . . . then . . .' the Captain said, answering the steward while trying to think at the same time. 'But . . . but . . . I'll need to have a little look at my rider first. She's been in a fall . . . *he's* been in a fall . . . I want to see if he's all right first. I don't want him bleedin' all over the place. How would that look, hey?'

The official nodded. He didn't care. As long as the plan was still the plan, he'd done his job and it didn't matter.

Up in the stable, Blue Eyes was having her own luck. It was the first place she looked for Jesus, and she found him. He was sitting in the straw, holding his gun. She had no time to tell him they needed to get back down to the track and put him on Thistle Queen.

'Leave that – you won't need that,' said Blue Eyes, who knew nothing about the police, or anything that had happened to Mary and Jesus before the morning they'd met on Bourke Street. 'Come with me. Quick.'

He didn't know how, but Jesus thought Blue Eyes must have known all about his troubles, and so she must have a plan for their escape. So he did what he was told.

If anyone in the overjoyed crowd had been watching for it, they would have seen Thistle Queen switching jockeys. But nobody noticed. When the horses came off the track, the Captain pulled his horse from the procession, so he could check his jockey for injuries.

'Quick,' he said. 'Get down off there.'

'Did you bloody see that, Captain?' Mary came out of the saddle with a leap. Her blood was pumping from the race and she was still drunk on the speed.

'I did,' he said. 'Let's have a look at ya.'

The wind had blown the dirt and grass from her face but there was still enough of a gash to show where she'd landed. Yet there was nothing wrong with her. Far from it. She was jumping with excitement.

'We've got to do a swap,' the Captain told her. 'Understand?' And she did. He knew he wouldn't need to explain the plan.

They could see Blue Eyes running towards them with Jesus.

'Soon as they get her, you bugger off,' the Captain said, talking out of the side of his mouth and looking around to see who was watching. But they were all too interested in the horses and their betting tickets.

'Mate, were you watching? Did ya see?' Mary asked Jesus when he arrived. For a moment, Thistle Queen had two jockeys. Both the same height and skinny with green silks.

Jesus didn't have the chance to answer.

'Bugger off, I told ya,' the Captain broke in. 'Get up to the stalls. Run,' he said to Mary before he turned to Jesus. 'Get ya bum in the saddle, as fast as you can.'

Jesus didn't know what was happening, and before he could think or ask he was on Harry Horse being led through the crowd to the front of the grandstand, where he could see a metal box surrounded by guns and police.

That's when Jesus began to doubt the plan.

*

Mary's legs pushed her up the hill. Her head was still giddy from the race and she thought she was alone. But she wasn't, she was being chased.

She got to the stall, closed her eyes and let out a howl. It was the loudest sound she'd made in her life. Every emotion she'd been feeling in the last twenty minutes came out with one noise. Panic, delight, physical pain, disappointment, determination, triumph. It all came sprinting out of her.

When Mary opened her eyes, the thing that had been chasing her up the hill jumped at her.

It was Harry Logan's dog.

'Mate! What the bloody hell are you doin' here?'

The dog put its paws on her stomach and barked, as it accepted every pat, rub and word of welcome.

Mary had thought he'd been kicked to death by the Brown Coats, and she'd never feel the soft fur of his face again, but if ever there was a day for the impossible to happen, it was today. She'd already had a miracle on the track, and now her old mate, the dog, was still alive.

'Mate, hey, guess what. I think we just bloody won the Melbourne Cup. How 'bout that one, hey?'

The reunion continued for a few seconds more, before Mary realised the implications of the dog's appearance.

'Hang on a sec, where's the boss? He here too?'

It was no wonder Jesus looked the way he did. But it couldn't just be Harry Logan who'd made him so frightened. There had to be something else. Or someone else.

Mary looked around, trying to think, and on the straw she saw the gun of Andre Noble.

*

In front of the grandstand, Donovan was getting ready for his great show. The steward from the finishing post hadn't told him the winner yet. He'd asked him not to. He wanted to save it for the final bit of drama. He had Thistle Queen and Archer put on the grass in front and asked the police to place the box of gold in the middle on a table. He wanted everyone to see it. And he made sure the constabulary were standing guard.

Inspector Frederick Rourke was still so delighted with the thought of winning his bet that he offered to do the job himself, and asked Tom Addington and Harry to stand with him.

Harry was so numb from the surprises that he just did as ordered. And as he stood beside the box of gold, with his rifle and revolver, he looked across at his grey horse that was now just twenty feet away. It was standing next to an old man with a white beard and a tiny child with sharp blue eyes at the bridle.

The animal turned its perfect head and looked at her old master. Harry Logan almost expected a wink. Then he looked at the horse's jockey, expecting it to be Mary, but it wasn't. Harry tried to see under the jockey's cap. There was a white neck and

271

white chin, and then the head turned just enough to give Harry a better look. It was the boy. It was Jesus Whitetree!

And now the insanity of Constable Harry Logan was complete. He wanted to shout out and make the world stop. Just for a few minutes. So he could think and try to understand what the bloody hell was going on.

But the world wouldn't stop. The world was too excited for the result. Thousands gathered around the grandstand for the announcement, pushing forward and standing up on their toes to see. Some were still on the grass, some on the track, and some still up in the stand.

'Harry, Harry?' Inspector Rourke said, flicking a hand in front of his Constable's face. 'What's wrong with ya? Up straight, mate. The boss is watching.'

In the stand, Donovan stood in the middle of the front row and motioned to the crowd for silence. He was overdoing the drama, but there would be no complaints. Everyone was intoxicated, either from the grog or the spectacle of the race. Donovan tried to make his voice boom with authority as he announced the two horses and their teams. He introduced Archer, emphasising with syrupy pride that it had come all the way from 'Sydney town'. Then the trainer, an impressive-looking young man with the grand name of Etienne De Mestre, and the jockey, John Cutts. The people applauded and Cutts waved and accepted the glory as if he'd already won.

'And to my left . . .' Donovan said. He was starting to sound more like he was preparing the crowd for a boxing match. 'My lords, ladies and gentlemen, trainer Captain Laurence Flynn, and with him, the jockey of the mighty local hero Thistle Queen, Mr Harry Grey!'

Harry Logan could only stand still and hope that one day he would understand what was happening. Harry Grey? Who the hell was Harry Grey?

'I shall now call for the result of the Melbourne Cup,' trumpeted Donovan, and he waved to the steward to come to him with the winner's name. The official walked very slowly, as though he was travelling down a church aisle to be married.

Donovan leaned forward, the steward whispered to him, and Donovan nodded his understanding. He called for silence again, but he didn't need to. The crowd was ready to hear the name.

Donovan checked the approving faces of the Chief Commissioner and the Governor, before turning back to the crowd. He held out his arms like he was about to sing. The people didn't know what was coming. It had been a close race. It could be anyone's. The only thing they didn't expect was the blast of gunfire.

But that's what they got.

*

In the weeks before the Cup, as the Pink Gang moved along the coast, Samuel LaBat thought of little else but the robbery and how writing the story would move him into immortality. He imagined letting the red ink flow as he described the weapons and the fear and the gold. Yet he didn't want it to be just a rowdy affair – there needed to be some grace, drama and poetry. That's how you make a proper story.

But before there could be any words, there needed to be a strong plan. The gang would be outnumbered and outgunned, so they must have a strategy of surprise and deception.

The twins were to arrive first and pose as entertainers for the children, and when the time was right, they were to grab one as a hostage. Or maybe two. And as the Fox boys moved through the crowd, Mother Pink and Camilla would seat themselves in the grandstand, just behind the Governor. Camilla would carry a small calibre revolver and Mother a shotgun that she'd stolen from a farmhouse near Geelong. She'd sawn the double barrels down to the stock and cut off the butt, so she could hide it like a long handgun under her dress, and strapped it to her plump thigh with two rose-coloured garter belts. When she was ready, she'd pull it out and stick it in the Governor's face.

LaBat and Carrigan were to arrive just as well-armed, but by wagon. It was a vehicle they'd permanently borrowed from the same place Mother got her shotgun, and had once been used to transport pigs. It had high wooden sides that could act as cover if there was any shooting. It was perfect for the job, but unfortunately still carried the assaulting stink of pig shit.

Jack Pink himself was the last part of the plan. The bushranger was to ride in hard, fire a shot into the air, and then give the crowd a speech. LaBat had written the words for his leader, and they were magnificent. It would make Jack sound like a Shakespearean king, yet it was not without a certain delicate humility.

Jack would tell the people of the Melbourne Cup about how he was just a simple boy from the country, and how the police had harassed his family without mercy or justice, and that the races were just a sport run by the highborn to take money from the purses of the working classes.

It was beautiful, and LaBat knew, when the speech was done, that everyone in the crowd would be cheering for Jack to get away with the gold. It would be as though he was claiming it on behalf of all of them.

The plan was perfect. It had surprise, deception, fear and inspiration. And no-one needed to die. There'd just be a wagon full of gold, and a bloody great story.

But that's not what happened.

When the day was over, the gang would have the gold all right. And three people would be dead.

*

The plan went to hell fast, and the chaos began with Mother Pink.

She and Camilla found good seats just behind the Governor, with a clear aim to the back of his head. The women weren't the drunkest at the Melbourne Cup, but they'd consumed enough wine to make most things funny, as they giggled their way through the afternoon.

Every few minutes, Mother would feel down between her legs to touch the shotgun with her finger. The cold metal had been warmed by her flesh, and the stroke was almost sensual.

When the race finished, Mother and Camilla cheered along with the crowd and waited for the result. And waited. Where was the gold? The gang had worked too bloody hard to hang about like this. But just as Mother's impatience peaked, the metal box arrived. She smiled as she watched three stupid policemen struggle to carry the heavy treasure. When it was time for the gang to take it away, she thought, they would only need Carrigan.

The two winning horses were brought to the front with the gold, and a man in a top hat began making announcements.

Mother touched her weapon again and thought about what she needed to do. She was to fire one shot in the air and aim the next at the Governor's skull. The gun had two hammers that she'd need to pull all the way back to cock them in place. They were stiff, and though Jack had given them a good oil, they were still tough work for her old thumbs.

This was it. It was time. Mother Pink looked at Camilla.

'Are you ready for this, lovely one?'

'Yes, Mother,' she said and gave a sure smile that made Mother even more excited for what was to come.

Then with far more speed than she intended, Mother reached under her dress and grabbed the shotgun, but as she pulled it out from the garter belts, both hammers caught in the lace of her new dress. She began fiddling to get it out and was soon wrestling with it like she was trying to grab a flapping bird in a box. Mother rarely swore but she now muttered the worst word she knew.

When she finally got the weapon free, Mother flicked away the hair that had fallen across her face and put both thumbs on the hammers, trying to cock both barrels at once. Camilla went to help but she was waved away by an annoyed hand. As Mother tried again, the shotgun was aiming at the man right in front of her, only inches away. He was a wool merchant from Bendigo, and if her thumb had slipped, he'd never have known why the sunny day suddenly went black. But despite the arthritic throb in her knuckles, she managed to get the hammers to click where they needed to be.

Mother Pink puffed three quick breaths before she whispered the second worst swear word she knew.

'Come on, old girl, come on,' she said to herself. 'This is the fun part, remember.'

She pointed the gun towards the roof of the grandstand, closed her eyes and pulled down on the trigger. The sound was monstrous. Far louder than she remembered. And Mother realised she'd used too many fingers and accidentally let off both barrels at once. The force of the double blast ripped the gun from her hands, and the noise deafened everyone around her, including Camilla and herself.

Mother elbowed the girl and signalled for her to lift her revolver to the crowd, but Camilla had turned away and was holding her ears in pain and shock. Mother then fumbled under her seat to find the shotgun. She was no longer catching birds, she was now like a woman standing in a river trying to grab a swimming cod. She finally found the weapon, but as she stood up it caught her lace again. There was more wrestling to get it free before she tried to break it open for reloading.

Mother hadn't practised reloading the shotgun, and though she had extra cartridges in her purse, she didn't think she'd need them, and now they were too hard to find under her liquor flask and make-up. After two unsuccessful attempts, she abandoned the chunky weapon and grabbed Camilla's revolver.

When Eddie Donovan heard the blast, he stopped right in the middle of announcing the winner. He turned to look back at the grandstand. It was a frantic sight.

Harry Logan looked up too, and like the rest of the crowd, he had no idea what was happening. There was a loud blast and some commotion, but it could have been part of the show, and while he tried to get a better look, Mother started screaming.

'Bail up, you mongrel bastards!' Mother shouted. She was far louder than she needed to be, but it felt like her head was underwater and she couldn't even hear her own voice. 'Bail up! Come on! Or I'll bloody put a ball in your Government's head!'

She said 'Government' instead of 'Governor', but when His Excellency saw the revolver pointed at him from three rows behind, he soon understood. And in a move that would have been quick for a man twenty years younger, he covered his face with his hands and dropped down to use his seat as cover, while those around him scrambled to escape the revolver's aim.

'Shit!' cried Mother, as she lost him under the seat. He was supposed to bloody well stay still. 'Get up, ya mongrel.'

In front of the grandstand, while everyone was trying to understand what they were seeing, a wagon cut through the parting crowd, carrying a scruffy man and a giant.

LaBat and Carrigan pulled up on the grass in front of the gold, and with far more skill than the gang's matriarch, LaBat produced two revolvers. One he pointed at the crowd and the other at the three policemen around the metal box. He could hear Mother screaming and swearing from above, and she sounded more enthusiastic than he'd expected. He couldn't see the Fox twins, but he couldn't look for them – he had to keep his eyes on the three armed policemen. He could only hope everyone was doing their jobs.

Everything would be all right, LaBat thought, Jack Pink would be here soon.

*

Harry Logan's brain was still ruffled from lack of sleep and the discovery of Mary, Jesus and his horse at the Melbourne Cup. But now there was gunfire and a revolver was being pointed at him.

The sight of the scraggy man and the big bloke made his skin turn like ice. But his fear wasn't just for himself. He was frightened for all the faces he could see – astonished women, confused children and men who didn't deserve to have guns poked at their families.

'Don't move!' Harry called out to the spectators, putting out a hand like he was trying to calm a spooked animal. It was the first thing he could think to say. 'Just stay still. Everybody. Don't move.'

'That's right, don't bloody move,' LaBat said, aiming at Harry's face. 'You're a smart bloke, hey? But don't get too bloody smart, though, will ya? That clever brain might get a bullet in it.' It was a good line, and LaBat hoped he'd remember it for later when he was writing the story by the fire. 'Drop that rifle, smart bloke. Put it down. And go easy.'

It took a moment for the words to make sense in Harry's head, but he did as he was told. He bent his knees and lay the carbine on the grass.

'And get those hands up. All three of ya. Up, up, up.'

Harry, Sergeant Tom Addington and Inspector Frederick Rourke lifted their hands to their shoulders.

'Everyone be still,' said Rourke, echoing his Constable, and his nose twitched with the sudden stink of pig manure. Despite the distractions of the day's racing and a mild addiction to gambling, Rourke was a hard and reliable policeman – and apart from the

Chief Commissioner in the grandstand, he was the highest rank at the course. Although rank meant very little when loaded guns were being pointed.

In a second, he knew what was happening. It was a robbery and these people wanted the gold. So it was his job to make sure it remained just a robbery. Not a murder. Not an assault. Just a robbery. There should be no blood. He tried to calm the situation, but with that woman screaming in the grandstand, it was going to be difficult. The sound of it echoed over the crowd in the late afternoon. And she was yelling things that didn't sound like words. She was far more like a trapped animal than a woman.

LaBat had first been pleased with the way he'd started the hold-up. He'd pulled up the wagon just where it needed to be, his aim was good and steady, and he'd said a couple of memorable lines. But now it was more than a minute later and he felt the panic of the moment. Jack was late, Mother didn't sound in control of her hostage in the stand, he couldn't see the twins, and he was worried that Carrigan's last dose of opium was too much. He could feel the big man slumping at his side. Labat began to worry that the only story he would tell from the day was how he ended up in jail with no Melbourne Cup gold to show for it.

But then he heard the thump of Jack's horse behind him, and the gasps of the unsettled crowd as the bushranger arrived at the front of the grandstand with his revolver drawn.

Bloody hell, thought LaBat, as the black horse spun twice for the audience, what a magnificent entrance.

*

When he got to the front of the grandstand, Jack looked around for his mother. It had been a long day waiting to be with her again. He was hoping to see her standing bold and lethal with her shotgun pointed at the head of the Governor. Instead, she was screeching like a mad woman and climbing over the seats. Her arms were thrashing and she was struggling with Camilla. They were a scramble of limbs, hair and white lace.

He looked at LaBat, who was holding up his revolvers. The expression on the writer's face was one of relief and expectation. Jack knew he needed to take command of the robbery and that he should start talking, but he couldn't remember the first line of the great speech.

The tall, strong bushranger, who could outshoot, outride and out-punch anyone south of the Murray River, felt alone and foolish in front of the thousands of faces staring at him. And with Mother still crying out from above, his embarrassment soon became fear. There was no sun. It was like night. As dark as the world can be.

So Jack did the only thing he could think to do. He lifted his revolver, pulled back the hammer, and fired into the belly of the nearest policeman.

*

The crowd screamed and scattered. A thousand ran up the hill, others rushed around the side of the grandstand, while those in the seats above either ran back into the dining-rooms or jumped over the barriers to escape. Another thousand ran onto the track and sprinted in the same direction as the horses had twenty minutes before, as though it were some crazed re-creation of the race. The atmosphere that had been so exciting and blissful only minutes before was now thick with fear.

Eddie Donovan and his wife leapt from the side of the grandstand and his ankles felt like they'd been pulled out of his feet when he landed. He knew he was too old to jump from such a height, but he was also too young to be shot and killed.

The Captain yelled at his Cockies to run and they did what they were told, except Jesus and Blue Eyes who stayed beside him with Thistle Queen.

Constable Harry Logan didn't run and he didn't cry out. He didn't a make sound. He'd been shot in the gut.

Harry had watched the man on the black horse arrive. It was a frightening sight, and not just because of the guns and confusion, but because Harry now knew who was responsible. It was Jack Pink. And the crazed female in the stand could only be Mother Pink.

Fate had twice helped Harry Logan avoid the Pink Gang. Once in Mull Creek after they'd put a knife to a baby's throat, and the second time when they'd set the Bacchus Marsh church on fire and blasted a path out of town. But there was no avoiding them today.

Just like his Inspector, Harry hoped the gang were only there for the gold. So they would let them have it. Harry had no reckless illusions of starting a gunfight or trying to save the prize.

Bugger the gold.

But with no warning, Jack Pink had lifted his gun and aimed at Harry. The moment froze and Harry felt like he'd walked through the front door of hell and the devil was pointing him out for some special torture. Then the devil fired and the gun disappeared in its own cloud, and an orange flash came from the smoke.

Harry's eyes and ears told him that he'd been shot. And his skin was alerted to a sharp poke just under his ribs. But his brain tried to tell him something different.

'Nah, you're right, Harry, old mate,' he told himself. 'It missed you by a mile. Not a worry.'

And he stood for a moment, still believing his brain and feeling a warm numbness in his belly. But then came another feeling. It was as if someone had slipped a dying ember under his skin and started puffing on it to make it glow. The glow became a flame, and the flame set his body on fire, before his legs buckled from the pain. And as Harry fell, Tom Addington caught him and lowered him down.

Just like everyone else at Flemington, Samuel LaBat had never seen a man get shot before. It was not beautiful. There was no grace and no poetry. It was nothing like he'd expected, or wanted. But there was no time for disappointment or to wonder how he could describe it better in red ink. And there was no time to wonder why Jack had done it.

Mother Pink had abandoned hope of holding the Governor for a hostage. She ran down to the steps and to the front of the grandstand to be with her boy, waving the revolver and scream-ing at anyone in her way, and dragging Camilla, who was still deaf and stunned from the double blast of Mother's shotgun.

'Get the bloody gold! Get it!' Mother yelled at Carrigan, pointing at the metal box. The big man came to life, like a cattle dog that only took commands from one master. He climbed off the wagon and scooped up the box in his massive arms and loaded it in back behind Labat. They had the gold, they just needed to get away.

But as Carrigan put it down, the old prostitute did something that got her killed. Mother Pink lifted her gun to cover Carrigan, and aimed it at the two policemen kneeling over the body of their comrade. She had no intention of firing, but Inspector Frederick Rourke didn't know that. He'd just watched his Constable gunned down, so he plucked the revolver from his belt at the sight of Mother's weapon. He was a lean man and quick, and despite never being in a gunfight, he'd been a lot like Jesus in his youth and practised each day when he was alone.

The Inspector's first shot was a true one, hitting Mother in the chest, an inch above the lace that covered her breasts. There was no blood at first, just a small black mark. She kept her gun raised and Rourke fired again and it hit closer to the heart. The woman had no time to feel the same glowing embers as Harry; instead, her flames raced over her like a bushfire in a north wind, and she fell back dead.

Although the racecourse was covered with the noise of gunshots and panic, everyone still heard the howl of misery that came from Jack Pink when he saw his mother killed. It was a long single cry that echoed off the grandstand and out across the track.

Jack jumped from his horse and let his gun fall to the grass as he ran to his mother's body.

'Jack, Jack,' LaBat said over and over, trying to get the bushranger's attention back onto the robbery. But he knew his words would be useless. And he knew Jack would be nothing without his mother. Fast Jack Pink was no longer a part of the plan. There was no plan anymore. Mother was gone, the twins had disappeared and Camilla was crying with her hands over her ears.

LaBat felt like a playwright who had tried to create a beautiful scene but none of the actors knew their parts.

He only had Carrigan left. The giant lifted Mother with the same drugged expression as he'd carried the gold, only this cargo had Jack slumped over it looking for a hint of life. He lay the body down in the dry pig shit and Jack followed her in.

Jesus Whitetree hadn't moved from his spot. He was still there with the Captain, Blue Eyes and Harry Horse in front of the grandstand. He didn't know why they'd stayed. Perhaps because the gun in the hand of the wagon man was waving at them. Or maybe it was because Jesus didn't feel as though he was really there. It was as if he was still watching everything from the hill. But when he saw the kind Constable Harry Logan get shot, he was back in his own body again. And he wished, more than anything the world could give him, that he had his gun in his hand, and that he knew where Mary was.

Perhaps, Jesus thought, each gun was only supposed to save a person once, and his had already saved Mary and Harry and himself. Maybe it was all used up. He didn't know. But he knew there were five shots left in the gun once owned by Andre Noble.

*

Before Harry and Mother Pink were shot, Mary was in the stable and couldn't sit still. She was worried about seeing the dog, and her head rolled with questions. What was Harry doing here?

What was he looking for? Did he just like the races? He didn't look like the kind of bloke who liked the races.

But until a few months ago, Mary had never been to a real race herself, so maybe she didn't know what all racing people looked like. And if the Constable boss was here, he'd have seen his old horse, for sure. Harry was a bit bloody hopeless and always got lost, but he still had strong eyes and would've found his grey animal.

She wished she could see his face. Mary knew she'd only have to look at Harry to know if he was chasing her.

And while Mary worried about the dangers of the afternoon, and the new troubles that may come for her and Jesus, her body was still jumping from the race. She'd loved every moment of it, even the fall that smashed her head into the ground. She loved chasing down the pack, and the look on the dumb jockeys' faces when she moved through, and the dash to the finish.

She wanted to win. She wanted it than more anything she could imagine. More than Jesus wanted gold. Because if she won, it would always be hers. It would always be true. If she had irons on her ankles again, it would be true. If she was back with the bloody farmer, or in the cold cell with no sky at Mull Creek, it would be true. Even if she was dead, it would be true. She would have won the Melbourne Cup.

So she listened for the announcement. And when Mother's shotgun blasted, Mary thought it was a cannon. She'd never seen a cannon fired, but she'd been told they were for special days. And what could be more big and special than today?

Then there were more cannons and the crowd cheered and squealed with the joy of the occasion. It wasn't until the howl of Jack Pink that Mary knew something was wrong. The dog gave a whimper and its tail stopped moving, and the vibration of Jack's cry travelled up through the ground.

Mary came out from the stall to see people running. There were hundreds of them and she knew they were terrified and running from something awful. The dog took off down the hill, weaving between the legs coming towards him, and Mary turned back, grabbed Andre Noble's gun and ran after him. She could smell the stink of danger as she got to the side of the grandstand and saw the Captain's children scattering with the crowd.

When Mary came around the corner, the first thing she saw was a giant man carrying a woman flopped across his arms, and another man with a long beard trying to grab the woman's head. Then she saw Harry Logan. He was on the grass, and Mary knew that one of the shots she'd heard was for him. He was holding his belly and the blood on his finger was darker than any blood she'd ever seen before.

Every face Mary could see was just as frightened as hers. Jesus, the Captain, the policemen, including the cruel one she recognised from Mull Creek, Blue Eyes, a man in a wagon with two revolvers, and everyone running away.

They were all terrified.

Mary thought about lifting up the gun in her hand. But she didn't know where to aim. Apart from her obvious mates, anyone else could have been a friend or enemy. So she kept it at her side.

*

In the wagon, Samuel LaBat felt a wet patch between his legs and realised he was pissing his own pants. It was warm for a moment and then turned cold when it found the air. He had thought he would feel powerful at this moment, but he didn't. All he could do was keep his guns on the police.

'Go!' Inspector Rourke said, aiming his revolver at LaBat and moving to stand in front of Harry and the others. 'You have what you came for! Now go! No-one else needs to go down!'

Rourke had a clear shot at LaBat but he wouldn't take it. It was too dangerous. He still had to worry about Jack Pink. Though he'd never seen him before, and he was now in the back of the wagon with his mother, Rourke had heard enough to know he would lose any gunfight or fistfight with the bushranger. So it was better to just keep talking.

'Look, just turn your wagon and leave here,' Rourke said, lowering his voice to LaBat. 'You've got the box. I don't care about the gold. I won't shoot. We will let you leave.'

'Drop that gun,' LaBat tried to demand.

'No, I can't do that.' Rourke could hear the shaking in LaBat's voice, and it made the Inspector more frightened of what the man could do. 'But I won't shoot. Not if you go.'

'Drop ya gun.' LaBat's voice almost broke with tears.

'No. But it will be all right. We won't shoot. We won't ride after you. We'll all just stay here. The path is clear. You will be allowed to pass.'

Frederick Rourke felt better hearing his own voice. It reminded him that he was still alive. He wanted to swear and scream and run, but he couldn't. He could hear his constable groan from his wound and the sergeant comforting him, and Rourke also knew there were children behind him. So he had to keep using his words. And it was working. He could see the scruffy man thinking, and that he was being told he could leave and not get killed. Rourke knew that was all he'd be thinking about. The man was frightened and just wanted to live. And this policeman was telling him he could.

Inspector Rourke repeated his calm plan and his voice was almost a whisper now. LaBat darted his eyes around and found Carrigan.

'Get in,' LaBat said and the big man did. Then he found Camilla. She was clutching her ear and still sobbing from the confusion. 'Get the horse. Get Jack's horse,' he told her. LaBat had to say it five more times before she moved and climbed into the saddle. She looked like a crying child who had been forced into riding lessons. To hell with the twins, LaBat thought, wherever they were.

'Go now,' Rourke said again. He tried to tell himself to stop talking. The gang looked as if they were preparing to go, and if he kept talking he might just anger them, so Rourke pushed his tongue into the back of his teeth to keep it still.

LaBat gave one of his revolvers to Carrigan, who held it more like a stick than a gun, then LaBat grabbed the reins to turn the wagon around. He fumbled at the leather straps but Rourke held up a hand to show they could take as much time as they needed. All was well, he said without words. No hurry. Just go.

Thistle Queen had been still. Although Archer had been spooked by the blast of Mother's shotgun, the grey didn't move. She stayed with the Captain, Jesus and Blue Eyes, who were all just as still, and grateful the policeman was doing his job so well. They didn't see Mary standing behind them. No-one had time to think about where other people were, they could only think about the pointing guns, the shots fired, and the bodies that had fallen to the ground, dead or wounded.

As the gang's wagon started to turn, the afternoon became quiet. All they could hear was the squeak of the ungreased wheels under the load of gold sovereigns and bodies.

But then Mary heard stamping feet behind her, and she turned to see two enormous babies. She was being grabbed again, but this time the men weren't Brown Coats coming from the dark; instead, their chubby hands were coming at her from a bright sky.

Before she could lift the revolver or have another thought, she saw the flash of a knife and one of them grabbed her and put the blade to her neck. And the gun dropped from her hand.

The other baby-man had a revolver but it was small and looked like a toy in his fat fingers. He waved it at the Captain and Jesus to keep them back.

'Yes! Yes! Yes!' cried out LaBat. He was almost hysterical. He was winning again. He had no bloody idea where the twins had been, but they were here now.

'Yes!' he called to them. 'Get a child! But no, not that one, she's worth nothing to us, Wellington! No! Get that other one!' LaBat pointed at Blue Eyes and the twin moved fast to follow the orders. Wellington flung Mary out of his arms, with the blade just missing the side of her neck by half an inch, before he grabbed Blue Eyes and put the tip to her throat.

The Captain could only watch and curse his useless hands. He'd rather have been dead than stand there while his Cockies had knives held under their chins. What good is it being big when your bloody hands don't work?

Jesus looked at his revolver on the ground. As much as the Captain wanted hands, Jesus wanted to get that gun. But it was too far away. He'd never make it.

'No, you're not taking the child,' said Rourke, looking between Wellington Fox and LaBat. He tried to maintain his calm tone but was failing. 'Leave the child. You're not taking her. You've got the gold. Just put her down!'

'No!' LaBat screamed back. He had no control over himself. 'You don't say! I say! I say now!' He sounded like an angry child as the piss chilled in his trousers. 'Bring! Bring her!' he said to the twins as they dragged a fighting Blue Eyes to the back of the wagon. Wellington loaded her up and got in too. It was crowded, with Jack, the dead Mother Pink and the gold.

Inspector Rourke tried to negotiate again, but he was outgunned and LaBat wasn't listening anymore.

The wagon rolled towards the hill and Winston tried to climb up onto Jack's horse with his sister. After the first attempt, he handed the gun to Camilla so she could cover them. After four more tries, he was in the saddle and they went off after the wagon.

Inspector Frederick Rourke kept his gun on the gang as they left. The sight was almost comical. On another day, it might have made him laugh, but his constable had been wounded and a small child was kidnapped. Nothing was funny.

The Pink Gang was almost free, and halfway up the hill, when Winston Fox lost the grip of his sister's laced dress and fell from the back of Jack's horse. The animal kicked him in the gut on the way down and he landed on his head. The weight of his solid body snapped his neck and he was dead less than a minute later. There was no room left in the wagon for his corpse, so he was left behind.

When they got to the top, LaBat halted and looked down on the first Melbourne Cup. Two members of his gang were dead and Jack was in the back sobbing and wailing, but at least they had the prize and a hostage. It was time to go. But just as he flicked the reins, Jack Pink stood up in the back, stumbling as he clutched the side of the wagon.

'Listen to me!' he called out to the grandstand.

'Bloody hell,' LaBat muttered to himself. 'It's too late for the speech, Jack. We're done.'

'You will cry!' Jack shouted down. 'All of you! While I live, you will cry!'

*

Harry Logan was dying and the sun was almost gone.

After the Pink Gang left, some spectators started to come out from their hiding places, like dawn lizards over rocks. But they weren't seeking warmth or food, they were looking for an understanding of what had just happened. Most had already escaped the racecourse and would never return. They got out any way they could. They stole horses, hung off coaches, jumped onto moving boats, swam across the river, or just ran through the long grass. Anything to get away from the firing guns. But some had stayed and found a place to hide.

Sadly, of all the people who were still there, none was a doctor. Inspector Rourke had hollered for one to help his constable but he got nothing. Not even a nurse.

Harry lay in the same place he fell. Tom Addington took off his own coat and rolled it up to put under Harry's head. Then he ripped his shirt to make crude bandages.

'Move ya hand, mate,' Tom said to Harry. 'Let's have a look at this.'

Tom lifted Harry's coat to see the wound.

'Shit,' Tom said, putting a scrunched-up right sleeve over the hole in his friend. The cloth soaked it up like it was being lowered into a bucket of black liquid. 'Bugger me.'

'Is that all you got to say?' said Harry, coughing as he talked. 'Well, that doesn't sound too good then, does it?'

'Nah, but you'll be all right.'

Sergeant Tom Addington only had lies to tell as he switched bandages and pressed down to stop the leak.

Harry's face had lost every colour except white, and his skin was bright with sweat. He closed his eyes. It was the only thing that was easy to do. Everything else, like breathing or moving, was either painful or impossible. And the darkness felt good. Then something wet and cool touched his ear hole. He heard a loud sniff and knew it was his dog.

'G'day, mate,' he whispered and kept his eyes shut.

'Boss?' a voice said. 'Constable boss?'

Harry let his mind think it was the dog talking but then he opened his eyes and saw the faces of Mary and Jesus over him.

'How are ya doin', boss?' Mary asked.

They were all he could see. They covered everything. And Harry almost laughed at the sight of them, but all his body would allow was a tiny snorting sound.

'Mary, Mary, Mary,' Harry said over and over a dozen times. 'What the hell are you two doing here?'

'Hey, boss, you're gonna be all right. You'll get fixed.'

Tom Addington almost felt like he'd been shot himself. He couldn't believe what he was seeing. He was already in shock, but now, as his hand drowned in Harry's blood, that skinny kid who he'd whipped in Mull Creek and the native girl were sitting there next to him over his mate's wounded body. The same two wanted for the murders of three mining executives, and who had been on the run for months. He should be putting them in cuffs and locking them in the guard room. But he couldn't. And stranger than anything, Harry Logan wasn't even surprised to see them. Far from it. It was bringing him comfort. What the hell was happening?

'You want something to drink, boss?' Mary asked. She hated seeing him in pain and wanted to do something to help.

'Yes, please.' Harry realised that he did. 'But stay here with me, Mary. Don't go anywhere.'

'Give him nothing to drink,' Tom Addington said with no emotion. 'It's a gut shot. No water.'

Mary didn't reply – she just kept her eyes on Harry.

'Bugger, boss. I wish I had some ginger beer for you. Have you had some? It's bloody good stuff that.'

It was all Mary could think to say. She wanted him to hear her talk. And she smiled just so he could see her smile. Harry Logan was a good bloke, maybe one of the best she would ever know, and his life was leaking out of him. And no-one could help him.

'Boss. Boss.'

'I'm still here, Mary.'

'You remember that big bastard splinter? Do you remember that?'

'I do,' he said and let his eyes close.

'Look at me. Do you remember? At the fire?'

'Yes.'

'We got that mongrel out. You'll be better, boss. You'll be better again.'

'Constable?' said Jesus. He had no story to tell, he just wanted the kind policeman to know he was there. 'Are you good?'

'Good as gold.'

*

The Captain had been all over the course gathering up his Cockies, and now he was chasing the Inspector to make a plan to get Blue Eyes back. The old man wanted to weep at the thought of her being taken by low men like this. They had already shot a policeman for nothing. What would they do to a child? But he didn't have time to waste with tears.

Eddie Donovan had also been walking around. He was still dazed from the event and limping from his fall. He stood near the dying policeman and looked at the bloodied cloth around him. What a magnificent day it could have been. And what a terrible day it was.

A young man approached Donovan. He was tall and well dressed, and he was smiling as though he had just arrived and was untouched by anything that had happened.

'Hey, Mr Donovan, who won the race?'

'What?' said Donovan. 'What did you just say?'

'The race? The Cup? Who won it?'

Donovan answered without thinking and with no joy. 'The grey did. Thistle Queen won the Cup.'

Jesus and Mary heard the answer and looked at each other. They had done it. They had won the gold. But they knew they'd never see it. It was long gone over the hill. And soon the Sergeant of Mull Creek would have them back in chains.

Harry whispered Mary's name again.

'What is it, boss? You can't have water. You'll be better soon.'

'Mary,' he said and opened his eyes to see her and Jesus and the shirtless Tom Addington. 'What the hell are you two doing? You should be gone.'

'It's all right, boss.'

'Why didn't you run? Why are you here?'

'We're here for the Melbourne Cup,' Jesus answered.

'And did you hear that?' Mary said. 'We won the bugger.'

Mary shrugged at him and grinned and Harry could only snort another laugh.

'And we were on your old horse, boss. She's a bloody cracker, that one. Did you see her running? She's just over there, see?'

'I know,' Harry whispered and his eyes closed. 'I can see her. Alice is there.'

'What's that, boss?'

'Alice. She's in her.'

Harry Logan didn't want to die. The Constable had a strong desire to stay on this earth, if only to hear the story of how Mary and Jesus came to be here.

How did they run off after that awful night and then go on to win the biggest race in the history of the colony on the back of his police horse? He wanted to know. It must have been one hell of a yarn.

And he didn't want to die knowing Mary and Jesus were now

in the kind of trouble that would ruin them. They were set to hang or die in jail. He had to fix it, but he was almost gone.

'Where's Tom?' Harry asked, trying to lift his head.

'I'm here, Harry, mate,' Tom said, coming closer to Harry's face. 'I'm still here. Stop moving.'

The Sergeant and Mary and Jesus stared at each other across Harry's body. Looking like warring tribes over a peace table.

'Tom, leave them alone. Leave these two alone. They didn't do anything. They never did. Leave them.'

'All right, Harry. Don't worry about that now. And don't flamin' move. We're trying to get some help.'

'Leave them. Leave them. Leave them,' he whispered and repeated until the two words became one. 'L'em, l'em. Promise.'

'Yes. Be still now.'

'They never did anything, Tom. Promise me you'll leave them.'

'I promise, mate.'

The sun was almost gone and Mary put her hand on Harry's cheek and she started to cry.

'You need a shave there, boss. That's not like you.'

Harry tried to smile for her, but it didn't show. Mary's hand was soft on his face and he felt the sniff of the dog at his ear.

'Boss??' Her voice sounded like she was running away from him, but her skin didn't leave his cheek. 'Boss? Boss?'

The day had been still until then, but now a breeze came across Harry's face. And it was just like a spring wind should be, yet it didn't carry the scent of blossoms. It was better than any flower. He pulled the soft air into his nostrils and could only smell warm butter and pears.

'Boss? Boss?' Mary was almost too far away to hear, and her voice became something new but familiar.

'Boss? Harry? I can see you, Harry. Can you hear me? Come on now. Come on, sweet one. You'll never get lost again.'

*

The news of Constable Harry Logan's murder, the kidnapping of a small child and the theft of the Melbourne Cup gold spread through the colony like a disease carried on the back of rats.

The papers filled their pages with story after story until there was nothing new to tell. And then they told it over again. Barrels of ink were used to write about the witness accounts, official statements, reactions from the other colonies, descriptions of the gang, possible sightings, reward offerings and criticism of all authorities involved.

Very few embellishments were needed when the story was being told. The images of the baby-men, the screaming woman with the shotgun, the giant carrying the gold, the waft of pig shit and the killings were fanciful and grotesque enough to capture any reader. And there were so many witnesses that the tale remained consistent from telling to telling. This made it even more frightening.

Within days, the story of the Melbourne Cup was in every town, goldfield, farm and sawmill in Victoria. Only those with the most solitary lives were left uninformed.

The story of the race itself was a different matter. Such was the shock of everything that followed, the result was only written as bare fact. The newspaper stories read more like reports on wool prices, rather than an account of one of the greatest rides ever seen. There were no decorations around the words, there was no mention of the fall, and nothing about how the local grey recovered and came from well back to beat the Sydney favourite in a finish that was so close only the official on the line could call it. And the rumour that an Aboriginal girl was riding the winner faded.

There was just a small article on the race, simply announcing Thistle Queen as the winner, with Archer, Mormon and Prince as the place-getters. The Victoria Turf Club had also asked the papers not to include the organisation's name in any of the stories.

And those who had backed the grey didn't brag about their pick. They quietly found their bookie, collected the winnings and folded the notes in their pockets. To flash the money and cheer after such a horrifying day almost felt like they were in on the hold-up.

The kidnapping of the child made all mothers twitch with fear. The newspapers didn't have a name to report. They only knew that it was a girl. Some said she was just an orphan street child, and others heard she was somehow connected with the stable of the winning horse, but that didn't seem likely. One witness told the papers they'd seen the little one's face as she was taken away in the bandits' wagon, and they had never seen a person with eyes so blue.

For most, the worst part was the death of the policeman. Since the colony's beginning, other troopers had been killed in the job. Some drowned, some fell from horses, and others were stabbed by drunks in the dark or shot by surprised thieves. But the killing of Constable Harold John Logan was something worse. It was like a public execution, a savage attack on the community they had all made together.

Most in the colony came from convict blood, and there was still bitterness from the mining riots of '54, but the police were seen as hardworking men who were often paid less than themselves. And though there were good ones and bad, the troopers were not part of the aristocracy. They didn't make the laws or set the taxes.

The word went out that Harry Logan was a fine man who'd been killed by the cold Jack Pink. And his death affected everyone in Victoria. It made them unwell, as though they'd eaten something bad and their bodies were trying to throw it up. They didn't fall asleep as easily or wake as fast. And they were haunted by the words of the bushranger as he escaped. 'You will cry! All of you! While I live, you will cry!' Until he was caught and in his own grave, they wouldn't be safe.

Police Chief Commissioner Standish shared all these feelings, but as the man responsible for upholding the laws, and as the Chairman of the Turf Club, he was also crushed with embarrassment. The day of the Melbourne Cup was supposed to be a glorious festival to celebrate the colony's greatness, but instead the gold prize had been stolen, one of his men murdered, a child taken, and the thousands who came to enjoy the event had run from it screaming in fear.

And it had all happened in front of the Governor. It was a bloody disaster.

Standish knew the awful news would soon be known by the whole world, and his face blushed red at the thought of Her Majesty Queen Victoria receiving the details as she sat by her fire.

The best he could now hope for was the gang's capture and some fast, hard justice. He demanded that the next delivery of news to London be about trials and hangings.

So he needed someone well motivated for the job of finding the Pinks. Inspector Frederick Rourke was to be his man.

Until the Melbourne Cup, Rourke's career as a policeman had been unremarkable, but now he was the day's only hero. The official reports recorded the Inspector's calm manner and leadership as he negotiated with the gang, and how he took down Mother Pink before they had the chance to kill again. Some of Melbourne's old crooks had tried to muddy the policeman's actions by spreading a story that Mother Pink was unarmed, and was executed just for the amusement of the toffs in the grandstand. But there were too many witnesses for the rumour to survive. So Frederick Rourke was given the job.

He began by collecting intelligence on the gang. From the blood-hungry Jack Pink to Samuel Henri LaBat, the horse thief with the weak bladder, Rourke had a file on each. Even the dead ones. And then it was time to track them.

Rourke was a city man who'd spent little time in the bush. He was born with the stink of the streets and had even been proudly ignorant of anything that happened out in the fresher air. So he needed a country man. That was Sergeant Tom Addington.

Addington was still jolted by the events of the Melbourne Cup. He hadn't returned to duty nor had he made the journey back to Mull Creek. After the race, he wrote the required reports, was interviewed by superior officers, and then spent his days and nights swallowing cheap rum at a rotation of Melbourne's public houses.

Addington had seen dead bodies before. He'd even watched a man killed by a falling branch when he was a boy. But he'd never sat with someone and seen their eyes change from life to death. And so much blood came from Harry's gut that he couldn't believe it would fit into just one man. Also, he and Harry were wearing the same uniform. It was like watching himself die, and the image festered in his head. He wondered if all soldiers felt that way when they were surrounded by lifeless bodies dressed in the same colours.

And he couldn't stop thinking about the dim boy who called himself Jesus and that native girl. They were right in front of him. If it had been a couple of months earlier, he would have taken them both by the neck and had them in cuffs without another thought. But with his dying mate between them, he could do nothing. And the promise he made to Harry was like a ghost that followed him into every room. He couldn't return to Mull Creek. The Brown Coats would know. They knew everything. And they controlled everything in his life. The food he ate, the bed he rested in, and every step he walked in Mull Creek's dirt streets.

Jesus and Mary, and his promise to Harry, had made him a man without a home.

When the rum stopped working, Tom Addington went to a doctor. He was careful to find a surgery away from the main streets and he kept his face down as he entered. The physician described him as being 'highly disturbed', but had no tonic for him other than 'bed rest'. Tom could have told him that being still in a bed only heightened his disturbance.

So he returned to the rum. And it was in the darkest of Tom Addington's public houses that Frederick Rourke found him.

The Inspector bought the Sergeant a large pour of dark liquid from the bar and watched him drink it in one desperate swallow.

'I hope you like that, Addington. Because it's your last for a while. Time to work.'

For their search party, Rourke and Addington enlisted three bush constables who always rode together. They weren't brothers, but the mistake was often made. They assembled along with two black trackers, one old and one young, and a man from the detective branch who wore glasses and had been overfed by his second wife.

And so on the last spring day of 1861, with Inspector Frederick Rourke leading, the eight men rode into an orange sun to find the murdering, thieving kidnappers from the first Melbourne Cup.

*

Back at the Captain's stable, the breakfasts were no longer noisy and cheerful. The children woke and worked in silence, and the Captain moved like his legs were becoming infected by the same accursed affliction that had taken his hands years ago.

The horses were fed and exercised as usual, but it was only from necessity. They were not trained for any coming races and when they ran the track at dawn, it was without the black watch of Blue Eyes to judge them.

And though the weather was warm and almost perfect, and they'd just won the Melbourne Cup together, they all felt like they'd lost everything.

Mary swore less and spent her days trying not to forget her mighty ride. She'd never felt anything like it before. It was as though her body had been transformed into lightning. And she wished there was some way she could watch herself in the race, just like Jesus had from the hill.

But the memory dimmed a little more with every new morning. Mary tried to keep it alive by standing alone in the stable with Harry Horse. She'd pretend to brush the coat, but instead she'd press her nose against the grey body, breathing in the animal's gentle blend of hair, skin and sweat. Sometimes it was enough to take her to a better place, where the memories of them running together would flick at her as fast as cinders from a spitting fire. But other times, no matter how much she filled her nostrils, no good thoughts would come.

Other memories, the bad ones, were always there. They never stopped spitting. She could see Harry on the grass and his blood and the feeling of being grabbed by the baby-man and then watching him take Blue Eyes. And the way she looked when they took her away.

Why were the good ones hard to remember and the bad ones impossible to forget? Why did it have to be like that?

And while Mary was trying to tame her memories, Jesus was feeling something new: anger. With all the life he'd lived in these fifty years, he could never remember feeling angry. He'd been hungry, lost, injured, lonely, determined and often confused, but he was now feeling true and helpless rage.

Even when he and Mary were grabbed by the Brown Coats, he didn't remember feeling this anger. He was just desperate to stop them. And when he'd killed the man with the cloud face, it wasn't wrath. It was from fear and protection.

But now he was angry. And he no longer wanted to use the five remaining shots in Andre Noble's to defend, he wanted them for justice. He wanted to avenge the killing of the kind constable, to bring Blue Eyes home, and get back their gold.

The gold, the gold, Jesus thought with his hands vibrating as fists. He was the owner of more gold than he could have imagined. A thousand pieces of it. A box full. So much that it needed a giant to carry it away. It was his. And it was theirs. They could have bought softer beds and sweeter food and bigger stables, and he and Mary could have gone anywhere they wanted, but it was gone. Someone else was using it for a better life.

He'd never even got to touch it, or find out if it had a smell.

Jesus wished that it wasn't really his. He wished they'd never won. And then it would be just like every other piece of gold in the world, underground or at the bottom of a river or in someone else's pockets. But knowing it was his, and that it was gone, implanted a violent frustration in his bones.

One evening, when it was time to eat, Jesus and Mary remained outside. They sat on the fence, listening to the horses settle and the insects wake up, as Harry's dog wandered about for a final pee and sniff before bed.

Mary told Jesus how she was sad. He told her he was angry. And they looked out at the size of the world in the soft light of the ending day. They wanted to wake early and find the killers and the thieves and make everything right that had gone wrong, but they just didn't know where to start looking.

Mary asked him, 'What's the bloody good of having a gun and a saddle and the fastest horse in the world when the bastard world is so big?'

*

In the days after the Melbourne Cup, the Pink Gang travelled without rest. The leather reins barely left the hands of Samuel LaBat, as his eyes dropped closed and sprung open through the days and nights that he drove the wagon.

He pointed the horses towards the north-east. It was a part of the colony that none of the gang were familiar with, so he hoped no police would think to look for them there. It had always been the strategy to travel that way after the robbery, and now it was the only part of the plan that was going as expected. Apart from the gold.

They tried to stay off the roads and tracks as best they could, but the bush wasn't as thick with protection as they'd hoped. And the wagon was weighed down with bodies and gold, so they had only one pace: slow.

They didn't look like a gang of criminals who'd just come from a grand robbery that terrified an entire colony. To anyone seeing them move across the open ground, they were more like a family of travelling carnival folk who were weary from too much travelling and too few carnivals.

Thanks to the warm spring days, the urine in LaBat's pants had long since dried. And he was no longer just the gang's biographer and poet, he was the acting leader. That thought, as he looked over the people now in his charge, was both frightening and embarrassing.

Carrigan sat beside him. His size made the wagon slant, forcing the writer to lean against him. The big man said nothing, but LaBat could feel the body twitch when it needed more opium. He'd been rationing the last of the drug, and was hoping a search of Mother's cold body would produce more, but there was nothing. LaBat feared the twitches would become something far more violent. There was enough opium for a few more days. Perhaps.

Wellington Fox sat at the rear of the wagon with his eyes searching the trees. But he wasn't scanning for danger, he was looking for his brother. And through each day, with every moment, he kept watch as though he expected his twin to run from the scrub to join him.

Camilla Fox remained on Jack's black horse. She was now more alert than she'd been immediately after the Cup, but LaBat had no luck talking to the girl. He couldn't tell if she was silent from grief over her brother's death, or still deafened by the double blast of Mother's shotgun.

Jack Pink, however, was not alert, and he'd hardly opened his eyes since they left Flemington. After he'd cried out to the crowd – something that thrilled LaBat's bones – Jack lay down in the dried pig shit with his dead mother, clinging to the laced corpse like it was a buoy in a rough ocean. He wasn't asleep nor was he awake; he only muttered without proper words and cried without tears.

But LaBat hoped the real Jack Pink was still in there. The writer had once heard of different stages of grief when a loved one was dead. It was something he didn't know himself because he'd never loved anyone enough to miss them. But he'd been told that mourning moved from sadness to anger. So he was hoping Jack's anger was still to come, along with his speed and ferocity. It would be needed if they became surrounded by troopers.

LaBat tried to believe there were still great things coming for him and the gang. Things that could be written in red ink.

But something was siphoning his positive thoughts. Each time he turned to the back of the wagon, the child hostage was staring at him. She sat with her arms folded and resting on her knees. She didn't cry, she didn't ask questions, she made no demands of her captors, she never looked around for a saviour, and her sharp blue eyes never moved from the back of LaBat's head.

He tried to turn fast to catch her out, but she was always looking at him. Even when it was dark.

LaBat decided the child's eyes were the only thing about her that was bright. She was a stupid mute who would bring him no harm. His only concern was a child like that would not be missed by her family. They were probably even glad she was gone. So she'd be worth nothing as a ransom. But she could be used as human armour if they were caught in a stand-off with the police. So as much as LaBat wanted to smack her stupid face and throw her down a ridge, she might yet be useful.

But her glare, pecking at the back of his head, made him tired. So, at the beginning of the sixth night, LaBat stopped the wagon in a dense area and made a fire.

Carrigan climbed down and the angle of the seat became even again without his weight. He then unloaded the gold and put it by the fire. LaBat didn't give the order, but days before the robbery, Mother Pink had instructed the giant.

'Now, Ben, darling, I want you to watch that gold,' she'd said to him. 'That is our life.' And even though the woman had no life anymore, her instruction was still obeyed.

Then Carrigan carried Mother's body and sat it upright on a log by the fire, and Jack followed to sit with her.

The surviving members of the Fox family came close to the

flames. And when everyone was finally settled for sleep, the child stepped from the wagon and sat across from Samuel LaBat.

LaBat knew the witless girl wasn't doing it for warmth or for rest; she was there so she could keep staring at him with those cursed eyes.

He was too tired to care. Just before his mind escaped for the night, he whispered a prayer to any god that could still be bothered with him.

'Please just let me get away it. I can't promise that I won't sin again, but I'll try. Just let me escape with some gold and a good ending to the story.'

*

Wellington Fox was the first to disappear.

Samuel LaBat woke in the morning and the fire was dead ash. The first things he saw were the eyes of the child. It seemed that she hadn't moved. She was staring at him just as she'd been when he went to sleep.

'Imbecile,' he said to her in a hiss. 'Cretin. Do you know what that means? Do you know those words? No, I would not think so.'

She could stare all she liked, he thought. He would win. Why wouldn't he? He was the one with the guns and the gold and the horses. This child only had the stupid eyes in her stupid head, and if he wanted to, he could dig them out of her skull with his fingers.

LaBat sat up, wiping a hand over his face as though he'd dipped it in water to clean himself, and looked at the rest of the gang. The corpse of Mother Pink was against the log, and the soft light of dawn made her look even more dead than the dark. Jack still clung to her, his misery unchanged. Camilla was asleep, curled up like a small child. And Carrigan was asleep in the back of the wagon with his huge legs hanging from the end.

But Wellington Fox was not there. LaBat looked around. Perhaps the twin was collecting wood or trapping their breakfast.

Blue Eyes could have told LaBat that Wellington was not coming back. Three hours before, the baby-man had sat up in the dark and looked into trees, like a dog that heard a rabbit move in a bush. Then he jumped up and ran after it. She heard his feet kicking up the dried leaves and bark until the noise faded.

But only Wellington Fox knew why he ran. He'd been dreaming of his brother, and when he'd woken up he'd seen his twin's image amongst the red gums. It wasn't like a ghost, it was as clear as a reflection. So he'd chased it, and it had kept moving away, like a mirror strapped to the last carriage of a train.

Later, when the sun was at its highest, Carrigan woke. As usual, there was a flicker of violence from the man before he had his first taste of drugs. LaBat had wanted him to move the gold back into the wagon first, but Carrigan was not ready to receive instructions, and LaBat became worried the flicker might become a blaze. So he went to the supply.

There was three days' supply of opium left, maybe more, but as LaBat was measuring out the narcotic breakfast, Carrigan's big arm came around, shoved LaBat and took the lot. And before LaBat could attempt a negotiation, Carrigan had absorbed every drop into his system. He then returned to the wagon to enjoy his coma.

The long day ended. Camilla made herself into a ball near the fire, Jack clung to his rotting mother, the child stared at LaBat, and LaBat prayed once more that he would be delivered from this situation.

*

In the morning, Ben Carrigan was gone. And so was the wagon.

'Where is he?' LaBat asked the staring child.

But Blue Eyes said nothing. She didn't even turn her head in the direction she'd seen the big man disappear just two hours before. She had watched him wake, then search every bag in the camp and frisk the body of Mother Pink, before he got into the wagon and drove it through the trees. Making no more noise than the wind. And he took no gold.

LaBat yelled at the child.

'Curse your bloody gormless face and your dead brain. Answer me. Where is he?'

He kicked the dead fire with his boot and soft ash flew and came down like snow. Some landed on Blue Eyes' lashes but she didn't blink it out. She just kept looking at LaBat.

But as angry as the writer was, he also felt some relief. He had nothing to give Carrigan for the day, and he'd yet to decide what to do about it. LaBat had visions of the giant killing everyone in the camp when his unsatisfied blood could not be drugged. And LaBat would have been first. So the poet was at least still alive. But he no longer had access to Carrigan's strength, and they didn't have a wagon to move the gold.

And that bloody child kept looking at him.

But he still had Jack Pink, and the hope that the bushranger's sadness could yet turn to anger. While there was Jack, there was always a chance for glory.

*

LaBat waited by the fire for a week, but the anger didn't come. And while Jack remained useless with misery, Camilla stayed in her silent world. The gold was still immovable, the blue-eyed hostage continued to stare, and Mother was really beginning to stink.

But it was at the end of the seventh day, just when LaBat thought his future held nothing but poverty or suicide, that his brain flashed with the solution. And he realised, with some embarrassment, that Mother Pink had already prepared them for this moment. He'd just been a little slow to see it.

'Yes, of course,' LaBat said, pointing at Mother and giving the dead prostitute a smile. 'Clever old girl.'

Then he moved to the other side of the fire and sat down with Camilla. The young woman was still wearing the identical dress she'd bought with Mother before the Cup, but all the fancy had been rubbed off from sleeping in the dirt.

'Do you hear me?' LaBat asked. Camilla just blinked and sniffed up a glob of snot that was resting under her nose. 'Can you hear my voice?'

Then he asked again, even louder. And once more, loud enough that it could almost reach the place where Mother had gone.

'I can hear you,' Camilla said. It was only half-true. She could hear a little but LaBat's shouting voice buzzed in her broken ears like a blowfly in a curtain. So she watched his lips to get the words.

'Then listen. It's you, understand? It's you. You're the only one who can bring him back.'

The girl nodded.

'You're the mother now. Understand?'

She did.

LaBat helped Camilla stand, then he straightened her clothes and touched her hair, like a father preparing a bride for her waiting groom.

'Come and sit beside him.'

She did, and LaBat took Jack's arms from around Mother. A fresh waft of death was released, but the poet sucked in his breath and did his best to ignore it as he moved Jack towards Camilla.

The girl unbuttoned the front of her race-day outfit, and the warmth of the fire touched her bare breasts. As expected, they were a younger and smaller pair than Mother Pink's, but they were also fresher and looked ready to nourish Jack back into the world.

LaBat didn't bother to look away. Their lives had become far too primitive and brutal to bother with the usual manners of a polite society.

'Yes, that's the girl,' LaBat said as Camilla put her hand behind Jack's head to guide him down. 'That's it . . . Mother Fox.'

Here he comes, thought LaBat. Here comes Jack Pink. The real Jack Pink. The hard-riding, quick-shooting, charming, ferocious Jack Pink who scares people like a snake in their bed.

He laughed, and even though the cursed child with the blue eyes was still watching him, he didn't care. She would be a witness. And this was going to be a hell of a story.

*

On that same night, at another fire not far away, Inspector Frederick Rourke, Sergeant Tom Addington and their search party were resting around the low flames.

They were close to the Pink Gang. So close that a watchful bird in the right gumtree could have seen the orange glow of both camps. And Rourke knew they were close because he'd been told by the old tracker just before sunset.

It would not be long now.

The Inspector always had trouble sleeping in the bush. He was a city boy who was used to the distant bells and chatting voices and hooves on cobbled stones. Every rustle of the grass sounded like a brown snake, and the sea of twinkling lights above was only a reminder that he was unprotected by a roof. So he was always last to close his eyes. But tonight, knowing the gang was so near, he would get no sleep at all.

Finding the gang had been far easier than he and Addington had expected. They'd thought it would be a long, and even hopeless, expedition. But between the trackers, the three bush constables and the detective, they were able to follow the Pinks' trail through the colony.

Rourke had expected nothing but lies and disinformation from the people they met along the way. Most had an inherent distrust of authority, and even those willing to obey the law themselves were often unwilling to give evidence against a person who didn't. But no-one wanted to protect the Pink Gang. The killing of Constable Harry Logan and the kidnapping of a tiny child had made the colonials ashamed of ever enjoying the newspaper stories of Fast Jack Pink. So every witness gave over any detail, rumour or guess they thought could assist the hunting party. And if they had no information, they'd offer supplies and shelter.

And now the gang was close.

Tom Addington also wouldn't sleep tonight. He was troubled by the things he wanted and the things he didn't want. He wanted to fill his belly with rum and he wanted to be back in his old life at Mull Creek, and he didn't want to be chasing criminals or to be troubled by the oath he'd made. So as he rolled over on his thin bush bed, Addington settled on a plan for himself.

It was a plan that went beyond simply finding the gang. He decided that if he could be the one to kill the man who murdered his friend, he no longer needed to keep the promise he'd made to Harry Logan. Things would be even. He could then return and find that boy called Jesus and the native, and take them back to Mull Creek for justice. And then his old life would be his again. He could grow old and drink as he pleased and be protected by the Brown Coats once more.

But they needed to take the gang first, and when they did, he needed to put a bullet in the head of Jack. For Harry. And to be free of the pledge.

Addington looked at the stars. It would be dawn in a few hours.

*

At the Pink camp, Camilla held Jack to her chest for hours. For night after night, the young woman had watched Mother Pink do the same thing. It had always seemed so natural and easy, like a calf finding its mother in a paddock. Jack would lock onto the old woman, she would hum a song, and the brutal world would become soft and peaceful.

Camilla thought that when it was her time, it would be the same. She would feel powerful and needed, as though she were the centre of a coronation.

But it was not to be.

From her first attempt, Jack fell off Camilla's nipple like a leech from a cold rock. She tried again, clasping his head with the dried pig shit in his hair between her fingers, but it failed. And through the night she tried again and again. Each bid was more desperate than the last.

LaBat watched on, and his hopeful expression dropped lower with each attempt, until Camilla finally gave up an hour before dawn. She flopped back with exhaustion and made no effort to cover herself, as Jack rolled over and put an arm around his mother's rancid carcass.

Bloody Mother Pink, LaBat thought. That abominable, fearsome, hellish bloody woman. She was worse than a witch. Or perhaps that's just what she was. This world would have been better if she'd been smothered as a child. She had been the fountain of milk and opium, but now the fountain was dust. Nothing was meant to survive after she was gone.

'All is lost,' LaBat said to himself.

The fire was dead and the child was still staring at him.

*

LaBat collapsed and slept long past sunrise. And when he woke, Camilla was gone. So was Jack's raven-black horse. He knew she would leave. He'd even dreamt about it.

But now he had no wagon, no horses and no way of carrying a fortune of gold to a place where he could spend it. All he had was a dead body, another body that was as good as dead, and that stupid child looking at him.

'All is lost,' he said again.

So it was time to go. There was nothing left to write about. The glorious tale was now just a sad story. And no-one wanted sad stories. That's not what would make him immortal. People wanted to read about heroes and revenge and glory. They wouldn't want to know of the harsh times he'd had in the last few months. He'd had to live it. The thought of writing about it as well made him sick.

'All is lost,' he said straight at Blue Eyes, but she gave no acknowledgment of his words. 'All is lost, you ugly little halfwit. All is lost.'

LaBat collected his red ink and paper and Bible, and stuffed a revolver into his belt. He stepped over the cold ashes and almost kicked Blue Eyes on his way to the gold. Until now, LaBat hadn't opened the metal box. He hadn't wanted to. He was saving the moment for a time when he could spend it. But the plan was different now, so he lifted the heavy lid.

LaBat had expected a strong, yellow glow to come from the box, as though there was a chunk of the sun inside. And he thought the coins would almost squirm with life. But when he opened it, no light was shining on his face and the round coins just lay together, like any other coins.

He picked up a single piece, squinting at the image of the odd-looking horse with the spike coming from its forehead.

All is lost, he thought.

But what the hell, it was still gold and it was still his. And one day soon he'd be in clean clothes and far away from the dead gang and the constant blue stare. LaBat put a big handful in each of his pockets, adjusting his belt to allow for the extra weight, then another two went into his writing bag with his Bible. He gave the wretched camp a last look before he turned and started to walk away.

Then he heard a voice. It was quiet, but the shock of it was like a scream in his ear.

'What?' LaBat said, spinning around.

'I said, that's not yours, Samuel LaBat.'

It was Blue Eyes. She was looking at him just the same way she had since they'd stolen her, but now she spoke.

'That's not yours. It doesn't belong to you. Put it back, Samuel LaBat.'

He started to say something but they were not real words. Hearing the child use his name with such cold intelligence made LaBat more terrified than anything else that had happened in this baffling and dangerous year of 1861. The stupid mute girl had heard and seen everything. And she was not frightened.

'That's our gold, Samuel LaBat. If you're going to leave, return the sovereigns to the box. And then you can go.'

'It's mine!' Labat hollered back, spitting the words at her and pulling up his gold-heavy trousers. 'This gold is mine!'

'No, it is not,' Blue Eyes said without hesitation.

'Yes, it is!' His words echoed like a whip crack.

'Return the sovereigns. And then you can go, Samuel Labat.'

Who was this child, he thought. Who was this bloody child? She had nothing. No guns, no mother, no brother, no sister, no milk, no drugs. She was alone. So who was she to make him afraid? And who was she to say when he could stay or go?

'I'm taking this! I don't have to explain myself,' he said, explaining himself. 'Do you know what I have done to get it?'

'We will get it back,' she said softly, looking away from LaBat for the first time.

'What did you say to me?'

'We will get it back. We will get it *all* back, Samuel LaBat.'

'Don't say my name! I don't want you to do it!'

'I know your name. And everything you have done, Samuel . . .'

'Don't say it!'

'. . . LaBat.'

He pulled the revolver from his pants. His fear, anger and shame made his thumb fumble as he cocked it.

Why should he have just a little of the gold, he thought. Why shouldn't he have it all? Even if he had to stay here and fight for every sovereign.

He pointed the barrel a foot away from Blue Eyes' right ear, and although his hand shook, he would not miss.

'Do you think I'm frightened to stay? You don't know what I can do. You don't! I do! I write the stories! I do!'

Blue Eyes turned to him, with the barrel now at the middle of her forehead.

'We will get it back,' she said. 'We will get it all . . .'

It was the last thing she said to him.

*

Two days later, the search party was only a hundred yards from the Pink camp. The trackers had done their job well and the smell of pig carried through the trees.

Inspector Frederick Rourke knew it would be best to raid the camp during the light. There was always a temptation to use the nighttime for surprise, but the reality was different. People were always too alert to noises and dangers in the dark, and if one of the gang ran off, they'd lose them in the bush and could be ambushed later at dawn. So Rourke and Addington decided it should be done the following afternoon, when the warmth of the high sun made the gang sleepy after their lunch.

That evening, Rourke's men lit no fire, had a cold meal, and went another night without sleep. They cleaned and oiled their guns, checking the movement of each mechanism, and winked through the sights at imaginary targets in the bush. Each man thought about the times their weapons had misfired, and prayed that it would not happen tomorrow.

The detective wrote a sweet and brief letter to his wife. 'I will be loving you from where I am,' he scrawled, before he folded the page and put it in his boots, so it wouldn't be ruined by blood if he was shot.

And Sergeant Tom Addington just looked into the dark, determined to stay with his plan. The plan that would take him back to his old life.

*

The next day came and so did the afternoon of the raid. The party surrounded the camp, taking more than two hours to creep to their positions. Frederick Rourke put himself behind a wide log and checked his watch every minute until the minute arrived.

For weeks, through the quiet nights and the long days of riding, the Inspector had considered what he'd say at this moment. He'd made many arrests but he'd never surrounded the hideout of kidnappers and killers.

He couldn't just say 'Come along then'. There needed to be some authority and aggression. And he couldn't shout 'Throw down your arms', because he might be mistaken for a criminal himself. He wanted it to sound like there were hundreds of police surrounding the camp. He needed Jack Pink, the giant Carrigan, the scruffy poet LaBat and the surviving Fox siblings to feel as though their situation was hopeless.

So Rourke finally settled on something that he prayed wouldn't sound too comical when it came from his lips. He checked his watch, blessed himself, squeezed the handle of his gun into his palm, and called out to the camp.

'Surrender! Surrender in the name of the Queen!'

Rourke waited. There were no panicked voices, no clicking of revolvers and no scurrying feet. He waited, then repeated, 'In the camp! Surrender, I say. In the name of . . .'

But before he could finish the request for Her Majesty, a blast cracked out through the bush. And before the echo could die, there came another. Rourke heard the shots and jumped from behind his cover.

Within the hour, the Crown search party had taken the camp. And when they did, they found only two alive.

*

Two weeks after the raid, it was the eve of Christmas. Sergeant Tom Addington flicked the reins of a police coach and two mares pulled him through the gates of the Richmond Depot.

The coach was a vehicle of unwelcoming appearance. The solid metal frame was painted black with no windows at the side, just a rear door made from bars. It was the only way in or out. It was the coach they used for the transport of prisoners, and as Addington drove it through the city streets at dawn, those who saw it pass knew there was either someone dangerous inside, or there soon would be.

Addington's face was grim. A shotgun rested across his lap and a revolver was wedged between his thigh and the hard seat so he could grab it fast.

His three bush constables were still with him. After the capture of the Pink camp, they'd remained in Melbourne for this one last job, at his request. They were just as well-armed as their Sergeant and positioned themselves across the top of the coach so they could see what was coming from all sides.

Addington whipped the straps again, as he turned onto the road that would take him to the Captain's stables.

*

Mary, Jesus and the Captain didn't know Tom Addington was coming. They were at the fence by the track watching Harry Horse on a run. She was slow this morning. Anyone who didn't know the animal would think she was good for nothing more than farm work, or transportation where urgency wasn't required.

But these three knew better. They also knew they were unlikely to see her flying at full stride again. Not unless she was surrounded by a breakneck field and a sea of spectators to cheer her through. And not unless Blue Eyes came home again.

On this day before Christmas, all these things seemed impossible.

'Bloody show-off,' Mary muttered, watching the horse come around. It was something she said when she wanted a reminder of the Melbourne Cup. And the memory always gave a quick splash of joy before moving back to sadness.

It had been almost two months since the race, and they'd received neither good nor bad news about Blue Eyes. The only official visit they had was from Eddie Donovan. The committee man arrived one afternoon to congratulate them and confirm, officially, that they had indeed won the first Melbourne Cup. And to inform them, officially, that as the gold was stolen *after* the completion of race, it was, officially, no longer the responsibility of the Victoria Turf Club. Instead it was, *ipso facto*, the legal property of the owners or representative of the winning horse, i.e. them and Thistle Queen.

To help him deliver the news, Donovan read from a letter by a Collins Street solicitor. He didn't mention that the lawyer was also on the board of the Turf Club.

'So I'm sorry but the prize cannot be replaced by the committee,' Donovan said, folding the letter. 'That is now a personal matter between you and the Victoria Police.'

And there was still no actual cup for the Melbourne Cup. So they got nothing.

'But,' Donovan said, trying to leave the property with a smile, 'it was still a terrific ride.' He stretched out his hand towards Jesus, who paused before he took it. 'I want to tell everyone

I meet that I shook the hand of Harry Grey, winning jockey of the first Melbourne Cup. Good for you, son. I've never seen a ride like it. Maybe we'll see you there next year.'

That was now more than a month ago. And tomorrow was Christmas. But it meant nothing to the stable. They knew it would be just like the all days they'd been living since Flemington.

Harry Horse finished on the track, and a small Cocky brought a large bucket of water for Mary to wash down the animal. Then Harry's dog barked. It was the bark that warned of danger. And the dog of Constable Harry Logan had known enough danger to recognise it.

The large wooden gates opened and a black metal coach came through. It was the kind of vehicle that could only bring bad news. It looked like a rolling cloud carrying a thunderstorm. As it got closer, Mary saw it was bristling with armed police. And closer still, Jesus found the face of Tom Addington at the reins. The cruel Sergeant.

The wagon came straight at them and they only had enough time for fear. The scars on Mary's ankle began to itch and Jesus gulped for air as he felt the imaginary rope tighten around his throat.

The dog kept barking and tried to snap at the wheels, until Addington pulled the horses to a stop. He took the revolver from under his thigh and shoved it back into his belt, before jumping down with the shotgun. His constables did the same, their hands close to the triggers as they stood like soldiers.

Tom Addington looked at Mary, Jesus and the Captain. His face was rough and serious, and his eyes were red and wet from driving through the cooler air of the morning.

'You remember me?' Addington asked, walking to the Captain. 'You know who I am?'

The Captain could only nod. Seeing the Sergeant made him afraid, just like Mary and Jesus, but it wasn't fear for his own life – he was afraid of what he was about to be told. He knew that one day someone would come to tell him his blue-eyed Cocky was dead. He'd tried to convince himself that it was better to know than to never discover the truth, but now that he was about to hear it, the feeling made him wish he was dead himself.

'Come with me,' the Sergeant said and he walked the three of them to the rear of the coach. He nodded to a constable, whose face was just as rough and serious. The bushman released the bolt on the door. They heard a gentle bang against the metal walls inside. Something was in there.

Mary thought it was just more police and she could feel her ankle scars glow purple. She knew she'd soon be in the back of the black wagon with Jesus. Swallowed by the storm.

There was another soft bang before a little body stepped out into the sun.

It was Blue Eyes.

The child rubbed her face, like a person waking from a good sleep. Then she saw her friends.

Sergeant Tom Addington watched the reunion. He'd never seen someone greeted with so much love. The child gripped the old man around the waist, and the boy Jesus and the native girl joined them. They all had expressions of desperate gratitude, like they'd been living inside a burning house and suddenly found the front door.

Dozens of children came running and cheering from the stables and the farmhouse. And the dog barked with a different tone and jumped around them.

It had been two weeks since Tom Addington and Frederick Rourke captured the Pink Gang's camp. And the Sergeant was unlikely to ever forget what he saw when he got there.

On the afternoon of the raid, Addington found cover behind a log – just like Rourke – and checked his own watch and waited for the moment. He'd tried to imagine what they'd find at the camp, and he'd had a dream of seeing gold sovereigns sprinkled around like decorations and the gang in various states of depravity. He didn't know. But he did know the gang wouldn't go easy.

Addington tried to clear his mind and just think of his plan. He needed to get in there first and kill Jack Pink before anyone else had the chance. And he couldn't let Pink be taken alive. That would not do. Pink had to be killed, and it had to be done by himself. It was the only way to be free from the oath. It was the only way he could get back to Mull Creek.

With two minutes to go, Addington's heart had never felt in so much trouble. He just wanted this to be over with. Why was it so bloody hard? Why did he make a promise over a stupid child and black girl? And why did it take so much to get out of it? Why was it so hard just to go home?

As Addington checked his watch again, he heard Inspector Rourke call out, 'Surrender! Surrender in the name of the Queen!'

Addington's blood rushed through him and he panicked. As Rourke called out again, he jumped from his cover and fired at the camp. He started running and almost fell twice and he fired again. He fired once more then he broke through into the small clearing of the camp, ready to shoot anyone he needed to just to get to Jack Pink.

But what he saw there could not be imagined.

Ten feet from the blazing fire was a mound of freshly turned dirt, the size of a human grave. For the headstone, there was a crucifix made from two crooked sticks tied together with a strip of white lace. At the edge of the flames was a pot of food on the coals, its lid rattling from the steam.

And there were only two people alive. One was Jack Pink. The bushranger was sitting on a log. His eyes were open and his face was calm and there was nothing in his hands. His hair was combed, his beard was trimmed and every button had been fastened. He looked like a good man ready for a Sunday morning.

The other survivor was the kidnapped child with the blue eyes. She was standing beside her captor with a bowl of food and a wooden spoon that she'd been using to feed him. She didn't look frightened or surprised.

'Good morning,' she said to Addington, as the Sergeant lowered his gun. 'We'll be ready in a minute.'

Now Blue Eyes was home and Tom Addington watched her being surrounded by affection. He waited until they broke away, then he walked to Mary and Jesus.

'Come with me,' Addington said. This was not done with. The armed constables came closer and Mary and Jesus knew they couldn't run. They'd be shot in the back or chased or one of the children might be hurt.

The Sergeant led them to the back of the coach and opened the heavy door. But before the prisoners could step in, the constables put down their weapons and went in first. There was more banging. It was louder this time as the three policemen dragged out the metal box of gold. They lifted it down and put it at the feet of Jesus and Mary.

'Here,' was all Tom Addington said. His face was just as rough and just as serious as when he'd arrived. Then he nodded his respect towards the Captain, climbed back into the coach and started to leave. There was nothing more to be done.

He was almost at the gate when Mary called after him.

'Hey, Sergeant Boss!'

'What?' Tom said, pulling up the mares. He was frustrated and still unsure of the decisions he'd made. He may have kept the promise to his old friend, but he had no home anymore.

'What do you want?' he said to Mary.

'Are ya stayin' for breakfast?'

*

Samuel LaBat's pockets were heavy with gold that he couldn't spend. He was afraid that if he tried, the first shopkeeper would know all about the Melbourne Cup and the sovereigns with the funny-looking horse head. And that would be all he'd need to get caught.

So for a month he'd travelled north, scrounging for what he needed and keeping away from roads and towns, until he got to the big river at the border. He'd never seen it but he knew it was there. It was wider than he'd imagined and the current was quiet but strong.

LaBat hadn't just been afraid of someone recognising the horse-head sovereigns. The words of that bloody child had haunted him every mile of the journey.

'That's not yours, Samuel LaBat. We will get it back.'

He kept hearing her voice and everything that was blue, including the sky, was like her eyes watching him.

'It's mine,' he'd repeated to himself each night before he tried to sleep, hoping it was how he'd feel in the morning.

He should have killed her for the way she talked to him. He knew that. But he also knew that if he'd squeezed the trigger and put a ball of lead in her skull, he would have been splattered with a curse that he could never clean away. So he'd taken what he could and left the camp.

But today, on a sandy bank by the Murray River, he wanted nothing more to do with the past. He suddenly felt lucky. As though he was about to be free. It was a new year. It was now 1862. He was going to a place under a new sky where he could change his clothes, spend his gold and never come south again.

He just needed to get to the other side.

LaBat had always been a weak swimmer and would have battled to get across, even if he had nothing to carry. But he had his revolvers, his paper and pens and ink, his Bible, and two pockets full of metal that would pull him down into a river that looked as deep as hell itself.

Yet he still felt lucky. He would rest and wait. He knew a solution would come. And it did.

LaBat slept on the bank and dreamed of the life waiting for him on the other side. He woke to the sound of a splash. The noise was like a rising fish but it was the oar of a small boat. The vessel was carrying just one man, cutting through the dawn colours shining off the soft water.

'Ho,' the man said to LaBat, coming for the bank. 'I say, ho there. Good day to you.'

'Good day to you too, sir,' LaBat said, trying to sound like an honest man. They were his first words to another person in a month, and his first smile in two. The expression felt foreign to his face but he kept it while the man got out and walked up the sand.

'Such a beautiful-looking morning, isn't it?'

LaBat agreed and shook his hand. The stranger was a thin man with a large white patch over his left eye. There was something about the rest of his face that was familiar to LaBat. But then again, LaBat had seen so many faces since this time last year.

The man sat on a log, rolled a smoke and talked to LaBat for almost two hours without pause. He talked of politics and fishing and crops, and food he wanted to eat but which was unavailable. And LaBat just listened with patience. He could have shot the man and stolen the boat, but the writer wanted to enter the new world with as much purity as he could gather.

Eventually there was a break in the man's monologue and LaBat asked, 'Can I trouble you for some assistance?'

'If I can,' the man said, lifting up his hands to show he was ready to help.

'Would you take me across?'

'Across? Over there?'

'I'd be most grateful to you.'

'New South Wales?'

'Yes. Just over the water.'

'You want to go to New South Wales?'

'I do.'

'How will you get back?'

LaBat tried not to touch the handle of his gun under his coat or look annoyed. 'I will arrange something for my return, but for now, I need to cross. Can I ask for your help?'

'Yes, you can.'

'I have nothing to give you for it.'

'It would be my pleasure. Please climb aboard.'

The man got in first and set the oars, while LaBat pushed them off the bank and then sat down.

'Do you want to know something?' the boat man said.

'What's that?'

'You're already in New South Wales.'

'What do you mean?'

'The river belongs to New South Wales. The bank is the border of the colonies.'

'I didn't know that.' LaBat smiled again as they drifted to the middle and towards the other side. He was almost free. And the smile was the most joyful one he'd felt on his face for years.

'Tell me something, friend, do you like the races?'

'What?' LaBat lost his smile at the question.

'The races? The horse races? Do you fancy them?'

'No, I don't much.' LaBat eased, realising the man had just found another topic to yammer about.

'Well, I love them,' the man said, pulling back on the oars. 'There's nothing like the races. I don't care where they're running – if they're running, I'm there. I'm surprised you don't like them yourself. You look like a fella who'd love the races.'

'Well, I don't. They're not for me.'

They were almost across and the current eased them sideways as they went.

'You didn't go to the Melbourne Cup then, I suppose?'

'What?' The name of the event made the writer's heart pound.

'The Melbourne Cup? Did you get there yourself?'

'No, I didn't.' LaBat tried not to sound sharp. 'I wasn't there.'

He was almost across.

'That's a shame. I was there.' The boat man stared at LaBat and his talkative face became serious. 'I was there. And it was one hell of a day.'

'I suppose it was.'

'It was. In the name of the Queen.'

'What's that you say?' LaBat asked.

'I said, in the name of the Queen.'

Before LaBat could ask again, the stranger lifted an oar with both hands and swung it at the poet, cracking the side of his head. LaBat's world went black and he slumped over the side of the boat, his bloody nose dripping into the water. And as he fell, the small ink bottle in his coat pocket cracked open and spilled.

The two reds blended together as the current carried them downriver.

*

LaBat woke in the crude lock-up of a bush police station, his head bandaged and aching. Then he was put in chains and transported back to Melbourne.

His trial was short. There was no-one to speak to the better qualities of his character, the newspapers were unkind when describing his appearance, and the outcome was easily predicted by the hundreds who crowded the court to watch the verdict.

The judge ordered LaBat to be taken from the dock to die in prison. When he died was up to LaBat himself.

They put him in a different gaol to Jack Pink, but he didn't know that. The bushranger could just as well have been in the cell right next door and neither would have been aware. The walls were thick and painted white and each man counted his days alone. As though the facility was made just for them.

LaBat was no longer a part of the world. He had no access to news or gossip, and no-one wrote him letters. So it was only luck that, one morning during his first winter, he heard about the death of Jack Pink.

Two warders were near his cell door discussing the outlaw's execution in excited voices. And one had either been there when it happened or he was just good at telling stories. LaBat put his ear to the small hole in his door and listened. He heard how Jack had received three visits on the night before he died. One was a bush storekeeper with his infant child, then a priest and his wife, and just before midnight, two well-dressed policemen with a dog. None stayed for more than ten minutes.

The warder told how Jack Pink had been woken the next day, his arms strapped with leather belts and irons clapped to his ankles, before he was made to shuffle through the prison court-yard. It was a grey morning, so his final view of the sky gave him no sweet colours to take to the gallows. The rope was put around his bearded neck and a white hood over his head. The lever was pulled and the trap opened and Jack Pink dropped until the knot broke his neck.

'And it sure was a beauty of a crack,' the gaoler said, popping the knuckles of his own fingers. 'You could hear every bone.'

When the story was finished, LaBat yelled through the hole.

'What did he say?!'

The warder was accustomed to prisoners shouting and had learnt to ignore it, so LaBat almost screamed until his voice broke.

'What is it? What are you yapping about in there?' the warder said, walking to LaBat's heavy door. 'What do you want?'

'What did he say?'

'Who?'

'Jack Pink. What did he say? I need to know. What were his last words? Did he say anything?'

'Yes, he did say something.'

'What did he say? Please, I must know.'

'Well, I'll tell you. Just before they pulled the floor on him, he cried out for his mummy.'

The warder laughed and repeated 'Mummy, mummy' as he walked away, the words echoing off the cold surfaces.

LaBat knew he was being taunted, but he also knew Jack Pink, so the story was probably true.

*

For five more years, LaBat sat in his cell without words or activity. And each day he would consider the average lifespan of a human male, then he would calculate how much longer he had to go.

But one morning in the spring of 1867, Samuel LaBat, the poet, thief, liar and kidnapper, began to write again. With only short pencils, thin paper and uneven surfaces to work on, he filled one page after another. He wrote of the courage, charm and scholarly intelligence of Fast Jack Pink. He wrote about the maternal kindness of Mother Pink and her concern for the common people of Victoria. He wrote about his own wisdom, integrity and literary gifts. And he recorded the incidents of harassment endured by the Pink family at the hands of the gold-greedy government and its corrupt constabulary, and how he was outnumbered by forty to one by the troopers at his glorious last stand.

For seven years, LaBat wrote and rewrote the tale. And when it was time to quote Jack Pink's last words, it took him six months before he was finally satisfied. It needed to be perfect. It must be something memorable and quotable, and when people repeated it, it must be something they felt about their own lives. LaBat settled on just three words as Jack's final statement, and when he wrote them, he danced in his cell.

And then he was done.

It might take a hundred years or more, but LaBat knew someday people would be looking for a hero and they would find his writing. History is made by those with the best words.

'The truth belongs to the poets!' LaBat shouted through the small hole in his door, and he laughed until he was told to shut up.

His final manuscript was more than a foot high. He sat it in the only corner of his cell that didn't get damp, and placed his Bible on top to weigh it down.

And under the Bible was the title page. In large, dark grey print it read: 'GOOD AS GOLD: THE TRUE STORY OF THE JACK PINK GANG.'

*

On the day of the 1930 Melbourne Cup, an old woman rode the train to Flemington. Every seat in every carriage was taken, so she stood in the aisle, holding on as they swayed over the tracks. She was accustomed to standing while others sat, and although she was well into her eighth decade of life, her back was straight and her feet were sure. A walking stick was her only hint of frailty.

The racecourse was the end of the line, and the Melbourne Cup was the only reason anyone was aboard. They arrived at the platform and the other passengers rushed around the old woman to get out into the sun for the horses, drinking and betting.

But she was in no hurry. She'd come here for just one purpose. And there was still plenty of time.

It was almost seventy years since Mary had been at the Flemington racecourse. The crowd was bigger, the grandstand was grander, and the grass and flower beds were trimmed like it was a king's garden. But even if she'd arrived in the middle of a night, she'd still know exactly where she was.

Mary entered the gates and moved through the crowds and down to the track, where they were about to start the last race before the Cup.

Even though she'd only spent one day at the track in 1861, it felt like she'd lived five lifetimes there. The memories of Harry's murder, the gang, the gunshots, the fear, and her great ride were still so clear, it was as though it could all happen again right in front of her at any moment.

The stalls clanged open on the other side of the course as the race began, and when they got close enough, Mary could see a lone grey in the middle of the field. They were all in tight and the smoke-coloured animal was looking for a gap. Mary lifted her chin to get a better look, and as they came by for the final sprint she was surrounded at the fence by people cheering and holding their tickets. Mary smiled. She could feel the thunder of the horses shaking the ground, and as the grey broke away to win, she felt like she was on its back, holding on as they went past the posts.

Then she was standing alone again. But she was still smiling.

Mary searched her pocket and took out a coin. A gold sovereign. It was the last one she owned. The last of her share. And it was the one she'd been carrying since the Christmas Eve of 1861. The words and emblems were still clear, but it was gleaming from the decades of polish between Mary's fingers.

She'd rub it when she needed to concentrate or steady her mind. She'd rub it to ease bad memories. She'd rub it to remember the friends who were long gone. And she'd rub it to keep her life lucky.

And what a life it had been. After the hanging of Jack Pink, the rescue of Blue Eyes and the return of the gold, the Captain's stable prospered. The newspapers started to write about the race itself rather than the crimes, and people began talking about the mighty run by Thistle Queen and her jockey.

'Perhaps there will never be another Melbourne Cup,' one report said. 'Or this may yet be the prologue to a tradition that will last one hundred years. Whichever will not matter. The spectacle of our local boy Harry Grey, with no whip in his hand, astride the magnificent Thistle Queen as she chased them all down, will remain a singular miracle in our Colony's story.'

The Captain and his Cockies were then famous. Every thoroughbred owner wanted their horse trained by the stable, hoping the same miracle that had propelled Thistle Queen could soak into the muscles and bone of their own animals.

The racing community in Victoria and beyond hummed with talk of the Captain's methods. The feed he was using, his treatments for injury and the way he could pick a fast one even before it hit the track. They wanted to know it all.

At the property, more stables were put up and a new house was built for the ever-growing number of Cockies. And before the century was over, they'd trained another three Melbourne Cup winners. By then, the Turf Club had finally made a real cup.

But none of the new wins were from Thistle Queen. The animal that carried the breath of Alice Logan never ran another race. Instead, she became a police horse again.

After Jack Pink was executed, Tom Addington was promoted to the rank of inspector and made the commander of Melbourne's mounted branch. Tom remained a regular guest at the Captain's breakfast table, and on the morning after his promotion he asked Mary and Jesus if he could buy back Harry's horse for the Crown.

Mary and Jesus knew the worth of the famous grey. They'd already been offered unthinkable money. But they also knew this is what Harry Logan would have wanted. And so the Colony of Victoria purchased Thistle Queen for a second time and she went back to the job with Tom Addington on her back. She spent the rest of her days clopping the streets of the city, where people would come out from their homes and shops just to put an apple under the nose of the first Melbourne Cup winner.

Tom took good care of her, and although he still kept a rum flask in his saddle bag, he was known in the city as a fair man who was quicker to show kindness than force. And for the next twenty-five years he helped guide the lost children of the streets towards a new life at the Captain's stables.

Though Inspector Frederick Rourke remained a hero after his actions, he took no promotion. He stayed at the Richmond Depot until he retired. But his life was not always quiet. Two decades after Jack Pink and Samuel LaBat were in handcuffs, Rourke had to hunt down another bushranger. And so he slept under the stars one last time.

The Captain died in May of 1866. His bed was surrounded by the Cockies and their love, and in the last minute of life his frozen hands bloomed open like two morning flowers. Blue Eyes held one and Mary the other.

The stables went on without him. The new children came in and when each was grown, they'd leave to begin their own lives. Including Mary and Jesus. And when each left, they were given their share of the 1861 Melbourne Cup prize.

So the sovereigns were used to buy homes, open businesses, raise families, or to board ships that would take them to the other side of the world.

And the coins became their own legend. They were given the nickname of 'Old Spiky' because of the strange ear sticking out from the horse-head emblem. But others knew them as 'The Orphans' Gold'. And with each year, the sovereigns became rarer and more valuable.

With her last piece of Orphans' Gold in her old hand, Mary put her walking stick on the lush grass and moved through the crowd to the place where Harry Logan had been killed seventy years before. There was no memorial or statue on the spot, there was just more grass and a young couple sitting on a blanket. They were well dressed but not wealthy, and the man was pouring a drink for his wife and she was slicing a piece of green fruit to put in his grinning mouth.

They looked up to see Mary staring at them.

'Good afternoon,' the young woman said, smiling.

'Would you like to sit down?' the husband said, starting to clear a space. 'We have the room.'

It took Mary a moment to realise they were talking to her. She'd been thinking about Harry on the ground with the blood coming through Tom Addington's fingers. She'd wanted to stand there and honour him by remembering his last moments. But then she could only see the young couple, sitting so close that they looked like the one person, and throwing around their love like it would last forever. Mary decided they were the perfect memorial for the Constable boss.

'There's plenty of room,' the husband said again.

'No thanks, love,' Mary said, returning their smiles. 'Just thought I was meeting a friend.'

Mary had thought about Harry Logan many times in the last seven decades, and for the first twelve years she'd had his dog at her feet as a reminder.

She'd married in 1872 and become Mary Cooper. Her husband was a shearer when they met and, in more than one way, he reminded her of Harry. He had no sense of direction and would easily trip over when there was nothing in the way but his own feet. Yet he was a handsome bugger, a hard worker and a good father for their five children.

They bought a pub together at Creswick and he worked the bar while Mary ran the kitchen. And no-one ever knew that the 'best tucker north of Ballarat' was cooked by the real jockey of the first Melbourne Cup winner.

But Mary's husband knew. He knew most of her secrets.

He died when they were both just fifty-one, and a year before he went he'd said to her, 'You had a busy life before you met me, love. I hope I didn't make things too boring for you.'

She held him in their bed and said, 'I'll take every bit of boredom I can get.'

She missed him. And there was more grief when two of her grandsons were killed in France at the same battle. One boy had been writing her long letters. The words became more despairing as the war went on. And then they stopped coming.

But Mary had long known that great grief always came after great love. That was the price.

In 1901, Victoria joined the federation and Australia became a country of its own. That same year, Mary was reading the newspaper in her kitchen and there was a story about a woman who'd been travelling the world, training thoroughbreds. She was known in all the great stables of England, Ireland, France, Spain and America. She was greeted by presidents and princes, and honoured by the horse-loving new King.

Her name was Margaret Flynn but very little was known about her early life; just that she was one of the greatest horse trainers who ever lived and she was born somewhere in the Colony of Victoria. And everyone who met her could not help remarking at how blue her eyes were. The bluest they'd ever seen.

'Cocky,' Mary whispered as she read the story. 'Bloody hell. Our blue-eyed Cocky.'

And then there was Jesus Whitetree. Jesus never went looking for gold again, and he never had need for the five remaining shots in Andre Noble's revolver. And when it was time to leave the stables, he left behind his share of the Melbourne Cup prize. But he didn't leave his new name behind. After the Cup, everyone knew him as Harry Grey, the jockey of Thistle Queen. So that's what he called himself. And it was a name he knew he wouldn't forget. He wouldn't need to repeat it three times around his fire.

But he didn't look much like a 'Harry' and soon his friends started calling him 'Harold'.

Harold Grey became a driver on the railways. For more than fifty years, he shovelled the fireboxes and drove steam trains to every part of Victoria. No-one knew more about the engines than him, and when each new line opened, they always asked Harold Grey to test the virgin track.

And Mary remained his friend. She never had to stand in the aisle of any train driven by Harold Grey. He would always reserve the best spot for her in the first-class carriage. Though she rarely used it; instead, she'd ride up in the cabin with him.

On their first ride together, once they got up a good speed and the dark smoke flooded the sky, Mary leaned out and let the air hit her face and looked out over the country they both knew well. The country he'd travelled hoping to find gold and she'd walked in chains. Now they were as free and as rich as they ever needed.

Mary would ride with Jesus at least once a year. The last time was just before he retired and they were both slower getting down onto the platform at Flinders Street Station. They walked out together and stood under the clocks at the entrance and the city that had almost starved them was still alive with people, but starting to smell better.

A young man and his son approached them. They removed their hats and spoke with a quiet respect worthy of a war hero or champion cricketer.

'Pardon me, Mr Grey. My boy here wants to meet you.'

'Good afternoon, mate,' Jesus said. The boy was too nervous to reply.

'Young Jim wants to be a jockey too.' The lad was a little plump to ride, but his enthusiasm was clear. 'Do you have any advice for him, Mr Grey?'

Mary jumped in first. 'Try to keep ya bloody eyes open, mate,' she said.

After they walked away, Jesus said to Mary, 'You've got to let me tell people.'

'Tell them what?'

'Tell them you're Harry Grey.'

'No thanks. If I'm Harry Grey, who are you gonna bloody be?'

Then she looked over the hundreds of faces in front of them as the people of Melbourne walked, traded, rode on carriages, or checked the clocks for their next train.

'Nah,' she said, showing a smile that he never got tired of seeing. 'They're not ready for a yarn like that yet. The shock would kill 'em. You and I know. That's enough.'

Later that year, the newspaper announced the retirement of Harold Grey. It said, 'He was the boy we knew from the first Melbourne Cup and he became the grand old gentleman of the railways. He traded the racetracks for the train tracks and he never failed us on either. And by this publication's arithmetic, Harold Grey has travelled more miles than any man in the history of Australia.'

Six years after that, the paper announced his death.

Mary went to his funeral. And so did the Chief Commissioner of Police, the Premier, the Victorian Railways Commissioner and the Cockies of the Captain's stables – both the small ones and the hundred who'd grown.

Harold Grey's family filled the first two rows of the church. Mary went up and embraced his widow. She was a small woman and always had been, but now Mary could almost put her arms around her twice. And Mary could never imagine how Mrs Grey got so many children out of such a tiny body. But their children were a good mob. They were farmers, grocers, teachers, physicians, and two worked on the railroads and looked just like their father. They all had names that they never feared forgetting and birthdays that were always celebrated.

At the funeral, Mary watched Jesus' sons and grandsons carry him from the church and she cried. Paying the price again.

When she left the church, the priest was greeting people as they came out of the door. When he got to Mary, he said, 'Jesus loves you.'

'Yes, Father,' she said, smiling at the thought. 'I think he did, the mad bastard.'

Now, at the 1930 Melbourne Cup with her last gold sovereign in hand, she still felt the words the priest had told her. She felt them every day.

She walked from the young couple and towards the parade ring. The horses for the main race were being brought out for display and soon the fence was covered with people wanting to get a look at their tip. There was a crowd of bookies nearby, taking bets and talking fast, and with the race only minutes away, punters rushed about searching for the best odds.

Mary stood back and looked over the collection of book-makers until she found the one she wanted. He had a new hat and a hard face and a nose that would have been broken more than a couple of times. Judging by the early indications of his personality, Mary thought he'd have deserved each break.

She waited for her turn as the bookie grabbed money with one hand and used the other to scribble on betting slips.

'Don't bloody stand there, woman,' he snapped at her. 'Get out of the road.'

'I'll have a bet, thanks,' Mary said, with a patience that wasn't returned.

'No, ya won't. Bugger off.'

'Ya sure?'

'Of course, I'm sure. Take ya pennies somewhere else. I'm busy.'

He kept taking bets while he talked to her. It was like he was using one side of his mouth to give odds and the other side to bark at Mary. He was annoyed. The Melbourne Cup was always his biggest day of the year, and the New York stock crash meant that very few had money to throw around. So the bookie had to grab it while he could. He didn't have a second to waste on a woman like this.

'Just a quick bet,' Mary said, always keeping her smile and now blocking the path for others to get to him.

'Christ, will ya move? I'll grab a copper if ya don't.'

'Just a bet.'

'With what?'

'How's this one?' Mary asked, opening her hand. The sovereign flashed at him like a mirror catching the sun.

The bookie stopped moving when he realised what it was.

'What . . . where the bloody hell did you get that?' he said and checked over his shoulder, as though it was about to be stolen from both of them. The bookie knew exactly what it was, but he'd only seen one once before, and it was locked in a glass cabinet.

'How'd you get a flamin' Old Spiky? Did you nick that?'

Mary didn't answer the question. She just said, 'So, are we havin' a bloody a bet here or what?'

'Watch ya language with me, woman. Where did ya get it? Tell me.'

'Will this do ya? Do you want it then?'

He wanted it all right. He had always wanted it. Ever since he was a boy, when his nose was straighter, he'd wanted a piece of the Orphans' Gold. And by the year 1930, everyone else wanted one too. The story of Jack Pink and Mother Pink was now folklore, as well known as any story on the continent, and the tale of Harold Grey and Thistle Queen became bigger with each year. Especially now that everyone who was there that day was surely dead.

'Yes, all right. What's ya pick?' The bookie tried not to look too eager. A lesson he'd learnt from his father on that very spot.

'Hang about, though,' Mary said, closing her fingers on the sovereign. 'I want some better odds.'

'Just tell me ya pick. Come on.'

'And I want this bugger back.' She gave him another flash of Old Spiky.

'What?'

'When I win, I want my winnings *and* I want this back too.'

'*When* you win? Bugger me. *When* you win?' The bookie couldn't help himself. 'What would someone like you know about winning the Melbourne Cup?'

'So you can cover it then?'

'Yes, bloody hell, yes, I can cover it.'

And he could. But only just. If he lost, it would almost clear him out. But he could cover it. It was worth the risk. More than worth it. He would never have another chance to own a piece of the Orphans' Gold.

'What's ya pick?'

'Well, let me have a look.' Mary turned to watch the horses in the parade ring.

'Bloody hell, hurry up.'

'What's that one there?'

'What one?'

'That one?' She pointed.

'What one?'

'That one. I like the colours on the jockey.'

The bookie allowed himself a smile. He was flushed with joy. If the old Aboriginal was picking horses just from the silk colours, Old Spiky was as good as in his pocket. He would never forget this day.

'Where?'

'The one there in red. With the black-and-white sleeves. What's that horse? I'll bet on her. What's her name?'

The bookie felt a hard lump come to his throat when he realised her selection.

'*His* name,' he said, almost choking on the words. 'It's a gelding.'

'What's *his* name then?'

'That's Phar Lap.'

AUTHOR'S NOTE

I'm in the debt of all the mates, mentors, experts and comrades who helped make *Good as Gold*.

This novel is written with my full respect for the first people on this continent. As a non-Indigenous writer, I don't pretend to have created something that embodies the journey of the First Nations people. That's not my story to tell. The character of Mary is her own tale. For their guidance, thank you to Yorta Yorta man Daniel James and Samantha Richards of the Wurundjeri and Dja Dja Wurrung people.

For their historical counsel, thank you to novelist and racing historian Dr Andrew Lemon, and Stuart Duff and Ralph Stavely from the Victoria Police Historical Society. But it's important to note that any historical overreaching or poetic mangling of the truth are things for me to answer to, not them.

Thank you to Andrew Rule, Sam Doran, Nick Rye, Ray Kitchingman, Sarah Hall, Gavin Robertson-Glasgow, Rachael Skipper, Kirsten Lim-How, Emily Webb, Wade Kingsley, Lachy Hulme, Peter Delaney, Amy Johnston, Ash Yargi, Vanessa Till, Irene Forsyte, Trevor Smith and Tom Andronas.

For turning a story into a book, and for always making something better, thank you to publisher Ali Watts and senior editor Patrick Mangan at Penguin Random House.

And to Hannah, Emily and Merryn, thanks for the love. Keep it coming.

ABOUT THE AUTHOR

Justin Smith is a Melbourne author, journalist and broadcaster. He's won various awards for his work and is the acclaimed author of *Cooper Not Out*.

JUSTIN SMITH

COOPER

NOT

OUT

THIS SUMMER,
AN UNLIKELY
HERO IS ABOUT TO
REWRITE HISTORY.

In the Australian summer of 1984, in the small country town of Penguin Hill, Sergeant Roy Cooper is making a name for himself. He's been batting for his local cricket club for decades – and he's a statistical miracle. He's overweight, he makes very few runs, he's not pretty to watch, but he's never been dismissed.

When local schoolgirl Cassie Midwinter discovers this feat, she decides to take the matter further. The remarkable story finds its way into the hands of Donna Garrett, a female sports columnist who's forced to write under a male pseudonym to be taken seriously.

That summer, the West Indies are thrashing Australia, and the Australian people's love of cricket has never been lower. But Donna's columns on Roy Cooper capture the imagination of a nation, and soon there's pressure to select him for the national team. This would see him playing at the Melbourne Cricket Ground, carrying the spirit of every small country town in Australia along with him. Could such a miracle actually happen?

This is sport, after all, and who doesn't love a good story?

Cooper Not Out is a funny, heart-warming novel set within real events. It is a moving and highly original tale about friendship and belief, and the joy of discovering your greatest potential.

Read on for a sneak peek of Justin's acclaimed novel
Cooper Not Out

Roy Cooper lived in the town of Penguin Hill. It was two hours and 50 minutes from Melbourne and the unimpressive sign on entry read 'POPULATION 2400'. This was not true. The real figure was more like 1200. A mistake was made in the 1981 census by a federal government official with a drinking problem, a recent divorce, and a lump on his neck that had yet to be tested for cancer. The locals knew the number was high, but they liked being over the 2000 mark so no-one asked them to count again.

The earth around Penguin Hill was flat, and the horizon was a straight line only broken by trees and fences. There was one sealed road coming in and the same one went out. In the middle of town, between the newsagent and a butcher, was the police station.

As a sergeant, Roy Cooper was Penguin Hill's highest-ranking police officer. He lived 10 minutes' drive out of town in a red brick home that had once belonged to his parents. His long driveway came off a dirt road and the property was surrounded by gum trees, with no close neighbours.

In early November of 1984, the days were getting warmer and Roy Cooper moved through his house with only a towel around his waist. In his bathroom, water was running into the four-clawed tub as he ironed a clean shirt and hung it with the rest of his uniform.

Roy was 48 years old and six foot three, and had a moustache that bent to his chin. He'd been slim as a young man and was considered the fittest in his academy squad when he trained at Melbourne's St Kilda Road police depot. But with each new uniform they sent him, the sizes increased and his belly gave the towels less material to tuck in.

The floorboards squeaked under him as he went to his stereo, pressed 'PLAY' and turned up the smooth silver volume knob. The first bit of tape made a hiss before Bob Marley came on singing about three little birds. The handwritten label on the cassette read 'SUNDAY AFTERNOON #23', and the spools moved to match the rhythm of the reggae man's voice as he assured that every little thing was gonna be all right. Roy hummed and sang a couple of words without really opening his mouth, as he carried a plate of sliced fruitcake from the kitchen and put it on the bathroom tiles within easy reach. Then he made another trip to get six cans of Melbourne Bitter and a pewter mug. He turned off the water and mumbled another line from the song, then dropped his towel.

But he wasn't alone in the big bath. At the other end was Barry Midwinter.

He was two years younger than Roy. They were born in the same hospital and went to the same schools. Barry had a wiry build that didn't collect fat in the usual middle-aged places.

And below his elbows and knees the skin was leathery brown from the sun and there was a sunburnt V shape high on his chest. But the rest of him was white and lightly freckled. He sat in the water, only wearing his orange towelling hat, and the level lifted to his nipples when Roy got in.

Roy groaned and sucked in some air.

'Too hot, mate?' asked Barry. 'You all right?'

'Nah. Nah, good, mate. No worries.'

Roy reached over the side and got a beer and Barry's mug and passed them over. Barry opened the ring pull and a few drops fizzed into the water before he poured it into the pewter. Roy drank from the can. They sighed and lowered into the bath.

'Hey, I got a new telly,' said Roy, looking at the ceiling.

'Hey?'

'I bought a new TV. Got it on Wednesday.'

'You bought a new telly?' Barry stretched his neck to see out of the door into the lounge room. 'You did?'

'Yeah, Baz. Didn't you see it on the way in?'

'Nah.'

'Ha. Jesus, you're a blind prick.'

'I wasn't looking for it. How am I supposed to see it?'

'How did you miss it? It's twice as bloody big as the old one.'

'Oh righto.' He tried to look again, lifting himself up. 'Nah, didn't see it.'

Roy reached down and got the fruitcake. He'd sliced it thick into four pieces. Barry took one with his rough fingers and made a good bite.

'That's not like you, mate,' said Barry through the mouthful. 'Treating yourself to a major appliance. And a big one at that.'

'It's a big one all right. I didn't need one that big, but . . .'

'Nah, good for you, mate. Good for you.'

Barry finished his slice and washed down the strong mix of flour, dried fruit and brandy with two gulps of beer. Then he gave a smiling groan before he eased back into the tub.

'I heard a little rumour about you, mate,' Barry said.

'Oh yeah, what's that?'

'Something to do with Saturday.'

'What?'

'Retirement. Your retirement.' Then Barry dropped his voice to impersonate his friend's deeper tone. '"Oh, oh, I don't think I'll play again."'

'Piss off.'

'"It's getting a bit hot out there,"' Barry mocked. '"I'm getting a bit bloody old. Don't think I'll go around again."'

'I'm gonna get this all week, aren't I?'

'I'd say so.'

'From every prick?'

'That's a fair guess.'

Roy smiled and held the plate again for Barry. He took another slice and half disappeared with the first chomp.

'Hey,' Roy said, rubbing a wet hand across his face, making his moustache fall flat on his lip. 'You don't even have to get up to change the channel.'

'What?'

'The new telly – you don't even have to get up.'

'Hey? How does that work?'

'You just . . .'

'I don't understand.'

'It's got a remote.'

'A remote?'

'It's a little box on a cord that you plug into the TV. And you can change the channel without getting out of the chair.'

'Shit hey.'

'Yeah, I know. It's good.'

'Oh yeah, righto. I think I know what you mean. I might have heard about that. What is it, like a big bloody knob or something?'

'No, it's a button thing,' Roy said, wiggling his thumb to demonstrate. 'There's a button to go up the channels and another to go down.'

'One to go up and one to go down? Bugger me. Nice. Gee, you *have* lashed out, mate.'

'Yeah, a bit silly, I know.'

'Not at all, mate,' Barry said and looked almost serious. 'Sounds nice. Very modern. Good for you. Why shouldn't you have it?'

'Thanks, mate.'

Barry poured the rest of the can into his mug and sucked at the froth before it could spill.

'Roy,' Barry wondered. 'We only get two channels, but.'

'Yeah.'

'And you only ever watch one.'

'Yeah.'

Barry took a good drink and shrugged. 'Good for you, mate.'

'Thanks, Baz.'

Discover a
new favourite